Praise for
The Gate Keeper

"As always in this singular series, the mother-and-son team who write as Charles Todd position their mystery within the broader context of a nation frozen in postwar depression. . . . The melancholy tone that distinguishes the Rutledge series is a reminder that war never ends for the families and friends of lost loved ones. It just retreats into the shadows."

—Marilyn Stasio, *New York Times Book Review*

"Readers can't ask for more than Todd's masterful plotting, terrific characters and one of the finest protagonists in modern suspense." ~~k in Mystery~~

"The best one yet ~~~~ ook this far into a series can still su~~~~ ~~~~ what *The Gate Keeper* does. Highly recommended for historical mystery fans." —The BOLO Books Review

"In a series known for intelligent plots, Todd's 20th novel about Ian [Rutledge] excels. *The Gate Keeper* delivers an emotional novel . . . as well as an involving story about how the war affected other former soldiers and the families and towns to which they came home." —SouthFlorida.com

THE GATE KEEPER

ALSO BY CHARLES TODD

THE IAN RUTLEDGE MYSTERIES

A Test of Wills
Wings of Fire
Search the Dark
Legacy of the Dead
Watchers of Time
A Fearsome Doubt
A Cold Treachery
A Long Shadow
A False Mirror
A Pale Horse

A Matter of Justice
The Red Door
A Lonely Death
The Confession
Proof of Guilt
Hunting Shadows
A Fine Summer's Day
No Shred of Evidence
Racing the Devil

THE BESS CRAWFORD MYSTERIES

A Duty to the Dead
An Impartial Witness
A Bitter Truth
An Unmarked Grave
A Question of Honor

An Unwilling Accomplice
A Pattern of Lies
The Shattered Tree
A Casualty of War
A Forgotten Place

OTHER FICTION

The Murder Stone
The Walnut Tree

THE GATE KEEPER

An Inspector Ian Rutledge Mystery

Charles Todd

WILLIAM MORROW
An Imprint of HarperCollinsPublishers

P.S.™ is a trademark of HarperCollins Publishers.

HarperCollins books may be purchased for educational, business, or sales promotional use. For information, please e-mail the Special Markets Department at SPsales@harpercollins.com.

A hardcover edition of this book was published in 2018 by William Morrow, an imprint of HarperCollins Publishers.

FIRST WILLIAM MORROW PAPERBACK EDITION PUBLISHED 2018.

Library of Congress Cataloging-in-Publication Data has been applied for.

ISBN 978-0-06-267872-0

18 19 20 21 22   LSC   10 9 8 7 6 5 4 3 2 1

For Tubby, with a heart twice his size.

For Marla too, whose heart and home have sheltered so many cats over the years, not even counting those in the wild she has fed and tended.

And for Biddle, dearest Biddle, who walks on tiptoe and has a sense of humor.

THE GATE KEEPER

I

December 1920

Ian Rutledge drove through the night, his mind only partly on the road unwinding before him. He was north of London, and a little to the east of it as well. But he had no particular destination in mind.

At this late hour, he should have been asleep in his flat in London. He'd gone there with that in mind, but as soon as he'd crossed the threshold it had felt different. Stuffy. Claustrophobic. Almost alien. It was where he lived—but it was not his home, had never really been his home. In the end, he'd tossed a razor and a change of clothes in a small valise and returned to the motorcar. Telling himself that he'd be back in London in time for breakfast with Melinda in the morning.

His sister, Frances, had been married that afternoon, and the reception afterward had gone on until close to midnight. But he remembered the day only in snatches, moments that seemed to loom out of the darkness, to fill his thoughts.

Standing at the foot of the stairs, waiting for Frances and her attendants to come out of her room and walk down to join him. Thinking that his parents should have lived to share this moment with her. That his father should be the one to give her away, and that his mother should be upstairs with her now, putting the final touches on whatever was keeping them. Her hair or her gown. Bridal nerves.

And then Melinda Crawford was coming to the head of the stairs, heralding his first glimpse of his sister in her gown.

It had been a shaft to the heart to see her, as beautiful as she had ever been and happier than he'd remembered her being for a very long time. There had been someone during the war, while he was in France. An officer. She had loved him very deeply, but he had been killed, and she'd never spoken his name afterward. Rutledge had found out about him quite by chance, and never mentioned what he knew. There had been another man after the war, one she'd thought she loved. Rutledge had been through the aftermath with her, offering what comfort he could. But this time, he thought, she'd made the right choice.

Then he was sorting the wedding party out as they got themselves and their gowns into the line of motorcars waiting to take them to the church, much laughter and confusion as Frances remembered something blue, and Melinda had had to go back upstairs to find the ribbon that had once belonged to their mother.

He'd been afraid from the start that Frances might choose St. Margaret's for her own wedding. It was very fashionable—and rather beautiful as well. But the last time he'd seen Jean, the woman he'd expected to marry, she'd been coming out of St. Margaret's after conferring with her bridesmaids over some detail of her own wedding. But not to him. To a man who was being posted to Canada, taking Jean with him to a very different life from the one a shell-shocked former officer of His Majesty's Army could hope to offer.

Frances, tactfully, had chosen St. Martin-in-the-Fields instead, a church his parents had often attended, particularly for Evensong. It had significance for Peter as well. His ancestors had been Navy, and St. Martin's was the Admiralty church.

It was just off Trafalgar Square, not very far. He couldn't remember much about that drive, except for his sister's hand holding his, and nervously squeezing it sometimes.

His next clear memory was of walking through the doors of the church with Frances on his arm, seeing the bunches of silk flowers decorating the pews, ribbons trailing to the floor, and everywhere, candlelight, the scent of melting beeswax perfuming the air. The organ was playing, and with a last smile for Frances, Melinda was being led down the aisle on the arm of one of the groomsmen. The music changed, and it was the turn of the bridesmaids, a sea of faces smiling as they passed.

Peter was standing by the altar, his face turned toward the door, but he couldn't see Frances yet. There was happiness there, and a sense of wonder, as if he couldn't believe this day had come at last.

Waiting for the signal, Rutledge could feel his own heartbeat, and then Frances had looked up at him, tears in her lashes, smiling. He brought her arm closer to his side.

"It's beautiful," he said softly, "and so are you."

It was what his father might have said, and he knew at once it was the right thing.

And then they were pacing down the aisle to the rhythm of the music, and when it had stopped, he took Frances's hand and placed it in Peter's before stepping back.

He remembered his lines, when the question was asked: "Who giveth this woman?"

"Her parents and I," he'd said firmly, because that was what his sister had wanted.

He found his seat next to Melinda Crawford, and she reached out to rest her hand on his arm for a moment, as if she knew what was in his heart.

She probably did. Melinda was one of the most unusual women he'd ever met. As a child, she'd been caught up in the Great Indian Mutiny of 1857, a heroine in the bloody siege of Lucknow that had cost so many lives. And she had never looked back, her life taking its course through marriage and widowhood and years of travel before she returned home to England. She had been a friend of his parents, and she had been close to him and his sister throughout their childhood. She had been there when news came that their father and mother were dead.

What he didn't know, sitting there beside her as Frances and her fiancé spoke their vows, was just how much Melinda cared for him. But he thought he could guess. He was the son she'd never had, for she had never remarried.

And then Frances was turning from the altar, her eyes lit with joy, and the new husband and wife went up the aisle together, leaving him to follow.

She would have other allegiances now. Husband, please God children of her own, and he would take his rightful place in the background of her new life. Much as he wished her happiness, the sense of loneliness he'd felt since her engagement was still raw. He wanted her to marry. He wanted her to move on. And yet he would miss the knowledge that she was there if he needed her. He hadn't. Not in the two years since the end of the war. He'd made a point *not* to need her, *not* to draw her into the horror of his war, the shell shock, the voice he carried in his head. He had never told anyone but the doctor who had treated him and saved his sanity. Most certainly not Frances. Still, she had been an anchor in his life that he'd needed badly once Jean had deserted him. A sense of responsibility for someone else, when the desire to end it all swept him in the darkness before dawn.

It had been Frances, uncertain why he was locked away in the silence of his mind, who had brought Dr. Fleming to see him. He would never be able to tell her how grateful he was for that decision. Without Dr. Fleming, he would have been shut up in a clinic for incurable cases.

His next memory was of the reception at the Savoy beneath those splendid chandeliers. Frances, dancing with her husband, and then with him, in his father's place. Afterward he'd danced with Melinda, and she'd made him laugh. He'd wondered if she knew how much *he* cared for her, and how much he didn't want her to know the truth about him. She was Army, she would not look lightly at shell shock.

To his surprise, Kate Gordon was a wedding guest. She was Jean's cousin, but so very different from Jean. He'd always liked her. But one awful night in Cornwall, he'd found out just how much courage she possessed. And how much she had cared. He'd avoided her since then, not wanting to hurt her, not wanting to drag her into his world. She too was Army, both her father and her uncle and most of her friends.

Still, they'd danced a number of times, and he'd done his duty with the bridesmaids, the wallflowers, the older women who remembered his parents and commented on how much they would have loved this night.

And then he'd danced again with Kate, the strain of Cornwall gone, and her presence in his arms feeling very natural.

The bride and groom had left after the dinner and more dancing, running out of the hotel's ballroom in a shower of rice and good wishes. It was late when he'd said good night to everyone, driven Melinda back to the house that had been his parents' and now belonged to Frances. Melinda had asked him to come in for a cup of tea, but he'd smiled and said he was tired. She'd looked at him with that direct gaze that seemed to see through the wall he'd put up to prevent her from guessing what he kept from her, and how he felt at this moment. And she'd said, quietly, "My dear, you were a tower of strength today. Come and have breakfast with me in the morning."

Instead here he was, on a dark road somewhere—he thought in Suffolk. He seemed to remember a sign reading CAMBRIDGE an hour back.

Too many memories . . .

Tired now, having to blink his eyes to keep them from closing, he knew he'd have to find somewhere to sleep, and soon, if he wasn't to run off the road into a ditch. And that, he told himself, he could not do. Nothing must cloud Frances's happiness.

Hamish had—blessedly—been silent all day. As Rutledge was getting dressed, driving to the house to meet his sister, then to the wedding, the reception, it was the one thing he'd feared, that the war would come back and shame him, frighten Frances and her guests, and expose his nightmare for all the world to see. Somehow, he'd held the past at bay. It had taken all the will he possessed, but somehow it had worked.

Now, tired as he was, lonely as he felt, he was vulnerable, and suddenly Hamish was there in the motorcar with him, sitting in the seat behind him, a voice in his ear. Corporal Hamish MacLeod was dead, buried in France. Rutledge was as sure of that as any man could be. After all, he'd shot Hamish, and watched the light fade from his eyes as he died. He'd heard the young Scot's last whisper before he'd pulled the trigger in the coup de grâce: *Fiona*. The woman Hamish loved and wanted more than life itself to come home to. And yet, knowing the cost, Hamish had refused to lead any more men into the teeth of the machine-gun nest that had already killed too many of them. And Rutledge had had no choice but to make an example of him. It had to be done, or none of the men in his command would have followed him over the top again. What's more, they would have faced court-martial and, most certainly, another firing squad. Sacrifice one man to save many. Send them over the top to silence the machine gun, before it killed more men tomorrow when the big push began.

He shook his head, trying to shove those memories back into the shadows. Trying to stop Hamish while he could, but it was too late, and the brightness of the headlamps became the flashes of artillery fire, followed by the machine guns. And the war was back.

He fought it, and never knew how many miles he'd driven by rote, unaware of where he was and what he was doing, his hands gripping the wheel as he'd gripped his revolver and his whistle.

The screams of the wounded and dying filled his mind, and he shouted to his men, encouraging them, urging them on, and all the while he cursed himself as one by one they fell.

Without warning, the sounds began to recede and the darkness in his mind once more became the bright beams of his headlamps probing the night.

And almost too late he saw what they picked out just ahead of him.

A motorcar was stopped in the middle of the road, its doors standing wide. He'd hardly taken that in when he realized there was a woman in the road too, bending over the body of someone—a man—lying haphazardly at her feet.

Rutledge was already pulling hard on the brake, bringing the heavy motorcar to a skidding halt not twenty feet from the rear of the other vehicle. It was then he saw one more piece of the tableau in front of him.

There was blood on the woman's hands.

The woman looked up, staring toward him in dismay, fright filling her eyes as she stood there like stone, all color washed out of her face, and the blood on her hands black in the brightness bridging the gap between them.

2

Rutledge, recovering from the shock more quickly than the woman standing in the road did, switched off the motor and got down, walking swiftly toward her, forcing his mind to concentrate on what he was seeing.

"What happened here?" he asked, the voice of authority, of a Scotland Yard Inspector, taking over from habit. The voice didn't seem to belong to him, somehow.

And then he was once more in control.

She couldn't speak, her fear constricting her throat.

He stopped. He could already see that the man was dead. And no weapon was visible. Both the woman and the man on the ground were wearing evening dress.

"It's all right," he said more gently. "Just tell me what has happened."

"We were driving back to the village. There was someone standing in the road," she said, her voice trembling, uncertain, as if she hadn't been there but had heard the story from someone else. There was the slightest hint of a Scots accent as she went on. "We had to stop. I thought he must be in trouble, and we could help. Stephen told me to stay in the motorcar, and he himself got down. The figure didn't move at first. He—he just stood there. It was—I was beginning to be frightened. And Stephen was saying something like 'Do you need help?' I think he asked twice, because it seemed that the other man didn't grasp what he'd said. The man started forward, then, and I realized he had a revolver in his hand. He just walked up to Stephen, said something I didn't hear—and he—he brought the weapon up until it pointed at Stephen's chest, and he *shot him*. Just—*shot* him."

Rutledge could see the black patch across the front of the dead man's shirt, open to the night. Not a lot of blood—his heart had stopped beating quickly.

The woman looked down at her hands. "I opened his coat, I tried to stop the bleeding with his scarf. But I think he—I think he was already *dead*."

Rutledge glanced around, saying, "Where did he go? This man? Did you see?"

"He just turned and walked across the road—that way—" She pointed to her left. "And vanished. I didn't care, as long as he was gone. I had to help Stephen."

"What's your name?" he asked her.

"Elizabeth . . . Elizabeth MacRae." She was beginning to shake now, in the aftermath of shock. Clasping her hands together to still them, she went on in rising hysteria. "I've never watched someone die. It was horrid."

Keeping her within his line of sight, Rutledge moved toward the man, knelt beside him, and felt for a pulse. The action was perfunctory, but it had to be done. The body was quite warm. This had only just happened. And it appeared that the man had been shot. Just as she'd described. He glanced quickly under the motorcar. If there was a revolver there, he couldn't see it.

"Is he—*is* he alive?" she asked, a flare of hope in her eyes.

"I'm afraid not."

She leaned against the frame of the door, looking faint.

Rising, he took Miss MacRae's arm and guided her away from the body to the far side of the motorcar. "Where had you come from? Where were you going?"

"We—we were dining with friends. It was rather late, they—they urged us to stay the night. But—but Stephen had plans for tomorrow. To-today." Her teeth were chattering now, and he looked into the rear seat of the motorcar, found a folded rug there, and draped it around her shoulders. She clutched at it, pulling it closer.

He thought she was on the verge of being sick, but he said, "Stephen?" She had no rings on her left hand.

"Stephen Wentworth. He—he lives in Wolfpit. Lived." She began to cry, and he handed her his handkerchief. She buried her face in it.

Rutledge walked to the front of the motorcar and examined the road for any evidence that might support her account. But he couldn't find any footprints. The deep winter ruts crisscrossed each other in irregular patterns, making it impossible to pick out details. Still, he searched carefully, even walking to the verge to look for signs that someone had passed that way. Or that a revolver had been tossed into the high grass there as soon as his headlamps were visible in the distance.

The greatest danger, he knew, was that she was telling the truth. *Was the killer out there somewhere, watching? Still armed . . .*

If, of course, he actually existed.

It could as easily have been a lovers' quarrel that ended in murder. But how many men carried a weapon in their motorcar? If it was a service revolver, had this Stephen Wentworth been afraid of something? Was that why it hadn't been locked in the boot? Why wasn't it put safely away in an attic or box room, with other reminders of the war brought back from France?

His own was locked in the trunk under his bed . . .

Rutledge walked back to Miss MacRae. She had stopped crying, her face streaked with tears and the blood from her hands, but he thought she was nearly at the end of her strength. She was leaning against the cold metal of a wing, head down, eyes looking inward. She raised her head, but said nothing.

Rutledge was in a quandary. He could hardly shove Wentworth's body into the rear of his own motorcar and leave this one where it stood. He had done a cursory examination of the vehicle, it was too dark for more than that, and he didn't relish leaving it in the middle of the road where anyone might come upon it. Or the killer return to it.

He said, "Can you drive?"

"I—yes." She stared at him, uncertain what he was asking.

"How far is Wolfpit from here?"

"Tw-two miles, I think. Three at most."

"Does it have a policeman?"

"Yes. Constable P-Penny."

He considered her. She was wearing a rather pretty dinner gown, shimmering gold under a matching wrap, and gold slippers, muddy now. There were feathers in a spray, held by a pin in her fair hair. Hardly proper attire for driving a large motorcar.

"Will you take my motorcar, drive to the village, and bring back the local Constable? Tell him there has been a death, and we'll need the doctor. He'll know what to do."

"I don't think I can manage it," she said, anxiously gazing up at him. "Is there any other way?"

"I'm afraid not." He let that take root in her mind, then asked, "Are you sure you didn't recognize the man in the road?"

"I don't know that Stephen did, either. He was just—there. In the middle of the road. Waiting."

"What was he wearing?"

"I don't think I noticed. You don't understand—it happened so quickly. There was no time really to look at him."

He let it go for the moment.

"And you didn't hear what he said to Wentworth?"

She shook her head.

"Did Wentworth reply?"

"I don't think so. No, he must have done. Just a word or two. But I didn't hear that either."

"We must have the police, and the doctor. I'm reluctant to leave him lying there, but I don't want to move the motorcar. Not yet. You'll have to go in my place. Or else stay here alone."

That was all the persuasion she needed. "No." She shook her head again, the feathers dancing. "Anything but that."

He led her to his motorcar, turned the crank, and collected his torch from the boot before helping Miss MacRae into the driver's seat. She looked around for a moment, as if she had never seen gauges before. He waited, giving her time to collect herself. Finally, setting her mouth resolutely, she pulled her skirts aside so that she could reach the pedals, then put her hands on the wheel.

With some trepidation he watched her drive slowly around Wentworth's motorcar and carry on toward the village.

In a matter of seconds, he was alone on the road.

He stood there, staring at the scene, dark now without his own headlamps to light it. Wentworth's beams probed the shadows ahead, catching movement as a predawn breeze stirred the dry grasses. A fox's muzzle poked out of the undergrowth, sniffed the air, then vanished as quietly as it had appeared.

What had he heard or seen as he was coming up to Wentworth's motorcar?

He tried to remember. Had he heard a shot? Or a woman's scream? He couldn't quite believe he'd missed the sound of a shot. Not even in the throes of nightmare.

The problem was, he couldn't be sure.

Had it been the approach of his own motor that had sent the killer away? If whoever it was had stayed, would he have killed the only witness too?

Why hadn't he killed her, come to that?

Rutledge went back to the body lying in the road, switching on his torch. A single shot, almost point-blank range. Meant to kill, not to frighten or wound.

The dead man was fair, of medium height and build, a gentleman from the quality of his clothing, and reasonably attractive. There were laugh lines around his eyes and mouth, smoothing out now in death, but just visible.

Who had wanted to see him dead? Did someone know that he would be coming down this road at this hour of the night, and wait for him? This wasn't a main thoroughfare, just a narrow road through fields joining two small villages. It wouldn't have been heavily traveled, not at this hour.

The killer couldn't have been at the party that Elizabeth MacRae had attended—she would have recognized him. And the same was true of the village. If he lived in Wolfpit, she would very likely have known who he was. Not by name, perhaps, but certainly able to identify him.

Still, in Rutledge's experience, it was odd that in a random murder like this, Wentworth was dead—and Miss MacRae still alive. Surely there had been time to fire at her before disappearing?

There was another explanation. Either the killer was looking for Wentworth, or he thought Wentworth was the man he sought. Had he been mistaken? And if he had been, would he stand in the road another night, and kill again, until he found the victim he wanted?

Hamish spoke suddenly, loud in the quiet of the night.

"Or it was the lass herself. Miss MacRae?"

Rutledge had to keep that in mind as well. It was, in fact, far more likely that she had shot Wentworth than that someone had appeared out of the darkness and killed him. A quarrel, Miss MacRae threatening to get down, the motorcar stopping abruptly in the middle of the road. Wentworth getting down as well, as the quarrel escalated into a shouting match . . .

The problem was the revolver. Where had it come from? There was no indication that they'd fought over possession of it. Those elegant feathers in Miss MacRae's hair would surely have been the first victim of any struggle.

Rutledge began a thorough search of the vehicle. But there was nothing useful to be found. Wentworth's hat, lying on the rear seat with his gloves. Miss MacRae's purse, lying on the floor of the passenger's seat, a beaded affair on a silver chain that was far too small to conceal a revolver. But there was a coat in her seat as well, with deep enough pockets.

You didn't carry a revolver with you in your coat pocket to a fashionable dinner party. Not unless you expected to need it. For protection. Or in anticipation of a quarrel ending badly. But then she might have left it out of sight in the motorcar before going in.

Hamish said, "Jealousy?"

If Miss MacRae had carried it with her—where was it now?

Finishing his search, Rutledge scanned the road on either side. It was relatively flat here and open, no hedgerow or straggle of trees to make a killer's disappearance easier. To his left, he could just see hay stacked in the field beyond the fallow one closest to the road, eerie humps in the darkness. On the far side, a shed of some sort, shapeless and swaybacked, as if it had been there a very long time and was near to collapsing.

Which direction had the killer taken? Surely he would have gone the shortest distance, toward the hayricks? Still, he might have doubled back once he had got clear, to throw searchers off.

The field of hay would take longer to search. Torch in hand, Rutledge set out toward the shed. The ground was rough, muddy in some places. He thought, as he nearly lost his footing for a second time, that this had been a pasture plowed up during the war to grow a crop, then abandoned at war's end. Every bit of arable land had been put to the production of food, once submarines in the North Atlantic made it nearly impossible to bring in sufficient supplies from overseas. He cursed the field now. When he finally reached the shed, he saw that the door was half off its hinges, hanging crookedly inside the frame. He swept the interior with the torch, but it was empty save for scraggly weeds that had survived for a time and then died, leaving behind skeletons of their past.

Although Rutledge looked closely, he couldn't find footprints in the dry soil of the interior. He looked on the outside as well, circling the shed in the hope of spotting where someone might stand out of sight and watch for passersby. In the end, reluctantly, he ruled out the shed.

He had just reached the road again when he saw his motorcar approaching. A Constable was driving, the shield on his helmet gleaming in the reflection of the headlamps. Beside him, looking exhausted, was Miss MacRae.

They pulled up well ahead of the dead man's motorcar, and the Constable got down, striding forward to meet Rutledge.

"Constable Penny, sir," he said. "What's this about a body?"

Rutledge took him to see where Wentworth was lying, and heard the low whistle as Penny recognized the dead man.

"Know him, do you?" Rutledge asked.

"He lives in Wolfpit. Owns a bookshop there. But who shot him? I couldn't quite make out the story the young lady was telling me. Did you see what happened? I understand you came along only moments later." There was a detectable hint of suspicion in the policeman's voice.

"Unfortunately I arrived just after the shot was fired. By that time the killer had vanished in the darkness, according to Miss MacRae."

"Do you know her, then?"

"No, I don't," Rutledge answered. He indicated the interior of the motorcar. "No weapon that I've been able to find. You might have better luck in daylight."

"That was wrong of you, sir. Meddling with the crime scene."

"Yes, well, we don't know where the shooter went, and I'd rather be in possession of his firearm than find it pointed at me when my back was turned."

"That's very brave of you, sir." There was a hint of sarcasm in the Constable's voice.

He went to stand in the open door of the motorcar, peering inside, poking around. Rutledge wondered if he'd come to the same conclusions. "What brought you along this road tonight, sir?" he asked, withdrawing from the vehicle and taking out his notebook.

What *had* brought him along this road? He couldn't have said. Nor could he explain himself to this man. Rutledge looked back the way he'd come, and finally answered, after examining the map in his head, "I was on my way to Ipswich."

"And your name, sir?"

"Rutledge." He reached in his pocket, and found that he'd left his identification in the London flat. "Inspector. Scotland Yard."

"Can you prove that, sir?"

"I was on personal business this evening. Morning," he added as he looked toward the eastern sky. But the first faint rays of false dawn hadn't appeared. "I don't have my identification with me." He realized he'd driven much farther and much faster than he'd expected. London seemed a very long way behind him. And the wedding had receded in his mind, driven out by the return of the war. What had made that stop so abruptly? Had it been the sound of a real shot close by? Was that why he couldn't actually recall hearing it?

"I see, sir," Constable Penny was saying.

Rutledge knew that the man couldn't possibly begin to understand. "Is the doctor coming?"

"Yes, sir, Dr. Brent is on his way. Although he'll not be able to help this one."

Miss MacRae had remained in Rutledge's motorcar. He could see the pale oval of her face, the color drained even more by the brightness of his headlamps.

Turning back to Penny, Rutledge said, "I've walked out to the shed you can see over there. No sign of anyone hanging about, waiting for Wentworth to come along. But I haven't gone in the other direction. Now you're here, I'll have a look."

"I'd rather you waited, sir. For the doctor."

"That's my motorcar, Constable. I'm not likely to walk away and leave it."

As if he hadn't recognized the dryness in Rutledge's voice, Penny nodded and then began to examine the scene for himself, studying the ground, the position of the body relative to the vehicle, and finally walking along the verge.

Rutledge stood to one side, watching him. Penny was making much the same survey that he himself had done. A competent man, he thought, and unwilling to take anyone's word for what had happened here. He himself had already contaminated the ground, but it couldn't be helped. Still, there had been damned little to find.

As a place to commit murder, this was ideal. No habitation in sight, the road relatively straight in either direction, making it possible to see vehicles approaching long before the killer could be spotted.

And that brought up another point. Had the killer known that it was Wentworth's motorcar? Had he recognized it? Or just stopped it at random, the first to come along after he'd chosen his spot?

How had he come to this place? By bicycle? Motorcar? If so, where had he left them? Or on foot? But that would slow his escape, walking across fields without a torch.

Any chance of finding Wentworth's killer was rapidly fading. Rutledge still had his torch in his hand, and ignoring Penny, he started toward the hayricks. But just then lights came around the slight bend in the direction of Wolfpit, and the Constable squinted to see who it was.

"That'll be the doctor, sir. Dr. Brent."

Rutledge stopped and turned around.

The doctor pulled in behind Rutledge's motorcar and got down. He paused for a moment to speak to Miss MacRae, then nodded and came on toward the two men waiting by the body.

"All right, Penny, what do we have here?" he asked as he approached. He was a man of medium height, graying, and sporting the trim mustache affected by many officers during the war. "And who is this man?" He nodded toward Rutledge.

"Mr. Rutledge, sir. He came along from the other direction, just after the shooting."

Satisfied, Brent moved around them and inspected the body. "You don't need me to tell you he's dead." Kneeling, he began to examine Wentworth. "Probably by the time he hit the ground. Dead center shot, close range. I'll be damned if it didn't go straight through the heart. But we'll see about that, won't we? And still relatively warm, despite the cold air. Killed in the last hour, I should think." He shook his head. "A damned pity. Wentworth was a fine young man. Who closed his eyes?"

"I did," Rutledge said. "I was first on the scene. It appeared that Miss MacRae had tried to revive him. There was blood on her hands. No sign of the weapon."

Dr. Brent looked up sharply. "You aren't saying that Miss MacRae shot him?"

"She told me that there was a man standing in the middle of the road. Wentworth got out to speak to him after he refused to move out of the way. They appeared to exchange a few words, and the other man shot him without warning, then disappeared while Miss MacRae rushed to Wentworth's assistance."

"Description?" The Constable and the doctor asked the question almost simultaneously.

"She didn't recognize him. She didn't think Wentworth did either. Or he gave no indication that he had. She was so shocked she couldn't give me much more than that."

"Small wonder. I'm amazed she's held up as well as she has," the doctor said.

"And the weapon belonged to the man in the road?" the Constable asked.

"Apparently he brought it with him. If what Miss MacRae told me is true. He simply pulled it out and fired. There was no anger, no shouting, no warning."

"What was said between the two men?" the Constable wanted to know.

"She didn't hear."

Constable Penny looked toward Rutledge's motorcar again, then turned back. "I have to ask, sir. Do you believe the witness is telling the truth? Or did she kill the victim?"

"I don't know," Rutledge said truthfully. "She was in such a state when I arrived that my first impression was that she had not. And we haven't got a weapon. But of course if she had, she might have been shocked by what she'd done and refused to believe what had happened. Or—she's a very fine actress."

"Nonsense," the doctor said, in his turn glancing toward Miss MacRae. She was still sitting in Rutledge's motorcar. "Besides, where had she come by a revolver?"

"It could have been Wentworth's," Rutledge said. "Was he in the war?"

"Yes, he was," the doctor responded shortly. "Captain in the Royal Navy."

"He would still have had a sidearm," Rutledge answered.

"Where had they been, where were they coming from? At this hour?" the doctor asked, looking into the darkness in the direction Wentworth and Miss MacRae had come from, as if somewhere there he might find an answer. "Dressed for a dinner party, from the looks of it."

"I don't know precisely where that was. It's best to ask Miss Mac-Rae."

"Well, that can wait. We've been lucky no one else has come along. Penny, can you drive this motorcar back to Wolfpit? I wasn't able to bring a stretcher, but I think between us we can get him into the rear seat."

"Do you know Wentworth well?" Rutledge asked as he bent down to lift the dead man's feet.

"Fairly well. I know his parents, of course. They live just outside Norwich now, to be closer to their daughter and her children. Her husband was killed in the war. Stephen went to Cambridge, read the classics, and wanted to travel. He was in Peru when war broke out.

Came home and joined the Navy. Ship went down under him three times, and he survived." He shrugged. "Only to die within sight of home. Or nearly so. Sad."

They lifted the body, heavier in death than in life, and got him into the rear of his own motorcar.

The doctor closed the door, then said to Rutledge, "You'll bring Miss MacRae back to the village?"

"I'd also prefer it if you did," Constable Penny added. "To help with this inquiry, sir?"

"He doesna' believe ye're an Inspector," Hamish put in, startling Rutledge.

Recovering quickly, he said, "Unless she would be more comfortable traveling with you, Dr. Brent?"

"No, no. She doesn't need to be bounced from motorcar to motorcar," he answered briskly.

Rutledge walked back to his own vehicle to turn the crank, then waited while the doctor reversed his, before getting behind the wheel to do the same. The Constable was already starting Wentworth's, preparing to bring up the rear.

Miss MacRae was huddled in the corner of her seat, still clutching the rug he'd given her. Rutledge asked, "Are you warm enough? Your coat and evening purse are still in Wentworth's vehicle. Shall I fetch them for you?"

"No, please. I-I just want to go home. To my aunt's house," she amended.

As the three-car convoy started toward the village, she turned to look at him.

"They think I killed him, don't they?" she asked after a moment. "They kept looking this way. I saw them. And it wasn't very sympathetic."

He smiled grimly at her. "I think there's an even chance in their minds that if you didn't kill Wentworth, I did."

3

Rutledge had never been to Wolfpit. The unusual name, he learned later, came from a pit used centuries before to hold captured wolves. For some reason it hadn't been changed, though it certainly no longer fit the pretty village he found himself driving into.

It was still quite dark, and the church clock was just striking five.

"Are you sure you don't need to have Dr. Brent give you something to help with the shock? I can stop by his surgery," Rutledge asked Miss MacRae, but she shook her head.

"I don't think I could bear to see Stephen's body one more time," she said. "Please? I'm staying with my aunt. Just there, beyond the church."

He could see the church—could in fact hardly miss it, for it was quite large with a tall, slender spire piercing the night sky. Turning away from the other two motorcars, he drove in that direction.

"Why were you so long at the dinner party? They generally end at ten or eleven o'clock."

"We stayed on. Mrs. Hardy's son was expected. He'd sent a telegram earlier from Dover, saying he'd been delayed in France. And so we waited. We sat and talked for a while, and I expect we lost track of the time. We had just gone down to the kitchen to make tea when her son arrived. But we had to leave soon after, and I hardly had a chance to do more than meet him."

She pointed to a house on her right, and he pulled over.

"This one?" He couldn't see a light showing.

"Yes, please."

"These were your friends you were dining with?"

"No. They were Stephen's. Evelyn's brother had known him for ages, and of course everyone was eager to see Mrs. Hardy's son. Stephen had invited me to this dinner because he needed to have someone with him—the numbers, you see, at table." Her voice caught on a sob as she remembered, and she hurried on, changing the subject. "I'm staying with my aunt for a bit. I often come to visit her. That's how I knew Stephen, through my aunt. There's no attachment, you understand. Just a friendship. I think that's why he feels—felt—comfortable with me, and I enjoy—enjoyed—his company."

It was said simply, and he believed her.

He'd studied her as she spoke. She was attractive, a pretty face, silvery fair hair that she wore in a becoming style, and blue eyes. Hardly a last resort to make up numbers, he thought. Whatever Stephen Wentworth might have led her to believe.

Had he chosen Miss MacRae because she *was* quite so attractive? Was there someone at the dinner party he wanted to see him with a pretty girl on his arm? It would be worth considering.

Hamish had said it. Jealousy.

"When did you first meet him? How long ago was that?"

"I was here one summer—it was just before he went up to Cambridge—and he was looking for a tennis partner. I was fifteen, but a good player. My aunt suggested me. And we continued to play, whenever I was in Suffolk. Sometimes we went to lunch or dinner. And, of course, my aunt knows his parents." She clapped a hand over her mouth, leaning toward him, as if for comfort. "Oh dear God, what am I to do? Someone will have to tell them that Stephen is—is dead. I can't bear it to be me."

"That will be the duty of the police," he told her gently. "Although you might wish to write to them later—to give them the peace of mind of knowing he didn't suffer."

"Oh. Yes, of course. I shall do just that." Her relief was so great that tears came to her eyes. "I didn't *love* Stephen. But I was quite fond of him. It was a friendship I cared about. We are both great readers, and I was fascinated by his stories of his travels. He showed me photographs, places I'll never see, exotic and exciting and romantic in the larger sense. There was an ancient fortress outside of Cuzco, and in it was a throne-like stone structure. The altitude was terrible, thirteen thousand feet, and he found it hard to climb up to the throne. Even after taking days to get to Cuzco, over the mountains, he hadn't acclimated. And in the desert, down at sea level, there were lines that made no sense, just stones set in what appeared to be an aimless pattern. But when you climbed high enough in the surrounding hills, they weren't aimless at all. Birds and spiders, all sorts of designs. You'd have to be a bird yourself to see them properly. How had these ancient people managed such a tremendous plan? It was stunning, beyond belief."

She had changed as she spoke, animated by the memory of what she'd been shown, her face alight. And then the light dimmed as she remembered. Catching her breath on a gasp of pain, she turned and opened her door before he could come around to help her, and still holding the rug around her shoulders, she hurried up the path to the house door, letting herself in without looking back.

He watched until a lamp was lit in a room on the ground floor. She might not have been in love with Stephen Wentworth, but she had been caught up in the excitement of the life he'd led, and how short a step would it have been to love the man as well as his stories and photographs?

Rutledge found the doctor's surgery easily enough. Wentworth's motorcar was standing in the front of a fair-size house just beyond the triangular square, and there were lights on in one of the wings.

He went to the door and tapped lightly. Constable Penny came at once, saying as he let Rutledge in, "We were beginning to worry."

"I made certain Miss MacRae was safe," he said. "Has Dr. Brent found anything of interest, examining the body?"

"He's given it a preliminary examination," Penny said reluctantly, "but prefers to wait for morning to do more. I was just leaving to go back to my own cottage."

"Someone will have to let Wentworth's parents know he is dead."

"Yes, sir, I'll see to that." He nodded across the square. "There's a fairly decent inn just there. I'll rouse the clerk, if you like, and make certain you have a room."

"Very kind," Rutledge answered, and leaving the motorcar where it was, he crossed the square with the Constable.

"No luggage, sir?" Penny asked when Rutledge made no move to collect a valise.

"It's in the boot."

"You said Ipswich. How long were you expecting to stay?"

Exasperated, although he knew the man was only doing his duty, he said, "I don't know, Constable. My sister was married today. Yesterday. I went for a short drive to clear my head, and it just seemed the right thing to do to keep on driving. I'm not expected back at the Yard until Tuesday. I'm on leave until then."

"I see." They had reached the inn. Rutledge looked up at the sign. A swan in black wrought iron. After stepping through the front door, the Constable disappeared through another one behind the desk and came back in a few minutes with a very sleepy woman.

"You're wanting a room?" she asked.

"Yes, I am."

"Well, there's no one staying here just now. Would you like a front or a back view?"

"Front, please."

She opened a drawer, found what she was after, and handed him a key. "Number two, that is. Will you be wanting breakfast this morning?"

"Please."

"We begin serving at seven. Through there." She pointed to a room to one side, set with tables and chairs designed for meals. And with that, she turned and disappeared through the door, shutting it firmly behind her.

Bidding the Constable a good morning, Rutledge took the stairs two at a time and found himself in a very dark passage. Wishing for his torch, which was in the motorcar, he paused to let his eyes grow accustomed to what light there was, and saw a door just in front of him. The key fit, but he discovered that the door wasn't locked.

The light from the windows helped him find a lamp, and after two tries, he managed to locate the matches. As the glow brightened, he saw that he had found number 2 quite by chance, and he shut the door before walking to the window. The street was quiet. Apparently Constable Penny had gone home, and the only light that Rutledge could see was from the bakery down the street—faint enough that it must be shining through the windows from a back area where the ovens were.

He drew the curtains, undressed, and went to bed. He hadn't realized how very tired he was. His eyes seemed to close of their own weight, and he was asleep.

It was a little after eight, just after dawn, when Rutledge woke. He could feel his beard rasping against his hand as he rubbed his chin. And he hadn't brought in his valise, he thought ruefully. It was still in the boot. What the hell had he been doing, driving cross-country like that? And yet at the time it had seemed the best thing to do . . .

Hamish, in the back of his mind, would have none of it.

"Face it, man, ye couldna' settle. Else, why did ye bring yon valise? A half hour around London doesna' require a razor and a change of clothes."

Rutledge tried to shut him out. He wasn't prepared to look too deeply into last night.

He got up, dressed, and went down to the dining room, where he poured himself a cup of tea and drank it down. Then he went out to his motorcar and retrieved his valise.

While he was shaving, he considered what to do about Stephen Wentworth's death.

He was the best choice to take over the inquiry—after all, he'd been first on the scene. He had a feeling he would have to convince Constable Penny that this was *his* decision.

But he found, when he arrived at the police station, that the Constable had been busy with his own arrangements.

"I've sent a message to Inspector Reed in Stowmarket, sir, asking him to come to Wolfpit and take over this inquiry. It's for the best. I don't know that I can be objective enough, having been acquainted with Mr. Wentworth as long as I have. And to tell truth, I don't know that I find what Miss MacRae told us to be convincing. An odd story at best."

Rutledge quickly changed his mind about arguing with the Constable, given what he'd just said. It would do no good, and could potentially do a great deal of harm.

Instead, he commented, "It might be best to ask the Chief Constable to call in the Yard. Since the party Wentworth and Miss MacRae attended probably isn't in your jurisdiction or Reed's."

"Sir, I considered that too. But you're a witness after the fact, and I don't know that it would be right to ask you to conduct the inquiry. Still, it's out of my hands. The Inspector will know what's best to do."

"How well does he know the village?"

"He's been here a time or two, just looking in. He took over Stowmarket in 1919, after the war. Inspector Gray had been set on retiring before the war but stayed on for the duration, as many of us did. I daresay he was very glad to hand over to Mr. Reed."

"Much trouble here?"

"The usual miscreants. Nothing to speak to Inspector Gray or Inspector Reed about. Much less the Chief Constable. The last murder here was in 1910. Jealous husband. We didn't have to look far to find out who did it. He was standing in the kitchen with blood all over him and a butcher's knife in his hand. He was in no state to answer questions then, but the next morning he confessed readily enough. I think it was a relief, in a way, to get it off his chest. I always felt I should have seen it coming, but his own mother hadn't, nor his wife—the victim. I don't know to this day whether there was an argument precipitating what he did, or if wondering and not knowing had driven him to be done with it."

"Had she been having an affair?"

"Yes, sir. With the postmaster. He was nearly twice her age. Odd choice, if you ask me. But there's no accounting for tastes, is there?"

"No." Changing the subject, Rutledge asked, "Any word from the doctor?"

Penny hesitated. "I don't know that I should tell you, sir. Seeing that you're a witness."

"I hardly think Dr. Brent has uncovered any earth-shaking information," he countered dryly.

"Well, as to that, he hasn't done anything but examine the gunshot wound. It was close range and straight through the heart, just as he expected." Penny paused, looking around the spare little room that was his kingdom. "Which says to me that it isn't likely a stranger shot him, not coming in that close."

Rutledge said, pulling out the only other chair and sitting down, "It's also rather surprising that a woman, having an argument with her escort of the evening, was such a good shot."

Penny raised his eyebrows. "I hadn't considered that, sir. *Did* they have an argument?"

"I've no idea. But both parties were out of the motorcar when I arrived on the scene. Either something had happened on the road, just as Miss MacRae has claimed—or they had argued, Wentworth had stopped the motorcar, and one of them got out, followed by the other."

It was clear Penny hadn't got that far in his own thinking. And Rutledge had a feeling that it was because he knew Wentworth but not Miss MacRae, just as he'd said.

"How did you become acquainted with the victim?" Rutledge asked, intentionally not using Wentworth's name, but driving home the point that he could no longer be viewed as simply another inhabitant of the village.

"He owns the bookshop down the street. Owned. He was well off, he didn't need to earn his keep, but he bought the shop when old Mr. Delaney took ill and wanted to sell, and he's made a go of it. During the war, he asked Mrs. Delaney to keep it open, and to her credit, she managed to do it, even after she lost her husband, poor woman."

"You're a reader, then?"

"I am, sir. I'm fond of biography, and Mr. Wentworth made a point to look out interesting titles for me. The latest was about King Harold, and what might have happened if he hadn't had to race north to stop the King of Norway's army, then south to face William of Normandy. Quite a rousing account, even though it's only speculation."

"When do you expect to hear from Inspector Reed?"

"By ten o'clock, I should think, sir."

"Have you spoken to Miss MacRae this morning?"

"I did step around to her aunt's house, but there was no one awake at that hour."

Rutledge rose. "I need to find a telephone. Is there one in the village?"

"Mr. Wentworth had one put in for his shop just last year. He said it was the coming thing, and paid for it out of his own pocket."

"I should like to use it. Do you have Wentworth's keys? Or are they still at the surgery?"

The Constable hesitated. "I don't think it would be proper to give you the keys to his shop, sir. Not until Inspector Reed has had a look."

"He wasn't killed there. And I shan't disturb any evidence. I simply need to use the telephone," Rutledge answered, quelling his desire to swear.

Reluctantly, Penny pulled out the drawer in the table he used as his desk and brought out a small ring of keys. "That's to his house, farther along The Street. The High, if you will. This is to the shop."

"How did you know?"

"I tried them this morning, in order to label them for Inspector Reed."

Rutledge kept his voice level as he took the keys and thanked Penny. With a nod, he left the police station, and after walking one way then the other along The Street, he found the bookshop. A sign hung above his head, an iron book with lettering that read DELANEY'S. And just under it, as if stamped into the outer corner of the cover, was a silhouette of a wolf's head, muzzle raised in a silent howl.

Inserting the key and turning it, he opened the door and stepped inside, closing it behind him.

The shop had that particular smell of books, and he saw that there were shelves arranged precisely around the interior space, with two tables displaying a range of stationery, cards, and diaries. On the wall just behind the counter was a telephone, but Rutledge walked through the shop before using it.

It was spacious, with two smaller rooms in the back, one containing a desk with ledgers and, in one of the side drawers, what appeared to be bills for books ordered and sold. In the center drawer there was stationery, with an ornate *D* at the top, with a similar wolf's head inside. A cabinet against one wall held other accounts, and unopened boxes were set in a stack against another wall. The second room, the smaller of the two, was more a sitting room, with a comfortable chair and a lamp on the table beside it. On a shelf were cups and saucers, tins of tea, and a small, half-empty bottle of milk as well as a china sugar bowl.

This room looked well used, as if Wentworth preferred to sit here to read or work, rather than at home.

Out back was a shed and a small garden, winter dead but obviously well tended. There were an iron table and a pair of chairs under a section of the main roof that had been extended to protect them.

In the public area of the shop, Rutledge did a brief survey of the shelves and recognized many of the titles. To his surprise, he even discovered a small volume of poems by O A Manning. *Wings of Fire.* He knew it well, had carried it with him in the trenches. And after the war, he had been called to look into the death of Olivia Marlowe, who was actually O A Manning. A woman whose poetry haunted him still, as she herself did.

Abruptly turning away, he walked to the telephone and found it to be working. He put through a call to London, to the Yard.

It was Sunday, and he hadn't expected to find Sergeant Gibson on duty. But he recognized the Sergeant's voice as soon as he answered.

"Good morning, Sergeant. Rutledge here. I'm in Suffolk at present—"

"I thought your sister was to be married this weekend," Gibson said, alarm in his voice as he interrupted Rutledge.

"Yes, that was last evening." He hesitated. *Was it only last evening?* "I had business in Suffolk, and I've stopped in the village of Wolfpit."

"Sir?"

"Wolfpit. An old name, Gibson. Recall the tale of the green children? They came from here."

"Indeed, sir, my mother read me a story about them. They were found in a field, as I remember, and their skin was as green as grass. No one knew who they were or where they came from." He paused, confused. "Is that why you're telephoning, sir? Something to do with those children?"

"There's been a murder here, Gibson. I happened on the scene just after it had occurred. And I've reason to believe it should be a matter for the Yard."

"Have the local people requested assistance, sir?"

"No, not yet. But I have a feeling the Chief Superintendent ought to speak to the Chief Constable. Wentworth is the name of the victim. Stephen Wentworth. He's a man of some importance here. And the circumstances around the death are unusual." He went on to describe what he'd found in the middle of the road.

"If you're a witness, sir, it might not be the wisest thing to take over the inquiry."

Rutledge wanted to tell him that he wasn't ready to return to London. But he couldn't, not without explaining more than he cared to have Gibson know.

"I didn't witness the actual murder. But I was first on the scene, minutes after it happened. I expect that gives me an edge over the local people."

"I don't know," Gibson said slowly, considering the explanation.

"Then leave it to Markham to decide what should be done. But since I'm already here in the village, it seems pointless to have someone else travel down from London."

"There's that," Gibson agreed. "We've been at sixes and sevens here, on another inquiry, and we need all the men we can bring in. That's why I'm in here of a Sunday morning."

"I shan't have access to this telephone on a regular basis. But keep trying until you reach me."

"Aren't you still on leave, sir?" Gibson asked, remembering.

Rutledge took a deep breath. "I am, but my business in Suffolk can wait."

"All right, then, I'll see what Himself has to say. He won't be in until later in the morning."

"Yes, thank you, Sergeant."

He rang off.

Standing there, he admitted to himself that he'd been intrigued by Miss MacRae's account of a man waiting in the road, and coming up to Wentworth, speaking to him, then shooting him. It wasn't the sort of thing that someone generally made up, not on the spot. If Miss MacRae had intended to throw the police off the scent, she would have claimed a botched attempt to rob them, highwayman style. It would have made more sense, seemed more plausible.

What's more, unless she had planned ahead to kill Wentworth, why attend the dinner party with him? Or had that precipitated any quarrel?

He had the strongest feeling that if Penny didn't believe her account, neither would Inspector Reed.

Locking the door after him, Rutledge listened to Hamish mocking his explanation to Sergeant Gibson.

"Ye havena' met yon Inspector Reed. Ye canna' be certain he's no' the man for this inquiry. It's your ain self ye're thinking about. This murder willna' be solved in a day, and that will keep ye oot of London until ye're prepared to go back."

"Damn it, I was *there*," he answered the voice in his head. "I came on the scene whilst Miss MacRae was still in shock, before she'd had a chance to think clearly. Even if I give the police a statement, setting down what I saw and felt at the time, I'm not sure Penny will give it much weight. As it is, he probably thinks I'm a party to Wentworth's murder. After all, I could have disposed of the weapon while Miss MacRae went for the doctor. They'd have to sweep the fields and sift through all those hayricks before they could be sure. And Reed is more likely to listen to Penny than to someone claiming to be Scotland Yard and unable to prove it."

"Aye, ye've persuaded yourself just fine."

Rutledge returned the keys to Constable Penny, then went back to The Swan for his breakfast. Until Reed came to the village or sent word of his intentions, there was very little he could do.

Through the dining room window, he could see people dressed for morning worship making their way toward services in St. Mary's, in family groups, children dressed in neat coats and caps against the winter chill, their faces well scrubbed and pink with cold. A woman passing his window wore a very fetching hat, an upswept brim framing her face and a dashing feather curling down one side.

It reminded him of Frances, who adored smart hats and was tall enough to wear them well. He could imagine her choosing just such a one for her trousseau.

And that reminded him that he'd promised to meet Melinda Crawford for breakfast . . .

Well, it was too late—and too far from London—to do anything about that. With any luck, Melinda would assume that he'd been tired enough to sleep through their arrangement, and leave a note for him at his parents' house before departing for Kent.

On the other hand, Melinda Crawford was sharp enough that she might well come round to his flat in search of him.

What would she make of finding him gone?

He answered his own question. She would be worried.

He cursed himself for not thinking of that sooner, and using Wentworth's telephone to put in a call to his parents' house, Frances's house now, where Melinda had stayed after the wedding.

All would be well if Melinda didn't call out the cavalry. He had no doubt at all that she would manage to find him, drawing on resources that never ceased to amaze him.

He couldn't chance it. Hastily finishing his tea, Rutledge went back for the keys, then on to the bookshop to put through a call to the house.

Melinda herself answered.

"I called to apologize—" he began, but she cut across his words.

"Are you all right, Ian?"

"Yes. I'm in Suffolk. In a village called Wolfpit. There's been a murder."

"Then there's no need for an apology, my dear."

He had to be truthful. "I wasn't called here."

Down the line, he could hear her soft chuckle. "I didn't imagine you had been. But never mind. I'm sad for the victim, but perhaps it's Fate."

Rutledge wasn't certain just how to take that. "I promised you breakfast."

"I've had mine. Ram is here with the motorcar, and my boxes are already taken out. I've closed up the house, and made arrangements for it to be opened when Frances comes home from her wedding journey. She asked me to see to it."

"Thank you. Er, could you do a favor for me, before you leave London?"

"I'll be happy to."

He told her where to find the key he'd given to Frances when he first took the flat. And where to find his identification. "Could you post that to me, in care of The Swan, here in Wolfpit, Suffolk?"

"Of course. Consider it done. And Ian? Come to Kent, when you've finished your inquiry. We were all so busy with the wedding. You and I haven't had much time together. You must have a few days left of your leave?"

He had avoided long visits with her since leaving Dr. Fleming and the clinic.

Rutledge smiled, hoping it would be reflected in his voice. "The Yard may have something to say to that."

"Then I'll just have a word with the Home Office. Mallard is a dear friend."

Horrified, he said, "No, you mustn't. Truly. I'll do what I can."

"I look forward to it. Is there anything else, my dear?"

He thanked her and rang off, standing there by the telephone for a long moment. Perhaps Hamish was right. Perhaps he'd leapt at the excuse to prolong his absence from London.

On the other hand, he'd know soon enough how competent Stowmarket's Inspector Reed might be.

Still, all his training, all his experience as a policeman told him that this wasn't the usual village murder.

A horseman came up The Street from the direction of the Stowmarket Road and stopped in front of the police station. Rutledge could see just enough of the door to realize that this must be Reed coming to find out what was afoot in this outlying patch, and his responsibility toward a death here. Or more properly, not a death—a murder. Wentworth hadn't shot himself . . .

He left the bookshop and made his way to The Swan without passing the police station. Wentworth's keys were still in his pocket, and he hoped that Reed wasn't anxious to search the bookshop.

After several minutes, the horseman came striding across The Street toward the inn.

Rutledge had hastily taken his hat and coat up to his room as soon as he'd realized he was to have a visitor. By the time he'd come down the stairs again, Reed was just stepping through the inn door. A man of middle height, strongly built, with curling hair the color of burnished copper.

He looked Rutledge up and down, then said, "Well, now, well met if you're Inspector Rutledge."

"I saw you as you came to the station. I was just on my way there." Only partly true, but it would do.

The inn's pub was closed of a Sunday morning, and they took a table near the bar, where the light was good.

"Penny tells me you witnessed Wentworth's murder." Reed studied the man opposite him.

"Not entirely true," he said and explained once more.

"What were you doing on the road at that hour?" Reed asked. He had cold gray eyes, probing and suspicious.

"I couldn't sleep. I was driving through to Ipswich."

"And what took you there?"

"I have a few days of leave. I decided to get out of London for a bit. My sister was just married, and the past week was rather hectic. Duty done, I thought I might slip away."

"Odd place to choose to slip away to. Ipswich."

"Chosen randomly, I'm afraid. Mainly, I expect, because I'd never led an inquiry there." It was the truth, in a way. He'd been trying to put London behind him, literally, and there were no memories, no reminders in Ipswich. Of course, he'd had no goal in mind. But Ipswich was beyond Wolfpit, toward the coast, and it sounded reasonable enough to be his intended destination.

Reed considered him, one hand fiddling with his riding gloves.

"You don't have any identification, I'm told."

"That's correct. This journey wasn't a Yard matter. I saw no need to bring it with me."

"Then how do I know you're who you claim to be?"

Exasperated, Rutledge said, "I'm told Wentworth had a telephone put in his shop. I suggest you go there and put in a call for Sergeant Gibson at the Yard. Ask him whatever you like. I've worked with him for some years." Belatedly he remembered that he still had the keys.

"Why do you want to take over this inquiry?" Reed's eyes were hard.

Rutledge wondered what Constable Penny had told this man.

"Because I'm here. Because I was a witness, on the scene earlier than Penny and much earlier than you. It makes good sense." As he said it, he had a sudden memory of the smell of boiled cabbage from last night's dinner still drifting from the kitchen passage of the inn as he'd climbed the stairs, his mind on the bed waiting for him at the top of the flight. Was Reed a family man, with responsibilities at home that would pull him in two directions, duty and hearth? Taking a gamble, he added, "Of course, if you want to handle it yourself . . ."

"I don't," Reed said shortly. "I was married two weeks ago. I've hardly had time to realize it. And there's much to be done, settling her into my cottage. It's larger than her own. Besides that, she's from Wolfpit. She knew Wentworth."

Alert now, Rutledge said, "Then it must be a problem for you."

"Not for me. For her." Something in his voice led Rutledge to think that there was more than a passing acquaintance in the word *knew*. "I wanted to be wed last summer, but she preferred a winter wedding. She said she would need the extra time."

"Not surprising," he replied casually, without emphasis. "Brides generally make more of wedding than a man."

Reed looked away. "Yes, well." After a moment, he added, "Do you think this Miss MacRae is telling the truth?"

"I don't know. It's too elaborate a lie, if you think about it, when a simpler one would do."

"Women tend to exaggerate."

"I think in this case, it was closer to the truth. She didn't have time to concoct a plausible story. And where's the murder weapon? Which brings me to the point of asking if Wentworth had enemies."

Reed got up, pacing. "How the hell would I know? Ask Penny."

"He's of the opinion that Wentworth was the sort of man everyone admired."

"Well, there may be some truth to that." There was bitterness in his voice, as if he believed his wife held the same view. "Those born with a silver spoon generally are admired. Or hated."

After ten more minutes of beating about the bush and going nowhere, Reed left without settling the problem of who was in charge of the inquiry.

Wentworth's motorcar was in the yard behind the police station now. Rutledge went out to have another look, but he found nothing of interest. The vehicle was well kept, tidy inside, and there were no personal belongings in any of the pockets that might shed a light on Wentworth—or Miss MacRae. Her coat and purse had been removed.

He drove out of the village the way he'd come in last night, and pulled to the verge well before he came to the place where the shooting had happened.

Although he had searched rather thoroughly by the light of his torch, he got his bearings from what he'd seen in the fields, then paced up and down the road in a regular pattern, looking for anything that might have been missed in the dark. The ruts were deep, even along the shoulders. And late autumn grasses, dry and easily snapped, had encroached here and there. In London this work would have been done by a line of Constables an arm's length from each other, walking in the same patterns. But not here in the countryside. There was no one to call in. He had no authority—yet—to ask for assistance.

Halfway through he'd still found nothing of interest, but he persevered, patiently making certain that he kept his lines straight.

And then in one of the deeper ruts, he noticed an odd shape that was not a stone. Raising his head, he checked his bearings again. About here, he thought, the man must have been standing when Wentworth's headlamps picked him out.

He knelt and with his pocketknife carefully dug out whatever it was. Brushing off the caked mud, he realized that it was a small wooden carving in the shape of a wolf howling at the moon, head raised, ears back, tail curled around its haunches. And not more than two inches high. Yet the workmanship was of excellent quality, and he thought, from the smoothness he could feel, he would find once it had been cleaned, that it had been well polished.

Either an expensive toy for a child or a small treasure, he thought, turning it this way and that. But how had it come to be here? And how long might it have been lying there, lost?

Certainly anyone in Wolfpit might have owned it at one time. That wouldn't be surprising. He had noticed, etched into the glass of the inn's pub window, a wolf in a pose very much like this, and just the head had been depicted on the bookshop sign.

Dropping the carving in his pocket and dusting off his hands, he completed his pattern without finding anything else but a ha'penny.

That done, he walked across the fallow fields to the hayricks, taking his time searching for any sign of the shooter. If there had been footprints, they were gone now, and there was nothing to indicate that anyone had waited here until the flash of headlamps down the road warned of someone driving toward Wolfpit.

Rutledge paused. What if his own headlamps had been the first to come out of the darkness? What then? Would he have been stopped in the middle of the road and faced with a man armed with a revolver?

It was an interesting proposition. Wentworth had been delayed into the early morning hours. Anyone might have passed this way before he appeared. How long had the killer waited? And how had he been sure that it was Wentworth before he'd stepped into the road?

Rutledge cast about again. A waiting man paced—kicked at the straw—showed signs of impatience . . .

Frustrated, he finally turned to go, and as he passed on the far side of the rick closest to the road, he could have sworn he caught the faintest hint of tobacco. It was almost ephemeral in the damp morning air, and for a moment he wasn't quite certain where it was coming from.

"No' a cigarette," Hamish said quietly in the back of his mind.

And he was right, Rutledge thought. It was more like the aromatic pipe tobacco that some men had blended especially for them in shops in London.

He searched, to no avail, and then, just as he was about to give up, he saw it. A small pile of ash and unburned tobacco, no larger than a sixpence, at the very edge of the nearest rick. He squatted beside it and studied it, then touched it gently with one fingertip. Smelling it, he knew he was right. Someone smoking a pipe had stood here, waiting.

"No' verra' clever, pipe ash around hay."

"An unexpected conflagration would have put a spanner in his plans," Rutledge agreed, rising.

Had the killer known where Wentworth's motorcar might have been coming from?

Rutledge went back to his motorcar and drove on, backtracking Wentworth. It had been too dark last night—and he'd been too deep in the throes of nightmare—to notice what lay along the road. Slowing as he passed first one, then another house, he considered them. Both too small for a dinner party that lasted into the early hours—one was hardly more than a tenant cottage. Continuing down the road, he saw the roof of a larger house, possibly a manor, set in a park of trees. There was an elegant *H* on the open gates. Did it stand for *Hardy*? That was the name Miss MacRae had mentioned.

Cursing the lack of his identification, his authority to ask questions, he turned in the drive and came to a stop at the black-painted door of a lovely Georgian house with three stories and a pretty portico. The winter-bare branches of rosebushes set in small gardens on either side were dull green.

He lifted the heavy brass knocker and let it fall.

A middle-aged maid in crisp black answered the summons. Rutledge smiled at her.

"Good morning," he said pleasantly. "My name is Rutledge. I'm looking for Miss MacRae. I'm told she came to dinner here last evening with Stephen Wentworth. She didn't attend morning services, and I wondered if they'd decided to stay the night."

She responded to the smile, some of her stiffness fading. "She was here, sir. They left about two in the morning. Mrs. Hardy's son arrived late from France, and several guests stayed on because they know him."

"And she and Mr. Wentworth left at two, you say? Are you sure about that?" If they had, they would have arrived in Wolfpit long before Rutledge reached the village.

"Yes, sir. But he volunteered to take Miss Hardy home first. She's Mrs. Hardy's niece. Her husband's younger brother's child."

And that would explain much.

The maid was beginning to realize what Rutledge was asking. "You might inquire of Mr. Wentworth. At his family's house. He keeps rooms there. The rest is closed up."

"I hadn't thought to look there," he said, apparently embarrassed. "Thank you."

He turned to go, but the maid added, "Miss MacRae wasn't particularly happy about driving to Wickham first. She was tired and wished to be taken home. She and Mr. Wentworth argued while Miss Hardy went upstairs to fetch her coat."

She shut the door smartly before he could reply.

Rutledge had the distinct feeling that she didn't care for Miss MacRae.

4

The later morning services had just ended as he drove into the village. Rutledge watched as families came out the church door, speaking to the Rector. He could see that while there were quite a number of young children, some of them without their fathers in attendance, young people in general were missing, as they were beginning to be a vanishing breed in quite a few towns and villages. The young men had gone to war and the young unmarried women had discovered more freedom in the larger cities and towns where there was war work to be done. England had already changed while he was in the trenches, and it was still changing before his eyes.

Shaking off his darkening mood, he looked for Miss MacRae among the churchgoers. He didn't see her, but there was another woman, very likely in her early forties, tall, elegantly dressed, who left the church and walked briskly through the churchyard toward the road, waiting for him to pass before crossing it. She was alone, and a good candidate for Miss MacRae's aunt. He hadn't seen the aunt when he dropped Miss MacRae at her door, and it was purely guesswork, for there were others going in the same direction.

When she turned up the walk to the house that Miss MacRae had entered, he drove on, giving her time to go inside, and then went back to leave his motorcar at The Swan.

Five minutes later, he was standing on the small porch, waiting for someone to answer his knock.

She had taken off her hat and coat, but her cheeks were still pink from her walk in the cold air. "Yes?" she said coolly.

"I was calling to see how Miss MacRae was this morning. It was rather late before the Hardy dinner broke up."

"Then you're out of luck," she replied. "She's still asleep. I looked in her room when my little dog woke me around three, and she wasn't there. Apparently he heard something in the back garden and told the world to come and see the neighbor's cat out hunting. But she was in her bed at eight, when I came down to breakfast."

Before Rutledge could speak, she went on.

Considering him, she said, "It was Stephen Wentworth who came to collect her for the dinner party. Did he not bring her home? And who are you?"

"My name is Rutledge. I met Miss MacRae last evening."

"Did you indeed?"

"I'll return later, when she's awake."

But she was an intelligent woman, and quick to sense that Rutledge wasn't a new beau eager to pursue last night's introduction. "There's something I don't know about, isn't there?" she asked calmly, her gaze intent on his, trying to read what he was not saying. "Three is rather late, isn't it, to return from a dinner party?"

"I'm sure Miss MacRae will explain when she's awake."

"I'm asking for explanations now."

"Audrey. It's all right."

Rutledge could hear footsteps coming down the stairs, and Audrey turned, then made to close the door.

He put out a hand to stop the swing just as Miss MacRae came into view.

"Mr. Rutledge," she said. He could see the toll the night had taken. Her face was pale, strained, and her eyes were red from crying. "I didn't think I could sleep at all. But I did."

"Sometimes that's best," he said, and stepped into a wide hall. He could see the stairs to his right, and beyond them a passage with doors. There was a large green plant on a table to his left, and a chair beside it. Overhead a pretty chandelier caught the sunlight outside and sent prism reflections around the ceiling.

"My dear, you look terrible," Audrey said, trying to conceal her irritation. "And since Mr. Rutledge appears to have invited himself inside, we might as well be civilized about this. You need to sit down." She took her niece's arm and led her toward one of the doors. It was a sitting room, done up in the palest yellow, bright and cheerful. Rutledge closed the outer door and followed them.

Audrey had rung a bell after Miss MacRae had taken a chair covered in a pale green-and-cream chintz. "I think we need tea. Mr. Rutledge, do make yourself at home. I shall be interested in talking to you. Ah, Lily, we'd like tea, if you please. Lunch can wait."

The maid disappeared, closing the door behind her.

"Now then. Enlighten me," Audrey said affably, glancing from her niece to Rutledge.

Miss MacRae turned to him, her eyes pleading, asking him to answer for her.

He said, "I'm sorry, I don't know your name."

"Audrey Blackburn," she replied.

"Miss Blackburn. I'm afraid Stephen Wentworth is dead. He was shot last night while bringing Miss MacRae home from the dinner party. She was a witness to the killing, and is important to the police inquiry."

"Merciful God," Audrey Blackburn said, turning to stare at her niece. "I was thinking . . ." She coughed a little, and then went to Miss MacRae, sitting on the edge of her chair and putting an arm around the younger woman. "My dear, I am so sorry. I had no idea—why didn't you wake me up at once?"

"I couldn't talk about it. I wanted to forget." She was gazing up into her aunt's face, but Rutledge didn't think she was actually seeing her. "It was horrible. It happened so fast, and yet I remember every second. It runs over and over again in my mind. Over and over and *over*." She buried her face in her hands.

Miss Blackburn turned to Rutledge, shock in her voice. "Were you there? Did you see what happened?"

"I came on the scene shortly after it happened."

"Thank God, I can't imagine . . ." She stopped, but he knew what she was saying, that it was better for her niece not to be alone. "Thank you," she added as an afterthought.

He said, "I've come to ask Miss MacRae if she's been able to recall any more details of the shooting. I'm not officially in charge of this inquiry, but I'm an Inspector at Scotland Yard in London, and the sooner we can find this man the better for everyone."

But Miss MacRae was shaking her head. "He was just *there*, in the middle of the road. Our headlamps picked him out and Stephen slowed, waiting for him to move. That's what haunts me. The way he just stood there. As if only waiting for Stephen to step out of the motorcar. I've tried and tried to think what he could have said to Stephen. What sort of question he could have possibly asked that would be an excuse for murder. I was frightened. I wanted to ask Stephen who the man was, but I was afraid to speak. There was something—hideous—about all of it. The way the man stood, the way he spoke to Stephen, and then the coldness with which he *shot* another human being."

"Did you by any chance smell pipe smoke, when the man came closer?" Rutledge asked her.

"Pipe smoke?" She stared at him as if he'd lost his mind, to ask such a nonsensical question.

But sometimes scents carried in the cold night air, and the killer had apparently just finished his pipe.

"Looking for any possible clue to who he was," he answered quietly.

She nodded. "I do wish I could do more to help. He wore a hat, of course. That's why I couldn't see very much of his face, it cast a shadow."

"How was he dressed? Like a workman, perhaps, or a beggar?"

"No, not at all. He wore a coat. Dark. Black? Dark gray? It could even have been a dark brown. Not too different from your own."

A man of means, then. His own had come from Oxford Street, from the same tailor his father had preferred.

She added slowly, "He was rather—ordinary. And he put up a hand to shield his face from the glare of the headlamps until he stopped by the wing." Picking at a seam in her skirt as she spoke, she realized what she was doing and smoothed it again. "It was all such a surprise. I mean, there wasn't a house close by, no motorcar that had come to grief, just this man."

It was so often the case with witnesses. The shock of the crime, especially murder, wiped away any details that might have helped the police afterward.

Audrey Blackburn cast a glance at her niece, then said, "Why do you think this man is a pipe smoker?"

She was quick, he had to give her that. "We found a place amongst the hayricks on the far side of the road where he'd stood waiting and smoking. Pipe ash was left there where he'd emptied the bowl."

"And what if that's merely a ruse, to confound the police?"

Rutledge had the fleeting thought that he must introduce Miss Blackburn to Melinda Crawford. "There's every possibility that he *was* that clever," he answered her. "You must have lived here for some time. Do you know of any pipe smokers who might have had a disagreement with Mr. Wentworth?"

"Not at present," she admitted, "but I shall take that under consideration."

Lily brought in the tea tray, and Miss Blackburn busied herself with it. When her aunt wasn't looking, Miss MacRae threw him a pleading glance. He could tell that she hadn't fully recovered from what had happened, and talking about Wentworth's death, even in a roundabout fashion, brought it all back too vividly.

But it was clear, as Miss Blackburn passed Rutledge his cup, that *she* now had the bit in her teeth and was running with it.

"And how did this man arrive on scene? Or leave it?" she asked.

He answered before Miss MacRae could speak. "On foot, as far as we can tell. He went back across the fields, and so far there is no evidence of a horse or a motorcar."

"Clever indeed. Walking in a hay field would leave no prints. How far did you pursue this direction?"

"As far as I could, this morning. There's a copse just beyond the hay fields, and if you don't mind muddy boots, after the hay there is a fallow field of what might have been turnips or marrows."

Finally satisfied, she nodded. "I know the place you are speaking of."

Rutledge smiled at Miss MacRae, drawing her back into the conversation. "How tall was this man?"

"Oh—he was about the same height as—as Stephen. Not counting his hat, of course."

"Did he seem to weigh much the same?"

"I—he was wearing a coat. But yes, I should think he was about the same size."

"Young or old?"

She closed her eyes for a moment. "I don't know. Stephen's age, I should think. He didn't strike me as *old*. He walked—I don't know—easily."

Miss MacRae had seen more than she realized.

Remembering, he reached into his pocket and found the small carving. He held it out to her in the palm of his hand. "I found this on the road. Could it have been Stephen's by any chance?"

Miss MacRae examined it. "I don't think I've ever seen it before. It could have been Stephen's, I suppose. Are you saying it fell out as he stepped out of the motorcar?"

"It could have done," he agreed, keeping his tone light. "Or the other man might have dropped it as he pulled out his revolver."

She winced at the thought. "If he did, I didn't notice it," she said doubtfully.

Miss Blackburn picked it up from his palm. "Quite pretty. You found it on the road? You must have exceptional vision."

He ignored the comment, saying to Miss MacRae as he set his cup and saucer back on the silver tray, "I won't tire you with more questions. But if you think of anything else, I'm staying at The Swan." Miss Blackburn returned the little wolf, and he dropped it back into his pocket.

Thanking Miss Blackburn, he rose to leave, and it was Miss Blackburn who saw him out, not her niece.

"Elizabeth is very upset," she said. "Thank you for being kind."

"She's the best chance we have of finding Wentworth's killer. He may realize that as well, and rectify any oversight in leaving a witness alive."

Her eyes narrowed. "I appreciate the warning, Inspector. I will see that he has no opportunity to do any such thing."

Rutledge walked back to the square, watching a small boy of perhaps five or six rolling a hoop down Church Street ahead of him. The hoop hit a rut in the roadway and bounced, wobbled, and then went down.

Heedless of anything that might have been coming his way, the child dashed into the middle of the roadway and reclaimed his hoop. As he was coming back to the verge, hoop in hand, he looked up and saw Rutledge for the first time.

He stopped, his gaze on Rutledge's face.

"Hallo," he said as he reached the boy.

"Hello," the little boy said. And then, with the directness of a child, "Are you a policeman?"

"Yes, I am."

"You don't wear a uniform like Constable Penny," he said, still staring. "And you don't have a helmet."

Rutledge smiled. "No. I've come from London."

"Is that where you live?"

"Yes."

"Don't the police wear helmets there?"

"Some of them do. The Constables and the Sergeants."

"Oh. Do you know the King?"

"I have seen him."

Clearly disappointed, the boy went on. "Who will read to us on Saturday morning?"

Momentarily imagining King George, fully robed and wearing the coronation crown, reading to a small boy, Rutledge suppressed a smile as he realized that the child must mean Stephen Wentworth at the bookshop. Word of his death had begun to spread. "I don't know," he answered in the same serious tone. "But I imagine it will be sorted out soon."

The boy went on staring up at him.

Rutledge said, "Did you like Mr. Wentworth?"

He nodded.

"Tell me about him."

"I did. He reads to us on Saturday morning."

Rutledge waited.

And then the boy said, "He has a revolver in his desk. I saw it one day. He said I must never touch it, not until I am twenty. Then he would show me how."

Rutledge hadn't found a revolver in the bookshop desk.

"What else did he tell you?"

The boy shrugged. "How to say *hello* and *good-bye* and *please* in French. And how to tie my shoes properly." He held up a small foot. "And he told us The Well was haunted and we must not play there."

"The well?"

Ignoring the question, the boy added, "Sometimes he wrote letters after he read to us. I saw him while I was waiting for Mama. He frowned a lot then."

"Where does Mr. Wentworth live?"

The boy cocked his head. "I thought you were a policeman."

"A good policeman always asks questions, and checks every fact."

"There's a *W* on the gate. Mama says it's far too fine for just one person." He settled his hoop in his hand, and said, "Oh ree vor," with a cheeky grin and ran off.

Watching him go, Rutledge walked on. He had the key to Wentworth's house in his pocket, on the same loop as the bookshop key. It was time to have a look, before the family arrived from Norwich. Or Penny came to ask for them.

Hamish said, "It's no' yet your inquiry."

"Would you have me wait until the trail is cold? It will do no harm to proceed. I'm still a policeman. Even without a proper helmet."

He walked down the High, past The Swan, and soon found himself looking at a large house set back from the road. There was an iron gate at the end of the low stone wall. Within a wreathed circle in the center of the gate was a scrolled *W*. Rutledge swung it open and walked up the path between two narrow borders setting it off from the lawns. The door had a pediment above it and a large brass knocker, again in the shape of a *W*.

"We'll soon know if this is the right house," he said under his breath as he put the key into the lock, but it wasn't necessary. The door wasn't locked.

He opened it and stepped into a short hall, listening to the silence of the house around him. To his right was an open door showing a very elegant parlor, and on the left the matching door was closed.

He worked his way through the house, careful to leave no trace of his presence there. The family had money—that showed in the furnishings, the paintings, and the general air of comfort and ease. The ground floor appeared to be unchanged from Wentworth's parents' occupancy. There was an unlived-in air about the parlor, a study, a sitting room, and the dining room, as if no one ever sat in the chairs or stood at the windows. There was no dust—there must be someone who did for Stephen.

The kitchen did show signs of use: a cup and saucer on the drain board, a kettle on the cooker, and in a pantry, a small pitcher of milk and half a roast chicken.

Upstairs were six bedrooms. One belonged to the absent parents, another must have been the daughter's, judging from the feminine furnishings, a third was used by Stephen, and the rest kept for guests. He walked into each of them, to be certain he missed nothing.

The daughter's room and one of the guest rooms looked out over a terrace and gardens enclosed by three sides of an arbor walk. The vines were dead now, but they appeared to be wisteria, gnarled trunks growing around the supports and, at this season, rather picturesque.

The master bedroom suite took up the opposite side of the house. Rutledge walked to the windows and looked down on a private walled garden with a gate set in at the back. Roses and boxwoods, laid out in a circular pattern, surrounded a low terraced mound covered by ivy, still green here in mid-December. Atop the mound was an elegant sundial. Under bare-branched trees—spring blooming, he thought— was a wrought-iron seat, painted white. While it was probably a lovely view in summer, with the trees leafed out and the roses in full bloom, it struck him as rather somber now.

There was a pair of rooms facing the back garden that might once have been the nursery, although the larger of the two was now a guest room.

Stephen's room and another guest room faced the street. Rutledge went through these, looking in the tall chest, the tables by the bed, and a dresser between the windows. He found clothing and the odds and ends of a man's life. Cuff links, braces and belts, shoehorns—one with a handle in the shape of a ram's head—and the like. Photographs of what appeared to be his parents and his sister were arranged neatly on the mantelpiece, along with one of a young woman sitting in a Cambridge punt, smiling up at the camera. She was slim, fair, and attractive.

There were books on one of the tables by the bed, and a crystal carafe for water, the glass forming the top. Rutledge leafed through the books—a history and two biographies. He noticed that one of them was inscribed.

To Stephen, on his Birthday, with Best Wishes.
Evelyn

The script was very feminine, with graceful loops and curls in the capitals.

The girl in the photograph? Or not?

The guest room next to Stephen's room had been turned into a sitting room, with bookshelves and paintings of racehorses in the style of Stubbs. Rutledge thought one of them might actually be by Stubbs himself, for the horse could have stepped out of the frame, its sleek coat displaying the fine musculature beneath it. On a shelf were small pieces, strange faces and animals molded in a yellowish clay with red markings. Something the bookseller had brought home from Peru?

A desk against one wall held personal correspondence and household accounts, along with an envelope marked *Last Will and Testament*. It was empty.

The personal letters were from his father, many of them written before the war while Stephen traveled, and during the war when he was in the Navy. They were bundled in packets, and Rutledge found it surprising that Wentworth had kept them. He read one or two—formal accounts of daily life, the sort one might write to an acquaintance, not a son. One packet contained letters from Patricia, clearly Wentworth's sister, her childish hand growing into that of a woman over the span of years. They were more informative, mentioning the staff and the dogs, and a pet rabbit she had called Peter. But lacking warmth too.

The one interesting item was in the middle drawer. It was an engagement ring in a small black velvet-covered box. It was exquisite, a diamond with rubies on the shoulder. Who had turned it down? Evelyn? Or was it someone else? Rutledge found it intriguing that Wentworth had kept it, rather than returning it to the jewelers. The name on the satin inside the top listed a very fashionable London jeweler's address.

He found no sign of a revolver, not even under the bed pillows or in the desk. Remembering the tall shell decoration at the top of the armoire, he went back to check, reaching up and feeling behind it. And there it was, in a case. It was well oiled but hadn't been fired recently. The chambers were empty, but there were cartridges in a box closer to the decoration.

He wondered if Wentworth had brought it home from the bookshop after the child had discovered it in the drawer there.

Hamish asked the question Rutledge was already considering. "Why did he need it in the bookshop?"

Rutledge was on his way down the stairs when the outer door opened and a woman in a kerchief stepped in. She was wearing a heavy coat and sturdy brown stockings.

The daily. Looking up, she saw him on the stairs and drew in a breath. He thought she was going to scream, but she didn't.

She dropped the sack she was carrying as her hand went to her heart, and she exclaimed, "Who are you? What are you doing here?" It was a demand in a voice that was noticeably quavering.

"Sorry to frighten you. Inspector Rutledge, Scotland Yard."

"But why are you in this house?" she asked again.

"It's necessary to know more about Stephen's life, if I'm to find out who killed him." He walked the rest of the way down the stairs.

"Here! You're not to touch anything. His mother will be coming, and I'll not have you worrying her. Do you hear me?"

"Your name?"

"Lydie Butterworth," she answered defiantly, daring him to make anything of it.

She came farther inside and shut the door firmly.

"Tell me about Captain Wentworth. Was he a good son, a man who cared about his family? Or was he a troubled man, with secrets?"

"He was a decent young man who cared about a good many people," she said stoutly.

He gestured around him. "How did he come to be a bookseller?"

"He didn't need the money. His grandmother on his father's side had left him her fortune. But he was always in Mr. Delaney's bookshop, when he could escape from his mother's eye. When Mr. Delaney sold up, Mr. Stephen bought it, against his parents' wishes, because he loved books. He had no secrets, and he was shot down in cold blood by a madman who should be taken to the hangman directly he's caught. And the sooner the better," she ended pointedly, as if to remind him of his duty.

"How long have you worked for the Wentworth family?" It was clear that she knew a great deal about them. Listening at doors? Or trusted servant?

"I watched that boy grow to be a man. He might as well be my own family. I've wept for him. Now I have work to do." She marched off toward the back of the house.

He had seen what he needed to see. Turning, he started to walk out, then stopped. "Who is Evelyn?" he called.

She was already at the door down to the kitchen. "That's Miss Hardy. Evelyn Hardy."

"Is she also the woman in the punt—the boat? There's a photograph on the mantelpiece."

"Don't be silly. *That's* Dorothea. He wanted to marry her. But she didn't want to marry him. Before the war, that was." She pulled the door closed behind her.

He went after her, and called down the stairs, "What was her surname? Do you know?"

"Mowbray. Dorothea Mowbray."

5

"Twa women in his life," Hamish was saying. "There's trouble."

And there was Inspector Reed's wife as well. *And* the Miss Hardy who Wentworth had been set on driving to her home after the dinner party. Not to speak of Miss MacRae.

But then Wentworth was young, had come home from the war with all his limbs and no disfiguring burns or gassed lungs. And he was wealthy. Women would have found him attractive—and available.

"One of them might explain why Wentworth chose to go to Peru. If my memory serves, there's good work just now being done on the Inca. Did he own the bookshop then?" Rutledge mused.

He went to find Constable Penny, who was just sitting down to ham and roasted potatoes.

"I won't keep you long," Rutledge told him when Penny met him at the cottage door with his plate in hand, in his view a subtle hint. "Who minded the bookshop while Wentworth was in Peru?"

Penny said, "That would be Mrs. Delaney again."

"Where do I find her?"

Penny was torn between his cooling dinner and arguing with the man from London over meddling in matters he had no right to look into. His dinner won.

"She's just down The Street past the bookshop. Look for green shutters." Salving his conscience, he added, "She didn't come to services. It may be she's away."

Rutledge thanked him and walked on. He expected to find Mrs. Delaney at her own dinner, but he could see her through the window with the green shutters, sitting in her parlor, reading.

He knocked lightly at the door, and after a moment she opened it. "The man from London," she said, and swung it wider so that he could enter. "I've been expecting you."

She was a tall, attractive woman on the edge of fifty, her dark hair showing little gray. Patrician features, a firm chin—and eyes redrimmed from crying.

The parlor was a pleasant room done up in blues trimmed in white and an elegant white plaster medallion in the center of the ceiling. An ormolu clock on the mantelpiece stood between two Chinese-style vases in blue and white, and there was a pale blue Turkey carpet on the floor with rose and cream in the border. A little white-and-black King Charles spaniel looked up from a basket by Mrs. Delaney's chair and tentatively growled. "Dickens," she said quietly, and he subsided.

"You've come about poor Stephen," she went on, offering him a chair. "Dr. Brent dropped in early this morning. He was afraid I might hear the news if I went to services. And later I was told by a neighbor that someone had already been sent down from London."

He didn't explain that he was first on the scene. "I'm sorry. I understand Mr. Wentworth had bought the bookshop from your husband. You must have known him well over the years."

"My husband was terribly fond of him and felt that the shop was in good hands. It's such a lovely one. I don't know what will become of it now."

"Perhaps you would like to have it back again."

But she shook her head. "It was my husband's joy, and I supported him, of course. And I helped Stephen when he needed someone to step in. But I prefer my garden and my own books." She indicated the one lying on the small table at her elbow.

When Rutledge didn't immediately respond, she added, "I'm Tom's second wife. He and Josephine made the shop what it is today. I came along in its middle years, well established and well known." Anticipating his question, she went on. "Josephine died before I met Tom. Kidney failure. Oddly enough, that's what killed him as well. He was in London, appraising a private collection that was coming onto the market." Her eyes welled with tears. "He wanted to come home, but he waited too long. The wonderful, foolish man."

"I'm so sorry."

"And when Stephen asked me to look after the shop while he was in Peru, I almost turned him down." She refused to reach for a handkerchief, willing the tears away. "It was so sudden, you see, and I was still missing Tom terribly. But of course there was no one else, and so I agreed." She smiled wistfully. "We didn't have children, Tom and I. But I would have been pleased if I'd had a son like Stephen."

"I understand he had money of his own, that he didn't have to ask his father to help him pay for the shop."

"Yes, that's right. His grandmother—his father's mother—was still alive when he was born, and she left him her personal fortune. She lived until he was nearly seven, and so the money was put into trust for him through her bank in London. He came into his inheritance when he turned eighteen. His parents felt that that was too young for such responsibility, but the terms of the trust were explicit."

"Why did he go to Peru? There was the bookshop waiting for him."

"He bought the bookshop before he'd come down from Cambridge. You've never seen a happier man. It was his heart's desire, and Tom was getting along in years, he'd wanted to sell while he was still able to keep an eye on it. His illness only made that more urgent. A year later, Stephen wrote to me and asked me to take it on, because he was off to Peru. I was angry with him at first. I thought then that he'd bought the shop on a whim, and tired of it. But he hadn't. It was something else that changed him."

"Dorothea Mowbray?"

She stared at him. "However did you find out about *her*? But you're a policeman, aren't you, and no secret is safe from you. Yes, Dorothea. He wanted desperately to marry her, he'd even bought her the loveliest ring. He brought it along for me to see. And she refused. God knows why. Two days later he'd left England. The war brought him back."

"Where is Miss Mowbray now?"

"I have no idea. I doubt if Stephen could have told you either."

But Rutledge rather thought he might have known. The ring in the desk drawer told its own story about Dorothea. To keep a ring for a woman he might not have seen in some years meant he hadn't forgot her or stopped loving her.

It had taken Rutledge a long time to get over losing Jean.

Hamish said, "And there's Fiona . . ."

Rutledge winced at the reminder. But Fiona hadn't refused Hamish. And he would have come home to her if he'd lived.

Rutledge could still hear the dying man's voice whispering her name as he delivered the coup de grâce . . .

He'd lost track of what Mrs. Delaney was saying. "I'm sorry?"

"I was commenting that lately Stephen has been seen about town with the young woman visiting Miss Blackburn. Miss MacRae?"

He thought there was more behind the question than idle curiosity. A flare of hope, that Wentworth might be on the brink of finding happiness again? Or worry that he might have been making another wrong choice? He said, "Miss MacRae and Wentworth were driving back to Wolfpit after a party at a friend's house. About three in the morning."

Her brows rose in query. "That's rather late, isn't it, for a party to end?"

"I believe he was asked to take one of the other guests home first."

"Still . . ." Then she shrugged. "It doesn't matter. What does is, who could have done such a thing? Stephen had no enemies. I mean to say, one must hate or fear someone very much to want to kill him."

"Or perhaps envy?" Rutledge suggested.

And Mrs. Delaney frowned at that, but said only, "Booksellers seldom find themselves facing a killer. It's not that kind of work."

He left soon after. Mrs. Delaney had filled in some of the blanks left in reconstructing Stephen Wentworth's life since Cambridge, but he was no closer to the answers he needed. Most men he'd ever met—and he himself was a fine example—had secrets they would rather not see voiced by the town crier.

What were Stephen Wentworth's?

That brought Rutledge back to what the killer said to Wentworth in that brief exchange before the shot was fired.

"Ye ken, ye ha' only Miss MacRae's word for what happened on yon road."

Which was a point he was keeping in mind. It was a beginning, and not necessarily an ending. He didn't believe that Miss MacRae had killed Wentworth, but the circumstances might of necessity have been changed to protect someone else.

Her shock could have come from watching Wentworth die, or from seeing who his killer was.

She had protested taking the Hardy niece home that evening. It could have delayed their expected rendezvous with a killer.

But that was speculation and more suited to the future.

He was walking back toward the police station when he saw a motorcar draw up in front. A smart chauffeur in uniform stepped down and opened the rear door.

A distinguished-looking man in well-cut dark clothing got out. His fair hair was streaked with gray, but his face had remained young, and Rutledge knew at once that he must be Wentworth's father. The resemblance was striking.

A woman followed him. She was of medium height and slim, her back as straight as an arrow, and she was dressed in black and wore a black hat with a black veil. It obscured her face and hair, falling almost to her shoulders. Rutledge had seen Queen Alexandra in just such a veil at the funeral for Edward VII in 1910.

The chauffeur opened the door of the police station for them, and the pair went inside. He took his place by the motorcar, an elegant Rolls, to wait for them.

Rutledge crossed the triangular square before he reached the station. It was best for Penny to speak with Stephen Wentworth's parents. It was clear that they had been told of their son's death and had come to view the body and make whatever arrangements they could. Lydie Butterworth would have the house ready for them when they arrived there. Who had informed them? He thought it was very likely Dr. Brent again. It would have been kinder than hearing it from the police.

Dealing with the bereaved was one of the most difficult duties a policeman faced, and sometimes the worst. To tell a family that one of their own had been killed, whether by accident or murder, and then watch their faces as they realized that someone they cared for was never coming home, took backbone of a particular kind, and an enormous reserve of sympathy.

And there was still nothing one could say that would make it any better.

He walked into the inn's dining room, where he could sit by the window and watch the door of the police station. Ordering tea, he saw that the street was for the most part empty. It was Sunday, after all. And then a couple came strolling from Church Street, her hand in his arm. They were very young and appeared very much in love. His gaze followed them out of sight.

The woman who had served his tea was standing by his table, watching them as well. "Peter just missed the war," she said pensively. "He wasn't seventeen until the last day of November 1918. It's lovely to see young men again who aren't in uniform and on their way to war."

She was small and dark, with lively blue eyes. He put her age at thirty, perhaps even thirty-five. Stephen Wentworth's generation.

Rutledge was agreeing with her just as the police station door opened and the Wentworths stepped out, still speaking to Constable Penny. Then, after a word with the chauffeur, Mrs. Wentworth was settled once more in the rear seat, and Mr. Wentworth set off toward Dr. Brent's surgery. By the time he'd been admitted, the motorcar had reversed in the square and disappeared in the direction of the house.

"Poor lady," the woman beside him said as the motorcar passed the window. "Stephen came home from the war. She must have been so grateful he was safe. And now this."

"I hear she and her husband live in Norwich now, with their daughter."

"My heart aches for Patricia!" the woman said. "Jocelyn was such a handsome man. And kind as well. He was a solicitor, you know. Everyone liked him enormously when she brought him to Wolfpit. And they had two sweet children. He wanted to serve his country, and she let him go. She saw him once after that. Her parents went to stay with her when the news came, and then decided to live there."

"How did Stephen Wentworth feel about that?"

"He was at sea, and when he came home, he appeared to be happy enough about the arrangement."

They had kept their voices low, so as not to disturb the last of the diners. He'd noticed that most of them were single women, the majority of them in the black of widowhood. No Sunday family dinners for them, he thought.

The woman sighed. "I wouldn't say this to anyone else, but you're a policeman. I don't think the family ever quite forgave Stephen for buying the bookshop. And then going off to Peru. He got the idea from the bookshop, you know. The book that man wrote about finding a lost city. Bishop? I can't seem to recall his name." She smiled. "I remember the city sounded like mashed potatoes. I told Stephen that once, and he had a good laugh at me."

Rutledge searched his memory. "Hiram Bingham. The American who found Machu Picchu. In 1911, I think."

"You may be right. Stephen brought me back a photograph, and told me that I was closer to the truth than I knew, because Peru has more varieties of potatoes than any other place in the world. Some of them are actually purple. And there was a little pin he found in a market some-where. It was a sort of camel, he said, except that no one rode it, it was just a pack animal. And as nasty tempered as anything he'd ever seen."

"He talked to you often, I gather?"

She shook her head. "I love to read. That's the thing. I went as often to the bookshop as I could. That's where we talked about Peru."

A chair scraped behind her as someone rose to go, and with an apol-ogetic smile for Rutledge, the woman went to the counter to deal with the departing guest.

She's as lonely as they are, Rutledge thought. *And that's why she's serving dinner on a Sunday afternoon.* Women whose men never came home, like Patricia Wentworth.

He waited until he saw Mr. Wentworth leaving the surgery and walking toward his home. Then he rose, settled his own bill, and went across to the police station. He found Constable Penny sitting behind his desk, staring into space.

"Ah. Inspector. Did you find Mrs. Delaney, sir?" he asked, rising.

"Yes, thank you. How are the Wentworths?"

Penny shook his head. "I couldn't see her face through that veil, but I'm sure she'd been crying. The mother. Her voice was quite husky. Mr. Wentworth was bearing up well enough, but it was a strain."

"Could they tell you anything about their son that might be useful to us?"

"I didn't have the heart to ask, sir. They wanted to know if any progress had been made in the inquiry, and I had to tell them early days, early days." He looked at Rutledge. "*Has* any been made, sir? What did Inspector Reed have to say? I stayed here to wait for the Wentworths. Dr. Brent had informed me they would be coming."

"A little. I'm beginning to form an opinion of the younger Wentworth, and that's helpful." He paused, then said, as if it didn't particularly matter, "I would like to speak to his friends. Male friends. They might see him differently than the young ladies he was acquainted with."

Penny scratched his chin. "A good many didn't come back, sir. But there's Will Holden and Geoff Marshall. They were close when they were young."

"And not now?"

"I don't know, sir." He busied himself with his pen. "Some of the men who came back are changed. They keep to themselves. Stephen was a naval officer, he saw a different war. Perhaps that's it. Holden and Marshall were in France."

He understood what Penny was telling him.

"Where can I find them?"

"Marshall lives down Church Street, toward the end of it. You'll have no trouble finding the house. It hasn't been kept up all that well. His wife left him last year. She found him difficult."

"And Holden?"

"He lives in the house three doors down from Doctor's surgery. Are you sure you ought not leave these matters to Inspector Reed, sir?"

"I don't see him here in Wolfpit, interviewing anyone. I don't think he cared much for Wentworth. Not the best attitude with which to begin an inquiry."

"No, sir. But he did say he'd be back in the afternoon."

Rutledge thanked him and left.

Penny was right. He had no trouble at all finding the Marshall house. It was two-story and had a front garden gone to seed. The window trim could have used a coat of paint, and wisteria vines had taken over one side, clearly out of hand.

Rutledge walked up the path, bracing himself for what he was likely to find here. Shell shock? Burns? Amputations?

What he found when Marshall opened the door was a man who had turned to alcohol to hide what he feared most, his own mind.

His dark hair unkempt, his shirt not very clean, he stared at Rutledge. "And what do you want?" he demanded belligerently.

"Rutledge, Scotland Yard. I'd like to ask you about Stephen Wentworth."

"Do you need a personal reference before buying a book from him?"

"He's dead. He was killed Saturday night on the road, coming home from visiting friends."

The bleary blue eyes sharpened. "Are you telling me he's dead?" he repeated.

"I'm afraid so."

"Gentle God." He moved aside to allow Rutledge to step inside.

The house reeked of cigarette smoke and stale beer. Someone had made an effort to pick up in the parlor, but there was dust on the furnishings, and the drapes at the windows were heavy with it in the folds. The antimacassars on the backs of the upholstered chairs needed smoothing out and the hearth rug was rumpled. "Come in and see how a man lives when his wife deserts him."

Rutledge carefully chose where to sit. Dog hair covered the cushions of every chair. The hair's owner was curled up on a mat under the window, and snoring.

"I'd offer you a drink," Marshall said sourly, "but of course you're on duty."

"I'm afraid so. How long have you known Stephen Wentworth?"

"Probably since we were in leading strings. But when he was older, his mother sent him off to boarding school, while the rest of us went to the local grammar school. In the holidays, he'd escape her eye, and we'd play or wander in the fields beyond the village. He liked that, but his mother didn't care for him coming home covered in burrs and smelling of sweat."

"Did you like him, despite his mother?"

"I couldn't help it. He was an all-round sport. Never any airs. Of a Sunday, if he couldn't speak to us, he'd wink. And we'd fight to keep a straight face and not give him away."

"Did he make any enemies in the village?"

"We thought it *her* doing that he went into the Royal Navy when the rest of us enlisted. No burrs in the trenches, of course, but they were damned sweaty. Not to speak of the lice."

Rutledge said, "Being torpedoed at sea is no walk in the park."

"I expect Mrs. Wentworth never thought of that. All the girls were agog when he walked down the street in his officer's uniform." He shrugged. "It didn't go to his head. I will say that for him."

"Who shot him, then?"

The suddenness of the question caught Marshall off balance. "Here. You said he was killed—not that he was murdered."

"Did I not make it clear?" Rutledge had deliberately left out murder. "Who would want Wentworth dead?"

"I don't know that anyone would want to kill him. I mean, why?"

"Had you seen much of him since the war?"

"Not really. There was my marriage—and the marriage going sour. We didn't have much in common. And where was the time to read?"

"I'm curious. What went wrong with your marriage?"

"What else? My drinking. Betty calls it demon drink, but I drink because of the demons. Were you in the war? An officer, I take it?"

"Yes. The Somme."

"Then I don't need to tell you about demons. We were stepping on the dead, piling them up behind the trenches, watching men bleed to death because there was no time to help them. Listening to the screams and the cries. The smells—it was *July*." He shuddered. "How do I tell my wife about that? She can barely cut up a joint from the butcher's. How can I tell *her*, then watch her suffer from nightmares she ought never to know?"

"You can't. But you might make her understand that there are some things better left unsaid."

Marshall shook his head. "It doesn't work. She's led a sheltered life, my Betty."

Rutledge attempted to bring the conversation back to Stephen Wentworth.

"Is there anything else you can tell me about Stephen's life that might be helpful?"

Taking a deep breath, Marshall said, "I never understood why he went to Peru. When he'd just bought the bookshop a year or so before. When I asked afterward, he told me it was wanderlust. But he'd never shown any interest in travel until then."

"I was told that the books on travel in the shop had enticed him."

"Oh, he liked them well enough. I just never heard of him wanting to go badly enough himself. There's a difference between seeing something in a book and being curious, wanting to learn more, and rushing off to London to buy a steamship ticket."

There was some truth in that.

"Then what precipitated the flight to Peru?"

"There was a girl he met in Cambridge. She lived in the town. I don't know if she had anything to do with it, but he told me once that he wanted to marry her. Then I heard no more about her. Not even her name."

"Perhaps he asked her to marry him, and she refused." It was what Lydie had told him, and Mrs. Delaney as well.

Marshall grimaced. "Girls didn't refuse Wentworth. He could have had his pick. Betty liked him. I could tell." Something stirred in his eyes as he said it.

"Jealousy? Do you think that might have had a role in his death?"

Marshall got to his feet with an effort. "I have enough worries of my own. I can't take on Stephen's too. I'll thank you to shut the door when you leave."

And he was gone, climbing the stairs to the upper floor, making it clear he didn't expect Rutledge to follow him.

Rutledge let himself out. The dog lifted its head but didn't bother to bark.

He walked down the street, mulling over what he'd learned. There had been envy in Marshall's voice, but a defeated envy and an uncertainty about his wife's affections. Not a bleeding wound that might drive a man to remove the source of his pain.

But there was a corollary to that. Would heartbreak have sent Stephen Wentworth haring off to Peru just when he had bought the bookshop he had wanted so badly to own? Mrs. Delaney had made that connection.

He'd been young, just coming down from university, and such a rash decision might have seemed to be the right romantic gesture. And yet what people had been telling Rutledge about Stephen Wentworth painted the picture of a stable and considerate man.

It would be interesting to hear Will Holden's view of the victim.

A chill wind had come up, and villagers were hurrying along The Street now, no longer strolling in the sun. Several of them nodded to him. By now most of the men and a good many of the women knew there was someone from London looking into Wentworth's death, but he found it odd that none of them stopped him to offer information. Not even a "*Hope you catch the bastard. Wentworth was a good man.*"

He came to the Holden house. Like its neighbors, it stood directly on The Street. When he knocked, there was no answer. He waited, but there was no indication that anyone was at home. It was a little more imposing than Marshall's bungalow, and better kept. And there was a pram standing by the door, indicating that Holden's marriage at least had survived.

He walked on toward the end of The Street and as far as the smithy and a small brickyard, then turned back toward The Swan. The winter day was closing in, and he could feel the sharp edges of a little sleet jabbing at his face, but by the time he'd reached the inn, it had passed by, although there were dark clouds chasing the squall toward the North Sea.

He found himself thinking that before the war, Frances might have chosen Italy for her wedding trip. She had always wanted to see Florence. But she had picked Paris as the more sensible choice. He hoped they had fairer weather.

Last night he'd got very little sleep, and it was catching him up now. He climbed the stairs to his room, found his key, and even though it was barely four o'clock in the afternoon, he turned up the lamp and was about to carry a chair to the window when he saw an envelope lying on the bed.

Curious, he reached for it. The flap hadn't been sealed. Pulling out the poorly folded single sheet that had been stuffed inside, he unfolded it.

The scrawl was written in a water-thinned ink by a narrow point, and the word *spidery* came to mind. An attempt to conceal the handwriting?

But there was no mistaking the message.

Stephen Wentworth is a murderer. He got what he deserved.

Rutledge's first thought was the war, that something had happened during the fighting that had made Wentworth a marked man—and someone had come to see that he paid his debt.

The war hadn't all been heroism and glory.

Officers had been shot in the back, men had been sent out in hopeless charges and raids, with the expectation that they would die, and ranks had been reported for courts-martial on false charges. It was easy enough to find a reason to hate . . .

But Stephen Wentworth hadn't served in the trenches. On the other hand, he'd lost ships, and men had gone down with them. It was worth keeping in mind.

What if it wasn't the war? What if something had happened at Cambridge—and Wentworth had fled to Peru until he felt it was safe enough to come home?

The writer of the message in his hand had meant to leave the impression that Wentworth wasn't the man Rutledge had been led to believe he was.

Instead, it had opened doors that Rutledge hadn't yet found a key for. And that in itself was suspicious.

Hamish said, "Ye canna' ignore it."

I don't intend to, Rutledge answered silently.

But who in Wolfpit could tell him about Wentworth's time at university?

Constable Penny might have an answer for that.

A knock at the door brought him back to the present, and he turned to open it.

Melinda Crawford stood there in a dark red wool traveling dress, a fashionable ermine hat on her head and a matching ermine muff in one hand. Raised in the heat of India, she claimed that English winters tested her. He had wondered if they had also given her an excuse for indulging in pretty winter clothing. In spite of the long drive from London, she looked entirely fresh, and her dark eyes were bright with curiosity.

Behind her, Ram, her Indian chauffeur, carried a valise that Rutledge instantly recognized.

"I thought you might need a few things," she said, taking the valise from the chauffeur and passing it to Rutledge. "You'll find your identification in there as well."

He hadn't got around to thinking about the fact that he'd only brought one change of clothes. How had she known?

Collecting himself, he asked her to step into the room. "Have you had your dinner?" he asked. "I can't speak for the food here, but I owe you for this."

She walked in and took the chair by the window. "Wolfpit is a lovely village. We took the lane by the church to have a better look at it. Quite splendid. David would find it interesting, I think."

His godfather, David Trevor, was a well-known architect.

"I came here quite by chance," he confessed. "I couldn't sleep, and I went for a drive. And it went on longer than I'd expected."

"Yes, I thought that might be the case. But you wanted your identification. You said something on the telephone about a murder."

"I stumbled on a murder. Well, not *stumbled*. I was driving, there was a motorcar in the middle of the road, and a frightened woman standing over a dead man. He'd just been shot."

Melinda nodded. "And you've taken over the inquiry?"

"I expect to. I've asked for London's blessing."

She turned to look down into the street. "I believe I know the Chief Constable. He's the son of a very dear friend. We met in Hong Kong. We were very clever to take it over, you know. Hong Kong, I mean. Too bad we couldn't have owned it outright—a hundred years will pass in no time, and China will want it back after we've made something of it. But I was speaking of the Chief Constable's father. He had connections in Peking, and he took me to see the Great Wall." She smiled at the memory, then turned back to him, going on briskly, "But that's neither here nor there. Will you come and see me on your way back to London?" She added, "It isn't terribly far out of your way."

He knew what she was asking. To come and reassure her that he was all right.

"I'm happy for Frances, you know. And I like Peter."

"Still, you and Frances have drawn closer after the death of your parents, and it will be different now. For a little while." And then as she picked up her muff, she said, "I do like Kate Gordon. I'm so glad Frances invited her to the wedding. We had a chat over the champagne. She's quite fond of you, you know." And without waiting for an answer, she swept to the door and held up her face for his kiss.

As he bent to kiss her cheek, he said, "You see too much."

"My dear Ian, I don't know what you're talking about."

And she was gone, down the stairs to her waiting motorcar without giving him a chance to escort her.

Rutledge stood by the window, watching her drive away.

And then when he opened his valise, he saw that it was expertly packed, with the foresight and the efficiency of a soldier's wife. Her Captain Crawford had been a very lucky man, Rutledge thought. A tragedy that he'd died so young.

6

When Rutledge had stowed the valise in his armoire, he went down to Reception and rang the little bell to summon the clerk.

"There was a message waiting for me when I came up to my room. Before my visitor arrived. It's important that I answer it. Do you recall who brought it? Whoever it was, he or she would have had to ask for the room number."

"I only gave your number out once. And that was to the lady who just left."

"Was there someone else on duty earlier?"

"No, sir. That's to say I went to the kitchen to fetch my dinner. I wasn't away from the desk more than a minute or two."

"How would someone coming in off the street have known which room I'd taken?"

Unsettled, the clerk said, "I wouldn't know, sir. Perhaps he got it from Constable Penny?"

But he hadn't given out his number. He'd simply told people he was staying at The Swan.

He thanked the clerk and went to the kitchen, where the staff was clearing away. The woman who had brought him his tea and stayed to chat was finishing her own meal.

Rutledge gave the same account to them. The cook, a pot in her hands, shook her head, and her two helpers followed suit. The woman who had served him said, "There was a very elegant older woman who was coming down the stairs as I closed the dining room doors. Was it she?"

"No, she was a friend who called. Did you notice anyone else going up the stairs?"

They hadn't but volunteered the information that someone could have taken the back stairs. There was a door leading to them from the kitchen and another from the back entry into the rear yard.

"No matter," Rutledge said with a smile, thanking them. "If it's important, whoever left the message will find me again."

But he thought that whoever it was must have known about the back stairs. And it was possible that he or she had simply opened doors until the right room was found. It wouldn't have taken long—he was in number 2.

To be sure of that, when he had climbed the stairs again, Rutledge quietly opened the door to number 1. It wasn't locked, and one glance at the state of the room would have made it plain that it was not taken.

He tried number 3 and number 4 as well. Neither was locked.

But he had a key to his own room, and from now on, he would make a point of locking it whenever he wasn't inside.

After his dinner in the inn's dining room, Rutledge fetched his hat and coat, then walked down The Street to the Holden house.

He found them just rising from their own meal, and Holden carried Rutledge off to a small study after introducing him to his wife, Matilda.

She was a very pretty young woman with a square face, black hair, and merry eyes.

Will Holden was of the same height as the man on the road, but there any resemblance to Wentworth's killer seemed to end. Holden walked with a noticeable limp. He said, running a hand through his dark hair, "I still can't believe Stephen is gone."

Rutledge took the chair he was offered and sat down. The room was very masculine in style, with watercolors of dog breeds on the walls and heavy leather-upholstered chairs, reminiscent of a men's club in London.

"How well did you know him?" he asked, although Geoff Marshall had given him a very good idea of the relationship. Still, it was better to hear Holden's own version of growing up in Wolfpit with Wentworth and the other lads they'd known as children.

But Will Holden surprised him by saying, "I didn't like him when we were young. I really can't say why. He was nice enough, I expect. On the other hand, I was wild, and his was the more level head. At eight, it's hard to value someone who always has a very good reason to say *no, it's not on,* when you have your heart set on climbing the church tower and seeing the bells. My mother often held Stephen up as the font of all virtue, and that didn't help very much either. Later on, we had more in common than we did at eight, and I quite changed my mind about him. But he went off to a public school when he was twelve, and then to university. And we didn't see very much of each other after that."

There was an undercurrent in his voice that Rutledge heard, faint though it was. Envy again? Or something darker?

"Do you think Cambridge changed him?" It was a wider world than Wolfpit, and if it had made a difference somehow, Holden would have been the first to notice.

He frowned. "I don't know. The last summer before he came down, he seemed to be much the same person, a little older and a little wiser, you might say. But that last term he didn't come home and he didn't write to any of us. As soon as it ended, he was off to Peru." He shook his head. "I never quite understood that journey. It smacked more of running away than choosing to go away."

"Did he tell you why he was going? Why he chose Peru?"

"He didn't even say good-bye. I got a short note posted from South-ampton before he sailed. We'd talked about a walking tour in Scotland that summer, and he apologized for changing his plans. He didn't say where he was going or when he'd be coming back." There was an ag-grieved note in his voice now.

"I understand there was a young woman he met while he was at university. Did she live in Cambridge? Or closer to Wolfpit?"

"So I've heard, but he never spoke of her to me. I can't say where she's from."

"Could an unhappy love affair have spurred his decision to go to Peru? Was Wentworth the sort of man who would have felt that deeply enough to change his plans rather drastically? After all, he'd been ex-pected to come home to run the bookshop."

Holden shook his head. "They say still water runs deep. It did with Stephen. He seldom spoke about himself or what he was feeling. He was open, talking to people, a good listener, the sort of friend you could count on in a pinch. But sometimes I wasn't sure what he was thinking. He never said."

"A private person."

"I expect you could call it that. But it was almost as if he was afraid to let anyone see his weaknesses."

It was a perceptive remark.

"Did you spend much time with him after the war? Any idea how it might have affected him?"

"I came back from France with only one thought in mind. Marrying Matilda. By the time Stephen got home, I was a married man with a child coming. We were still friends and all that. But we had much less in common. I'd share a pint with him sometimes in The Swan, but we had less and less to say to each other." He shrugged. "It was sad in a way. Neither of us could afford to lose any more friends. As it was, we'd left most of them behind in the trenches. Or at sea."

"Any hard feelings that he enlisted in the Navy rather than follow-ing the rest of you into the Army?"

Holden frowned. "We'd have liked to have him with us. Of course we would have. Geoff—that's Geoff Marshall, another friend—always held that Stephen had chosen the Navy to please his mother, but he never struck me as being that close to her. Looking back, he never mentioned her the way the other lads did. 'My mum told me to be home by three—my mum gave me sweets to share around—my mum had something to say about tearing my shirt whilst climbing that tree.' Odd, in a way."

"What about his father?"

"I remember he bought Stephen a sled one winter when we had an unexpected snowfall. And there was a bicycle later on, I think."

"Can you think of anyone who might have wanted to see him dead?"

"Murder? He's the last person I'd expect to hear was murdered. I'm still shocked. You must wrong someone if they're to hate you. I can't imagine what it was that Stephen had done."

But in Rutledge's experience, hate was not always earned.

Although he talked with Holden for another few minutes, he learned nothing more. Thanking the man, he left. Walking back toward the inn, he crossed the street and went on down the road, almost to the eastern outskirts of the village. There were several run-down cottages there, and another larger brickyard, then the open fields. Here the sheep had run, making the village prosperous over the centuries, but he didn't see any of them now.

Coming back past the bookshop, he heard what sounded like the ringing of a telephone. He hurried to the door and got it open just as the ringing stopped. Making his way through the darkness in the shop, he reached for the telephone and asked the switchboard who had called. But all the woman at the other end could tell him was that the call had come from London.

He put through a call to the Yard, and Sergeant Williams answered, not Sergeant Gibson.

"Mr. Rutledge, sir? Yes, I did just try to telephone you. I've been asked to tell you that the Chief Constable has agreed to call in the

Yard in the case of the murder of Stephen Wentworth. However, Chief Superintendent Markham has questioned the request that it should be you in charge. You're a witness, sir. After the fact, but nevertheless, a witness. It might be best to send down Inspector Vernon."

"With respect, I think it's the opposite case. I was there at the start of the inquiry, I saw the body in place. It gives me a greater insight than arriving days later."

"Yes, sir, I can see that, sir. But what shall I tell the Chief Superintendent, sir?"

It was more a plea than a question.

"Tell him that I prefer to take charge at this point, but I will let the Yard know at once if I feel that my presence on the scene at the beginning is not helpful in pursuing my duties."

He could hear the smile in Williams's voice as he said, "Yes, sir, thank you, sir. I will quote you on that."

"Thank you, Sergeant. See that you do."

Rutledge rang off, then stood there in the darkness of the bookshop, looking around at the shadowy shapes of the shelving. What had changed Wentworth's dedication to this work, after he'd gone to so much trouble to purchase the shop?

But the shelves were silent.

He locked the door and left. In the distance he could hear a dog barking and remembered that this was once a place where wolves roamed. He found himself feeling some sympathy for the last wolf caught here, the last of his kind, alone and lonely.

There was no one in the police station, but a night lamp was burning on the desk. Rutledge found pen and paper, then wrote a few sentences telling Penny that it was official. He was the officer in charge.

Shutting the police station door behind him, he crossed to the inn. The street was empty, and his steps echoed.

Climbing the stairs to his room, Rutledge wondered why Stephen Wentworth had hidden his feelings, as Will Holden had suggested, and if he had lost the woman he was said to have loved because he couldn't break free from that inbred need for his own privacy. Or if there was some other reason for ending the relationship. He would have to travel to Cambridge sooner or later, to speak to her . . .

The next morning was dismally wet. It had warmed in the night, enough to bring an early fog with it. Nothing like the London fogs, which seemed to cloak the spirit as well as the clothing in a cloying mist that brought on coughing fits and left a damp grime behind. Still, this one was enough to keep anyone by his hearth who had no particularly pressing business elsewhere.

Rutledge stared out the inn window as he considered where to begin, now that he had been assigned the inquiry. The Wentworths would be finishing their breakfast. And before they went back to Norwich, he would have to speak to them. It wouldn't be a comfortable interview. The bereaved often saw their dead as someone more than human, above reproach, possessor of all the virtues. It was sometimes hard to sift the truth from the flood of memories in support of that belief. And yet the interview had to be done as soon as possible.

He lingered over a second cup of tea, to give them time to do the same, then set out briskly for the house, his umbrella tilted against a blowing rain.

When he knocked at the door, there was no immediate answer. And then Wentworth's father opened it, saying sharply, "Are you from the undertaker's?"

"Inspector Rutledge, Scotland Yard. I'm in charge of the inquiry into your son's death."

Mr. Wentworth stared at him blankly for a moment, then seemed to grasp what Rutledge had said. Face-to-face, Rutledge could see that while he resembled his son in coloring and features, he gave the impression that he was a weaker man. It was there in the softer line of the jaw and a short chin. There were circles under his deep-set blue eyes, signs of grief or of a long familiarity with pain. "Come in. My wife has just gone up to finish packing her valise. If you'll step this way." He gestured toward the parlor, and Rutledge walked ahead of him into the room he'd already seen. It felt more alive than it had earlier. As if the presence of the former occupants had rejuvenated it somehow.

"The Constable has told me how my son died. I hope you're here to tell me why he died."

"It's too soon for answers, when there are so many questions still to be asked," Rutledge replied quietly. "Your son is well thought of here in Wolfpit. There seems to be nothing in his past or his present that could have led to his death."

Taking the chair opposite the one he'd offered Rutledge, Mr. Wentworth said, "He was never the sort of person who caused anxiety. Not even as a child. A peacemaker rather than a troublemaker."

And yet Stephen Wentworth had chosen to own a bookshop when he could have enjoyed a life of leisure.

"Were you pleased when he chose to buy the bookshop?" Rutledge asked, following up on that thought.

"Not particularly. I thought it was more a whim than a lifelong passion. But he had spent a great deal of time there, and I expect it seemed natural to him to take it on when Delaney fell ill. He was always bringing home lost dogs as a child. None of which he could keep, of course, and I was sometimes hard-pressed to find suitable owners for them."

"Most boys grow up with dogs. Why wasn't Stephen allowed to keep one?"

"My wife—his mother—doesn't particularly care for animals. She felt they were unhealthy in a house."

Rutledge's parents had been more indulgent. He had had dogs most of his childhood, and not all of them had been pedigreed. The last, a white male called Rover for his ceaseless desire to roam the countryside at all hours of the day and night, had died at a ripe old age almost two years before the war, and in a London flat, with the hours he kept as a policeman, Rutledge had not replaced him.

"Tell me why Stephen chose to go to Peru after he came down from university."

Surprised at the change in direction, Wentworth shook his head. "I wish I could. It was sudden, unexpected. I wondered if it had to do with a young woman he'd been seeing in Cambridge. Her father was something to do with one of the colleges."

Here was new information indeed. A woman who might be considered unsuitable for the Wentworth heir . . .

"Did you and Stephen's mother ever meet her?"

"Only briefly. While we were there at the end of term, she left to visit friends."

"And how did your son seem? Brokenhearted? Unhappy? In a mood that might send him halfway across the world to recover?"

"In fact he seemed very much himself." He stirred uneasily. "Stephen was deep, you know. I sometimes wondered if I really understood him."

"Secretive?"

"No. 'Private,' I think, is a much better word."

"And yet people liked him. That's not usually the case if a man keeps to himself."

"You're twisting my words, Inspector."

"I'm trying to see your son through your eyes."

The door opened just then, and a woman dressed in severest black came into the room. "I've closed my valise—" She broke off. "I'm sorry. I didn't realize you had a guest."

Both men had risen as she entered. But Rutledge thought that Wentworth was more than a little put out by his wife's presence. As if he would have preferred conducting this interview alone. He covered it well, nodding toward Rutledge.

"Inspector Rutledge has come to ask questions about Stephen's life. The better to find answers to what has happened."

She stared at this man from London. Her face was not pretty, nor was it unattractive. Instead it was expressive of a woman who had been disappointed by life.

"I should think it's more to the point to learn about the man who killed Stephen," she said coldly.

"And that's one of the ways of going about it," Rutledge said pleasantly. "The more I learn about your son, the better able I am to find his murderer."

"That makes no sense to me at all."

"Nevertheless," Rutledge replied.

Raising her eyebrows at that, she looked him over a second time. Then, to his surprise, she sat down on the small sofa across from the fire and said, "He was always a disappointing child. And he grew into a disappointing man."

Rutledge stared at her. Here was a grieving mother, but she looked more like a disapproving headmistress discussing a recalcitrant pupil.

"How so?" he asked, trying to hide his distaste.

"He could never settle. He had to have that bookshop, and then he had to be off to Peru. It's all of a piece with everything he's ever done. He'd ever done," she corrected herself, remembering that he was dead.

"And yet he's your only son."

"He is not. His brother died soon after birth."

In a flash of insight, Rutledge saw the problem. The dead child had never lived to disappoint. The living child must have always been compared to what might have been. *If your brother had lived . . ."*

But what had Stephen done as a child to make him less acceptable than a dead memory?

Before he could respond, her husband broke into the conversation. "You must understand, Inspector, that we are still in a state of shock. This has been unbearably sudden, and we can barely face this news in our own minds."

Mrs. Wentworth glanced at her husband, opened her mouth to say something more, then carried on with the theme of shock. "Our daughter is waiting for us. She has the care of small children and had to stay behind. If we're to return here later in the week for the funeral, we must be on our way." She rose and turned toward the door. The two men got hastily to their feet.

Rutledge said, "It's possible that your son won't be released for burial for some time. There must be an inquest, for one thing, and questions to be answered first."

"That's ridiculous," Mrs. Wentworth told him sharply. "My husband will have a word with the Chief Constable." And before he could answer her, she was out the door.

Wentworth shrugged apologetically. "She's distraught—" he began, then with an arm outstretched to usher Rutledge toward the door, he added, "Another time?"

Rutledge found himself out on the step, the door closed firmly behind him.

It had been an interesting interview, he thought, staring at the brass knocker. He had seldom seen parents so untouched by a child's death. And that was something he would ask Constable Penny about.

Striding down the path to the gate, he heard Hamish say, "Look behind you."

Rutledge turned as he closed the gate, and he was just in time to see Mrs. Wentworth's face vanishing from view in an upstairs window. Stephen's room?

He found Constable Penny in the police station, and began with his own news.

"Did you find my message? I've been requested by the Chief Constable to take charge of this inquiry. It's official now."

Penny said, "Indeed, sir." As a comment it was as careful as the man could make his response.

"I've just called on Mr. and Mrs. Wentworth. They lived here in the village for most of their marriage. Tell me about them."

Reluctantly Penny said, "If we were to have a squire, I expect it would be Mr. Wentworth. Not the major landowner in these parts, of course, but the wealthiest man in the village. His word carries some weight."

"And his wife?"

"She came from York. Her father was the MP for the city. As marriage goes, it was advantageous for both of them. But Mr. Wentworth didn't have political aspirations, or so I've been led to believe. Mrs. Wentworth was more than a little upset by that, according to gossip. I expect she rather fancied a house in London while Parliament was sitting."

"Instead she had children."

"Yes, sir. She was rather strict rearing them. But Stephen grew up to be a fine man, so it didn't do much harm. The daughter was a pretty little thing, and she married well as you'd expect."

"How did brother and sister get on together?"

"I can only tell you what I've heard. Well enough, although never close. Patricia was a lively girl. She went her own way, made her own friends. It was at a party in Leicester that she met Jocelyn Courtney. Her husband. Late husband. He was from Norwich, up-and-coming young solicitor, or so I heard. A fine match."

"This was while Stephen was up at Cambridge?"

"Yes, his last year, as I recall. He came home for the wedding, but wasn't in the wedding party. There was some talk about that."

And Rutledge had just given his sister away, filled the role of her father as best he could. But of course Patricia had a father still living . . .

"What did the gossips have to say?"

"That the mother insisted on not having him in the wedding party."

"Odd, I should think," Rutledge agreed. But he had seen Stephen Wentworth's mother, and was prepared to believe this was true.

"Most seemed to think she was angry with him for wanting to buy the bookshop. Mr. Delaney wasn't well, he'd spoken to several villagers about wanting to sell up, and Stephen was eager to buy it while he could."

"Since it was his own money, he needn't ask their permission. Was that a cause for disagreement?"

"I don't know that it was the money so much as a Wentworth going into trade."

"Were there hard feelings between brother and sister over his exclusion from the wedding party? Did he perhaps feel that she should have insisted?"

"Now that's the odd thing. Mr. Stephen came to the wedding, danced once with the bride, the third dance, after her husband and her father. That's the custom. Was generally pleasant, and seemed not at all put out. He went back to Cambridge the next morning, having slept the night at a friend's house. Mr. Holden's, as a matter of fact. Well, the Wentworth house was full of guests. Still."

That also fit well into what Rutledge had heard from Mrs. Wentworth about her feelings toward her son.

"There were no other children?"

"I wasn't here until Mr. Stephen was seven or eight. But I never heard of any others."

"Who was here? The doctor? The Rector?"

"I don't believe so, sir. The sexton at St. Mary's might know. He's older. Or the Rector might be willing to look back in the church records. If it matters?"

"It's not important," he said, rising to leave. "Just filling in the family history."

"I don't know who would have it in for Mr. Stephen."

"So far, neither do I. But we'll see." He nodded to Constable Penny and left.

Rutledge walked up The Street, as far as the brickyard on the outskirts, then turned and came back. The village was not so large as to offer an unlimited number of suspects. But he wasn't quite satisfied with the possibility that one of the two friends he'd interviewed held a grudge that had suddenly flared into anger and murder. He decided to find out by asking Miss MacRae if she knew them and possibly might recognize them in the dark.

When he knocked on the house door, Miss Blackburn informed him that she had given Miss MacRae something to help her sleep.

"She was awake most of the night. I heard her walking about till all hours. So I stopped by the doctor's surgery and asked for something. He gave me some drops, and they appear to be just the thing. She's sleeping like a child, poor darling."

He didn't want to ask Miss Blackburn—he preferred to watch Miss MacRae's first reaction to his query for himself.

Hamish spoke suddenly, catching him off guard. "She's lived here an aye lang time."

"You don't approve?" Miss Blackburn demanded, bristling.

"Sorry, nothing to do with the drops. It occurred to me—how long have you known Mrs. Wentworth?"

Frowning, she considered. "Nearly twenty years, I expect."

"What can you tell me about her?"

"She's a spoiled, vicious woman who should have been given a taste of a belt when she was young enough to change."

Surprised, Rutledge said, "That's rather harsh."

"Not if you know the woman. I have had to suffer her presence in situations where I couldn't very well walk out of the room or the church, but I refuse to be polite to her. And her husband isn't much better. He will do anything to keep the peace in that house, letting her rule as she wishes. A weak and shallow man. I bid you good day."

With that she swung the door shut in his face, but not before he'd seen the flame of anger in hers.

Whatever her reasons were, it was clear that she wasn't about to discuss them. He thought perhaps he'd caught her off guard just as Hamish had caught him when he suggested asking her about Stephen's mother.

And he rather thought that Miss Blackburn wouldn't have been at all surprised to hear that Mrs. Wentworth had shot her own son, if the circumstances had been different.

The rain had let up for now, but lowering clouds promised more to come.

Folding his umbrella, Rutledge walked on to the church, crossing the street behind a farm cart laden with a half dozen unhappy pigs. Their noisy objections were bad enough, but the odor from the straw under them was foul.

The Sunday services had left behind a lingering hint of incense, but there was an emptiness that the echoes of his footsteps couldn't fill. He found himself wondering how long prayers drifted in the stillness of a Monday morning. There were holly branches among the greenery at the altar, and a splash of red berries that stood out in the dimness. Overhead, carved angels holding up the lovely wooden roof watched him as he walked down the nave. He looked around at the splendors that wool had built in churches like this. Many of them hadn't escaped the attentions of Henry VIII or Oliver Cromwell, but Rutledge had always loved fine architecture, and his godfather had cultivated this love, hoping that one day Rutledge would join his firm. But David Trevor's son, Ross, had been killed in the war, and Rutledge had chosen the police even before that. Trevor had tried to soldier on, but his heart hadn't been in it, and he sold the firm to take early retirement in Scotland with his small grandson, who was cared for by the young woman who had been the only family the boy, also named Ian, had known for the first few years of his life.

Pushing that memory away, he tried to imagine what these houses of worship had looked like before Oliver Cromwell's ravages. Before the Puritan spirit had torn out everything that smacked of Catholic imagery. Henry VIII had left many such architectural treasures untouched after he—with the help of another Cromwell—had decreed himself to be head of England's Church.

Rutledge quickly discovered evidence that the Wentworth family had been a large part of village life over the centuries, with plaques honoring them and brasses or memorials marking their resting places. They had been generous with their time and their money, but there was no indication that they had been good men—or bad, with a conscience guilty enough to offer up gifts to save their troubled souls.

But many men had lost their faith in the trenches and had had no place to expiate the horrors or the killing. One didn't build churches any longer, or give money toward a chapel, or pay for a fine new window. Sometimes one gave to repair a roof or deal with damp or replace an altar cloth—upkeep was expensive. But it was done as a charity and not as a hope for eternity.

Suddenly claustrophobic, even here in the spacious nave, Rutledge turned and walked back the way he'd come, taking a deep breath of the cold air as he stepped into the churchyard.

Hamish, all too aware of Rutledge's moods, said, "Ye canna' escape what's done." There was a harshness in his tone now.

"No." He hadn't realized he'd answered aloud.

He began to circle the churchyard, looking for the Wentworth plot, and he was halfway down one side when he felt that someone was watching him. He turned to glance over his shoulder.

There was a man standing some thirty yards away, near the tower. Rutledge would have sworn that he hadn't been there before, for surely he would have noticed him.

His hair was iron gray, his complexion ruddy, and he was wearing country clothes. High boots, corduroy trousers, and a flannel shirt beneath the heavy coat that was not buttoned up. He had no umbrella with him, but his hair and his shoulders were dry.

The sexton? Rutledge waited to see if he would come forward to greet him. But the man stared at him for several minutes before disappearing around the front of the church.

Rutledge went on with his search, and on the far side of the church, close enough for the graves to touch its outer wall, stood some twenty older tombstones incised with the Wentworth name, and almost like satellite clusters, later family groupings.

The voice behind him almost made him jump.

"Looking for the present family?"

He turned. It was the man he'd seen earlier. "As a matter of fact I am."

"They're on the far side. You missed them."

"Have I indeed?"

"Nothing to see there, anyway."

"I'm told the Wentworths lost a son. Many years ago."

"Who told you that?" His gruff manner was now almost menacing. Rutledge stood his ground. "Mrs. Wentworth."

"Well, now." The man turned away, looking toward a wood on the far side of the churchyard. "I shouldn't pry into a family's grief. Not now. Not when they have another cross to bear."

"How well do you know them?" Rutledge asked, deliberately showing interest.

"Well enough."

"Your accent isn't local."

"No?" He faced Rutledge again.

"In fact, you sound very like Chief Superintendent Markham, a Yorkshireman."

The man said nothing for a moment. "I spent some time there in my youth."

"I'd like to see the family graves."

"Have at it." He turned on his heel and strode away, not stopping until he'd reached the low churchyard wall and disappeared from Rutledge's view.

He spent another half hour looking before he realized he'd been searching for the wrong graves. Where would a child be buried? Not in a plot of its own but in that of grandparents? The problem was, with so many Wentworths buried here, more than a few of them children who had died young, he couldn't be sure which one might have been Stephen's brother.

Turning away, he walked grimly back to The Street.

Constable Penny was making his rounds, and Rutledge caught up with him outside a haberdashery.

"Looking for me, sir?" Penny asked, turning as Rutledge called his name.

"Yes. Do you know the names of Stephen Wentworth's grandparents?"

"Grandparents?" Penny frowned. "Why do you need that, sir?"

"I'll explain later. Do you know?"

"Um. I don't—I believe it was Howard and Patricia." He scratched his chin. "Patricia doesn't sound right. That's the granddaughter's name." Staring into the past, he searched his memory. "The family used to put flowers on the altar in their memory. I've seen the notice. On the occasion of the father's birthday. That stopped some years ago. Howard and—" He turned triumphantly to Rutledge. "Margaret. That's it, Margaret."

"Thank you," Rutledge responded, and was gone before the Constable could ask more questions.

But when he returned to the churchyard and resumed his search, it took some time to find Howard and Margaret Wentworth. When he did, he realized why he had found it so difficult to locate the right child's grave.

The marker was in the shape of a sleeping lamb, nestled between the stones of his grandparents, as if for protection, and half-hidden in the high winter grass. Rutledge knelt and brushed the dry strands away so that he could see the stone and what was written on the base beneath the lamb.

ROBERT EMORY WENTWORTH

And below that a date. 7TH JULY – 10TH DECEMBER 1890.

Rutledge rocked back on his heels. Robert Emory Wentworth had lived only a few months.

Thirty years ago. Had Stephen Wentworth done nothing to redeem himself in his mother's eyes in all that time? Or was it she who refused to relinquish the past?

7

Rutledge got to his feet, dusting off the knees of his trousers and then his hands.

The loss of a child was always dreaded. But early childhood diseases carried them off with heartbreaking frequency. His own parents had been fortunate, but as he was growing up, one friend had died of diphtheria, another of measles. During his first year at Westminster, typhoid fever had killed two boys at school, and another had died of a cancer. And he recalled vividly the stark, grieving faces of parents attending the memorial services. He had thought at the time how painful it must have been for them to walk into an assembly with so many active, healthy boys when they had just buried their own.

Lines from one of O A Manning's poems came back to him. The poet he and so many others had read over and over again in the trenches, because the poems somehow put into words what they all felt, officers and other ranks, waiting for the whistle to go over the top—and were afraid to say, when courage was expected of them. Profound courage sometimes, that they had never known they possessed.

In life we are in death . . .
The number of our days,
Long or short, troubling us
As we stare into the guns
And wonder, will Death come now?
Tomorrow? Next week? Or—
Not at all? Sacrificing
Some other mother's son
In our place.

Shaking off his dark mood, he looked up at the handsome tower for a moment, then turned and left the churchyard.

Who would talk to him about Stephen Wentworth and tell him the truth about the man some admired and at least one person had called a murderer? A man looked up to by some and envied by others? Who had gone his own way in the face of the dreams others had for him? Clearly independently minded, but socially accepted by his peers in spite of his decision to become a bookseller.

Somewhere in Wentworth's past surely lay the key to his death. But where to find that key?

He was about to turn toward The Street when he saw Miss Blackburn hurrying toward him. Stopping, he waited for her.

"Inspector?"

"Miss Blackburn?"

"Elizabeth has gone to the box room for her cases. She had a nightmare—it frightened her, so she wants to go home to Scotland. She says Stephen's killer will come for her next. Because she was *there,* you see, and could identify him."

"But she can't. She told me she didn't see his face clearly."

"Well, I know that, and *you* know that. This murderer does not. And in her dream he found her. And he shot her. She woke up just before she died."

"I'm sure it must have been terrifying. Dreams often are," he said, trying to ease her mind. "They wear off, sooner or later." It was a lie. He knew that sometimes they didn't. "Unless, of course," he added quickly, "there was something in her dream that she can't remember when she's awake."

"I asked her," Miss Blackburn retorted, as if he'd questioned her intelligence. "Be sure of that. If she had told me there was, and it put her in danger, I'd have fetched her cases myself and helped her pack them. Whatever Scotland Yard might have to say about it."

"Do you want me to go back to the house with you and reassure her that it was only a dream?"

"Easy for you to say 'only a dream.' You aren't the one who watched a killer fire at a friend, and thought for a horrified moment that he intended to turn and shoot you next!"

He had not seen her so rattled, even when he'd told her about Wentworth's death. He responded gravely, "You misread me, Miss Blackburn. But from my perspective, your niece is my only witness to this crime. At the moment only she can help me stop whoever it is from killing again. And she's far safer in Wolfpit than she would be traveling alone. You must realize that as well."

"Then you stop her, Inspector. Why do you think I have come out to fetch you?"

She turned on her heel and marched away, not waiting to see if he intended to follow her or not.

Rutledge had the feeling that Miss MacRae was suffering from delayed shock. In the pressure of the moment, she had answered his questions as best she could, she had even found the courage to drive his motorcar to Wolfpit to find Constable Penny. She had held up well later that morning when he'd come to interview her. But her dream, vivid and bringing into sharp focus her own danger in the aftermath of Wentworth's death, must have broken through the protective shell she had surrounded herself with, and let the demons in.

When they reached the house door, Miss Blackburn turned to him.

"You will be pleasant, if you please. No threats or callous disregard for her feelings."

It wasn't a question, more like the dictated terms of the owner of a dwelling, be it house or castle. The price of admission.

"I have nothing to gain by threatening her."

"Precisely."

She turned back to the door and opened it, once more leaving him to follow. At the foot of the stairs, she called, "Elizabeth? Inspector Rutledge would like to have a word with you."

She waited, but there was no immediate answer.

"Elizabeth?" More sharply now.

Then, with a suddenly fearful glance over her shoulder, as if to see how Rutledge was taking the silence from the head of the stairs, she went up them quickly and turned down the passage to Elizabeth's room.

Rutledge waited, tense, by the handsome newel post. In the back of his mind, Hamish was warning him to be prepared.

"*Inspector!*" Miss Blackburn's cry filled the ominous silence, and he took the stairs two at a time, turning in the direction she had taken. A bedroom door stood wide, pale light from the windows casting a paler glow across the polished floorboards.

He went into the room prepared for anything, and found Elizabeth MacRae lying on the floor in a widening pool of blood.

M iss Blackburn, her face gray with shock, was kneeling by her niece, trying to find a pulse. She looked up as Rutledge came through the door. "She's not dead," she said, keeping her voice steady with an effort he wasn't meant to see.

He was already scanning the room: window closed, no sign of a struggle, but there were half a dozen jumpers lying scattered at her feet, and a silk stocking was tangled around the heel of her shoe.

"She tripped," Rutledge said, coming to kneel by Miss Blackburn. "And her head caught the edge of the bed as she went down." He could see the cut, deep enough to bleed freely, just above her left eyebrow. "Towels? And some cold water?" he added in an attempt to give Miss Blackburn something to do to take her mind off her fright.

"It's your fault," Miss Blackburn said, suddenly losing her temper. "She was so upset by this business that she wasn't watching what she was doing. And this is the result. Look at her. See what you've done."

He didn't answer her directly. This angry outburst was a way of coping with her fear. "It doesn't matter whose fault this is. Do you have any smelling salts? They will help bring her around."

"No, I don't," she snapped. "I'm not given to fainting." But she got up and went to find what he needed, coming back almost at once with towels and a pitcher of water.

Bathing Elizabeth MacRae's face while Rutledge wiped up the blood on the floor, she said, "Darling, it's all right. You tripped. There's an ugly bump on your head, but no harm done."

Miss MacRae's eyelashes fluttered, and she threw out an arm, as if to catch herself from falling, and then her eyes opened and she looked up at Audrey Blackburn with alarm.

"What am I doing on the floor?"

"No, don't try to sit up just yet, darling. Catch your breath first."

She realized there was someone else present, turning to stare at Rutledge, on one knee beside her. He had moved the bloody towels out of sight.

Then, before they could stop her, she put up a hand, touching the wound and wincing. As she drew her hand away, she saw the blood on her fingertips, and Rutledge thought for a helpless moment that she was about to be sick.

"Oh dear God," she said faintly. "Stephen's blood."

Miss Blackburn said bracingly, "Nonsense. It's your own. You tripped and took a nasty spill, my dear, and you will probably have a headache too. Such a fright you gave me. I thought the ceiling had fallen in, and rushed up the stairs to see why you were rearranging the furnishings." Over her niece's head she glared at Rutledge, daring him to contradict her.

But there was no answering smile. "I was trying to pack, wasn't I?" She struggled to sit up, and felt a wave of dizziness. She put up her hand again, and this time touched the lump on her forehead. "Oh."

"I was downstairs," Rutledge was saying. "I'd just called. Can I help you to my motorcar? I'll be happy to take you to be seen by Dr. Brent. It might be a very good idea. You were unconscious for a bit. He may worry about a concussion."

The color was coming back into her face, and the dizziness appeared to be receding. "I've bled all over my shirtwaist. How awful."

Taking up the bloody towels, Rutledge said to Miss Blackburn, "I'll be downstairs. It will take only a few minutes to fetch the motorcar." And then he added to Miss MacRae, "I'm glad you're all right." With a nod, he left the room.

As he walked down the passage, he heard the younger woman say, "Why was the Inspector here?"

But he was too far away to hear Miss Blackburn's answer.

Instead of leaving, he stood in the center of the parlor, where he could be seen at once from the doorway, and after some minutes, he heard footsteps coming smartly down the stairs.

Miss Blackburn. Miss MacRae was surely still too shaken to leave her room. He stepped forward, and spoke before she saw him, so as not to frighten her.

"Why are you still here?" she demanded at once, keeping her voice low.

"I wanted to be certain she was all right," he said. "In the event I need to bring the doctor to her."

"She will be, when I've made her a cup of tea. If I see anything to worry about, I'll go to Dr. Brent's surgery myself."

"Is she still determined to go back to Scotland?"

"I haven't asked her."

"She can't, you know. I've explained why. It will be better coming from you."

"Elizabeth is my niece," she retorted. "I will do what is best for her. Not for you."

"Would it be easier if I arrested her as a material witness? I will if I must."

She stared at him, clearly appalled. "You will do no such thing," she told him roundly.

"Think about that," he said, turning toward the door. Then he remembered what he'd wanted to ask her. "Who in Wolfpit knew Stephen Wentworth best? I've met his mother and father, and parents aren't always the best judges of their children. Is there anyone else I ought to speak to?"

"Mrs. Delaney, I expect. Show yourself out, Inspector." And she walked on down the passage, leaving him standing there.

But he'd already spoken to the widow of the former bookshop owner.

Closing the door behind him, he considered the short list of people he'd questioned. As a rule, the village Constable was a useful source of information, but Rutledge was not sure yet where Penny's loyalties lay. With the Wentworths? Or possibly even with Inspector Reed.

He decided to return to Mrs. Delaney. She had shown more grief than the dead man's mother. And she appeared to know more about the boy who had grown into a man with a love of her husband's bookshop.

He walked on to her door, but no one answered his knock. As he turned back toward the center of the village, he saw her just stepping out of Dr. Brent's surgery. He went to meet her, and saw that the reason she was hurrying with head down was that she was crying.

When he spoke to her, she tried to nod and pass him by.

"What is it?" he asked gently. "Shall I walk you home?"

"Thank you, no," she said, looking away.

But he turned to give her his arm, and she had no choice but to walk on with him to her house.

They had just reached it when she said in a gruff voice, "I asked if I might see Stephen. It's taken me some time to work up the courage. But that's more than his mother or father did. I thought someone should at least—but Dr. Brent told me that I was not his *family*." She looked at him, her eyes bereft.

"I'm sorry," he replied. "Still, it's for the best, I should think. Instead, remember the boy and the man you knew so well."

Mrs. Delaney took a deep breath. "Why should anyone want to kill him? I can't seem to wrap my mind around that. An accident of some sort—we're all vulnerable to fate—I would find shocking and grieve just as much as I do now. But the uselessness of it all, the sheer *waste* of murder appalls me."

"Who knew him best in the years before he began to come to the bookshop? When he was quite young and couldn't read yet?"

"His parents, of course," she said, frowning as she studied his face.

"Someone more—objective," he suggested. "His sister, perhaps?"

Mrs. Delaney shook her head. "Hardly objective. His parents saw to that."

Small wonder, he thought, *that the boy spent his leisure time in the bookshop, where he was welcomed and in some fashion loved.*

"In what way?" he asked her.

"Little ways. She was younger, of course, and so it must have been easy to show her that Stephen was not valued. It astonishes me still that he became the person he did. He must have drawn from some inner source of strength. Amazing, really. When you stop and think about it."

"Why?"

She shrugged her shoulders. "Who knows? I certainly never did, nor could I ask the child such a question."

"There was no one who stood by him? A grandparent, a favorite aunt, someone who helped him until he could find his own strength?"

"Only Nanny," she said, "but what could *she* do? His grandmother tried, she left him financial independence, which tells me she understood what was happening. I don't think she could do much more than that. She wasn't well in her last years, and died when he was still just a lad."

"Is Nanny still alive?" he asked, feeling a surge of hope.

"I think so. She went to live with a friend in the next village when Stephen was seven. He had a tutor until he was sent off to school, boarding school. Far too young, if you ask me. But perhaps that was the saving of him too."

Rutledge asked for directions to the house of Nanny's friend, and was given vague instructions on how to find her.

He waited until Mrs. Delaney had gone inside, shutting her door behind her, then went to the inn and his motorcar.

As it turned out, the little cottage was easier to find than he'd expected.

Winthrop was more of a hamlet than a village, down a narrow lane that turned off the main road and wandered a mile or so into the countryside before a string of cottages and shops appeared. It was barely eight miles from Wolfpit as the crow flies, but it might as well be on the moon, he thought. He wondered if it had started life as a collection of weavers' crofts, before the mills took away their livelihood, for many of the cottages were of a size to hold a large loom. The prosperity that had built Wolfpit had never reached here.

One of the last cottages on the lane was set in a garden. It had been painted a pleasing yellow at some stage in its life, and that had faded to a paler shade that blended perfectly into its setting.

It was, he thought, the rose-covered cottage that many British living abroad dreamed of for their retirement back in England. *Quaint* was one word that suited it. And *charming* was another. *English* summed it up well. A small sign by the white gate identified the cottage as PRIMROSE HILL, the name that Mrs. Delaney had given him.

The garden was bedded down for the winter, bleak but surprisingly tidy.

The woman who answered his knock was also a perfect example of an English nanny: round and soft, her graying hair pulled neatly back into a bun at the nape of her neck, and round glasses perched on the end of her nose. She was wearing a dark blue coat and held a matching hat in her hand.

Rutledge smiled. "I am looking for the woman who was nanny to the Wentworth child Stephen."

He expected her to name herself, but she said, "You'll be wanting Hazel, then. She's in the parlor reading. I'm just popping out to buy something for our tea." And with a nod, she stepped past him and went off down the path to the lane.

Bemused, he stepped into the entry and peered into the parlor. "Hazel?" he asked of the woman sitting by the fire in the hearth, a book in her lap. "I'm sorry, it's the only name I know."

She turned, examined him from head to toe, and rose. An angular woman, her back as straight as a board, and her hair salt-and-pepper gray, she had gray eyes to match.

Something in her expression made him feel six again, and in Nanny's charge.

But she said in a pleasant voice, "I thought I heard Sally speaking to someone. My name is Hazel Charing. And you are?"

He told her and even produced his identification, but she barely glanced at it. He thought she had learned more about him in that scanning glance than his card could have told her.

"Close the door and come in. The chair there, across from me."

He did as he was asked, and joined her by the fire. The day was still gray and cold, although the rain was holding off. The fire's warmth felt good.

"I understand you were once nanny to Stephen Wentworth, when he was a lad."

"You're the policeman who found him," she countered.

"Sadly, yes." He hadn't expected the news to have traveled this far, but he rather thought Winthrop was deceptive. "I've heard a great deal about the man. I'd like very much to know more about the boy."

"You mean, you wish to know why his parents hated him so?" she asked bluntly.

"In fact, yes."

She set the book aside. "I was hired as nanny before the birth, when it was learned that Mrs. Wentworth was to bear twins."

He hadn't intended to interrupt her, but he said, "Twins?" in his surprise.

"Yes. She went into labor some six weeks early. Robert was born a little before midnight. Such a lovely child. He had fair hair, almost golden in the lamplight, and his eyes were blue. Perfectly proportioned. The ideal baby, and a boy as well. When he was put into his mother's arms, she cried out in delight, and held him to her, calling him her Robbie, telling him how sweet he was and showering love on him. Mr. Wentworth was overjoyed, laughing and crying tears of happiness. It was several hours later that Stephen was born. We'd had to take Robbie away when she went into labor a second time. And then the second son came into the world." She turned to stare into the fire. "Such a different baby. Angular and with a shock of ugly black hair. It was as if he hadn't been quite finished but had hurried to be born anyway. They were not identical, of course, but the difference was rather startling." Turning back to him finally, she continued. "When we had bathed Stephen and wrapped him in a blanket, we gave him to his mother in his turn, and she refused to take him. She exclaimed that he was hideous and couldn't have been hers. And she asked us to bring Robbie back to her. I took Stephen, while the doctor handed her Robert, and she made over him until she was tired, and we let her sleep. The crib closest to the bed was his, and Stephen's was against the far wall, out of sight. By the time we had cleaned up the room and taken everything away, Mr. Wentworth went over to the crib where Stephen was lying, and bent over it. 'A pity,' he said, shaking his head, and he walked off to the study to wet the boys' heads with a glass of brandy."

She looked at Rutledge as she finished, to see what his reaction was. "You didn't know they were twins?"

"No," he said. "No one mentioned that to me."

"I expect after all these years most people have forgotten," she said, nodding.

"But what happened to Robert?"

"Ah. You've spoken to his mother. He was the most beautiful child. Angelic. She had a portrait done of the two of them, mother and son, by a famous London photographer when the boys were two months old. But Robert was frail. While Stephen flourished, it was as if he sucked the life out of his brother. And when he was about six months old, Robbie was found dead in his crib, with Stephen curled up next to him."

Rutledge felt the jolt of shock. He was beginning to understand.

"Mrs. Wentworth swore that Stephen had killed him out of jealousy. It was rather terrible. Mr. Wentworth asked me to take Stephen away for a few weeks, for fear she would do him a harm in her wild grief."

Rutledge sat there, forcing down his anger at the selfish, mean-spirited woman, ungrateful that she still had a living child.

"What did the doctor have to say about the boy's death?"

"He was of the opinion it must have been a weak heart. But Mrs. Wentworth wouldn't hear of it or allow a postmortem. She sent him away. I heard her raging against Stephen, begging God to take him and let her boy live."

There would be no reasoning with such grief. And it had grown more vicious with time, instead of passing through the normal stages of mourning.

Miss Charing was still speaking. "He lived in the nursery with me after that, never coming down for tea or a good night kiss from his mother. No outings, no presents at Christmas, no invitations to visit friends. Mr. Wentworth came from time to time, doing his duty. He bought the boy a pony—then a wooden ship to float on the farm pond. A kite once, and a toy train that ran on wheels. He wasn't cruel. Just never kind. On school holidays Stephen came to visit me. I'd left by that time, and there was a younger girl set in my place when Miss Patricia was born. You would have thought Miss Patricia was their only child. It was quite remarkably cruel."

"Yet her husband condoned it, and the village turned a blind eye."

"Mr. Wentworth took great care that the village remained ignorant of her feelings. Even the Rector. As Stephen was old enough, he took his son for walks, he took him up in the carriage. He even took him to church services when Stephen was older. Only of course on Sundays when Mrs. Wentworth declined to attend. She was quite angry with God but put up a good public front of her own. She would have sent him away at seven, but for the fact that her husband forbade it."

"He never told the other boys in Wolfpit what his home life was like? Why was he allowed even to play with them?"

She smiled for the first time, giving her face a softness he hadn't seen before. "Ah, that was my doing. I protected him as best I could. And I tried to see that he lived a normal life. I took him out in his pram, I saw to it that he met other young lads his age and played with them. Out of his mother's sight, of course. Several families had nursery maids, and naturally they were quite happy to let their own charges meet the Wentworth heir. And in summer when he was at home, he would come here on his bicycle and then go off to play. Even after he discovered a second home as it were with Mr. and Mrs. Delaney, he came here often. I'd always told him that people would be curious about how the Wentworths lived, and he was to smile and say, 'Not so very different from the way you live, except that I'm to be sent off to school.' Mothers were the worst, asking prying questions." They heard the outer door open and close. Miss Charing waited until the other woman had gone to the rear of the house before saying in a low voice, "There were other problems, you know. And I think that added to Mrs. Wentworth's hatred of her son. The boys were not identical twins, as I've said. Stephen had been an ugly baby. Even I must admit it. But that thatch of stiff black hair fell out, as it often does, and in its place his hair grew back as fair as his brother's, and that scrawny body grew longer and stronger. That was the reason his mother swears he killed his brother. She called it sucking the life out of Robert, and when Robert died so suddenly, she swore that Stephen had got all he wanted from his brother and was finished with him."

O n the drive back to Wolfpit, Miss Charing's words echoed in Rutledge's head, and Hamish said in disgust, "It's a wonder she didna' kill the lad hersel'."

"I think Stephen's father feared she might. Especially in the years just after Robert's death."

"Aye. It was a dreadful secret to keep. How the family stopped gossip is a wonder. Unless yon servants pitied him and didna' wish the village to know, for his sake."

Rutledge remembered that Lydie, the daily, had wanted him to see that Stephen's killer was found and taken directly to the hangman. He thought it likely that Hamish was right. "But he's still the heir, isn't he? His father would have something to say to that."

"There are grandchildren to inherit. If one is a boy, it's no' sae difficult to change a name. And their father is dead and wouldna' be able to object. Even the mother would be tempted to see her lad raised up to heir."

Murder had been done for weaker reasons . . .

He had been too busy to think of lunch, and it was nearly four o'clock. He went back to The Swan and ordered sandwiches and a pot of tea. He'd have preferred something stronger after the disturbing conversation with Miss Charing. But he was on duty still, and the Yard frowned on anything that might reflect poorly on its men.

The son of loving parents himself, he couldn't imagine how Stephen had grown up in such an environment. But there had been those who cared for Stephen and tried to make his life better. The Delaneys, Nanny, even his friends, who took him at face value and didn't question the manner of his life. After all, he was in boarding school, he was bound to be different from them. And he let them believe that was all it was.

The question was, When had Stephen himself recognized that other lads had very different mothers? And how had he dealt with that? In books, in escape into other people's lives?

His tea came and he poured himself a cup, still thinking about Stephen.

Then Hamish warned him, and he looked up in time to see Inspector Reed crossing the dining room on his way to Rutledge's table.

Keeping a bland expression pinned to his face, Rutledge waited until the other man was near enough and said, "Reed," with a nod of greeting.

Without waiting for an invitation, Reed took the other chair at the table and sat down. "Any word?"

"Early in the day," Rutledge answered.

"Hmmm." He studied the scene beyond the window for a moment. "It has to be someone in Wolfpit. Stands to reason. Who else might know where Wentworth would be that evening? What about this MacRae woman? Do you trust her account of events? She might have been in touch with the killer."

"Where's the motive for her to kill her companion? Or to agree to tell someone else where to find him?"

"Still, she might know more than she's telling."

There was always a caveat to certainty. He had to consider the possibility that Miss MacRae had realized in her dream that she knew Wentworth's killer, and it had precipitated her decision to go home to Scotland. He couldn't put off questioning her about that.

"Women found him attractive," Reed countered sourly. "And he didn't seem to be interested in *them*. Makes you wonder."

"I was led to believe there was someone while he was at university who mattered," Rutledge said casually. "And it precipitated his decision to go to Peru."

"A man like Wentworth doesn't fly away to the ends of the earth over a broken heart. No, I don't believe that's why he went."

"Then why?"

"Because he's Stephen Wentworth, and spoiled into the bargain. He does what he feels like doing at the moment. Buy a bookshop. Go to university. Hare off to Peru. He doesn't have to earn his bread the way the rest of us do. He can indulge whatever whim strikes his fancy. And if you ask me, that's what led to his death. Whatever it was he fancied *now,* it got him killed."

It was, in fact, an interesting point.

Rutledge said, "You have an ear to the ground here. What do you think that new fancy might be?"

Reed shook his head. "How should I know? Playing fast and loose with another man's wife, for instance."

Rutledge kept his expression mildly interested even as he understood that Reed was probably talking about his own fear. "How would I go about finding out a name? His friends won't talk about his peccadillos. I can hardly ask his parents. Where should I begin?"

With a shrug, Reed got to his feet. "Damned if I know. It's your inquiry anyway. So I have been told." He couldn't keep the sarcasm out of his voice. And with an abrupt nod he walked away.

Rutledge watched him pass the window on his way to the omnibus stop that would carry him back to his own police station.

Jealousy was a very strong emotion. And more than one man had killed because of it. Reed was a jealous man who probably wished the killer of Stephen Wentworth well for removing a thorn in the side of his own marriage.

Hamish reminded him, "Wentworth took a lass home before bringing Miss MacRae back to Wolfpit."

Yes, and I think it's time to look into that, Rutledge answered him silently as he smiled at the woman who had come to take away his dishes. He remembered to mention that he might be in late for dinner.

There were signs of activity at the Hardy manor house. The new arrival had shaken up the middle-aged maid as well.

When she answered Rutledge's knock, he could hear voices and laughter in the background and there was even a slight flush in her face, as if all the excitement had brightened her own mood.

When she saw him standing on the steps, he could almost hear what she was thinking: *You again.*

He smiled formally this time, and her expression changed to wariness.

"It's urgent I find Miss Hardy," he said. "It's a matter of police business."

"What can the police have to do with Miss Hardy?" she demanded.

"Her direction, please."

Uncertain, she stared at him. "I can't give you that."

"Then I'll speak to Mrs. Hardy." He made as if to enter the house, and she stepped back.

"Here!" she said quickly. "Mrs. Hardy has guests. You can't come in."

"Then tell her, if you will, that Inspector Rutledge is here and would like a word with her about Stephen Wentworth."

Mrs. Hardy was middle-aged and still very attractive, with fair hair and hazel eyes.

She came into the drawing room where the maid had left him while she inquired if Mrs. Hardy was receiving.

"I understand you're looking for my niece. I should like to know why."

"I'm sorry to be the bearer of bad news, but Stephen Wentworth is dead, and I've been asked to conduct the inquiry into what happened. I should like to speak to Miss Hardy—I understand he and Miss Mac-Rae took her home after your party."

She was still digesting his news. "Dead? There must be some mistake. He appeared to be perfectly fine Saturday evening. What happened?" She frowned. "You aren't telling me that there was a crash—that there was a problem with the motorcar? But that's why I allowed him to take my niece home. He's a good driver, steady, reliable."

"I'm afraid it was more serious than that. Someone stopped the motorcar on the road when Wentworth and Miss MacRae were on their way back to Wolfpit. Wentworth got out to investigate and was shot. Miss MacRae was unharmed."

"Dear God." She had kept him standing, and now she pointed to a chair and sat down herself, as if the shock had left her shaken. "He was just *here*. I can't believe—I don't want to believe you." She blinked back tears. "Stephen is—Stephen was like one of the family. Why weren't we informed sooner? I have guests—my son—what on earth shall I tell them? Everyone knows him."

He said nothing, letting her come to terms with death. It was a measure of her concern that she hadn't been able to hide her emotions behind a social facade. The odd thing was, she hadn't heard about Stephen. But then it had happened over a weekend, no tradesmen or dailies coming in bursting with news.

"But who?" she asked finally, as the implications of what he'd said fully registered. "I mean, Stephen. He hadn't an enemy in the world. Why?"

"That's what I'm trying to find out. I need to speak to your niece. She was in the motorcar shortly before that. I'd like to hear how he looked and sounded, and whether or not he was worried. Miss MacRae is in no condition to answer questions just now."

Not quite true, but he wanted very much to speak to Evelyn Hardy.

"And I shall need a guest list from Saturday evening," he added after a moment.

She stared at him. "But surely you don't think that one of our guests—it's *preposterous*."

"Nevertheless, they were with him all evening, spoke to him, would possibly have noticed anything unusual in his manner, or heard him express any concerns he might have had. He could have said something that will help us find his killer."

"My guests—" she began, then realized the implications of what he was saying. "You think he *knew*—but he offered to take Evelyn *home*."

"She was in no danger. The shooting occurred after that."

"Stephen," she said again, then shook her head. "I can't quite— quite grasp this." She looked away from him, and then, resolutely, she rose and went to a very elegant little desk by the windows. Lifting a sheet of paper out of the drawer, she took up a pen and began to write. Halfway through, she stopped and stared at nothing before resuming her task. After looking it over briefly, as if to make certain it was complete, she held the list out to him, and he crossed the room to take it from her. Miss Hardy's direction was at the top of the sheet.

"I shan't say anything to my son and his friends," she said quietly. "Not just yet. It will spoil his homecoming. There's nothing he can do."

"And you yourself saw nothing Saturday evening that would have worried you?"

"No. Sadly no. Gentle God. Stephen."

"Thank you, Mrs. Hardy."

"I wish you had never had to come to my door." She rose and saw him out, shutting the door quietly as soon as he had stepped out into the drive.

As he turned the crank, he remembered the look on Mrs. Hardy's face. Death had come too close, and she had liked Stephen Wentworth, considered him almost a member of the family. After all, he had stayed to greet her son, in spite of the delay in his arrival. Late as it was. Rutledge wondered just how long she would be able to withhold the news from her houseguests. How soon they would read the shock in her eyes.

I t seemed that Miss Hardy lived with her widowed mother in the village of Wickham, just a few miles to the north of the Hardy household, and no more than ten miles from Wolfpit. He found the village easily enough, and then the house itself. It appeared to be a dower house, elegant and set back from the road by a low wall and a stand of tall evergreens that offered some privacy to the grounds. Like the houses around it, it had been built in a different era, and there was a certain air of gentility here on this short street that ran just off the High. If wool had built magnificent churches, it had also made the fortunes of those who knew how to profit from it. There was most certainly money in the Hardy family—where the senior branch lived, the estate had appeared to be well kept and prosperous. And the cadet branch had not done too shabbily here in Wickham.

Painted a soft yellow with white trim, the dower house was quite attractive, and as he left his motorcar by the road, opened the low gate, and walked up a flagstone path to the door, he couldn't help but admire the proportions and the decorations at the windows. A cake, he decided suddenly. With the loops and swags that pleased the eye, it could have been a wedding cake.

And that reminded him of Frances and London. He pushed the thought away.

The doorknocker was a beautifully polished brass pineapple. He let it fall against the plate, and waited.

It would have to be done all over again, this telling of bad news.

8

Another middle-aged maid answered this door, and he thought she might possibly be related to the one at the Hardys' house. Both women had the same square jaw and deep-set hazel eyes.

He asked to speak to Miss Hardy, and received a frown.

"May I ask who's calling, sir?" she inquired politely.

"My name is Rutledge. She doesn't know me, but I am here about Stephen Wentworth's death."

Her expression changed at once. It was clear that the news had already reached Wickham. He wondered who had carried it.

"Indeed, sir. I'll inquire if Miss Hardy is in."

A few minutes later he was being led to a small drawing room as elegant as the facade.

Miss Hardy was standing in the middle of a pale green Turkey carpet, and an older woman, who must be her mother, was seated by the bow window.

He could see that Miss Hardy had been crying earlier in the day. There was redness around her eyes, and a puffiness as well.

"Mr. Rutledge?" she said at once. "You asked to see me? Word came at breakfast this morning. The butcher's lad told Cook, and she told us. I hadn't heard—"

She stopped as if she couldn't trust her voice. The other woman rose.

"May I ask who you are?" Her manner was decidedly cool.

"Scotland Yard has charged me with looking into the circumstances of Mr. Wentworth's death."

"And what are these circumstances? We have only been told that something had happened on the road to Wolfpit." She indicated a chair and resumed her own seat, but Miss Hardy stayed where she was.

Rutledge sat down across from her. "He was returning to Wolfpit with Miss MacRae in the motorcar with him. They were stopped before they reached the village by a man standing in the road. He spoke to Stephen Wentworth, who had stepped out of the motorcar to ask what was wrong. And then without warning, Wentworth was shot. He died at the scene."

"Dear God," Mrs. Hardy said softly.

Her daughter cried out, "But how awful!"

"Do you have this man in custody?" Mrs. Hardy asked after a moment.

"Sadly, no. That's why I'm here."

"My daughter had nothing to do with murder," she retorted sharply. There was no particular response to the death of someone she knew, only a self-centered concern about her daughter. He had the fleeting thought that she and Mrs. Wentworth would have much in common. This Mrs. Hardy, unlike her sister-in-law at the house on the Wolfpit road, didn't appear to have shed a single tear over Wentworth's death.

"But she did know Mr. Wentworth," Rutledge responded with the firmness of authority, "and I have come to ask for any information about his life that might help us find this man."

"My daughter is engaged to Mr. Quinton."

He had seen Miss Hardy move suddenly, and he made certain that his response was innocuous. "That's not in question here. Anyone who was acquainted with Stephen Wentworth can add to my store of knowledge about the man. However little your daughter may know, it's still more than I myself have discovered at this stage."

Miss Hardy was still standing stricken in the middle of the room. Now she sat down in what could be interpreted as sheer relief.

"Mama, may I speak to Mr. Rutledge privately?" she asked then.

"We have no secrets, Evelyn."

"No, Mama, but perhaps Mr. Wentworth might."

Mrs. Hardy stared at her. "What are you saying, my dear?"

"Only that Mr. Rutledge might feel that I was betraying a confidence."

Her mother sat there, uncertainty in her eyes, but her daughter remained firm, her own gaze on Rutledge's face.

"For heaven's sake, Mama, I've known Stephen for years," she finally added in exasperation. "That's not a secret. My brother was in school with him. And it isn't Stephen that I'm engaged to marry."

Mrs. Hardy stood up. "Very well, my dear. Mr. Rutledge, I bid you good day. Please don't take advantage of my absence to upset my daughter."

"That was never my intent on coming here," he replied, rising as well.

When she had gone, Evelyn Hardy waited to hear her mother's footsteps crossing the marble floor of the entry hall, and then she drew Rutledge to the far end of the room, by the bow window.

"Will you keep my confidences?" she asked. "I have to know."

"In as far as I can. In a murder inquiry, anything that leads me to the guilty party has to be reported."

She shook her head. She was slim and fair, with a pretty face, and Rutledge found himself thinking that she suited this pretty house she'd grown up in, more than her mother did.

"*My* confidences," she repeated. "Not Stephen's."

"If I can. But I won't know until I've heard what you have to say."

She took a deep breath. "Very well. Mark Quinton and I had a quarrel on Saturday. It would upset my mother to know that. But sometimes he can be so very—very difficult. I wanted him to take me to the party, it was in my aunt's house, after all, and he wasn't happy about it. I don't know why. Well, I expect I do. He doesn't like some of my family. Still, he took me anyway, feeling rather put out about it, and before my cousin arrived late from France, Mark wanted to leave. I wanted to stay and see him. Mark claimed it was far too late to be out, he'd promised my mother to bring me home by midnight, and I thought he was being rude. Stephen offered to see me home, and Mark left in a huff." She hesitated. "Thank you for not telling my mother who actually brought me back."

The jealous man? Rutledge waited while Hamish stirred in the back of his mind. But she didn't go on, and finally he had to ask, "Why doesn't Mark Quinton care for the senior branch of the Hardy family?"

"Well, for one thing, they're very much into politics, and Mark isn't. Our grandfather was an MP, and I think my cousin Robin wants to stand for his seat as soon as our present member retires or resigns. He's in poor health, you see. And now the war is over, Robin can do just that. He survived the war with only a little limp, and he wants to have a say in the way things are being done. He's quite marvelous, you know, and very popular in the county. He was a fearless rider, very good at tennis, and just the kindest man. I shouldn't think he'll have much trouble winning the seat."

Listening to her, Rutledge had the feeling that any jealousy on Quinton's part had nothing to do with Stephen Wentworth and much to do with Robin Hardy.

"It was Robin who just arrived from France?"

"Yes. He's been back there several times. He got himself seconded to an officer involved in the peace negotiations, and he has rather strong opinions on what reparations will do to Germany. The people, not the army."

A good many people had discussed that, on both sides of the issue.

Belgium and France felt that Germany was responsible for the damage to their countries, the loss of towns and railways, the destruction of farms and villages, the displacement of millions of people. Returning Belgium and the northern part of France to their prewar state was going to be costly. But the problem was, Germany was in no better straits, and possibly worse. Reparations would keep her economically broken for years to come. And possibly that was exactly what the Allies, save the American president, had had in mind. But the Treaty of Versailles had been signed and ratified by all the parties—again, saving the Americans—in 1919, on the same date as the event that had started the war had taken place.

28 June 1914, the day he had proposed to Jean . . .

He brought himself back to the pretty drawing room with an effort.

"Tell me about Stephen and your brother."

"My late brother," she replied. "Harry was killed in France in 1916. He had gone to school with Stephen, and sometimes he brought Stephen home with him. I liked Stephen, and so did Harry. But I had a feeling he must not have a family that cared much for him, because there never was any trouble on his part to accept invitations."

"What was the problem with his family?"

"Harry and I talked about it once. We think Stephen must have disappointed his parents somehow. I don't quite see how. He was a good student, a nice young man. My father liked him enormously, and that counted for much in this house. Robin liked him too, although Robin was some years older and only knew him through Harry and me. Stephen never talked about his family, or only in the most general terms. I wondered sometimes if he really felt loved by them. But he must have done, don't you think? To have become the fine man he is—was?"

"I have heard that he was in love with a girl he met in Cambridge."

"Yes, and Harry liked her too. He thought she would be good for Stephen. I never met her, but she was the daughter of someone in the colleges, and Harry said she would not begrudge Stephen his dream of having the bookshop."

"What happened? Why did he suddenly decide to go to Peru? If it was likely that he might marry her after he came down?"

"It was the oddest thing. They were so close. Stephen told Harry he'd already found the perfect ring for her. He was quite excited about it. And on the night he was to propose to this girl, Stephen walked into Harry's room very late, looking as if he'd seen a ghost—Harry's words—and returned a book he'd borrowed. He said he was tired and was going to bed straightaway. And he left. Without another word. Harry thought there might have been a quarrel, and that it would be patched up the next day. But Harry didn't see him the next day. Or the next. And when he did hear, Stephen had already sailed for Peru. Harry tried to speak to the girl, but she wouldn't see him. He left Cambridge without knowing what had happened between them."

"What was her name?"

She grinned, surprising him. "It was not for me to know. Well, that was years ago, and I was still a schoolgirl. Harry was up at university, quite lofty and secretive. And then one day he forgot and said her name. Dorothea. That's all I learned. But after that, Harry did mention her from time to time. After I promised I'd never tell Stephen I'd guessed, of course."

"And you are the Evelyn who gave him a book on his birthday?"

She blushed. "How did you know that? But yes. I did. It was a book he'd expressed an interest in. And I thought, how perfect for his birthday. Harry teased me unmercifully about it later. Coals to Newcastle, he said, to give a book to a bookseller. But I loved Stephen as a friend, nothing more. He was like another brother. And when Harry was killed, Stephen sent me such a wonderful letter, all about Harry. I would have done anything to help him be happy. He deserved to be."

He had identified Dorothea and Evelyn.

But he'd got no real answers to help him find a killer.

And no question of Mark Quinton's jealousy over Evelyn Hardy. Come to that, both Miss MacRae and Stephen Wentworth would have known Quinton by sight. After all, he'd attended the same party. Even if Quinton had stopped Wentworth's motorcar to find out what Miss Hardy had done after his departure from the house, there would have been no reason for murder. A simple answer would have sufficed. Miss MacRae had also been in the motorcar, and the two women would have chaperoned each other, as far as propriety went. Even if Quinton was angry over the lateness of the hour.

"What was Wentworth's mood on Saturday evening?"

"He seemed to be in fine spirits. If something was worrying him, he gave no sign of it. He kept us entertained while we were waiting for Robin to appear, just chatting and laughing, helping Mrs. Hardy in any way he could. The servants had gone up, and it was Stephen's idea to adjourn to the kitchen and make tea."

"I've been told that Miss MacRae was put out over Wentworth volunteering to drive you back here."

She shook her head. "Not put out. She was afraid her aunt might be worried that she hadn't come home, and I think that privately she felt it rather childish of Mark to behave as he had, walking out and leaving me there. Robin stepped in and said he'd be happy to take me, but he'd just driven all the way from Dover, and he was quite tired. Besides, I knew Mark wouldn't care for that—he's taken a dislike to Robin and my other cousins. He couldn't complain about Stephen, not with Miss MacRae in the motorcar with us."

"Why do you think he's quite so jealous?"

She glanced toward the door, to be sure her mother couldn't hear her, then said with noticeable embarrassment, "Please don't think ill of him. It's just that Mark has had a stricter upbringing, and my Hardy cousins can be quite lively at times."

"I understand." But he thought it might be more than their lively natures. Whenever Evelyn spoke Robin Hardy's name, there was an unconscious warmth in her voice. And a man in love might not care for that.

He thanked Miss Hardy soon afterward, and left without seeing her mother.

What had Wentworth done to bring down such hatred on himself that someone had killed him? Aside from how his own mother felt, everywhere Rutledge turned people spoke well of him. Except for the man at the church in Wolfpit. The sexton, he thought. And Inspector Reed.

Unless Wentworth had a secret life that no one knew about, a wolf in sheep's clothing as it were, he appeared to be blameless.

Rutledge turned his motorcar and went in search of Inspector Reed.

R eed was not in when Rutledge reached Stowmarket at teatime. It was an attractive small town with a market charter going back to the Middle Ages, and he could see a handsome church closer to the river.

Reed wasn't in the police station, and the Constable there seemed to have no idea where to find him. With Hamish busy in his mind, Rutledge walked up one side of Bury Street and down the other to pass the time. The shops were busy, the street crowded. No one seemed to take particular notice of a stranger among them, although small children, muffled to the ears against the cold, stared at him from their prams. And then Hamish said, "There."

Rutledge looked down the street in time to see Reed just stepping into a tea shop with the speed of a man looking to avoid anyone searching for him.

Picking up his own pace, Rutledge reached the shop just as Reed was taking a table in the back, where he couldn't be seen from the street.

He glanced up and saw Rutledge bearing down on him, and his mouth twisted in a grimace.

"Good afternoon," Rutledge said affably, although it was going on five. "I was told you were out at one of the farms." Before taking the other chair, he turned and smiled at the woman behind the counter, and she came over at once to take their order.

With poor grace, Reed gave his, and Rutledge asked for a pot of tea.

When the woman had gone away, Reed said, "You've come to ask me to take over the inquiry. I expected it would be too much for you."

Rutledge felt like gritting his teeth. The man was a fool. And jealous . . . Not just about his wife, apparently. But then, an unhappy marriage could ruin the best of men.

Keeping his tone pleasant, he said, "I'll soldier on today, if you don't mind. No, I've come to ask if you know of any shooting similar to Wentworth's that has occurred in, say, the past six months? Or even the past year?"

The other man grinned, waited for his sandwich and their tea to be set down, and then said, "Looking for a way out?"

"Answer the question, Reed."

The change in tone from friendly to icy caught Reed off guard. He lost the silly grin and stared at the man from London.

"All right, then, I haven't inquired of other jurisdictions. But nothing of the sort has come to my attention since I've returned to Stowmarket. Mainly men taking their service revolver out to the back garden and ending it. Three amputees in the month of October. That was the worst. There's no work for them, and sitting around the house under the feet of wives or family begins to overwhelm them. There's a church group trying to help, but mostly it's people who weren't out there in France. They do their best, but they don't *know*. You were there, you understand what I'm talking about. It's sometimes bloody awful, looking back."

"You turned the corner. How did you manage it?" But even as he said it, he wondered if that was true. And wished he could take back the question. The edginess in this man, the jealousy, the provocative remarks might be the only way he could cope.

Reed looked away. "Never had any corner to turn," he said brusquely.

Rutledge commented without emphasis, "You're a lucky man."

"Lucky in many respects," he answered, nodding.

Rutledge knew he was speaking now of his wife. *What sort of woman is she?* he wondered. *And why does she let the green eye of jealousy fester in this man?*

But that wasn't his problem. He had a murder on his hands, and Reed would have to attend to his own woes. Unless or until they cast a shadow on what had happened in Wolfpit.

He finished his tea and prepared to go. "I'll be on my way. When there's any news, I'll let you know."

"*When,*" Reed said, his tone biting once more, "is what we're waiting for. Will you be holding the inquest any time soon? I'm told the Wentworths would like to bury their son."

"Possibly by the end of the week," Rutledge said, keeping it vague on purpose. "Where do you usually hold them?"

"Here in Stowmarket. Unless you insist on Wolfpit. There haven't been that many murders in a while. We're out of practice."

Rutledge made certain he paid for the tea on his way out.

O n the drive back to Wolfpit, Rutledge debated what direction the inquiry should take next.

So far there was no thread of trouble in Wentworth's background, save for the very personal family problems, to indicate enemies. And while Hamish was favoring Reed as his killer, Rutledge thought it unlikely. Reed might well fret over his wife's connection with Wentworth, but he hadn't given out the signals of turning to murder.

Now the question must be what his wife's feelings were. And Rutledge could think of no way to question her without sending Reed into a blind fury.

Hamish said, "Yon Miss MacRae or her aunt might know her."

"I don't want any gossip reaching Reed's ears." He concentrated on the road as he passed a farm cart carrying a boar. "It's possible she has a father or brothers who blamed Wentworth for what was happening between Reed and his wife."

It was long odds. But it would have to be explored. Sometimes the answer in a murder inquiry lay in long odds. He had always been rather good at following them up.

The question remained: How best to go about approaching Mrs. Reed with some delicacy?

He finally settled on Mrs. Delaney as the least likely person to gossip, though it was after six when he called on her.

"Mrs. Reed?" she asked in surprise, when Rutledge brought up the name.

"What do you know about her?" he said, holding his ground.

She smiled. "She grew up in Wolfpit, Inspector. Her father is the greengrocer. Her grandfather—her mother's father—owned a Suffolk Punch farm before the war, and he's trying to rebuild it now. But there isn't a call for draft horses, with vans and lorries taking their place. That's a horse, you know. Not a party beverage."

Rutledge laughed. "I know." Then he asked, "Would they step in if they had a feeling that her marriage was in trouble? Have a word with Reed, perhaps, or even with anyone who might be causing that trouble?"

"I hardly think so," she retorted, more than a little shocked. "They're a respectable family, and Mrs. Reed isn't that sort of woman. If there's a problem in that marriage, it's the Inspector's fault, not hers."

"Then why does he appear to be jealous of Wentworth?"

"Is he? Oh, you aren't thinking that he might have shot Stephen? He's a *policeman*."

He told her the truth then. "It's affecting his work, this obsession with Wentworth. I need to know why." A partial truth, but that was all she needed to know.

"Oh. I wish you'd told me that in the beginning. Let me see. She went to work in the milliner's shop, the summer of 1914. She was only seventeen but she was quite good with a needle, and did rather well there. It was something of a surprise, so the gossip claims, when she announced she was to marry Inspector Reed. She'd seemed intent on making the shop her career."

"I had a feeling when speaking to Inspector Reed that his wife had known Wentworth well."

"I expect she did. She was in and out of the bookstore as a child. Stephen was often there as well. She told my husband she wanted to broaden her world, which was rather sweet. I don't know whether she also had an eye on Stephen or not, but Mrs. Wentworth would probably have had something to say about that, even if she was hardly more than a child."

"Once he was back in Wolfpit after the war, did he show any personal interest in her? Was she in the bookshop more often than was usual? She wasn't a child then. Reed might have misunderstood."

"I haven't heard any gossip in that quarter, mainly because I don't believe there was any. I don't quite know where you're taking this, Inspector. I'm sure her family would have been overjoyed to bring the Wentworth fortune into the fold. But I really don't see Stephen being unkind enough to lead her on. In fact, he was very careful these past two years not to show interest in any direction. It wouldn't have been good for business, to have such a reputation. Has anyone else given you the impression that he was a flirt? No, I didn't think so! I do think that's why he enjoyed Miss MacRae's company. She's only a visitor here, you see, and they've been friends for ages. If you want my honest opinion, if it hadn't been for the girl in Cambridge, I expect he might have found himself looking at the Hardy girl."

"Yes, I've spoken with Evelyn Hardy."

If Stephen hadn't been close to Robin Hardy, had he stayed at the dinner party for Evelyn Hardy's sake, because he knew she cared for her cousin? And volunteered to take her home, when her fiancé deserted her? That spoke of a different kind of affection.

"Her brother was a lovely boy, and he grew into a lovely man," Mrs. Delaney went on with sadness in her voice. "The Germans took our best and brightest. It was unbelievably cruel. I shan't forgive them. Ever."

They lost their best and brightest as well, he thought to himself. But apparently that hadn't counted in the Kaiser's decision to go to war.

He nearly missed what she had to say next.

"It's Robin I always wondered about. He's come home, I hear."

Rutledge kept his voice neutral. "He arrived the evening Wentworth was shot. It's what delayed their return to Wolfpit, according to Miss MacRae and Evelyn Hardy."

"Did he now?" was all she said.

Probing, Rutledge commented, "Evelyn appears to be fond of him."

"Which doesn't surprise me. He's fascinating, is Robin. The younger son. People are drawn to him. And then they learn the hard lesson that he isn't what he seems. I don't know how to explain Robin Hardy. In the past he'd have been a highwayman simply for the devil of it. Or a pirate, perhaps. Something wild and full of adventure. You sense that in him. At least older people do. Younger people are often drawn in by that air of devil-may-care. It was once said of Lord Byron, I think, that he was dangerous to know. Robin isn't a dashing poet with a dark streak in him. But he would have enjoyed being such a one."

Frowning as he tried to read between the lines of her comments, he asked, "Was Mrs. Reed in love with *him*? Not Wentworth? Is that what you're avoiding telling me?"

Mrs. Delaney smiled. "My dear Inspector. I don't have any idea. I don't know her secrets. But you see, while Stephen was the lad everyone admired and loved, the sort of child you might wish to have yourself, Robin was wild and interesting and unpredictable. And women find that irresistible too."

R utledge quietly let himself into the bookshop, locking the door again behind him.

The telephone was out of sight from passersby. He took out his notebook, then put through a call to the Yard, asking for Sergeant Gibson.

When Gibson answered, his voice gruff, Rutledge said, "I'm in need of information, Sergeant. Can you look into names for me?"

The gruffness dropped half an octave deeper. "I'll do my best. Sir."

He read a list of names, spelling some of them carefully. The final one was Robin Hardy's.

Sergeant Gibson cleared his throat. "As to this last, sir. If that's the Hardy I'm remembering, he was up before the London magistrates a number of times before the war."

"Was he indeed?"

"He was taken up once for attempting to paint the Tower ravens a bright yellow. They can't fly, you know. Not far at any rate. He was nearly successful with the first one. And on another occasion, he was attempting to fly a kite from the rooftops of St. Paul's. He was charged with public drunkenness, but the Constable reported he was as sober as the magistrate was."

"High spirits? Or maliciousness?"

"I couldn't say, sir. Odd sort of chappie. He seemed to like the risk more than anything else. Paid his fine without complaint, no trouble to anyone, even apologized to the keeper of the ravens."

"Any other incidents?"

"I couldn't say, sir. Those are the only two that've come to my attention."

Which probably meant, Rutledge thought, that Hardy had chosen other venues for his eccentricities. Gibson seemed to know everything of importance that went on in London and half the counties as well.

"I'd like very much to know what sort of war he had."

"As to that, sir, I heard of one occasion when someone slipped behind the lines and stopped up the main guns on half a dozen German tanks before the alarm went up. They were taking bets in the Met ranks here that it was Hardy."

"Were they indeed?" He'd heard the same story in France, but without a name attached to the foray. There had been speculation that it was apocryphal, rather than an actual attempt to spike the guns.

Gibson was saying, "I'll get on to these names, sir. Anything to report to His Eminence?"

Rutledge smothered a laugh. The gruffness he'd heard at the beginning of the conversation was explained: Gibson had had a run-in with the Chief Superintendent and come away second best. He could imagine what it had been like at the Yard today, everyone creeping about and trying not to get caught in the cross fire. It also explained why Gibson was still there.

He was well out of it.

Hanging up, he stood there watching the foot traffic past the bookshop windows. Most people were preparing to sit down to their dinners, but a few men, holding on to their hats against the wind, were hurrying by.

Where was he to find the secret that would unlock the death of Stephen Wentworth?

It was there somewhere. A man like Wentworth wasn't killed without a sound reason. His death caused too many ripples in the fabric of a village's life, his family too important to be ignored by the police, the shock of the way he'd died too frightening to the people who knew him, and even those who didn't know him well were touched by the strangeness of time and place. The hunt would go on until the killer was caught—or found dead. Public opinion would demand that.

As the man in charge, Rutledge would much prefer that to be sooner rather than later.

The fact that a comment had passed between killer and victim worried him. It meant that whoever it was must be searching. And there was no way of knowing whether Wentworth was the right target—or the wrong one, who still must die because he'd been asked a question and couldn't be left alive to repeat it.

The only way to know which it might be was to wait for the next body to be found.

He left the bookshop and went to Miss Blackburn's house to look in on Miss MacRae. He was just coming to the short path to her door when he saw the sexton staring at him from the churchyard across the road. He recognized the shadowy silhouette.

Without altering his pace, he set out across the street and went through the open churchyard gate.

By the time he could see where the sexton had been standing, the man was gone.

Rutledge stopped and waited, but the sexton didn't reappear. And he wasn't in the mood to give chase.

He went back to The Street and the police station, found Constable Penny at his desk, and greeted him.

Penny looked up warily from the daily log he was finishing.

"Good evening, sir. Any news?"

"A matter of curiosity. Tell me about the church sexton?"

"Not much to tell, sir. According to my predecessor, Pace showed up one day looking for work. Oliver is his given name, but I've never heard anyone use it. He said he found the Yorkshire winters too cold and had decided to move farther south. He worked for a time at the ironmonger's, and then when the church sexton of the day had to retire because of his age, Pace took the position. There have been no complaints lodged against him that I know of. The church wardens are satisfied, and the Rector as well."

"He doesn't appear to be the friendliest of men."

"No, sir, and that's true enough. But we've got used to it, I expect."

"Did he have any dealings with the victim? Or with the victim's family?"

"None that I know of. That's to say, everyone knows who he is."

"There has never been any trouble between Wentworth and Pace?" he asked again. "In your position you'd have heard, if there had been?"

"No, sir. Pace doesn't spend much time on The Street. He comes to the ironmonger's or the butcher shop or the greengrocer's, makes his purchases and leaves. He doesn't frequent the pub or the tea shop, and I've never seen him coming out of the bookshop. Or walking the streets at night. He has a small cottage on the edge of town, grows vegetables in season, and largely keeps to himself. Confirmed bachelor. As the older ladies in Wolfpit can attest to. More than one set her cap for him, according to Miss Goodwin. But I find that hard to believe, because he was never much for social events. Keeps to himself, as I said. I think that's why being sexton suits him."

And no one would know when he was at home—or lurking in the dark on the Wolfpit road.

"Was he in the war?" A revolver could be a war souvenir, even if Pace had served in the ranks.

"No, sir, too old for it."

"And who is Miss Goodwin?"

"She plays the organ at St. Mary's. She stepped in for Mr. Havers—he was organist for more years than I care to remember—a number of times during his last illness, and it seemed quite natural for her to continue."

"Pace is from Yorkshire, you say? Did he know Mrs. Wentworth before she came to Wolfpit as a bride?"

"I never gave that a thought," Penny said in some surprise. "I don't believe so. That's to say, I don't recall I've ever seen them exchange a word in all these years. And Yorkshire is a large county."

"So it is," Rutledge agreed. But there was the note he'd found in his room. Not the sort of message he'd expect from most of the people who had known Wentworth. People who had admired him, people who knew nothing about his mother's accusations. Pace's attitude toward him since he'd begun the inquiry indicated a resentment of authority, and the man might just be bloody-minded enough to leave such a note, to complicate the inquiry.

Hamish, in the recesses of his mind, spoke, jolting him. "Ye ken, he might have left Yorkshire because he'd run afoul of the police there. And no' just the local Constable."

"Something wrong, sir?" Penny asked quickly, a frown between his eyes.

"Old war wound," Rutledge managed to say, and then added, "Did anyone look into Pace's background before he was offered the position of sexton? After all, he'd have access to the church and the communion silver."

"I don't believe the church wardens thought it necessary, sir. Here, you're not thinking Pace could have killed Stephen Wentworth?"

He'd been exploring the possibility.

"I'd be remiss if I didn't look into everyone, Constable." He rose. "Thank you."

"Yes, sir. Someone mentioned to me that you were noticed coming back on the Stowmarket road. Any news from there? Has Inspector Reed found any information that might help us?"

"Reed? No, he's found nothing new."

"Worst luck, that. I know the Wentworths are impatient to learn who it was killed their son. They made it clear when they called here. I've spent hours trying to find some reason for Wentworth's murder, and the more I think about it, the more unlikely it seems that *he* was killed. It makes no kind of sense, sir."

"It made sense to someone."

"It must have done to his killer, sir. Else he wouldn't have pulled that trigger."

Rutledge was nearly to the door. "We'll know when we have him in custody."

"Yes but, sir, where is he now? He's had time to cross half of England. He could be in Wales. Or Cornwall, for that matter, if he took a train. Well out of our reach. And there's no description to be going on with."

"I'm well aware of these possibilities, Constable." Rutledge wondered if he was hearing an undercurrent of Inspector Reed's voice in Penny's concerns.

"But I'm saying, sir, that we might never know who it was."

Rutledge turned, suddenly angry. "Who has been making these remarks?"

Penny flushed. "It's what I hear on my rounds, sir. People ask. They want to know. And I don't have anything to give them to stop them from worrying."

"Or was it Mrs. Wentworth, Stephen's mother?"

"Well, yes, sir, she was saying much the same thing herself. But I hear it elsewhere."

"She doesn't think we'll find her son's killer?"

"It's more a matter of being afraid we won't." Penny realized all at once that the matter had got out of hand, that he was on the brink of betraying a trust. And he shut his mouth sharply.

"She's asking you to request that I be withdrawn, and another man sent to Suffolk to take over the inquiry. When was this?"

"Before she left for Norwich, sir. I had to listen to her concerns, sir. She's one of the people I serve," Penny managed to say.

"Send that request to London," Rutledge responded, his voice as cold as his eyes, "and I'll see that you're withdrawn as well, Constable."

"She means you no disrespect, sir. It's her son, after all. You'd be in a state too—"

"—if I'd lost my son," Rutledge finished for him. "What does her husband have to say in the matter?"

"I don't know, sir. He never has much to say on any matter."

"And you would be well advised to follow his example. Hear me, Constable. I will have no more discussion about contacting the Yard to ask for a change in officers. From you, from Mrs. Wentworth, or from any other resident of Wolfpit. Or Stowmarket."

"Yes, sir. I understand, sir."

"I don't think you do, Constable. Just see to it."

And he stepped out into the street, closing the police station door with a firmness that was a pale reflection of his anger.

But it wasn't the Constable who was to blame, and by the time Rutledge had twice walked to the outskirts of Wolfpit in either direction, he regretted his own fury.

His anger was directed at Mrs. Wentworth. For her unfeeling, self-centered war with her own child, and for her efforts to undermine his work here. He wondered why.

It was the undercurrent in her comments that had troubled him most.

That she might know—or believe she knew—Wentworth's killer. And that she was willing to help him get away with what he had done.

Rutledge realized, when he came in sight of The Swan again, that it was too late now to call on Miss Blackburn.

9

It was time, he thought early the next morning, to pay a visit to Dorothea Mowbray. But how to find her? He wasn't sure even Lydie Butterworth could tell him that. Mrs. Delaney hadn't seemed to know which college Dorothea's father was associated with.

He would have to speak to the local police in Cambridge.

When he got there, the town was in the throes of Christmas preparations. Shop windows were brightly decorated in goods and gift suggestions, and streets in Town were crowded with people. And yet he could feel, this December of 1920, the sense of loss that still permeated so much of life in Britain. There were wounded on the street corners, begging. And more young women in the shops than men of military age. Older women still wore the black of mourning for sons and brothers and husbands. Among them were a scattering of students hurrying to tutorials, gowns flying like gangly crows, and young girls who were laughing and careless of passersby, enjoying an outing and the glances of anyone who would notice them.

Reluctant to announce himself to the police except as a last resort, to avoid the questions they would ask, he decided to try another possibility first. He found a bookshop just down the street from Wentworth's college and stepped inside, setting a little bell over the door to jangling softly. He occupied himself scanning a shelf of titles just inside the door while the man behind the counter wrapped a book for a customer and politely saw him out. He turned then and approached Rutledge.

"May I help you, sir?" the shopkeeper asked, peering over the rims of his glasses. "Looking for anything in particular, are you?"

"I am. I've been told that one of my cousin's tutors has written a book. Mowbray was his name." He had a sudden thought: What if Dorothea's father was a groundskeeper and not a tutor? The shopkeeper was waiting, and he took another chance. "A history, I think." If the man was connected with Stephen Wentworth, it was more likely to be through history than mathematics.

"You're thinking of a volume on the Great Mutiny. Just this way."

Rutledge followed him toward a shelf along one wall where he was handed a work bound in leather, beautifully tooled. "This is a rather fine presentation. A private printing for friends and family. And here of course is the actual publication." He pointed to the next book, in modern binding. "You have a choice," he ended with a quiet smile.

Rutledge bought the leather-bound copy, thinking it might please Melinda, and as he was making his purchase he asked, "Does Mowbray still reside in Cambridge?"

"Oh yes, in the same house. It's not four streets from here. Still threatening to retire, but of course he never will. He loves teaching too much."

"So my cousin told me. Could you write down the address for me? I'd like to send a note around before calling. It might be inconvenient."

Moving back toward the counter, the man peered at him again, this time with sympathy. "Lost your cousin in the war, did you?" He found a slip of paper and jotted something on it.

"I'm afraid so."

"We lost a good many from here. My own son among them." He

took a deep breath, as if shutting away the past. "There you are. Thank you for stopping in, sir."

Rutledge had some difficulty finding the house. It was mock Tudor and set back from the road behind a hedge. And the number on the door was hidden behind a large knot of black crepe. When he finally came back to the house, having counted backward to number 27, he left his motorcar on the street and walked up the short path to the door.

An older woman opened it, her brows rising in surprise to find a stranger on the doorstep.

"May I help you?" she asked, assuming he must be lost.

"I'm looking for the Mowbray residence. I'd like very much to speak to Miss Dorothea Mowbray."

"This is a house of mourning, I'm afraid. Miss Mowbray's brother has just died."

"I'm sorry to hear it. But I've come rather a long way, and if she can spare me a few minutes, I'd be grateful."

Hamish warned him in time to look up.

Behind the woman, in the recesses of the hall, a very attractive younger woman was just starting down the stairs. He recognized her from the photograph in Wentworth's bedroom. If it wasn't Dorothea, it must surely be her sister. He was certain of it.

"Who is it, Jane?" she asked, pausing on a tread, one hand on the banister.

"He hasn't give his name, my dear."

But Rutledge was already speaking to Miss Mowbray. "I've come about Stephen Wentworth."

There was an instant's stunned silence. He couldn't quite read her eyes, because she was retreating into the shadows at the top of the stairs, moving back up them without turning away.

"Shut the door, please, Jane. I have nothing to say to anyone today."

Jane began to swing the door closed, but Rutledge stopped it with his foot.

"Miss Mowbray? It's urgent that I speak to you." He was talking to thin air. She had turned and disappeared down the passage to her right. And he couldn't set aside this woman blocking his way and follow her.

He stepped back and let the door complete its swing toward him. And for a moment stood there face-to-face with the black bow on the knocker before turning and walking back to his motorcar.

Rutledge was just getting behind the wheel when he looked up at the house again. There were two faces at a first-floor window overlooking the street. He thought they were Miss Mowbray and Jane, but with tree limbs forming a tracery of shadow across the glass, he couldn't be sure. He stared back until they were gone, then drove on.

He reversed where he could and came back to the mock Tudor house, stopping some thirty yards away and well out of sight of its upper stories, with the hope that someone would come out and start up or down the road. But after an hour sitting in the winter cold, he turned the crank once more and drove away.

I t rankled, having to return to Suffolk empty-handed. And so Rutledge turned the bonnet not toward Wolfpit but toward Norwich, finding his direction by instinct. He came into the city from the Colchester road, having stopped at The Rose Inn for tea and a sandwich at eleven.

This time he went directly to the Norwich police station to ask for the address of the Wentworth house.

The Sergeant at the desk looked at his identity card and said, "Sad about young Wentworth."

"Did he come here often?"

"Not often, no. But my brother-in-law is Constable here and is walking out with one of the housemaids. A good family. A Dr. Brent came himself to break the news. And Inspector Reed has called. From Stowmarket. You must be the man from the Yard sent to take over the inquiry."

"I am."

"He appeared to be of two minds about that."

Did he indeed? And clearly not above advertising his feelings . . .

Rutledge smiled sympathetically. "I'm not surprised. But I saw him only last night. Going over the inquiry." As though he and Reed were comfortably collaborating at this juncture.

The Sergeant nodded. "Good man, Reed."

For the second time that day, Rutledge was handed a slip of paper with directions on it. But the Sergeant had more to say about the Wentworth household.

"Constable Browne tells me that the Wentworths have no plans to attend the funeral service, once the body is released to the undertaker."

"It must be too much for parents to bear, burying a child."

"I expect it must be. We did enough of it in the war to last several lifetimes. Memorial services, of course." He shook his head. "They tell me the cemeteries in France are being well looked after. It's a comfort of sorts."

"I visited one not long ago. It's taken time," Rutledge told him, "but the Commission is doing all it can."

"Too many to return to their families, I expect." He looked down at the papers on his desk to hide what he was feeling, then said, "Will that be all, sir?"

"Yes, thank you, Sergeant."

The winter daylight had faded by the time Rutledge had found the house, tucked into a street of fine houses. The streetlamps had been lit, casting shadows over the roadway and making it difficult to read the house numbers. As he walked up the steps at number 19, he could just see that there was no crepe on the door to indicate mourning.

He found he wasn't surprised.

Lifting the knocker, he let it fall against the plate, and waited.

After several moments, the door was opened by a maid who coldly inquired his business.

"I've come to see Mrs. Wentworth's daughter. I'm afraid I haven't been given her married name. I'm from Scotland Yard, I'm looking into the murder of her brother."

"Mr. and Mrs. Wentworth have gone to a private luncheon, sir. Mrs. Courtney is resting."

It was far too early to retire. And he was in no mood to be turned away a second time.

"I'm afraid it can't wait," he said pleasantly, moving to step around her. "If you will ask her to dress again and come down?"

The woman tried to block him, but she was no match for his determination. She closed the door with a firmness that indicated her displeasure and led him to a small drawing room on the front of the house.

There he cooled his heels for over an hour, with only Hamish for company. He had a feeling that the intent was to outwait him. Mrs. Courtney was going to be sadly disappointed. Finally the door opened and a young woman stepped in, a small black-and-white spaniel at her heels.

He could see a fleeting likeness to her brother—the same fair hair and fair complexion—but she was plump where her brother had been slim.

And she was wearing the black of mourning. But not for her brother, he thought.

He rose and gave his name.

"Yes, my parents have already told me about you," she said impatiently, coming in to stand by the cold hearth. "I don't know why you've chosen to call on me while they are out for the afternoon. I hadn't seen my brother for several months before his death."

"I'm looking into that death," he said, matching her in tone now. "And I've come here to ask you about any friends—problems—worries—that your brother might have spoken to you about. When he last saw you."

"He came to see his niece and nephew. It was Laurie's birthday."

"Then he took no opportunity to speak to you alone?"

"Why should he? I live here now, and have very little to do with Wolfpit. Norwich is my home."

He gazed at her for a moment, clearly making her uncomfortable by his silence. Then he said, "Your brother didn't die in the war or of an accident in his motorcar, Mrs. Courtney. He was murdered. Without warning or compassion. Whatever you may think of him as a brother, you must have some sense of the need to catch his killer if only because murder can't be tolerated. It's your civic duty to help apprehend this person. And that includes speaking to the police when they knock at your door."

She bit her lip. And he realized she wasn't made of sterner stuff, like her mother, but only pretended to be. "Stephen didn't confide in me. He was always away. University. Peru. The war. I grew up, married, and came to Norwich. We didn't have much in common, given the age difference. I didn't know his friends, nor he mine, after he came home. Growing up, Stephen stayed away from his family as much as he could, visiting with friends or spending his time in the bookshop. I didn't share in his life."

"Do you know why Miss Mowbray broke off with him? I've been given the impression that there was an attachment between them."

She was frowning. "I don't see how this has anything to do with his death."

"His murder, Mrs. Courtney."

"I don't have any idea why she should have done such a thing. Unless, of course, she had known him long enough to realize what sort of man he really was."

"And what was he, really?"

She gave him a blank stare. It was as if she had heard this remark repeated in the household so many times that she'd never thought to question it.

He pressed her. "You allowed him to come and visit with your children on their birthdays. Surely if your brother was as terrible as you believe he was, you would feel differently about him and any influence he might have on young children."

"Mother will tell you—"

"I've heard what your mother could tell me. I've come all the way to Norwich to ask what you can tell me."

She seemed to be at a loss.

Rutledge waited, listening to Hamish in the back of his mind, quarreling with him.

After a moment, she said, "It was always understood—that's to say, he killed his own brother. *My* brother."

"Then why wasn't he taken up by the police and dealt with accordingly?"

"I—he was only a baby—" she began, then broke off. "He was *evil*."

"And yet he brings gifts to your children on their birthdays. Surely such an evil man, a killer of one defenseless child, is too dangerous to be allowed near any other young children?"

"Our parents live with me now. I can hardly forbid him the door." Her face was flushing, and he could see that she felt cornered.

"Had your brother killed anyone else?"

"Well, no—at least I'm not aware—what are you trying to make me say, Inspector?" she went on, goaded.

"Mrs. Courtney, you can't have it both ways. What about your children? Do they enjoy his visits? Or do they hide in your skirts, frightened of their own uncle?"

"I—they—they're far too young to be told such terrible things."

"Which tells me they like him. It must annoy your mother no end."

He thought she would have liked to slap him, to stop him from holding up a mirror and making her look into it.

"You will leave at once," she said, gathering herself together. "Or I'll send my maid to find Constable Browne."

"I'm afraid I've just left the police station, Mrs. Courtney. They know I'm here and why I've come. If you want me to leave, simply answer my questions."

The spaniel, catching the strain in his mistress's voice or the intensity in Rutledge's, growled softly.

"I don't know any of my brother's friends, or why he went to Peru, or what he's been doing since he came back after the war. We don't *talk*. Didn't," she amended.

"Robin Hardy? Do you recognize that name?"

"I know who he is. My brother preferred the Hardy family to his own. I didn't have anything in common with them. Or with that Miss MacRae, who appears to have set her cap at him, or anyone else in his life." She added contemptuously, "Except, of course, Mrs. Delaney, who managed quite well after selling him the bookshop. She just wanted the money, and didn't care if it wasn't suitable at all for Stephen to go into trade. He had enough money to do as he pleased, travel, buy a bookshop. Or he could have done something important with his life, to make amends for what he'd done. To show the world he was contrite and feared for his soul."

Her voice was thick with anger and a certain jealousy as well. She herself had married fairly young and now had responsibilities that tied her to this house she shared with her parents. He wondered if it was Stephen's financial independence, his freedom from his parents' wishes, that annoyed her, while she on the other hand must have been dependent first on her father and then on her husband. Even her dowry would have gone into her husband's pocket, not hers. She might feel it was unjust for an evil man to be so fortunate.

"Why did your brother go off to Peru?"

"It was all of a piece with everything else he's ever done. He doesn't care about the family or his name or anything but his own pleasure. Didn't. The bookstore is just the beginning. He went to Peru because he knew it would be talked about. And make us look as if we cared nothing for him. It was the farthest place on earth he could think of from Wolfpit. I'm sure of it. Now get out of my house, or I'll scream and tell the servants you attacked me."

"No need, Mrs. Courtney. You've told me all I needed to know.

I'm glad I came here to interview you rather than leave it to Inspector Reed. Good day."

Mouth open, she stared at him as he collected his hat and coat, turned, and walked out of the room and out of the house.

Before he'd closed the outer door behind him, he heard her shout, "I told you nothing. Absolutely *nothing*."

But he didn't go back.

R utledge was in an angry mood all the way back to Wolfpit, aggravated by Hamish speaking from the rear seat, where he always sat, just at the edge of vision, like a wraith that never quite materialized. But Rutledge knew very well that he was *there*. After all, the deep Scottish voice had been with him since 1916, four long years. Never comfortable with its presence, never comfortable with the possibility of *not* hearing it. Of not keeping Corporal Hamish MacLeod alive as long as he could, even though he was dead and buried in France. Madness of a sort, Rutledge thought, because it was irrational. And yet so integral a part of him that he needed to hear that voice even when he dreaded it most.

As he moved from dark countryside to brightly lit villages and back to dark countryside again, he felt his isolation strongly. Alone in this motorcar, not a part of the lives of any of the unseen people behind their drawn curtains or the half-seen animals whose eyes glowed orange in his headlamps, he belonged nowhere. To no one.

Rather like Stephen Wentworth, who had a home but didn't belong there. An outcast. Possibly a killer.

Who had a need or desire to kill an outcast?

Or *was* it the outcast who had been shot? What if it was what that outcast might *know*?

It was an intriguing thought and worth pursuing.

The only question was, *how*?

It was Hamish who answered him in the darkness, his voice as close as it had once been in the long watches in the trenches. Kept low to prevent the Germans from hearing them and pinpointing a location.

"The question he was asked. What was it?"

Miss MacRae claimed she didn't know.

But what if she did, and was afraid to tell anyone?

He had intended to return to Wolfpit to speak to Miss MacRae. Instead, he drove directly to the Hardy manor on the Wolfpit road. Once there he sat in the drive for several minutes, listening to Hamish.

And then he got out and went to knock at the door.

But before he could lift the knocker, the door opened, and a man stood there in shirt and trousers, his face grim.

"Not here, man, for God's sake. I'll meet you. Down the road, two miles from here, is a tree with a branch that spreads across the road."

He shut the door in Rutledge's face, his footsteps echoing as he walked briskly away.

So much for speaking to Robin Hardy, he thought to Hamish as he turned the crank and got back into the motorcar.

"Aye. There were men like him in the ranks, ye ken."

"MacDougal was one," Rutledge commented aloud as he went back down the drive, then found a spot where he could watch the gates without himself being seen.

"Aye, MacDougal. Sergeant Scott never knew whether to shoot him or praise him. Braver than the brave, but never considering the danger he put his neighbor in."

MacDougal had been decorated—posthumously. Robin Hardy was still alive.

Then minutes later, a Renault came tearing through the gates and roared off in the direction of Wolfpit. The driver hadn't bothered to look to his left. Rutledge gave him a good head start, then followed.

Hardy was out of his motorcar and pacing under the long branch arching overhead when Rutledge came into view. He had put his headlamps on, and Rutledge did the same, creating a pool of overbright light under the trees.

"What kept you?" Hardy demanded.

Rutledge took his time getting down. "I wasn't aware there was any particular rush."

Hardy stared at him. "You came to interview me. I didn't want it to be overheard in the house." He wasn't as tall as Rutledge, with fair hair that was darkening into the color of wet sand, and there was a long scar across his left cheek, very much like the dueling scars that Prussian officers once prided themselves on. Only this one was not the thin sharp line of rapier or saber. It gave Hardy's face a sinister cast.

"Yes, you assumed that I'd come to speak to you. I wondered if perhaps that was an indication of guilt."

Hardy laughed. "All right, yes, guilty as charged. But guilty of nothing more. My cousin sent word that you might be calling."

"Then why were you afraid of being overheard? If you had nothing to fear?"

Taking a deep breath, Hardy said, "For one thing, it was my late arrival that kept everyone at the party. Everyone who knew me, that is. Some of the others had left. And I'm not a fool, Rutledge. Whoever shot Stephen either had the patience of Job, or knew precisely when he would be coming along this road. He had a young woman with him—Miss MacRae—and she must surely have told someone where she was going that night. How many did Stephen tell? And how many who left the party early knew he'd be late traveling home? That's a large number of people who could have planned to intercept him."

"Yes, but you overlook one thing. Of that large number, how many would have chosen to wait for him to appear, when it was a cold night and they could be safely home in their own beds?" It was dark enough now that their faces were oddly shadowed in the glare of their headlamps.

"All right. You have a point."

"Why didn't you take Miss Hardy home?"

"Because she's engaged, and happily so. I didn't want to cause trouble."

Something in the curt response wasn't right. And Rutledge realized the man in front of him was in love with her—had been for some time—and had kept away on purpose.

Rutledge decided to be obtuse. "I don't follow your reasoning."

"Damn it, man," he said, turning sharply away. "She's been in love with me since we were children. Or so she thinks. I didn't want to encourage that, now the war's over."

"That's not very gallant of you, is it, laying the blame at her door?"

Red in the face, Hardy swore. "Oh, shut up," he said savagely. "What has this to do with Wentworth's murder?"

"She appears to have known him nearly as long as she's known you. Her feelings might have deepened in that direction while you've been away."

Hardy was still angry. "Everyone liked Wentworth. He was that sort of man. Kind and thoughtful, never overstaying his welcome, and with something of the lost puppy looking for a home about him that made women in particular want to make him happy. He found in others what he never had from his family: a sense of belonging. I never quite understood it. Most parents would have given anything for such a son."

And that told Rutledge far more than Hardy realized. It explained his wild and careless ways. In his own family, he must have got more attention for being the dashing adventurer than a proper, dutiful son. The younger brother who had to make his own way in the world, and who let it be known he preferred that place in life. Or pretended to prefer it.

Rutledge had also known such men in the trenches. Volunteering for any dangerous duty that would get them mentioned in dispatches, not to prove their bravery so much as to prove they mattered. To show their officers that they could be relied on, that they could take on whatever came their way. Just as they'd tried to show their fathers . . .

"Why do you think Wentworth was killed?" Rutledge asked, satisfied now that he knew his man.

"Mistaken identity," Hardy said at once. "What else could it have been? Wentworth wasn't the sort to get himself murdered. One must *do* something to earn such hatred. And he never had. He never would have. It was beyond him."

"An interesting observation," Rutledge said. "Was that why he went to Peru? To avoid being hated?"

Hardy frowned. "I never quite understood that. He was happy, as happy as I'd ever seen him. And the next thing I knew, he was on his way to the back of beyond. The thing that struck me was his utter lack of any reason to go to such a benighted part of the world. In his shoes I'd have chosen Rome."

"I'm told he read about Peru as a boy. He found it a fascinating place."

"Yes, I'm sure he did. He always had his nose in a book. And when he needed to go away, he remembered Peru, and he saw that it was the perfect solution."

Rutledge was beginning to change his earlier opinion of Hardy. Beneath the dash was a brain. And that brought this man back into consideration as a suspect. Although he wasn't sure he knew why at this stage, except that Hardy *could* have planned and executed a murder. He had the ability.

"What did you do in the war?" he asked.

Surprised by the sudden shift in the conversation, Hardy shrugged. "A little of this and a little of that. Like everyone else, I got to be very good at killing people, and that was noticed in certain quarters. I'm not particularly proud of my war. By the same token, we weren't exactly winning, were we, and whatever we could do we did."

Not a sniper, shooting from a hide. That wouldn't have appealed to a man like Robin Hardy.

Rutledge spoke to him in German. "And what did you do behind the lines?"

Caught off guard, Hardy started to answer in German, and stopped himself in time. "Sorry. I've never had an ear for languages."

When Rutledge said nothing, Hardy shook his head. "You're wandering off the subject."

Rutledge looked away. He'd learned what he needed to know. "So we are." But he understood now why Hardy hadn't wanted this interview to be overheard. There were too many minefields in his life to risk having them explored where others might hear.

"Look, Rutledge. I had no reason to kill Wentworth. We didn't want the same things in life, Stephen and I, but we understood each other. Possibly because we were alike in some respects. I'd have given my right arm to inherit the family estate. My brother doesn't value it as I did—do, if you want the truth. I loved it. He merely sees it as his duty. It's rather like a woman, in a way. I'd have given her my heart and soul. He sees it as his duty to honor and protect her and love her as the mother of his heir. If I had it in mind to kill someone, it would have been my brother, not Stephen. Only then I couldn't inherit, could I? And so he's quite safe from me."

It had been a wrenching confession, but for once Hardy wasn't posturing. It was there in his eyes, the love and the loss of what he held most dear. Was that why he'd volunteered for the dangerous duties? Because he had nothing else to give his heart to, except excitement? Or because he thought it was the best way to die, without the onus of suicide?

Hardy walked away into the shadows and then came back. "You're a damned good listener. Has anyone ever told you? You hear too much. And if you ever say anything about any of this, I'll deny it to the end."

"My only interest in you has to do with whether or not you murdered Wentworth. If you didn't, you have nothing to fear from me."

"Yes, well, I'm on safe ground then. I hope you catch the bastard." With a nod, he turned toward his motorcar.

Rutledge let him go. But before Hardy opened his door and stepped in, Rutledge called to him. "She's marrying the wrong man. She'll be wretched if you don't stop it. I heard that too."

Hardy looked at him for one long moment. "She'll be safe with him." It was hard to read his expression.

"If safety is what matters," Rutledge replied. "For my part, I don't think it is."

"Married, are you, and speaking from experience?"

"No. She married someone else."

"Did she, by God. And was she truly happy?"

"I don't know. She died in childbirth. I didn't learn that until months later. She's buried somewhere in Canada." It wasn't all of that history. But it was all he wanted Hardy to understand.

"Was it your child?"

"No. It was his."

Hardy nodded. Then he got into the motorcar and drove away. This time without speed and panache. More with the air of a thoughtful man.

Rutledge watched his red rear lamps disappear. Hamish, just at his shoulder, asked, "Why did ye tell him that?"

"I thought it might help."

"Noo. Ye wanted to hear yoursel' say it, to see if it still hurts."

Rutledge went to turn the crank. "*Did* it hurt?" he asked.

"That was anither life."

Hamish was right. It was. The young man, wrapped in happiness, who had proposed to Jean in that almost-forgotten summer of 1914 when the world changed, seemed to be another lifetime, another man, one he'd liked once and remembered fondly but no longer knew well. And Jean had somehow faded into the past with that young man who had loved her. He was six years older now, four of them the bloody years of the trenches, two of them the nightmare struggle of finding his way back from the brink of madness, and never quite sure he'd made it safely—not even now.

He got into the motorcar, ignoring what Hamish was saying to him, and reversed it on the road, startling a badger that had just peered out of a sett under the hedgerow. It was too late to go on to Cambridge.

The next morning, reaching the Mowbrays' mock Tudor house, he left his motorcar some distance down the road and walked back to the door.

He saw that in spite of the winter's cold, it stood ajar, and he could hear voices inside speaking in hushed tones.

Rutledge stepped into the hall. He could see into the room across from the staircase now. Miss Mowbray was standing there next to an older man who seemed to be dazed with shock. They were listening to condolences from a man and a woman who had come to call. He could tell the visitors had nearly finished what they had to say and were about to leave. He waited.

After several more remarks, they turned and stepped out into the hall. The woman was clutching a damp handkerchief, the man with her holding her arm. The older man had come with them, courteously seeing them out.

He noticed Rutledge as he began to close the door after them.

"I'm so sorry," he began. "Are you from the undertaker's?"

"No, sir, my name is Rutledge. I'm from the police. As much as I regret having to speak to your daughter at a time like this, I have a duty to perform."

"Is it about young Wentworth?"

"Yes, I'm afraid so."

"Then of course you must speak to her." Raising his voice slightly, he called, "Dorothea?"

When she didn't answer, he took Rutledge by the arm and guided him toward the drawing room doorway. "She's been very upset by her brother's death. Be gentle, if you will."

And then he was gone, leaving Rutledge to confront Miss Mowbray on his own.

She was standing at the far end of the room, looking out at the drive, her thoughts on the two guests who were just now walking down it to the street. Without turning, she said, "I hope that's the last of the callers. I don't think I could bear to listen to anyone else telling me how wonderful Arthur was. It makes it all the harder to realize I'll never see him again."

"I'm sorry to intrude on your grief," he said quietly. "But there is another family grieving for a lost son. And I need to ask you a few questions."

She whirled. "Who let you into this house?"

"Your father."

She bit her lip, holding back whatever retort she was about to make. Then she said, "Well, be done with it. As for another grieving parent, how dare you compare what we feel to what the Wentworths must be thinking now."

"Are you so angry with Stephen Wentworth that you can't even speak kindly of him now that he's dead?" He let it sound as if he were merely curious.

After a moment she shook her head. "No. I expect you're right. Well, then, ask your questions and go."

"Why did Stephen Wentworth go to Peru?"

Her fair eyebrows flew up in surprise. "You mean to say you don't know? I should have thought his mother might have told you."

"If she knew, she didn't mention that she did."

They were still standing, and as if she suddenly became aware of it, she gestured to the nearest chair, and then sat down across from him. "We were engaged, Stephen and I, and my parents gave a small party for us. It was held here in Cambridge, where both Stephen and I had friends. His parents were invited, but he thought it was likely that they wouldn't be able to come. He seldom spoke of them, and I had the impression that he didn't care for them."

She turned to look out the window again. "What I didn't expect was that they didn't care for him. His parents arrived, stopping at a hotel. They came early to the party—we'd invited them to dine with us—and before dinner, Mrs. Wentworth asked if she might go upstairs and freshen up. I thought it odd, since they'd just come from the hotel. But I took her up to my room, and when we got there, she sat down on the edge of my bed, and she told me about Stephen. I couldn't believe his own mother—but of course she must have known he hadn't said a word to me. She told me she was certain he never would, but that if I wished to marry him, she would give us her blessing. But it was very likely that he had killed again, and there was no certainty that it had stopped."

"She told you about his brother?"

"Yes, of course."

"And who were the other victims?"

"I don't know. She said that he'd disappeared a few times over the years, and when he came back he was different each time. She told me she would give me the names of the people he'd claimed he was visiting, and if I cared to, I could speak to them. They would tell me how he had used them to cover up what he was doing."

Rutledge listened with fury rising within him. At Mrs. Wentworth for her cruelty, and for this woman who was so willing to believe, who had never questioned or wondered.

As if she had heard him, she added, "I wouldn't have believed it if it had been anyone else. But for his mother to tell me such things—I asked why the police hadn't stopped him long before this, and she said there was no proof. They hadn't caught him at it. I was horrified."

"But you had known Stephen for what? Several years, at the very least. Do you think he could actually be a murderer?"

"I didn't know what to think. I went down the stairs afterward in something of a daze. Stephen was just coming out of the drawing room, where he and my father had been talking. And he looked at me, he looked up the stairs where his mother was just starting down. His face was awful, I've never seen such an expression. And he turned on his heel, walked out the door, and I never saw him again. Ever. Why would he do that, if he *hadn't* done these things? He never tried to see me, he never wrote to me, he simply disappeared. Someone told me afterward—weeks afterward—that he'd sailed for Peru that same week. What's more, that night my mother had to call off the engagement party, telling everyone I'd taken ill. But the fact was, I was in shock, hardly knowing what to believe. And I waited—waited for him to come here and tell me *something* that might explain what I'd heard."

"Would you have listened, if he had come back that night? Or the next morning?"

She couldn't meet his gaze. "Yes—I'm sure I would have been willing to hear what he wanted to say."

But he wasn't as sure. Neither was she.

Why had Wentworth kept her photograph—and the ring—if she had treated him so shabbily?

It was Hamish who answered. "She didna' love him enough."

And Mrs. Wentworth had deliberately ruined any chance of happiness her son might have had with Dorothea Mowbray.

"And your parents? What did they have to say about the charges Mrs. Wentworth made?"

"I never told them," she admitted after a moment. "I couldn't. They cared for Stephen. I couldn't bring myself to say anything but that I'd had a change of heart. It was true enough, after all."

"Why do you think Stephen Wentworth was shot?"

"His mother told me the police never had enough proof to bring charges against him. I expect that someone decided to do something about it. What else can one think?"

"You were engaged to Wentworth—you were planning to marry him," Rutledge said, in an effort to understand. "You must have found something in the man that you cared for and trusted. Did that count for nothing?" He realized suddenly that he was asking her the questions he'd have asked Jean, if she had ever come to see him again, once he'd released her from their engagement. And he turned away.

She took that as his judgment of her, a condemnation she couldn't face.

"I was eighteen," she said hoarsely. "I was young and inexperienced—and it was his own *mother*."

She wasn't Jean, she couldn't know that Jean had been afraid and ashamed of him, the thin, haunted stranger who could hardly speak for fear of breaking.

Rutledge rose.

But she was still struggling to explain herself. "Everyone believed in the straw man he pretended to be. Even I believed in him. My parents. *Everyone*. If it wasn't true, why didn't he fight for me? Why did he dash off to Peru instead? He loved that bookshop more than he loved me. I knew that, I accepted it. And yet he abandoned it as well. Only a guilty man runs."

"Or a man whose world has crashed into splinters around him, wi' no hope of putting it to rights again." Hamish's voice was loud in the quiet room. But Dorothea Mowbray was looking at Rutledge, pleading for understanding.

He had never tried to see Jean again. Nor had she tried to see him. It was for the best. And he had come to terms with that.

Or had he?

He managed to thank her for seeing him and found his way to the door somehow, closing it behind him.

He could hear her crying before the door snapped shut, and remembered too late that she had just lost her brother as well. Perhaps she was crying for him, and not for Stephen.

The door opened behind him.

He turned and saw that it was Dorothea.

"He was gassed at Ypres. My brother Arthur. It took him all this time to die."

"I'm so sorry," Rutledge said, knowing it was inadequate. But he meant it.

"That's why I'm crying," she added. "I can't cry for Stephen. I won't. Do you hear?"

Her father's voice called from somewhere at the top of the stairs. "Is that the undertaker, my dear?"

"It's no one," she answered him. "No one." And shut the door firmly.

10

When Rutledge drove down The Street into Wolfpit, he saw at once that something had happened.

There were knots of people standing here and there, looking up warily as he passed.

He went directly to the police station, but Constable Penny wasn't there. Crossing to The Swan, he stepped inside, looking for the clerk who was generally somewhere about. But there was no one behind the desk in Reception.

Rutledge was about to go back into the street when a lad of about sixteen, tall, gangly, and red in the face from hurrying, nearly collided with him in the doorway.

"Inspector, sir?" he asked, falling back a step.

"Yes, I'm Rutledge. What is it?"

"Constable says, if I found you, please to come at once."

"Come where?"

"The Templeton house, sir. I'm to show you the way."

The lad had a bicycle outside, and Rutledge lashed it to the boot of his motorcar. Watching the knots of people staring their way, the boy said, "Should you say something, sir?"

"I can't tell them what I don't know. Get in, man!" He waited until they were driving on before asking, "What's happened? What's so urgent?"

"I don't know, sir. I was riding by on my bicycle when Constable stepped out into the road and hailed me. He asked me to carry a message back to the village—I was to wait until I found you, sir, and see you got it."

They were passing fields of dry winter stubble, but ahead of them Rutledge could see a house set back from the road in a stand of trees that was encircled by a waist-high wall. Following the wall now, he could see gates ahead, obviously opening into a drive. The boy pointed. "Just there, sir."

"Thank you."

Rutledge slowed, stopping well short of the gates. Getting out, he took the bicycle from the boot and handed it over to the boy, gave him a sixpence, then walked away, leaving the boy to stare after him.

The doctor's carriage was standing in front of the gates, blocking any view. Rutledge put a hand on the horse and ducked under his head. The boy, clearly disappointed at not learning more, pedaled on, still looking back over his shoulder as Rutledge started into the drive.

Constable Penny, his own bicycle pulled up just inside the gates, nodded as Rutledge came toward him. Just beyond him, Dr. Brent was speaking to a middle-aged farmer. At the farmer's feet a black dog growled as Rutledge approached, and the man spoke sharply to it.

Beyond them, another ten feet into the drive, lay a crumpled figure, and by the stillness of the body, Rutledge knew at once that the man was dead. His coat was of good quality, as were the gloves on his hands and the boots he was wearing. Nearby, a hat lay upside down.

Dr. Brent turned as Rutledge walked past him. "Took your time getting here."

"The boy found me in The Swan. Who is this?" He gestured toward the dead man.

Penny, catching him up, said, "Frederick Templeton. Gentleman farmer. He owns acreage here and closer to Stowmarket as well. That's his house you can see beyond the trees. Mr. Martin"—he gestured to the farmer—"was passing the gates on his way to Wolfpit, and his dog bristled at something and began to whine. This was about two hours ago, sir. Martin walked up the drive to investigate, and he found Templeton lying where you see him. Dr. Brent says he's been there since sometime last evening. Rigor is well set in. From what we can tell, he's been shot once. Through the heart."

Rutledge was already kneeling by the body, examining it without touching it.

Templeton looked to be in his late thirties, fit and healthy enough to have taken on his attacker. But it appeared he hadn't known he was in danger until too late.

Very much like Stephen Wentworth, who had stepped out of his motorcar without realizing that such a simple act would lead to his death.

Getting to his feet, Rutledge said, "You've trampled the ground around the body. Were there any footprints here when you arrived? Signs of a bicycle—a horse? And what was Templeton doing out here? Arriving home? He wouldn't have been on foot, surely. If he was leaving, he would have been in some sort of vehicle. Where is it?" He'd been scanning the terrain. Now he looked directly at the Constable. "Have you been up to the house?"

Constable Penny answered him. "I was making my rounds, and Mr. Martin found me over by the churchyard. I've looked, but there were no signs of anyone else having been here in the drive with Mr. Templeton. But then the drive is well used, sir, and not likely to show much in the way of prints. As for the house, we were waiting for you before walking up to the door." He glanced toward the roofline beyond the treetops. "I don't expect you could look out a window and see Mr. Templeton lying here, sir. Or the four of us standing here, for that matter. Else, someone would have come down to see what was afoot. Still, you'd think *someone* would have come looking for him before this."

"Indeed." He took out his watch. It was already half past three. A very long time for Templeton to be lying here. He looked back toward the gates. Passersby wouldn't have seen him, unless they had been intentionally looking this way. Even then, it was the dog who scented death and not the farmer.

He said to Martin, "Why did you leave him here to go into the village for Constable Penny? Why not go to the house instead and ask them to send someone?"

"He was dead," Martin said stolidly. "There was nothing to be done for him. And I could tell he'd been shot. I thought it best to look for Constable instead."

It was clear he hadn't wanted to be the bearer of such news. In his eyes, it wasn't his place.

Rutledge nodded, looking again toward the house. "Why did no one hear the shot? And come out straightaway to investigate?" He turned to Dr. Brent. "Have you seen everything you need to see?"

"Yes. The similarity to the Wentworth shooting is inescapable. Still, I'll know more later, but I don't expect any surprises."

"Was Templeton in the war?"

Dr. Brent nodded. "He was. Mostly in France. One of the Devon regiments. Attained the rank of Major before it was over, although he declined to use it when he came home." He hesitated, then added, "He's well known in Suffolk. Not politically inclined, but influential. He was interested in new farming methods, and was often asked to speak on the subject all over East Anglia."

Constable Penny added, "He's never been in any trouble as far as I know, sir. Respectable and respected, like Mr. Wentworth. The last person you'd expect to find murdered."

"Married?" Rutledge asked.

"Widowed, sir," Penny replied. "Mrs. Templeton died in the Spanish flu epidemic."

"Doctor, will you and Mr. Martin stay with the body? Thank you. Now, I think it's time to speak to the house."

He led the way on foot, walking briskly up the drive to the circle in front of the door.

It wasn't a grand manor, but certainly a substantial one, with wings to either side of the central block. The style was Georgian, handsome enough but without flourishes.

It was Constable Penny who stepped forward to lift the knocker and let it fall. When the housekeeper opened the door, she saw the Constable first, and then the man behind him. Her face changed.

"What is it, Constable?" she asked, suddenly anxious. "And is that the man from London?" she added, her misgivings deepening.

"That's right, Inspector Rutledge. May we come in, Mrs. Cox?" Penny asked gently. "It's best not to talk here on the doorstep."

For a moment she didn't move, and then she opened the door wider, allowing them to step into the spacious entry. Shutting the door behind them, she led the way to a room on her left.

It was a formal room, a pale lavender trimmed in cream and rose, far more feminine than Rutledge had expected. Mrs. Cox gestured to chairs, and they sat, although she remained standing, her hands folded in front of her.

"Something's happened to Mr. Templeton," she said, as if unable to wait for them to break their news.

"Where did he go, last evening?" Rutledge asked, without answering her directly. "Do you know?"

"Yes, sir. He left here just after dinner. A gentleman was stopping to take him to Cambridge to look at a young bull he was interested in. But Mr. Young was late, and Mr. Templeton thought he might walk down to the gate, to save a little time."

"And did Mr. Young arrive to collect him?"

"I assumed he must have done, sir. Mr. Templeton didn't come back."

"Did he take a valise with him?"

"No, sir. He was expecting to return by this afternoon."

"And no one has walked down to the gate since Mr. Templeton left?"

"No, sir. There's been no need." Her gaze shifted to Constable Penny. "Do you know what this is all about? I wish you'd tell me straight out. Is something wrong?"

Penny glanced uneasily at Rutledge, then said, "There's been an accident, Mrs. Cox."

Rutledge asked, "How did Mr. Young and Mr. Templeton arrange for this meeting?"

"It was three days ago, sir. Mr. Young has a motorcar and was to come by for Mr. Templeton."

"Did anyone else know about this arrangement?"

"I wouldn't know, sir."

Hamish said sharply, "Put the poor woman oot of her misery. She canna' help you."

Relenting, Rutledge said gravely, "I'm afraid Mr. Templeton is dead. We have just discovered his body near the foot of the drive."

As he'd expected, the shock left her speechless for a long moment, and then as the full realization of what he'd just said struck her, she put her hands to her face, then sank heavily into the nearest chair.

Rutledge waited. There was no comfort he could offer. It was several minutes before she recovered enough to speak to them.

"Was it his heart, sir? I can't bear to think of him going alone, there in the dark."

"He didn't suffer, Mrs. Cox. It appears that someone shot him. Dr. Brent tells me that he died instantly."

"I don't understand. Shot him? And where was Mr. Young? Why didn't he come to the house to tell us? Or summon Constable, here?"

"We don't know. Not yet. Can you tell us how to reach this man Templeton was meeting?"

Mrs. Cox shook her head. "Mr. Templeton never said. It was the advertisement about the bull—Mr. Young sent him a message saying he was interested in buying it, and would Mr. Templeton judge whether or not it would be a good investment."

"When was this?"

"Three days ago. It was all in the letter."

"Did Mr. Templeton keep that letter? Could you find it in his desk? Wherever he might have put it."

"I don't know, sir. I don't like going through his desk." A fresh wave of grief overcame her, and he offered her his handkerchief.

"This could be very important, Mrs. Cox. Will you tell me where I will find Mr. Templeton's study?"

She obviously didn't want to tell him, but Constable Penny said persuasively, "We must do all we can to find out who did this. If Mr. Young was to meet Mr. Templeton, he might be in harm's way too."

Reluctantly she got to her feet and led them back to the entrance and past the staircase, then down the passage to a room near the end. She stopped at the door but made no effort to open it. Rutledge reached past her and turned the knob.

The door swung open. The room was a working study, crammed with books and shelves, photographs of livestock and various vegetables, and several very fine bronzes of bulls.

Crossing to the desk, he looked first in the open cubbyholes in the back, then through the piles of correspondence and advertisements and sheets of notes that cluttered the blotter. Constable Penny waited quietly at his shoulder as Rutledge worked.

Mrs. Cox, standing in the doorway, watched him sift through the papers. "Please, sir, he wouldn't care to have his work disturbed."

"It's all right, Mrs. Cox. I only need the letter," he assured her, but clearly without relieving her anxiety. He was about to give up and turn to the drawers, when he saw what he was after.

The envelope was postmarked from Colchester on Monday morning, and the letter inside was brief, to the point.

Mr. Templeton,

George Davies has suggested that I write to you about a bull for sale at a farm outside Cambridge. Enclosed is the brochure. I should very much like your opinion on the animal's value. My aim is to improve my own stock, but I have no real experience in choosing the right bloodlines. I am driving to Cambridge on Tuesday next, and will be happy to collect you at nine in the evening, if that's convenient. I expect we shall be back from the sale by late afternoon. It will be my pleasure to pay for your accommodation in whatever inn is available. If I purchase the animal, perhaps you can tell me the name of the best carter to bring the bull to me. I am grateful for any assistance you might offer, and I shall look forward to seeing you shortly.

Harold A. Young

Rutledge read the letter again, this time aloud. Then he looked at Mrs. Cox.

"Was Mr. Templeton accustomed to receiving such letters from strangers, asking for his advice?"

"I wouldn't know, sir. I can tell you that he was often willing to advise people. And he knew Mr. Davies quite well. He would have been happy to do a favor for him."

The advertisement wasn't in the envelope, but after shuffling through the papers again, Rutledge found it. It seemed genuine enough, with a sepia-tone photograph of the bull. He was to be auctioned to the highest bidder at ten o'clock this morning.

"Do you know how to reach Mr. Davies?" he asked, looking up from the advertisement to Mrs. Cox. "We shall have to speak to him, in order to locate Mr. Young."

She nodded toward the top of the desk. "That box, sir. It's where he keeps cards on all his friends and acquaintances."

Rutledge took it down. Inside were cards filed alphabetically, each with names, directions, and a few notes about a person or firm Templeton had dealt with.

He looked first for YOUNG, but there was nothing under *Y*. Then he looked for DAVIES and found that under the *D*'s. He took the card out, read it, then pocketed it.

"Here," Mrs. Cox said, moving as if to stop him.

"I shall return it, I promise. But at the moment I need to borrow it." He gave a final glance at the desk, then said, "Who must we notify regarding Mr. Templeton's death?"

"I expect that would be his solicitor, Mr. Blake. Constable here can tell you how to find him."

Rutledge nodded, and then said, apparently out of the blue, "And you never heard the gunshot last evening?"

Surprised, she stared at him. "The staff was downstairs, clearing away from dinner. I doubt anyone could have heard. But there's only the five of us," she added. "And with Mr. Templeton away, we were all there. Cook, a kitchen maid, two housemaids, and myself. The gardener and his son have a cottage at the bottom of the garden. I can't think they heard anything—no one came up to the kitchen to inquire."

"Thank you, Mrs. Cox, you've been most helpful. Constable, will you speak to the staff? I'll see Dr. Brent back to Wolfpit, and Martin as well. They'll give you a statement about this afternoon."

Penny was about to argue, then thought better of it. "You'll see to notifying Inspector Reed, sir?"

"In due course," Rutledge said.

"What about Mr. Davies?"

"I'll see that he reports to you as soon as possible to give his own statement."

He was ushering Mrs. Cox and the Constable out the door of the study as he spoke, and shut it firmly before asking for the key to lock it. Again Mrs. Cox protested, but he smiled, assuring her that this was what had to be done.

Once he'd seen the housekeeper and Constable Penny to the kitchen stairs, he went out to find Dr. Brent and the farmer.

It was arranged that Rutledge would send out the undertaker, while Martin and Brent would remain with the body, then give their statements to Penny as soon as he returned to Wolfpit. Brent was not best pleased, protesting that he had surgery hours that afternoon, and Martin argued for a good ten minutes that he had matters to see to on his own farm.

But Rutledge wouldn't hear of any other arrangement, and a few minutes later was on his way back to Wolfpit.

The knots of people speculating earlier on what had taken the doctor and the Constable away in such a hurry had gone on about their business. Rutledge found the undertaker, went in to speak to him, and then set out for Colchester, where Davies had his own farm.

He was in a hurry, wanting to find Davies and question him about Young before the news of Templeton's death sped across the countryside.

Hamish was already busy in the back of his mind. Rutledge tried to ignore him. But he had the strongest feeling, one that wouldn't go away, that Young didn't exist. And Hamish was of the same opinion.

The Davies estate was on the far side of Colchester, with a brick house set behind a barrier of trees that protected it from the road and the east wind. The original house had been much smaller, but with time and prosperity, it had grown into a large and handsome residence.

When Rutledge knocked at the door, he was told that Mr. Davies was out in the fields with his steward and not expected back until dinner.

"I'm afraid it's rather urgent," he told the housekeeper. "And I can't wait until he comes in. Can you send word to him? Or better still, tell me how to find him."

She was a heavy-set woman with graying hair, and not given to haste.

"Mrs. Davies is in, sir, if you'd rather speak to her."

"I'm sorry, but it must be Mr. Davies. Tell me how to find him." This time the request was still polite, but the undercurrent of authority gave it weight.

She reassessed the well-dressed man on the doorstep. "There's a lane just before the wall ends. If you drive down that, you'll come to one of the barns. A path leads out into the fields from there. You should be able to see him fairly soon after taking that path." She considered his well-polished boots, mud from the turnip field erased by the magic of the boot boy at The Swan. "You'll need Wellingtons, sir. If you can wait a few minutes, I think there's a pair in the back hall that might fit you."

She was less than a few minutes, returning with a worn pair of Hunters from the trenches.

He thanked her, and carried them with him to the motorcar.

The lane was easily found, a simple wooden gate leading into it and standing open just now. It was wide enough for a hay wain, and the ruts were muddy from recent rains. He bounced over them for some distance, the barn the housekeeper had mentioned coming into view after the first bend. He reached it, pulled on the Hunters, and set out across the muddy fields. There had been more weather here than in Wolfpit, and he was grateful for the housekeeper's forethought.

He was halfway across the first large field, the fading winter light already close to dusk, when he saw two men coming toward him. The taller of the two, thin and slightly stooped, called to him when they were within hearing. "Looking for me, are you?"

"Mr. Davies?"

"Yes, that's right. How can I help you?"

But Rutledge waited until they had met in the middle of the next field before answering.

"It's rather urgent that I find Harold Young. There's been a death, and I've been sent to find him."

"Young?" Davies turned to his companion. He was older, graying, and stocky. "Do you know him, Bill?"

"No, sir. I'm afraid not."

"I don't know anyone by that name. What led you to believe he might be here?" Davies asked, turning back to Rutledge.

"I was told you'd recommended him to a man named Templeton. They were to visit a farm near Cambridge to look at a bull." He took the advertisement out of his breast pocket and held it out to Davies.

But it was already too dark to read it.

"Let's go to the barn," Davies said, gesturing toward it. "I know Templeton, of course, have known him for fifteen years. But I don't recall ever introducing anyone named Young to him."

They walked in silence back to the barn. It was full dark now, but in the cavernous confines of the building there was a small room where tack and lamps and a chest full of tools were kept. Davies fumbled with one of the lamps, found a match, and lit the wick. Light flared, dancing around the walls and giving a sinister cast to the faces of the men standing in a knot in the middle of the floor.

Davies spread out the advertisement. "I've never seen this before. Bill?"

The steward shook his head. "No, sir, I haven't either."

Davies turned to Rutledge. "I think you'd better explain yourself, sir."

Rutledge took out his identification and held it out. "Rutledge, Scotland Yard," he said. "I've just come from Wolfpit. It seems that Templeton went to the end of his drive last evening to meet a man by the name of Young, expecting to travel together with him to Cambridge to look at this bull." He reached into his pocket again and took out the letter from Young. "See for yourself."

Davies read the letter carefully. "But I never met this man Young, much less suggested he speak to Templeton."

"Templeton believed you had. He went out at about nine in the evening to wait for Young, and instead he was found earlier today lying in his drive, shot dead."

"Good God," Davies said blankly. "Bill, did you know anything about this?" He passed the letter to his steward, but he shook his head again.

"It makes no sense," he said. "I've never met this Harold Young. But why did he write to Templeton? What was the purpose of this letter?"

"To lure Templeton out of his house," Rutledge said. "Are you quite sure you've never met anyone by this name?"

"I'd almost swear to it. I can certainly swear that I've never given anyone Templeton's name, not like this. I'd have written to him myself and asked if I could recommend him to someone, giving him full particulars. He's got something of a reputation in understanding better farming practices. He was the first to use a tractor to plow, and his yield of corn and sugar beets has proven his theories do work. I've adapted some of them myself. But that means he's well known all over East Anglia. What disturbs me is that someone knew to use my name in this business. I don't like it by half."

Bill cleared his throat. "There was that article you wrote for the *Times,* sir. I believe you quoted Mr. Templeton several times in that."

"That was a good six months ago. It had to do with irrigating after the winter rains."

Rutledge said, "Someone looking to contact Templeton might have come across it."

"I don't like it," Davies said again. "For that matter, who in hell's name would wish to shoot Templeton?" Then to Rutledge he said, "Come up to the house. I want to hear more about this Young person."

"You know as much about him now as I do. And I'd prefer it if you said nothing to anyone else about my visit or any questions I might have asked about Young. For one thing, I don't want such information spread about, and for another it might be best if you aren't involved. Not until I have more to go on than this letter."

"Here. You're not saying I'm in any danger."

"Another man has already been shot. What his connection with Templeton might be, I've yet to uncover. But it's for the best, I think, to keep well out of this for now."

Davies studied Rutledge's face in the glow of the lamp. "Who was the other man shot? Anyone I know?"

"Wentworth. Stephen Wentworth."

"No. I don't know him. A farmer? Like Templeton and me?"

"A bookseller."

"Well, then, there you are. Very well, I'll do as you ask. But you'll keep me informed? I have a wife. Children. I'd rather not put them at risk. And I can vouch for Bill, here. He'll say nothing to anyone about this."

He blew out the lamp, and led the way through the darkness of the barn to the door standing wide to the night. "What did you say at the house?"

"Only that I had urgent business with you. I didn't give my name."

"Good, good. I'll let it be known you came about a piece of land I had been interested in buying. That will satisfy the staff and my wife."

"If you can find a reason to travel to Wolfpit, Constable Penny will take your statement. It will not be made public until the inquest."

"Too late tonight, of course. But I'll be there by noon tomorrow." He turned away to look across his land. "Shot. I find that astonishing, Inspector. I cannot think of anyone less likely to be a murder victim."

But people had said much the same thing about Wentworth.

They had reached Rutledge's motorcar. He thanked Davies, and gave Bill the Hunters to return to the house. The man and his steward were walking on, heads together in close conversation, when Rutledge rounded the bend and lost sight of them.

Hamish said, "It was a verra' clever ruse. And Templeton walked out to meet him."

"I wonder why. It would have been sensible to wait at the house."

"Aye, but ye ken, he had no reason to be suspicious."

And that was true enough. Still, it was odd, since Templeton had never met the man he was expecting to travel with.

Or did he believe he had met Young before? A chance encounter somewhere that made him feel he could trust Young?

Or—more likely—he had met someone by the name of Young, and assumed it was the same man . . .

But how had his killer known all this? Had he made a study of Templeton, before writing that letter?

As he had known, somehow, that Wentworth would be late coming down the Wolfpit road from the direction of the Hardy house on a Saturday evening . . .

It was the dinner hour when he reached Wolfpit, and he found Dr. Brent in the midst of his own meal.

"I've had no opportunity to examine Templeton," he said, irritation underlining his words. "I had hours that ended just before my dinner. Come back tomorrow."

Rutledge drove on to the Templeton house. Someone had already put a bow of black crepe on the knocker, and Mrs. Cox was red-eyed when she opened the door a narrow space before she recognized Rutledge.

"I was of two minds about answering," she said. "For fear he might have come back."

Rutledge didn't need to ask who *he* was. "I don't think you need fear anything from Mr. Templeton's killer. He has no reason to come back to the house."

"As you say, sir," she replied doubtfully, and let him in, leading him back to the drawing room. It was dark, no fire on the hearth, although the curtains had been drawn, and she lit two lamps before turning to him.

"Do you have any news, sir?"

"I'm afraid not. I wondered if you had remembered anything that might be useful. For instance, why Mr. Templeton went out to meet this man coming to take him to Cambridge."

"He sometimes liked a cigarette after his dinner, sir, and Mrs. Templeton had always disliked cigarette smoke in the house. He'd go out into the gardens instead. I expect he smoked one on his way to the gates."

A simple answer, then. And yet it must have seemed a godsend to the killer, his quarry coming to him rather than the risk of being seen at the house by one of the staff.

Would he have killed the housekeeper? But he hadn't touched Miss MacRae, had he?

Mrs. Cox was saying, "Have you spoken to the solicitor, sir? I don't know what I should be doing about anything. It's not like when Mrs. Templeton died, is it? With Mr. Templeton here to tell us what to do."

"Was he here when she died?"

"Yes, sir, he came home on compassionate leave, when I wrote that she was in a bad state. They were very close. It was always her fear that *he* would be killed. And God decided otherwise, didn't he?"

"I'll speak to the solicitor in the morning. Meanwhile, carry on as you would if Templeton were here. He'd probably wish you to go on."

"Yes, sir. Thank you, sir." She hesitated. "Will the undertaker be wanting proper clothes for Mr. Templeton, sir? I'll see to laying out what he might need."

"The solicitor will tell you what is necessary. But yes, I'd go through his wardrobe and choose something suitable."

She seemed relieved, as if having something to occupy her thoughts helped her forget.

As he rose to go, she said, "The house seems so—empty without them here. Mr. and Mrs. Templeton. Cook was asking what to do about the dinner she'd made, and no one to eat it."

She stood at the door and watched him turn the crank before getting into his motorcar. And only then did she shut it, as if reluctant to lose even so small a contact with someone in authority.

As he turned back toward Wolfpit, Hamish spoke in the back of his mind.

"Ye ken, they were both alone. Wentworth and Templeton. No wives or children."

"I don't know if that had anything to do with their deaths. But it simplified matters for the killer. Wentworth was on the road, and Templeton obligingly walked down to the gates."

He stopped at The Swan for a quick supper, then went to see Mrs. Delaney.

She was upset by the news of Templeton's death.

"He was such a nice man. And I adored his wife, Rose. She kept that estate running all through the war, and still found time to encourage us to do whatever we could for our men. I must have knitted hundreds of pairs of stockings, and of course I lost count of scarves. We put up food to last us through the winter months, raised chickens and geese for their eggs, and did what we could for those who lost their sons and fathers. That's how she contracted the influenza, taking food to families who were stricken, without a thought for herself." She shook her head. "She put us all to shame, caring so much. But she said it was all to make the time fly and bring her husband back to her all the sooner."

"Was there any connection between Wentworth and Templeton?"

"They knew each other, of course, but Frederick was nearly ten years older, and married. Not much in common there. The Templetons often came to the bookshop, of course. But that was mostly when my husband was the owner. Frederick sometimes asked us to find books for him, mostly on the subject of agriculture."

"Not even a shared interest in Peru?"

She smiled sadly. "Not even that." The smile faded. "You're looking for something that might connect these two men in the eyes of a killer. And so you must be thinking that the same person shot both of them. But why? Why these two? They were good, law-abiding, quiet people who did no one any harm. It's unthinkable that either one of them might be hated enough for someone to want to shoot them."

"But someone has, and I must find out why."

He left soon after, stopping by the police station. But Constable Penny wasn't in. Rutledge looked for him, thinking he might be on his rounds, then gave up and went back to The Swan after leaving a note informing Penny to expect to see Davies the next morning.

Tomorrow, he told himself, he would find the solicitor, and then he'd speak to Miss MacRae again.

Everything he'd learned about Wentworth's death had been turned on its ear. He needed time to consider what the death of Frederick Templeton had to do with Wentworth—or Wentworth with him.

He opened the door to his room, and stopped short in the doorway.

Inspector Reed was sitting there in the dark, waiting for him.

II

Silently cursing the man, Rutledge crossed the room and took his time lighting the lamp on the table by his bed. When the wick had caught well enough to brighten the darkness, he turned.

"Good evening. Who let you in?"

Reed's mouth twitched, and his eyes were angry. "The clerk. Thank you for coming to Stowmarket to inform me of Templeton's death."

Rutledge said easily, "I thought that was Penny's responsibility. I was in Colchester, as it happens." He went to stand by the window, so that Reed had to twist around in his chair to look at him.

"Yes, something to do with a man by the name of Davies. Did you find him?"

"I did. Apparently there's no such person as Harold Young. It was a ruse to bring Templeton to his killer. Just when he expected to shoot him I don't know. Templeton made it easy by walking down the drive in the dark. But I expect we know something about this man. He owns a motorcar. I found no sign of it where Wentworth was killed, but it could have been left anywhere, in any direction. The killer made certain it was well out of sight."

"What else do we know about him?"

"It's possible that he smokes a pipe. I can't be certain. What's more, he's patient, and he plans meticulously. This wasn't a crime of passion. A need to kill at any cost."

"Then what do the victims have in common?"

"You're the local man. You tell me," Rutledge countered.

Reed grimaced again.

Rutledge was fairly sure now that Reed had been sitting here in the dark room for some time, nursing his grievances. He hadn't been thinking about the inquiry or about the dead men.

"They must have known each other. Of course they did. Wolfpit is a small village. How much they had in common is another matter," he said finally.

"I could have said just that after a matter of days here. Why would a killer stalk either man? Or both?"

"Damn it, how can I speculate on that when you refuse to keep me in the picture?" The anger in Reed's voice was overlaid now with irritability.

"It isn't deliberate, I assure you. But it was important to reach Davies before Templeton's death became public knowledge. If Young was the man I was after, there was a chance I could find him sooner rather than later. Before he got the wind up and disappeared. I didn't want to believe he didn't exist. But I thought that it was very likely. And I was right. Still, Davies was the key."

"And you believe what he told you? That there was no such man as Harold Young?"

"I do. He had no reason to lie. He hadn't heard the news about Templeton. He was shocked by it. Why should he protect Young, knowing he was a killer?"

Reed shook his head. "You should have brought him in for questioning."

"I questioned him. Meanwhile he's worried that Young, or whatever his name is, will come after him or his family."

"Why?"

"If this man is ever caught, Davies can testify that he never introduced Young to Templeton. That the letter was a lie. It could be the difference between a conviction and acquittal for lack of evidence."

"That's not likely."

"Davies doesn't think so. He has a wife and children."

"Which brings up a point. Neither Wentworth nor Templeton had families. Templeton was married but lost his wife two years ago. Did that matter?"

Rutledge shook his head. "I can't see how it did. Nor did the war, as far as I can tell. Wentworth was in the Royal Navy. Templeton was in France."

Reed got to his feet. "The truth is, I'm glad it's your inquiry," he said sourly. "My wife is wondering what happened to me. I should have been home three hours ago."

"If you have any suggestions, I'm willing to listen."

Reed regarded him for a long moment. "Why should I make your road easier?"

"Because two men are dead. And before we've taken anyone into custody, there could well be more victims. I'd just as soon have this stop at two."

Laughing, Reed said, "I'm sure you would. But it's your inquiry, isn't it? You made that plain from the start."

Rutledge said, "You won't be rid of Wentworth just because he's dead. You'll always wonder, won't you? And you won't be able to ask."

The laugh vanished as his fists clenched. "Leave my wife out of this."

"It has nothing to do with Mrs. Reed. This is *your* ghost."

Wheeling, Reed walked out of the room, afraid to trust himself facing Rutledge any longer. The door slammed behind him, and Rutledge could hear his footsteps thudding down the stairs, fast and angry.

"Ye didna' need to make an enemy of yon Inspector," Hamish was saying in the back of his mind.

"He was already an enemy," Rutledge answered him. "I just made it plain that he was. And that I knew he was." He walked across the room and turned the key in the lock. "I would like to see Mrs. Reed. It might help me understand him a little better."

Rutledge undressed and got ready for bed. But once there, he couldn't sleep. His mind kept turning the few bits of evidence he had over and over again.

Had the killer spoken to Templeton before shooting him? As he had done with Wentworth? And if he had, was the answer to his satisfaction? Or would there be another death, and another, until he found the answer he was looking for.

What the hell was he after, this killer?

And what the hell was that question?

If it had been Reed there in the darkness, facing Wentworth on Saturday night, Rutledge could imagine what that question might have been: *Have you ever slept with my wife?*

That wouldn't apply to Templeton. He had loved his wife.

Hamish remarked, "Aye, true enough. Unless yon farmer was shot to throw ye off the track?"

Rutledge smiled grimly. "I'd be willing to consider that, if it hadn't been for the mysterious Mr. Young."

He tossed and turned, and finally, close to two o'clock in the morning, he got up, dressed, and went out to walk the streets of Wolfpit. Someone's dog walked with him for a while, then trotted off to his home.

The churchyard was filled with shadows, and his footsteps echoed on the streets. There were few lamps lit in the houses and cottages he passed, while the shops were dark.

Two murders in a matter of days. In a single village. And no one had seen the killer's face.

Rutledge looked up at the windows behind which people slept. Who was next? Or had the killer finished with Wolfpit—and moved on?

He walked for two more hours, and then, thinking he could sleep, he turned back toward The Swan.

Hamish said, "'Ware," as he had so many times on night watches in the trenches.

Alert now, Rutledge scanned the empty street. And then ahead of him, close by the Wentworth house, something flitted out of the shadows and crossed the road. He realized it was the friendly dog, and relaxed.

Then he tensed again as he realized the dog had come up to someone he couldn't see, tail wagging and demanding to be noticed.

There was a sudden movement, and the dog dodged away, yelping. It turned tail and set off in the direction it had come from.

Rutledge was already running flat out, cursing the echo of his footsteps in the silence of the night. And then someone else was running, but Rutledge thought he had an edge on his quarry, coming up fast. The echo picked up other feet—and then there were only his own footsteps.

Had his quarry stepped into a doorway? Slipped into a garden or between two houses or shops?

Rutledge slowed, then stopped. He was breathing hard, and trying to listen as well.

Hamish said, "He's no' there."

"He has to be. He can't have vanished into thin air."

"He has before."

Uncertain whether to stay in the shadows himself and wait, or to begin a thorough search, Rutledge stood where he was.

Was that the creak of a back gate?

He moved forward, found himself looking down a narrow service alley between two houses. It was pitch-black. But he turned into it anyway, wary with every step he took, and at the end of it, he saw a gate leading into a walled back garden. Rather than risk opening it and giving himself away, he put out a hand and vaulted it, landing silently in the grass on the far side. It was lighter here, open except for a tree at the bottom of the garden. He could see the branches move a little, then stop.

He tried to stay in the shadows by the garden wall, taking his time, his eyes on the bare limbs of the tree, searching for a thicker darkness that might be a person. Halfway to the tree, he realized that whoever had climbed it had used it to swing over the wall just below it. For he could see the trunk clearly now.

Swearing, he ran toward the tree, heedless of being seen, and swung himself up into it, to a point where he could see over the wall.

He was looking down into an alley that ran between this garden and the back gardens of houses, mostly small cottages, as far as he could judge, facing out toward what appeared to be fields beyond them.

Scanning the alley and the back gardens he could see into, he searched for movement. But whoever he'd been after, there was no sign of him now. As the clouds overhead opened and a crescent moon lit the scene, he went on searching. But it was useless.

Rutledge scrambled down from the tree, walked back up the garden to the gate, and vaulted over it again.

What had he seen? Someone up to mischief at this hour? An errant husband on his way home? Or a murderer looking for his next victim?

Impossible to say. If it hadn't been for the dog leaping out of reach of a kick, he would very likely never have seen someone there in the shadows.

As he entered the alley, he found himself thinking of the days when wolves roamed the outskirts of villages, picking off livestock, frightening travelers, and keeping people in their houses after dark.

The wolves had gone, but there had been something—someone—abroad this night.

He crossed the street and went into The Swan. Once in his room, he locked the door again and sat by his window for another hour, watching the street from the edge of his curtain.

But nothing moved except for a lorry coming up from the Bury road and trundling away into the distance.

Finally, accepting the fact that whoever it was had gone, Rutledge gave up and went to bed.

This time he slept without dreams.

Early the next morning, as dawn was threatening to break through the clouds, Rutledge went out again into the street. He retraced his own steps, then went back down the narrow alley and examined the back garden for footprints. But his quarry had been careful to stay on the grass, avoiding any muddy patches, and there was nothing to show that he had ever been there. Rutledge even climbed the tree again and looked carefully at the top of the wall. He was rewarded with nothing of interest.

Before the householder or his servants had risen, Rutledge had gone away. As soon as he thought Penny was on duty, he stopped in at the police station, then found him at home, toasting slices of bread over the kitchen hearth while waiting for the kettle to boil. Cooked eggs and a sausage were already on his plate.

He had hoped to ask the Constable to draw him a map of Wolf-pit and add the names of householders to it. Compromising, Rutledge found paper on the desk in the station and sketched out the center of the village himself. When he took it back, Penny was just setting his dishes in the dry sink. He looked it over, then said, "You're a fair hand at drafting."

He offered Rutledge a cup of tea, and then began to put names to the spaces.

The house with the back garden, Rutledge discovered, belonged to two young women, mistresses in the local grammar school.

"Lost their fiancés in war, and turned to teaching to earn their living," Penny told him. "Settled, well liked. I've never heard a word against either of them."

"Do they have friends who call? Or some attachment to a man in Wolfpit?"

"Women friends, from time to time. But there's no attachment to anyone that I've heard of. If you met them, you'd understand."

"And the men they were engaged to? Were they local?"

"Miss Frost is from London. She took over the lower school when Mr. Hobson enlisted. Hired by the board of governors because her father is something in the government. Miss Dennis is from Dorset. Miss Frost recommended her for the vacancy when Mr. Grady died of the influenza. The house belonged to Mr. Grady, and he left it to the school. A bachelor all his life."

Hamish said, "It was the nearest way off the High."

While Rutledge agreed with him, he had some reservations. It was still early, and he thanked Penny, rolling up the sheet and taking it with him.

Children were just making their way to school, and he found a vantage point by a milliner's shop where he could watch the Grady house.

Ten minutes later, two women came out the door, leather satchels in their hands, and turned toward the school. They weren't what he'd expected. While they wore black with sensible shoes, their hair pulled back severely beneath their hats in an effort to make them appear older than they were, it was harder to conceal the spring in their step. The taller of the two had dark red hair, while her companion was fair. They wore only powder, no color on their lips or cheeks. He wouldn't have called either of them pretty, but he thought that must have been deliberate. He remembered his sister's governess, an intelligent woman who had also made her living teaching, always dressed in plain dark gowns and wearing her hair in an older woman's style. And yet her eyes had held laughter sometimes, and it had changed her face completely.

Rutledge followed the two women at a distance, watching children here and there speak shyly to them as they met along the way. Others walked on ahead, all too aware of who was behind them, and a few—mostly the older lads—lagged behind the women.

The school was down the road past the church, and had once been a smaller building. He thought it had been enlarged in the early 1890s, for the newer roof was now nearly the same gray as the older one.

Once the teachers and the children had disappeared through the door, and the last laggard had hurried to catch them up, Rutledge walked on.

Miss Frost and Miss Dennis were safe enough for the moment.

Hamish said, "Ye canna' watch o'er them day and night. It's better to find yon murderer."

There was no answer Rutledge could make.

He retraced his steps to The Street and began to scan his rough map to locate the firm of solicitors. He found the brass nameplate beside a door just down from the bookshop. BLAKE AND SONS was written in a Gothic script that matched the elegant door set into the plastered wall, painted a pleasing shade of blue.

An elderly clerk admitted him, and told him Mr. Blake was available. He was shown into an office where the heads of game animals circled the walls, glass eyes gazing down at him from an array of trophies. Mostly giraffe, lion, water buffalo, and several gazelles, although a rhinoceros hovered high above the desk.

Blake, a man in his forties, smiled as he watched Rutledge's reaction. "Not mine, I'm afraid. My grandfather was an avid hunter. He was the *Blake* on the board outside. My father and my uncle were the *Sons*. I've never got around to adding *Grandson*. It seemed somehow cheeky to change it. Or to change *them*. I've only been here ten years. I did offer them to the school, but Mr. Grady politely turned me down. A pity. Think what a teaching tool they would have made. Africa, watching while the children did their tables."

Rutledge returned the smile. "Is there not a box room that would hold them?"

Blake laughed. "One of my clients would die of the shock. She still compares me to my grandfather." Rutledge had the feeling that he was speaking of Mrs. Wentworth. Then the laughter faded. "You've come about Templeton, have you not? Or Stephen Wentworth? Or both? My clerk greeted me this morning with the news of another murder. I'm not quite sure what to make of it. If I were asked, I'd have said that both men were the least likely people I know to have been murdered."

"Were they friends?"

"Acquaintances. But they moved in different circles. Templeton was older, married, a settled man. I'd have said Stephen Wentworth was settled too. Half the eligible ladies in the village would have been happy to attract his notice. He was polite, attentive, he'd dance with the wallflowers, but he showed no interest in a closer relationship. I'd heard that there was someone he'd met while at university, but as far as I know, nothing came of it. As for Templeton, his wife's death was too recent. He's kept to himself as a rule."

That fit with what Rutledge had already learned. "Who inherits, in each case?"

"Templeton has left everything to his wife's sister. She lives in St. Albans. Married, several children. The two women were close, and there's no surprise there." He looked up at Rutledge, suddenly stricken. "Dear God. I just realized. I shall have to go and break the news to her."

"And Wentworth?"

"He left the bookshop to Mrs. Delaney. Again, not too surprising, he'd bought it from the Delaneys. And I'm sure his parents wanted no part of it. They were against his purchase of it in the first place. Like Templeton, he made the usual bequests to the staff and to the church, as well as the Widows and Orphans fund. The sort of thing that was expected of him. But the bulk of his estate goes to the Bodleian in Oxford. Rather an odd choice, but there you are. It was his to do with as he pleased."

"Not to Cambridge?"

"Yes, that surprised me as well. I'd have thought he might have left something to his sister's children. A gesture. But he told me they were well looked after, and the Bodleian would be grateful for the funds. And I expect they will."

"How long ago did he make this bequest?"

"Oh, shortly after he came back from Peru. Before he enlisted. I asked him after the war if he wished to make any changes to his will, but he told me he was satisfied with it as it stood."

Rutledge could see that this was going nowhere. "And nothing in either man's life was unusual—nothing that would lead you to question his associates or his decisions?"

"I can't say there was *nothing*. I didn't know them that well. But I've lived here all my life too, and there's been no particular gossip about either man. I've heard that Stephen and his family were at odds, but I don't know if that's true. He did spend a good many of his holidays with friends. Still, he was quite popular and never lacking for invitations to stay. Perhaps that's how the rumors got started."

"Did they share an interest in racing—chess—fishing? Anything?"

"If they did, I never heard of it. Templeton loved his wife, don't get me wrong. But he was devoted to his land. He cherished it, worked to improve the soil and his yields, rotating crops, plowing with the contour of the land, looking for the best quality seeds. He's—was—a rather quiet man. He seemed to be most at home walking across his land, but he was in demand to talk about some of the innovations he'd put in place, and he was generous with his time in that regard."

Which, Rutledge thought, was why "Young" had made that arrangement to meet Templeton. He knew it would work.

"What you're telling me is that Templeton and Wentworth were random targets, and yet there's some evidence that the killer planned each death, patiently waiting for his opportunity. Stalking both men. I need to know *why,* because I have a feeling he'll kill again." He studied Blake for a moment. "Do *you* fit the pattern?"

Startled, Blake stared back at him. "Good God. Are you serious?"

"I don't jest about murder."

He straightened in his chair, sudden anxiety in his face. "I'm close to both men in age. Closer perhaps to Templeton. At the moment I live alone. My wife's mother is ill, and she's in Derby just now, staying with her for a bit. I'm hoping she'll be able to come back for Christmas, or I'll travel to Derbyshire instead. Meanwhile—what the hell should I be doing, meanwhile?"

"Be careful. Don't go walking out at night alone. Don't stay here after your clerk has left. Be judicious answering your house door. And if you get a summons to a bedside for a last change in a will, be sure it's genuine."

"This time of year it's dark early on. And I sometimes dine out, rather than eat alone in that empty house."

"You'll have to change your habits. Or ask your housekeeper to see that you have dinner waiting for you. Loneliness is better than leaving your wife a widow."

"Good God," he said again, then cleared his throat. "Surely—" Breaking off, he stared beyond Rutledge at the lioness above the door. "I expect I'm as brave as the next man, I spent three years in France, and I learned how to kill or be killed. But this is different. I still have my service revolver. I expect it's in my trunk." His gaze came back to Rutledge. "I ought to thank you for the warning. Somehow I don't feel suitably grateful."

"I understand."

"Damn it, what about you? Why aren't you a likely candidate your-self?"

Rutledge said, "I might well be, when he realizes I'm looking for him."

He left soon after. Blake had gone over everything he knew about Templeton and Wentworth again, searching for a clue to their deaths. But none of it was new information, and in the end, he had shaken his head.

"Will you tell me if you learn anything more? Anything useful, I mean. Anything that might make a difference?" Blake asked.

"I will." He made an effort to mask his own frustration, and out in the street once more, he asked himself if these killings *had* been random. Hamish argued against that, pointing out that some effort had been made to locate the victim in Wentworth's case, and to lure him away from his home in Templeton's. In Rutledge's experience that was unusual in random murders.

What then *was* the connection?

The killer had taken nothing from his victims. But he had asked a question of Wentworth, and presumably had asked one of Templeton as well.

What answer was he looking for?

Or perhaps more to the point, what was he searching for?

And had he believed it was necessary to kill those who had the right answer? Or had he shot each victim precisely because he'd given the wrong answer and therefore couldn't be left alive to tell anyone what the question was?

That, he thought, trying to ignore Hamish, might be worth bearing in mind.

Well, then, Rutledge asked himself as he walked the streets of Wolfpit, what was the question?

One searched for a person. Or an object. A man . . . or a woman. Something that was lost or taken. Even for a place.

Hamish said so clearly that Rutledge turned to see if anyone else had heard the voice, "Ye can search for a witness."

And that opened up an entirely different line of thought.

Rutledge hurried back to The Swan, and once in his room, he took out several sheets of paper and began to make a list of everything he knew about the dead men.

It was damned little. The only item on the list that both shared was living alone. Why should that matter? Neither man was killed in his house.

Rutledge flung his pencil down on the desk and stretched the tight muscles in his shoulders.

Collecting his hat and coat, he went down to the motorcar and drove out to the Templeton house, but stopped short of the gates. They were still standing open, as they had been the day before.

Beginning at the road, he quartered the drive up to where the body had been found, scanning for anything that might make a difference.

Hamish said, "Anither wolf?"

"Or bear—cat—crow," he answered absently, his eyes on the drive. But search as he would, there was no carving to be found. He did see, not far from where Templeton had fallen, the stub of a cigarette. Flattened and torn, it lay in the hollow of a rut.

Frustrated, he moved to the verge of the drive. And there, beneath a bough of rhododendron and a clump of grass just touching the edge of the drive, he saw it, so well hidden in the shadows that only a determined search had found it.

Feeling a surge of excitement, he reached for it, closed his fingers over it, and then straightened. In the palm of his hand was another, almost identical, wood carving of a howling wolf. He thought it must have been kicked there inadvertently by Martin or the doctor or even the undertaker, for it was clean and smooth this time.

Triumphant, he strode back to his motorcar and got in, after safely putting the second wolf in his pocket with the first.

Here was no coincidence. In his wildest imagination, he could find no reason for two such similar carvings to be found at the scenes of two different murders.

He decided to speak to Audrey Blackburn. She was sensible and not given to wild speculations about people. And she had lived here most of her life.

When he knocked on the door, the curtain in the nearest window twitched, and then someone was coming to open it.

Miss Blackburn said, "We've already heard. It's Mr. Templeton this time. Why aren't you out taking a killer into custody, instead of annoying two defenseless women?"

Rutledge laughed outright. "Hardly defenseless. May I come in?"

"Oh, very well."

As she led the way to the parlor, he asked, "How is Miss MacRae?"

"Better. She's coming to terms with what happened. And she's no longer threatening to go home."

"I'd wondered if perhaps her dream reminded her of something she might have forgot in the shock of that night. Something I might find helpful," he said. "The mind sometimes refuses to face horrors. And then brings them to the forefront in a way we least expect."

"In my view, she's worried about the fact that she lived. She didn't think about that as Stephen was shot, but now it looms large. Why did that man let her live? And there's the other worry. She's afraid that, in the end, for want of any other suspect, you might accuse her of killing Stephen. After all, she was there. His blood was on her hands. I know, I cleaned up the sink after she tried to wash it off. And for two days she was Lady Macbeth, scrubbing the guilt away."

"But she couldn't have killed Templeton." It was as much a statement as it was a question.

"Of course not. What a suspicious mind you have."

"It's necessary in this line of work. What do you know about Frederick Templeton that I might not have discovered yet?"

Her eyebrows went up. "You're the policeman."

"And you're the lifelong resident." He considered her. "You also may know more than you realize. What do you dream about?"

For a moment color flared in her face, angry and insulted. Then, to his surprise, she laughed. "I think I'm beginning to like you. But only beginning."

Rutledge grinned. "Yes, well, desperate times require desperate measures."

"What do you want to know about Stephen? Or Frederick Templeton? I know very little gossip about them. As a rule people don't gossip with me."

"Do they have any hidden vices? Do they gamble? Have an attraction to other men, drink too much, kick small children, steal from the poor box when no one is looking?"

"They were good men, both of them. I don't know of any vices. I've never seen either of them the worse for drink. I've never heard them say anything that might lead me to think they gambled. And they treated everyone with courtesy and kindness. I could have gone to either of them if I'd been in trouble of some sort. I could depend upon them to understand and not judge me. Is this what you want to hear?"

"No. Because these qualities don't usually get a man killed."

"Well, I can't make up something suitable." She studied him for a moment, then said, "You should look at it this way. It's possible that they were mistaken for someone else. Or someone led their killer to believe these were the men he was after."

For a moment he saw Mrs. Wentworth's face in his memory. Twisted with hate. Would she throw her own son to the wolves, figuratively speaking, if she were given the chance? And hope that whoever it was killed him for her?

It was not only possible but likely. Her hatred had become an obsession with her, and he wondered now if she could actually remember the dead child's face or voice. There was the portrait someone had told him about, but he hadn't seen it in the Wentworth house.

"Ye ken, she would ha' taken it to Norwich with her."

Yes, very likely. To fuel the fires of hate.

But that didn't explain Templeton's death. Unless he was the intended target from the start.

"You've thought of something, haven't you?" Miss Blackburn asked.

"I'm not sure."

She smiled at him. "Glad to be of assistance to the Yard." But he could see that she was curious and wanted him to tell her what it was that had occurred to him.

Instead, he said, "To move on to another matter. Did Templeton and Wentworth regularly attend church services?"

"Frederick's wife was fairly religious, and so he attended with her. But if she wasn't in town, he didn't usually go on his own. Stephen seldom attended. On the holidays, of course. Christmas, Easter, Whitsun. He doesn't sit where his parents always did. He prefers the back row."

"Then it's not likely that the Rector would be able to tell me much about either man?"

"Probably not."

"There's something else I've been wanting to ask you. Did Mrs. Wentworth ever speak to you about your niece? Warning her off Stephen?"

"Odd that you should ask that. What she said was so uncalled for, I didn't really wish to repeat it. I think I simply told you that I didn't care for her. You recall my saying something about Elizabeth playing tennis with Stephen on her earlier visits? Yes, well, it wasn't long after they began to play that Mrs. Wentworth came up to me as we were walking to morning services. She asked me several questions about Elizabeth that were no more than thinly veiled efforts to discover whether my niece could be considered a suitable match. That was unpleasant enough, as if I had been throwing my niece at her son with the hope of snaring him. And then she warned me about a young girl spending so much time in the company of an older boy. This was her own son, mind you! As though he might prey on impressionable girls. I was astonished and sickened. I told her she was a vile woman, and I walked on. I can assure you I heard nothing of that morning's sermon. I was seething with fury. Afterward, when I was cooler, I asked Elizabeth in a roundabout way if Stephen annoyed her at all. And I could see from her expression that she had no idea what I was talking about. What a foul way of trying to warn me off. I expect I should have stopped the tennis straightaway, but it seemed to me to be precisely what she wanted. And I was not about to give her that satisfaction."

But it hadn't been that. Not in the way that Audrey Blackburn had understood the conversation. It had been designed to deny her son something that he enjoyed and leave him to wonder why Elizabeth MacRae no longer wanted to play tennis with him. To unsettle him and make him unhappy.

"I'm rather glad you didn't," Rutledge replied. Changing the subject, he took one of the little wolves from his pocket. "Is there anyone in Wolfpit who might have been able to carve such a handsome little fellow? Or perhaps a shop that carries them?"

She shook her head. "Why is this so important? You've shown it to us before."

"So I have. But I'm still curious about it. Unlikely as it may be, as a clue."

"Then you're desperate for answers."

He was about to respond when they heard footsteps coming down the stairs, and Miss MacRae appeared in the doorway, hesitating on the threshold.

"Inspector," she said in greeting.

He could see that she wasn't herself. The blow to the head had left her pale, and he thought she must have a ferocious headache still. He was about to say something to her when he caught Miss Blackburn's eye. There was a warning there, and he thought he knew what she was trying to tell him: Miss MacRae hadn't heard about Templeton's death.

Smiling, he said, "I'm glad to see you looking rested." She didn't, but he thought she needed reassurance. "Do you feel up to a few questions?"

Resigning herself to the inevitable, she said, "Not really. But I expect you need to ask them. This has all been rather"—she searched for the right word, then gave up and went on with a shrug—"exhausting."

"I'm sure it has been," he said sympathetically. "But I need to know. Have you remembered anything else? Even details that might seem unimportant can help in an inquiry like this."

"I've tried, but remembering is very painful. I keep seeing Stephen there, just standing in the road, asking if he could help. He meant it, he was that sort of person, you see. He'd have done what he could." She broke off, biting her lip to hold back the tears. After a moment she went on, her voice husky. "I don't know that he even had time to realize what was about to happen. But I do, and I watch helplessly, over and over again, powerless to *stop* it. The worst of it is that there was no anger in the other man, no sadness, no emotion at all. He just shot Stephen and without looking my way, walked off. That's what's so horrid. *Efficient.* That's the word that comes to mind."

"Did he limp? Was he heavy-set or slim? Broad shouldered? Stooped?" He fired the questions at her, trying to catch her memory of that moment while it was recurring in her mind.

"Limp? No. Average, I expect. Young. The way he moved. No, young isn't right. But not old. I've told you that. Like Stephen, perhaps, just something—I can't explain it. Stephen liked tennis and cricket, he was active, and that's what I saw in the man."

She had told him more than she realized, though the words had been halting as she tried to explain herself.

"And you still have no idea what he said to Stephen?"

"I've gone over that too, again and again. He kept his voice low. Well, he was face-to-face with Stephen, wasn't he? He needn't raise his voice."

He had learned all he could. Smiling again, he thanked her. "Every little scrap of information is helpful. I'm sorry to press you, but you're my only witness."

"I wish I had never gone to that party," she said then, her voice rough with pain. "I wish I'd stayed at home. But I thought it might be fun, you see. Oh, God, *fun.*"

She buried her face in her hands, as if that would shut off the memories.

Rutledge said gently, "You can't change what happened. You had no way to foresee how the evening would end. And you were there when he died. He wasn't alone."

She lifted her head and stared at him. It had never occurred to her to see events through Stephen Wentworth's eyes. "I—I was. Wasn't I?"

He rose. "One final question. Did anyone pass you on the road

Saturday night—or Sunday morning, as it actually was? Or overtake you?"

"No. I remember saying something about that to Stephen. That even the motorcars had gone home to bed. He laughed, and told me he'd have to apologize for keeping his own out so late."

From the Blackburn house Rutledge went back to The Swan, collected his motorcar, and drove to Norwich, some two hours away.

He found Mrs. Wentworth at home alone. Her husband, she informed him, was having lunch with friends, and Patricia had gone to do her marketing.

He was just as glad, because he wanted to speak to her alone.

"Have you found my son's killer?" she asked, in the same tone of voice that she might have asked if he'd found a tailor to his liking.

"Not yet."

"Then you must not be a very good policeman," she said.

He smiled, although it didn't reach his eyes. He didn't care for her, and he found it hard to disguise that. "Actually I've come to ask you whether Frederick Templeton and your son were friends."

"Frederick Templeton?" she repeated in surprise. "How should I know?"

"There's an age difference, of course. But I wondered if there was a mutual interest in books."

"You aren't suggesting that Frederick Templeton killed Stephen?"

"On the contrary. No, I was more interested in the fact that there appears to be some connection between them."

"I find that hard to believe."

"Why?"

"Because Frederick was such a nice young man. His mother brought him to tea once when he was about ten. Lovely manners. One could be proud of such a son."

"I've heard people say much the same thing about Stephen."

"He was very good at hiding the sort of person he was. Of course they were taken in." Her voice was heavy with contempt.

"Surely Templeton had some vices as well."

"I never heard of any," she retorted. And then he saw her expression change as she remembered something.

"What is it?" Rutledge asked when she didn't go on.

"It was nothing. Some small problem at school."

"I need to know, Mrs. Wentworth."

"Why?" She stared balefully at him. "It has nothing to do with the man he became."

"You can't be sure of that, can you?"

"But I can. Look at the good he does with his knowledge of farming. He has compensated fivefold for that one lapse. I have heard nothing but good about him."

"He's dead, Mrs. Wentworth. Shot in the same way that your son was killed. In the dark, night before last, alone in his drive." He was blunt on purpose.

She stared at him, speechless. Had she thought that only Stephen could become a murder victim? That her son's killer was finished when he had fired that revolver at point-blank range? Was she that self-centered?

Rutledge waited. Finally she managed to say, "I think you're lying to me."

"I wouldn't be that cruel," he responded coldly.

She collected herself with an effort that he could see. "Who in heaven's name would kill Frederick?" she asked softly, as if still absorbing the sense of what he'd said.

"That's what I am endeavoring to discover. What happened when he was in school?"

"It was nothing—an argument on the playing fields. In the end, he hit the other boy with his cricket bat. He was twelve, and the other child had struck him first. He was just defending himself. Both boys were sent down for eight days, with an official reprimand on their records. Everyone thought it most unfair. His parents went to collect him and had a word with the Head. Of course it did no good, the punishment had been decided. But they made it clear how they felt."

Hamish said into the silence that followed, "Would she have done as much for her ain lad?"

When Rutledge didn't say anything, she went on. "He's—he was a grown man. That was long ago. He has—had—put it behind him. I doubt anyone even remembers the incident now."

Yet she had. And that brought up the question of how many others had remembered it? The other child, for instance. But did one hold a grudge that long? How many years since Templeton was twelve and defended himself?

That raised another question. In the dark, had someone mistaken Wentworth for Templeton?

"Did they attend the same school, your son and Wentworth?"

"No, of course not. Frederick was sent to Rugby. It was where his father and his uncle had been sent."

It was still possible that a mistake had been made.

He thanked her and rose to leave.

"You have told me the truth about Frederick?" she asked him for the second time.

"I have."

She nodded. He walked toward the door, but she didn't bother to see him out.

H amish said as he turned the crank, "It changes naething."

"No. I still must treat this as a random killing. Until we find out why. Meanwhile, I'll look into Templeton's war." He had connections at the Ministry, he could ask for information. But that might well take longer than he could wait.

There was the mysterious Mr. Haldane, who claimed to be a member of the Foot Police, but who knew far more about too many other subjects ever to have been a mere policeman. Rutledge had meticulously avoided putting himself in Haldane's debt a second time. He'd had no choice but to call on his services once before, in another inquiry. And so far Haldane hadn't asked for information in return.

Rutledge had been relieved. Still, there was the knowledge that the day would probably come. He had no illusions about that.

Hamish said, "Ask yon Sergeant in London."

But Sergeant Gibson was not an Army man and would have to go through channels. He had known about Robin Hardy's London escapades because they had attracted the attention of the Metropolitan Police. Army records were handwritten, and any search would take days. Rutledge might not *have* days.

He drove back to Wolfpit, still turning the matter over in his mind. Even so, he knew he had no choice.

He left the motorcar at The Swan and crossed the road to the bookshop. Haldane was on the telephone, and after some hesitation, Rutledge finally put through the call.

Haldane's servant answered—Rutledge had never been precisely sure what role he played, from bodyguard to butler to man of all work—and after he had identified himself to the man's satisfaction, Haldane himself came to the telephone.

Rutledge could hear the amusement in his voice as he answered, and silently swore.

"Good day, Inspector. How may I be of assistance?"

"There have been two deaths here in Suffolk. Apparently random. I'd like to find out just what a man by the name of Frederick Templeton did in the war. Anything that might have made him the target of a murderer. A Dorset regiment. Rank of Major. The other dead man was in the Royal Navy. Stephen Wentworth. Captain. At least one ship was sunk under him."

"Anyone else?"

Rutledge gave that some thought. Blake? Or Hardy? But there was no reason to include them. Not yet. The debt was great enough with only two names. "That's all for the moment," he replied, leaving the door open.

"Very well. How shall I reach you?"

Rutledge told him, and Haldane rang off.

Rutledge put up the receiver, his mind on what he'd asked Haldane. There was no proof that the war was involved, it had ended two years before. The eleventh hour of the eleventh day of the eleventh month. He had always thought of the poetic symmetry of that. Eleven, eleven, eleven. It suited the war somehow. But while it had ended, it hadn't gone away for many people. The dead were still dead, and families who had lost loved ones hadn't forgot. Nor had the wounded, or the nation as a whole, healed. Two years was not enough time to heal.

And then he found himself wondering how the war poet O A Manning would have addressed the peace. She had seen the war finished before she had taken her own life, she had been granted that one gift.

There was a line he remembered from *Wings of Fire,* her most famous collection of poems.

The scars of war go deep . . .

He himself could attest to that.

Although he knew there was no likelihood of Haldane calling him back straightaway, he stayed in the bookshop for almost another hour, searching it more thoroughly this time. The desk in the tiny office held only business correspondence, orders, payment records, and other matters relating to the bookshop. He persevered, even turning the desk drawers upside down to see if anything had been taped to the bottoms.

But Stephen Wentworth apparently had no secrets, no guilty conscience.

Rutledge went out to the back of the shop to look at the dustbins, but they had already been emptied. He came back inside, and on impulse he went to the comfortable chair where Wentworth could sit and read when there was no one in the shop browsing or if he preferred this to the emptiness and memories at home.

Lifting the cushion, he ran his hand down the side of the chair. His searching fingers came up with the two halves of a pencil snapped in two, a shilling, and a ha'penny. Moving to the other side, he found only a crumpled piece of paper. Smoothing it out on the table that held the lamp, he realized that it was nothing more than a scribbled list. There were titles of three books, and he remembered seeing them on a sheet of orders sent to the publisher Collins.

Turning it to the other side, he saw that Stephen Wentworth had written the words *Gate keeper* over and over again with increasing ferocity, the last time so deeply that he realized that the crossing of the *t* had nearly perforated the scrap of paper.

He looked at the broken pencil, and wondered if it had snapped at that point.

Not the title of a book, surely?

Rutledge went back to the desk and scanned the orders again. And didn't find it. He remembered seeing an inventory of the books on the shop shelves, took it out from under the counter where Wentworth dealt with queries and purchases, and went through that by title, searching first for the words, then under *A* and after that, *The.*

Nowhere was it listed.

He looked again at the words and the jagged edges of the broken pencil.

Here was the first sign of a deep anger in Stephen Wentworth, a part of him that no one else seemed to have recognized in the very nice young man they had described.

What—or possibly even who—was the gate keeper?

12

Rutledge locked up the bookshop and walked back to his motor-car, still thinking about the words he had seen on the back of the list of titles. He had taken the list with him, folded carefully into his notebook.

Who among Wentworth's acquaintances would know what the words meant? To whom would he have confided such anger? Even after it had cooled? Who would have been trusted with this particular secret? For it must have been just that. Something that mattered to him so deeply that he would write the words with increasing fury, then crumple the scrap of paper and shove it into his pocket, out of sight. But it hadn't stayed there. It had fallen out.

If he remembered it at all, Wentworth would have assumed he'd lost it somewhere. Would that have worried him? The titles on the other side might have told the finder the scrap had come from the bookshop.

Mrs. Delaney? Probably not. He turned to her for many things, many needs, but Rutledge wasn't convinced Wentworth would have shared this particular secret with her. And if he had, she would have mentioned it, would have told the police what had troubled him. She might even have known why.

Evelyn Hardy, then. It was less likely that Wentworth would have confided in her, but there was her brother, Harry. But before he could leave Wolfpit, there was one other matter.

School was being dismissed. He watched at a distance as Miss Frost and Miss Dennis walked home again. They had an easy way with the children they taught, without endangering discipline, and he thought they must be well liked. When they had closed their door, he turned back to The Swan.

Hamish said, "Ye ken, they do na' live alone. He wasna' looking for them."

Rutledge agreed with him. But he had wanted to be sure. Whoever it was, he had been too close to their house to ignore the possibility.

That done, he set out for Wickham.

Miss Hardy was just coming from the milliner's, a pretty bandbox swinging from its ribbons as she walked toward him. Then she recognized the man standing by her door, and her expression changed from happiness to wariness.

"What has happened?" she asked quickly. "Why have you come?"

He smiled. "Your maid told me you were out. I thought I'd wait. There are always more questions in an inquiry like this."

Relieved, she went to the door and unlocked it with her key. "Come in quietly. My mother is resting. She was down with a migraine last evening." Drawing off her gloves and setting them on a table by the door, she led him down the passage to his left.

She opened a door into a small, very feminine morning room, with birds and flowers in the wallpaper giving it a sense of being out in a garden, especially with the winter sunshine spilling across the floor from the pair of windows.

"This is really my mother's room," she said, "but it's also my very favorite in the house." She gestured to a chair and sat in one across from him. "I try to forget what happened to Stephen, and then something brings it all back rather forcibly. Is there a time set for his funeral?"

"Not yet. There's an inquest to be held first. And I'm not ready to call for one. I'm still investigating Wentworth's life, and speaking to his friends. And that's why I've come. In the bookshop I came across a reference to something that appeared to be important to him. But it makes no sense to me. I thought perhaps he'd mentioned it to you or perhaps to your brother. Just two words. I discovered it by the chair he kept in the bookshop for reading in his spare time." He had done his best not to make the words seem as ominous to her as they had to him. "'Gate keeper.' Nothing more. But they were repeated several times."

Evelyn Hardy frowned. "'Gate keeper'?" she asked, looking up. "The title of a book he wanted to remember—or perhaps was trying to order?"

"That occurred to me as well. I looked through his desk to see if he had placed an order for it. He hadn't. Nor was it listed in his inventory of the books on the shelves. I thought perhaps it had to do with something more—personal."

"I hate that you must go through his things this way. He was such a private person."

"If doing so will bring me closer to finding his killer, I'll go on searching."

"I know. I just find it hard to think about." She looked away, going back through memories and her own recollections. After a moment she said, "Harry asked him once if he would write a book about his time in Peru. He answered that it was an interesting time but not necessarily a happy time. But he might change his mind one day. Could that have been a title he'd been considering?"

Rutledge smiled encouragingly. "That's one possibility." And yet he didn't feel it was likely. Not by the measure of anger he had seen.

"I can't think what else it might mean. Perhaps Harry would have known . . ." Her voice trailed off as she mentioned her brother's name. "I feel wretched, not being able to help. Is it really that important?"

"Perhaps not. But there's no way to know unless one looks into it."

She said, "I don't think I'd like being a policeman."

She hadn't meant to hurt, but he felt it just the same. "I speak for the dead," he said quietly. "Who else can?"

Her face turned pink. "I had never thought of it that way. I shan't take Constable Burke for granted ever again."

Rutledge laughed. Then he said, "If you think of anything else, will you send word to me in care of the police in Wolfpit?"

Evelyn promised, and he left.

But while he was in the village, he called on three of the guests on the list he'd been given by the senior Mrs. Hardy. He hadn't expected to learn much from them, and he was right. They had left early, returned home, and hadn't heard about Stephen Wentworth's death until late the next afternoon. In each instance he asked if there was anyone who could corroborate the time they reached their respective homes, and in each case there was someone on the staff who had had to wait for them to return from the party. In one house it was a nursery maid who wished to report that a child had begun to run a fever, in two others it was the lady's maid who had stayed awake to put away the party gown and the jewelry that had been worn with it.

Afterward, Hamish said, "It's no' likely they'll cross their employers by telling the truth."

"That's very probably the case. But until I have other reasons to question their statements, I'll accept them. What's more, they hadn't heard about Templeton's death, and their shock seemed genuine enough. I couldn't find a clear motive for killing either man."

Hamish said, "Aye, but early days."

But it wasn't. Time was moving on. Or had Hamish been sarcastic?

The last set of names on the list was a Mr. and Mrs. Peterson, who lived only two miles from the house where the party had been held.

They had heard about Frederick Templeton's death, and Edgar

Peterson was incensed. "We aren't safe in our own homes. And the police seem to be doing little enough about it. I want to know when we can expect to hear this monster has been caught."

It took Rutledge three-quarters of an hour to calm them down to a point where he could ask questions. But the upshot was, he didn't think they had been involved.

Although afterward, Hamish was of the opinion that he would be satisfied if Edgar Peterson turned out to be the murderer. "But it's no' likely. He's all bluster."

Still, the guest list had had to be looked into, however much a waste of time it had been. Rutledge could have assigned the task to Constable Penny and Constable Burke, but it would have taken longer, and he had wanted to see the guests for himself and hear what they had to say about both victims and how the evening had been spent.

Where they were in agreement was the tenor of the party: all the guests had enjoyed their evening, and there had been no quarrels or upsets to mar Robin Hardy's homecoming dinner, even if he wasn't there in time.

No one mentioned Mark Quinton's angry departure. Either he'd had the good sense not to make his displeasure public, or Stephen Wentworth and Mrs. Hardy between them had seen to it that Evelyn wasn't embarrassed.

Back in Wolfpit, Rutledge went directly to the Templeton house. The staff, red-eyed still, and sniffing into handkerchiefs, seemed not quite certain what to do, or whether they ought to accompany him as he went through the house more thoroughly now, looking for anything that might offer a reason why its owner had been targeted by a killer. He examined the study again, and then Frederick Templeton's bedroom. He began to know the man as he worked. The estate books were in meticulous order, on a separate shelf that was within reach of the desk. Correspondence was in a drawer on the left, and accounts in the drawer below. He got to know the small but clear script as he searched, but when he discovered in the last drawer on the right a bundle of letters tied in black ribbon, letters from Templeton's wife, Rose, to him while he was in France, he put them back unread.

There were no surprises here or on the lines of leather-bound books that marched along the shelves. He scanned for *Gate keeper,* but there was nothing remotely resembling the words. A well-worn leather chair stood by the hearth, and on the table next to it was a decanter of whisky and a clean glass. The table on the other side of it held books that Templeton must have been reading, mostly to do with various aspects of farming. But there was also a handsome gramophone on a table by the window, and to Rutledge's amusement, there were popular songs of the day as well as classic pieces stacked beside it. The record on the turntable at the moment was "Roses of Picardy."

Rutledge quickly turned away. There had been a young Scots private with a fine tenor voice who sometimes sang softly in the evenings, and one of his particular favorites had been "Roses of Picardy." He'd been badly wounded in the second battle of the Somme, and died in an ambulance on the way to hospital. Often in the silence before dawn, Rutledge's men swore he still sang. By that time Rutledge himself had already begun to hear Hamish in the back of his mind, and he was certain they were all on the verge of madness.

Upstairs, in the master bedroom was a portrait of Templeton's wife in a very becoming gown of silver and midnight blue, and Rutledge could see that she had been very attractive. And very loved. In her dressing room her clothes still filled the mirrored closets, and there were quite beautiful pieces of jewelry in the tall slim chest next to her dressing table.

He was reminded of Evelyn Hardy's comments about going through the belongings of the dead, and closed the drawer he had just opened.

In Templeton's dressing room he found country clothing as well as evening dress and half a dozen suits from London tailors in Oxford Street. And although he lifted the shirts and handkerchiefs and under-clothing in the drawers, there was nothing that appeared to be hidden or, at the very least, kept out of sight. And then among the array of cuff links and shirt studs, at the very back, he found a photograph of a man in uniform. He was very young and very anxious, reminding Rutledge of the many raw recruits sent to the Front too soon. Turning it over, he looked for a name on the other side, but there was none. He went back to the photograph. A private in a Territorial Army that had been called up early in 1915, he looked nothing at all like Templeton. A nephew? His wife's sister's son? Rutledge put it back where he'd found it, and gave a last glance around the room before closing the door and walking out into the passage. And startled one of the maids hovering there in case he needed anything.

He asked where Templeton's Army trunk might be stored, and wound up in the attics, where it had pride of place at the top of the stairs. But it too held nothing of real interest. There was a small photograph of Templeton, six years younger, in the uniform of a Lieutenant, staring back at the camera with a serious expression. They had all had their photographs taken in uniform, officers and other ranks. Rutledge had given his to Jean in a silver frame. Templeton was older than most of the young men who had rushed to enlist. His was a mature face, early thirties, attractive in a way, with dark hair and a strong chin. What had this Lieutenant done in his war, to have risen to the rank of Major in four years?

"Survived," Hamish said bitterly, and it was true, so many deaths had offered rapid advancement to those who lived.

Nothing here that would point to his dying two years after the war had ended, at the hands of friend or foe.

Rutledge closed the trunk and latched it, then stood up to dust his hands and his knees. As he did, he glanced around the attic. The sun had gone in and there was very little light coming in the windows at either end. He noticed a plain wooden chair, silhouetted against the far window. Something about the way it stood there, in the middle of an open space, was sinister. Rutledge walked over to it, and looking up, saw that it was directly under one of the crossbeams of the roof over his head. In the chair, neatly coiled, was a length of rope, heavy hemp, the sort of rope that might be used to lash goods onto a wagon or tie up something in a barn.

Or form a noose.

It was Hamish who put it into words. "He didna' use it. But he had it ready to hand. When his wife died?"

"Yes. I think it's likely."

But why hanging, when there was a well-oiled revolver in his trunk, and a box of cartridges beside it?

Mrs. Cox found him sitting in Templeton's study, staring at the shelves of books. Five minutes later she came back with a tray of tea.

"You look like you could use it, sir," she told him, setting it on the desk in front of him. "Have you found anything that would tell you who killed Mr. Templeton?"

He thanked her for her thoughtfulness and added, "Sadly, no. Was anything worrying him, or was he angry with anyone? Had there been any trouble with the staff or a neighbor?"

"He'd been different after the war. Not something you could put your finger on. But I expect it was rather terrible out there. He never spoke of it, at least not to any of us. And he wasn't the sort of man to quarrel with anyone. Of course Mrs. Templeton's death was a shock to him. He said once that he hoped it wasn't his fault. But how could it have been? He wasn't here when she took ill, although he managed to reach her before she died. That was a comfort to her. Such a lovely lady she was too. You'll have seen her portrait? There in the master bedroom? It had hung in the drawing room, but he had it taken down and carried up to his room. He said he wanted it where he could see her the last thing before he closed his eyes at night and the first thing when he opened them in the morning. My only comfort has been that she went first. I don't know how she would have borne his loss."

There were good men in the world, he thought, like Wentworth and Templeton. Quiet, steady, going about their lives without trouble. Many of them men who had created the Empire. Men who had mapped countries, built bridges and railroads, brought law and medicine in their wake, and sometimes found a nameless foreign grave as their reward. Others had stayed home and opened bookshops and bettered the yield of corn or sugar beets, improved the bloodlines of cattle or sheep.

He finished his tea and left soon after, feeling a sense of failure. Where was the link between these two murders? Two very different men whose lives had ended in the dark, at the hands of a cold-blooded killer.

He wished he could find an answer.

Back in the village, it occurred to him that Mrs. Delaney lived alone, a widow. He turned toward her house, and told her what he had told Mr. Blake.

"I'm too old to change my ways," she replied. "And I can't think of any reason why anyone would wish to harm me. Besides, Mr. Rutledge, I'm not a man," she pointed out, smiling.

"You knew Stephen Wentworth very well," he told her, "and I still don't have any answer to give you about why he died. Or Templeton."

"I know, Inspector."

"Just—be careful."

She smiled. "If it will ease your mind, yes, of course. I will be."

He left her then. Walking back the way he'd come, he heard the telephone ringing in the bookshop as he passed, and unlocked the door in haste, racing to catch it in time.

But it was a call from Ipswich, a customer of the bookshop wanting to order a title. He put them off and hung up. Standing there by the telephone, he told himself it was too early to hear from Gibson or Haldane, but it didn't lessen his disappointment.

He was still there when the door opened, and Sergeant Penny stepped in.

"I saw you come in here. I thought I'd ask if there was any news?"

"Regrettably, none," Rutledge answered. "I've searched Templeton's house. He lived as quiet and steady a life as Wentworth did. People who are murdered usually have secrets."

"I don't know of any. There's the Army in Templeton's case, of course. He never talked much about his war. In November, on the first anniversary of the Armistice, there was a service of remembrance, and he was asked to say a few words about what it was like in the trenches in the last days of the fighting. And all he said was, 'It didn't matter how you died, I expect, but as the end of the war came nearer and nearer, dying was bitter. The lucky ones didn't linger. For some few, it was relief. I saw enough of death to last me the rest of my life, and I will not walk behind another cortege. Ever again.' And he sat down then, his head bowed. I don't think I'll ever forget that morning. We didn't quite know how to take his words, but then most people said afterward that he was still grieving for his wife. And what a pity it was that she was taken like that."

But Rutledge, listening to him, heard something else. What had happened to Templeton out there? Something must have done.

Penny was expecting a comment, and Rutledge said only, "All of us saw too much death."

He moved toward the door, and Penny perforce had to turn and leave as well. "What's to happen to the bookshop?" the Constable asked.

"I expect it will be sold, when the estate is settled. Someone else may be prepared to take it on."

"I hope that's true." He sighed. "I had taken to liking reading, myself."

Rutledge locked the door, then replied, "Did Wentworth ever recommend a book called *The Gate Keeper* to you?"

Penny scratched his chin. "I'm not saying he never did. But I can't recall such a book, not offhand." Then he turned to Rutledge, frowning. "Odd how that rings a bell. But I don't quite know why."

"Try to remember. It could be important."

"I don't see how."

"Nor do I at the moment, but you never know." He looked up at the sky. The clouds were gathering. "I think we may be in for a storm."

"Not like the last one, I hope. Rained for two days, with some flooding in the meadows."

"Keep an eye on several houses during your evening rounds if you will. Mrs. Delaney, Mr. Blake, and the two schoolmistresses."

Constable Penny rounded on him. "That's saying that this isn't finished, that we're likely to see more killing."

"I don't know that it's *likely*," Rutledge said, giving the impression that he'd been considering the question. He didn't want to put the wind up the entire village, and yet some precautions had to be taken. He had warned Mrs. Delaney and the solicitor, but he still wasn't certain enough to speak to the two young women. "But under the circumstances, we need to keep our eyes open."

Penny nodded. "That I'll do. Inspector Reed can let us have more men. He told me as much. Shall I send for reinforcements, just in case?"

"It would do no harm."

"Then I'll pass the word. Thank you, sir." Hesitating, he finally added, "Have you given any thought to an inquest, sir?"

"I have. At the moment, it will end in 'person or persons unknown.' I'd rather have someone bound over for murder."

Surprised, Constable Penny said, "There's that, sir." Touching his helmet, he hurried away, intent on duty, and Rutledge watched him go.

Hamish said, "If yon Inspector sends men to Wolfpit, they're likely to be his creatures, and willing to spy for him."

"Yes, I'd thought about that. But if there's another murder, it's likely Reed will try to persuade the Yard that I'm not the best man to deal with this. From the start, Chief Superintendent Markham had questions about the suitability of letting me take it on."

He was walking back toward The Swan. The sun had vanished behind that heavy bank of clouds, and the light was quickly fading. He turned to survey the village. And as he did, he glanced in the direction of the church. He saw the sexton watching from the gate into the churchyard.

Rutledge wasn't quite certain what it was about the man that disturbed him. It went beyond dislike, for there was something that drove the sexton. He wasn't convinced that it had anything to do with the two murders, but it was possible that he knew something—had seen something—or was aware of something that Rutledge didn't know. And had no intention of sharing it.

The sexton was the first to turn away when he realized that Rutledge had seen him. He walked on down the road without looking back, a studied arrogance in the way he moved.

Hamish said, "He's from Yorkshire. And so is Mrs. Wentworth. If she kens what he did there, blackmail might persuade sich a man to kill for her."

"An interesting thought." He changed direction and went to the police station where Penny was writing out his request for more men.

The Constable looked up from the sheet of paper before him as Rutledge came through the door, bringing a swirl of cold air with him. "Sir?"

How did you explain intuition? Or that Hamish had given him a thought worth pursuing?

"The sexton. Pace," Rutledge began, choosing his words carefully, "gives me the impression of a man with something on his mind. Or his conscience. I think it might be a very good idea if you asked him a few questions. He knows you, he might speak more freely."

Penny said, "What sort of thing, sir? I can't think what it might be."

Changing tactics, Rutledge said, "Perhaps he's seen something he might not feel comfortable telling Scotland Yard. For fear he may be wrong. And that's what is bothering him."

"He doesn't live anywhere near either victim, sir. What could he have seen?" Pace had never been a troublemaker. And that was how Constable Penny had classified him over the years: not someone he needed to keep an eye on. Or question, if there was a problem.

Rutledge himself, as a Constable patrolling streets in London, had done much the same thing, assembling information about the people living there. He passed a few minutes with dustmen and nursery maids, workmen and cabbies, greeted householders and their families, and kept an eye on deliveries, until he knew the routine and the habits of nearly everyone on his rounds. Anything untoward got his attention. It worked quite well as a way to keep the peace, but he'd learned quickly that it didn't always take into account that people were human and therefore not always predictable. Penny was a good man, but he had got comfortable with his patch, and that could be dangerous.

"Keep it in mind, please, Constable. Or if you'd rather, I'll speak to him myself."

The threat worked.

Penny nodded. "I'll make an opportunity, sir. Straightaway."

But Rutledge intended to make certain that Pace would prefer dealing with Penny rather than the man from London.

He consulted his rough map of the village and found the cottage at the outskirts that was marked with a *P*. He was fairly certain it belonged to the sexton.

Two could play at intimidation. He strolled from the police station to the church, paused there to stare up at the tower, then continued to walk on past the school and to the straggling end of Wolfpit. Ahead of him stood the small neat cottage he was after.

It was as plain as the man, the paint a weathered gray, without a single garden to offset its austerity. Behind it Rutledge could see a large patch of turned earth, fallow at this season, where Pace grew his vegetables when not attending to church duties.

He walked up the narrow path to the door and knocked.

Almost certain Pace was in the house, even though there was no lamp lit in the front room, Rutledge waited and then knocked again.

But no one came to answer the summons. He'd have been surprised if Pace had.

Rutledge turned and left. As he walked down the path to the road and headed back to The Swan, he could feel eyes on his progress almost to the school. From one of the windows of that cottage, Pace was watching him go.

Let Pace wonder, he thought, why the man from London had wished to interview him.

After an early dinner, Rutledge went back to the bookshop, lit the lamp in the small room where Wentworth usually sat to read, then began to search the shop again. He had nearly finished, coming up with nothing to show for the time spent on the task, when the telephone rang.

When he answered it, the switchboard wanted to know if he was Inspector Rutledge, and then put him through to the Yard.

Sergeant Gibson was on the other end of the line, and he sounded tired.

"There's been a development, sir. I thought you ought to know as soon as possible. There was another shooting reported to the Yard this afternoon. Happened in a small village in Surrey. Very similar to the one you reported there in Wolfpit. A man was walking home from the pub, it was shortly before closing, and the streets were empty. No one heard any altercation, just the shot, and when someone stepped out to investigate that, the killer was gone. Victim's name is Harvey Mitchell, sir, Doctor says the weapon was a revolver. Nothing was taken, the body left where it had fallen. Mitchell was a quiet sort, no known enemies. We've dispatched Inspector Stevenson to deal with it, at the request of the Chief Constable. It seems the Chief Constable was a friend of the victim."

"That should be my inquiry," Rutledge said, stifling an urge to swear. It wasn't Gibson's fault. There was no point in blaming him.

"Yes, sir, I mentioned that to the Chief Superintendent. But he felt that it was too far away to be connected to your murder. All the same, I thought you should be informed."

"There's been a second death here." He gave Gibson the particulars. "And very little to go on. I ought to be in Surrey. Were there witnesses?"

"No, sir, this was late, and there was a cold wind coming out of Wales. Not a night to linger outside. First a householder and then two men from the pub came out to see who was shooting, and that's when they found him. He was already dead, died on the spot. No sign of the killer. How he managed to get away is uncertain. The thinking is, it must have been a bicycle. Fast and silent."

"What do the police there know about Mr. Mitchell?"

"A solicitor, sir. In the war, serving in France. It was his clerk's birthday, which is what took him to the pub that night. As a rule, he stays in most evenings with his wife and three children. Well, the eldest has just turned thirteen. The Chief Constable is with the family now. The local man has been thorough, likely because the Chief Constable knew Mitchell."

Rutledge hesitated, and then asked, "Was there a small wood carving found somewhere near the body? Possibly an animal."

"Wood carving, sir? I'm not sure what you mean."

"Will you ask Inspector Stevenson to look out for it? Small, perhaps two inches high at most. Well executed and polished." But there wouldn't be, he told himself. It would connect Mitchell's death with the two in Suffolk. And the killer wouldn't want that. Would he?

"What does that have to do with the murder, sir? Did it belong to the victim, or the killer?"

"I'm not sure. Just—mention it to Inspector Stevenson, if you will. And keep me informed, Gibson. If Markham is wrong, then what I know here in Suffolk will matter."

"I will, sir. As for the other information you asked me for, I've not found anything I thought might be worth passing on. Have you considered a random killing, sir? It might suit the circumstances, in light of what happened in Surrey."

"I've considered it. It's still possible. But that may be what the killer wants us to think. Meanwhile, we can hope that Inspector Stevenson finds answers."

"Yes, sir."

"And while I have you on the line. There's a man named Pace here, but he's originally from Yorkshire. Oliver Pace. Older, lives alone, grows vegetables. Can you find out if he has any record of trouble there? Thank you, Gibson."

"Yes, sir."

He rang off. Rutledge put up the receiver, standing there, staring into space.

If the killer in Surrey was the same man who had shot Templeton, then he would have to own a motorcar. Train schedules wouldn't have put him there soon enough to find and kill Mitchell. He'd have had to change trains in London . . .

Hamish said, "Unless ye ken, he's already found his victims, already knows enough about them to be at the right place when they're alone and vulnerable."

It was true. How else could he have been waiting when Wentworth left the party that Saturday night? Or known when the solicitor's clerk would be celebrating his birthday in his local—and that Mitchell would leave the party early, unaccustomed as he was to late nights in a pub drinking? Templeton had had to be winkled out of his house with a request he wasn't likely to turn down. But the killer must have *known* that such an approach would work.

Why these three men? What had they done?

Pushing the questions away, he finished searching the bookshop. It had been a useless exercise, but Stephen Wentworth lived in a house where his parents might take it into their heads to appear at any time. And where there was a housekeeper who worked alone, without supervision, and she could indulge her curiosity whenever she chose. Hadn't she known the names of the women in Wentworth's life? Happenstance or opportunity?

And so any secrets, any pieces of his life that he wanted to keep to himself, would have had to be hidden here.

There appeared not to be any.

Hamish said, "Ye ken, this is a bookshop."

Rutledge went to the shelves and looked for any books on the subject of wolves, either in history or in real life. The only one he could find had to do with the history of domesticating dogs, which included a section on wolves and their role as ancestors to the breeds of dogs that the English kept by their firesides.

Well, then, if not real wolves, what about the little wooden ones? How did they figure into the decision to murder two men? Besides the fact that both victims lived in a village associated with wolves.

Were the wolves gate keepers in any mythology or religious stories? Searching his memory, he couldn't recall any such association.

In the end he blew out the lamp and left the bookshop, going back to The Swan and his chilly room. The fire had gone out, and he set about rebuilding it, all the while remembering a sentence in the book he'd just scanned.

Dogs that return to the wild will either starve because they have been too long accustomed to food in a bowl and have lost their hunting skills, or they will revert to their ancestry and in packs are no longer trustworthy . . .

But this killer didn't hunt in a pack.

13

He slept poorly that night, restless and drowsing by turns. When he did dream it was of the war, this time standing in the cold rain, water quickly filling the trench beneath his feet, staring at the hands of his watch as he waited for the signal to launch an attack across No Man's Land. The bombardment from the English artillery was to cease at four minutes before four o'clock, and the signal would come thirty seconds later.

It was going to be a disastrous attack, designed by HQ on the large maps covering the table while senior officers offered their viewpoints, but no one had looked out the window to see the sheets of rain coming down. For one thing, that made the black mud as slippery as ice, and for another, the distance his men would have to travel in the teeth of enemy fire was too far to charge in these conditions. Instead of a wave of men, there would be a jagged line as one after another they lost their footing, and the curtain of fire as they ran, intended to keep German heads down, would be more sporadic, allowing the Germans to kill at twice the casualty rate that had been predicted. But the artillery stopped firing on schedule, he could hear whistles up and down the line, and blew his own, sending men up the ladders, over the flattened wire, and into unexpectedly fierce resistance despite the heavy shelling of the German trenches. He realized almost at once that they were running headlong into a trap.

He began to shout at them to turn back, recalling them, as a machine gun opened up. And in slow motion, he watched them fall one by one: the middle-aged Sergeant, the two raw recruits who had just been sent forward, the Private who brought him his tea and shaving water every morning, the Corporal who went for the rum ration. He kept shouting, swearing at them, ordering them to come back, even as the bullet struck home, spinning him around, sending him into spiraling darkness.

He came awake with a shock, rising up in bed and gasping for breath. It was several minutes before he was completely free of the dream, his pulse rate slowing and his breath coming evenly again. Putting a hand to his head, just above his right ear, he felt for blood and then for bandaging, and touched only his hair, thick and dark. The wound had healed long ago . . .

Rutledge could hear Hamish mocking him, and fought to shake off the last remnants of the nightmare. Sitting on the side of his bed, his head in his hands, he waited for peace.

The next morning heavy clouds obscured the sunrise, and a cold misting rain greeted him when he stepped out of The Swan and looked up at the sky. He was just in time to see the two schoolmistresses begin their brisk walk toward the school, their umbrellas shielding their faces. Rutledge didn't follow them this time. He still didn't know if they were targets, but they were safe enough on the street, with children all around them.

He turned to look at the solicitor's office, and watched the clerk arrive to open the door. Blake must still be at home. Rutledge idly wondered if the heads of dead beasts filled the man's house as well as the firm's walls. It wasn't a pleasant thought.

He went back into the inn and ordered his breakfast, his mind on the inquiry that must be going on in Surrey. Had Inspector Stevenson even bothered to look for a carving? He was a good man, steady, but more than a little stiff-necked with Scottish pride. He might not have cared to have another policeman second-guess his search for evidence.

Hamish said, "It doesna' matter. Ye've enough on your plate here. Surrey can wait."

And Hamish was right. Except that it could mean that the killer here was already well out of reach south of London.

Rutledge called on Dr. Brent to ask what he'd found when he examined Templeton.

"Little enough. Like Wentworth, he was in good health. More's the pity, dying so young. Some scars from his war, of course, but nothing that would have shortened his life. Single shot, straight into the heart. Dead before he knew what had happened, very likely." He frowned. "That's interesting to me. Most people would fire at the chest, and there's a chance their shot would find the heart. If not, or if they were anxious or frightened, they'd break the ribs and hit a lung. They might even be lucky enough to strike one of the great vessels. But it's a haphazard business. Especially in the dark, when a man's wearing a heavy coat against the cold. It's possible this man, whoever he is, has had medical training. An orderly in the war. Much as I hate to suggest it, even a doctor. He seems to have known what he was doing."

"Interesting indeed," Rutledge said. "I'm also intrigued that he was satisfied to shoot to kill instantly. If it's revenge, there's usually a desire to make the victim suffer, to give him time to recognize why he is going to die."

The doctor reached across his desk for a pen, twirling it between his fingers. "Is that always the case?"

"No. But more often than not. Where is the satisfaction in a quick death?"

"Miss MacRae was with Wentworth," Brent pointed out. "Indulging in revenge would very likely mean having to kill her as well. And in Templeton's case, the killer was lucky no one in the house heard the shot. He couldn't have counted on that."

"Even if the staff had heard the sound and realized it was a shot, the killer would have been well away before they found Templeton."

"Well, yes, there's that."

"This killer wanted both men dead. Fast, efficient, and before Miss MacRae's shock wore off, he'd made his escape. It goes along with what you were saying about knowing how to place his shot. I wonder what's driving him, if it isn't revenge?" He frowned, considering the possibilities. A bookshop owner, a gentleman farmer, and now a solicitor . . . "It must be something they know, perhaps only in part. But if it was ever put together, this knowledge, it would endanger someone. And they have to be stopped before they realize what they have in common. It's the only thing that makes sense."

"God knows." Brent sighed. "Surgery hours have begun. There will be a line waiting." Then he said, "Anger. That might be what drives him. A fury so deep he's already lived with it long enough that it has burned cold."

Rutledge nodded. "Yes, you could have something there. It makes as much sense as my theory. Thank you, Doctor."

The morning was still young. Rutledge had purposely called on Brent before surgery hours began, and by now, most people would have finished their breakfast and begun their day. He had asked Mrs. Delaney for a list of people who might have known Templeton well enough to be helpful, and she had given him three names.

Returning to The Swan for his motorcar, he drove out to the house of Templeton's neighbor, a Mrs. Wilma Smythe.

She was a war widow who had been close to Templeton's wife, Rose, and she led him into her sitting room with the usual platitudes about a man's death. Before he could ask her about Templeton, she said, "She was such a lovely person, always volunteering wherever there was a need. She did what she could for the children who had lost their fathers, organizing them into what she called her helpers, sending them out to take a basket of food to one family or turn over the vegetable garden for another, whatever needed doing. It took their minds off their own sorrow, you see, and let them know that they weren't alone in their suffering."

He had a difficult time bringing her around to Templeton. "My husband liked him," Mrs. Smythe finally told him. "And he helped Tom with an irrigation problem. He even got down into the ditch with Tom and found the perfect place to set up a pump. Tom had been struggling with that field for two years."

Rutledge came to the conclusion that Mr. Templeton had avoided her. Her stock-in-trade was gossip, and she rattled on about Rose Templeton in terms that made him suspect she hadn't been as close to her neighbors as she claimed, although she had assured him that they were "dearest friends."

His next stop was at the home of an older couple who had been friends with Templeton's father. They lived on the outskirts of a village on the Ipswich road. Mrs. Farrow asked if he'd care for tea, but Rutledge thanked her and launched into his questions about the dead man.

They remembered the boy with affection, the man with respect.

"Did he have any enemies?" Rutledge asked George Farrow.

"Nice people don't have enemies. I don't think it was possible for anyone to dislike him. He was the last person to cause trouble. He and Stephen Wentworth reminded me of each other, in a way. They went about their lives quietly, never expecting too much of others, and never shirking their own duty."

But it was Mrs. Farrow who said, "Something happened to him in France. Not just the war, something that touched him personally. Rose saw it too, and we talked a number of times about what it might have been. There was a very odd letter that she showed me. All it said was, 'My God, they've got it wrong. So damned wrong. I'm ashamed.' She was quite surprised that it had got past the censors. We decided that they must have believed he was responding to some domestic issue his wife had asked about. But that wasn't the case at all. Rose was completely bewildered."

"Did he ever explain what he meant?"

"I don't know if she ever found out. When he came home on compassionate leave, she was dying."

"What happened to the letter?"

"I don't know. I told her to burn it, that he wouldn't want to be reminded of it when the war was over."

"Was there anyone who would have profited from his death?"

Mrs. Farrow answered him. "Frederick? No. I can't imagine how. George and I have known him since his fourth birthday. He was a good man."

"And the war? Was there anything there that might have come back to haunt him?"

"He never talked about his war," George Farrow spoke then. "I let it be known that I'd listen if he ever wanted to look back, but he told me he had put it behind him. For good."

Rutledge had known men who said much the same thing, and hadn't in the two years since the Armistice found a way to live with what had happened to them.

He didn't need Hamish, stirring in the back of his mind, to point out that he himself was one of them.

Rutledge's last call was on the Rector of St. Mary's in Wolfpit, Thomas Abbot, a tall slim man with a pince-nez that gave him the air of a Cambridge don. When Rutledge found him in the rectory, he was just finishing his sermon for Sunday, and he said, leading Rutledge back to the study where he'd been working, "How shall I find the words to express what we feel about the loss of two men like Stephen Wentworth and Frederick Templeton?" He indicated a chair by the fire, and sat down in the matching one himself. Behind him was a mahogany desk cluttered with books and papers and correspondence.

"I understood that neither of them were in regular attendance at St. Mary's."

Abbot smiled. "I don't count that as the only virtue worth noting about a man's life."

Rutledge returned the smile. "Indeed. Tell me about Templeton."

"He was a fine chess player. We have played at irregular intervals for some years now. Frederick even sent me occasional moves from the trenches. And we were evenly matched. Which made it all the more challenging."

"What were his other interests?"

"You must know the answer to that, if you've looked into his life at all. His work was all-absorbing. It began when he was a young lad and asked his father why one of their fields was not producing as well as others next to it. His father's answer didn't satisfy him, and he began coming in on market day and asking some of the local farmers how they dealt with similar problems. He brought in a new variety of apple, French as I recall, and started a small orchard. When it began bearing, he set up a cider press. It was the way his mind worked. See the need, find an answer, and when you have that answer, find a way to better it."

"What sort of officer was he during the war?"

"He knew how to handle men. Well, he'd had enough experience dealing with farmers and their tenants, some of whom still did things the way their grandfathers had done them before them. Judging from the letters he wrote, I'd say he was a popular officer. But after a time the endless killing and maiming made him bitter, and what he saw of the destruction by the Germans during their retreat made him angry."

Rutledge had seen it too, a land laid waste. The thinking was, it would slow the Allied advance, but much of it was nothing short of viciousness on the part of a vanquished foe.

Was this what Templeton had written about so passionately to his wife, in the letter that Mrs. Farrow had been shown?

Abbot was saying, "He came back a man who had seen the worst that men could do to each other, and it didn't help that his wife died of the Spanish influenza. I thought it would change him. Instead, he threw himself into his work with a desperation that was pitiable. I don't know that his death wasn't a release for him."

It was an interesting remark from a man of the cloth, but Rutledge had a feeling that the Rector was a realist, who didn't turn away from the truth.

And it gave him a better view of Templeton than anyone else had done.

Rutledge took the opportunity to ask about the sexton. Surprised, the Rector said, "He keeps to himself. I have wondered if his previous life was unhappy. But he's trustworthy and a hard worker. And so I leave him in peace."

As Abbot walked him to the door, he said, "Have you visited our church? Wool money, of course. It has the most exceptional double-barreled vaulting with angels. If you care about such things, you'll be glad you stopped in."

Rutledge thanked him and left.

Hamish said, "You havena' found what you were after."

"I don't think I'm going to. Not here in Wolfpit." He had left the motorcar at The Swan when he came back from calling on the Farrows, and he went to collect it, driving out to the Hardy house and asking to speak to Robin Hardy.

This time his quarry came to the door.

"The houseguests have all gone away. I can be seen in the company of a policeman," he said wryly.

"That's helpful," Rutledge said, and went to shut the door of the sitting room where the housekeeper had left him while she looked for

Hardy. "Have you heard that Frederick Templeton is dead? In very similar circumstances to the killing of Stephen Wentworth. Did you know Templeton?"

"Not well. To be honest I had no need to consider growing marrows and finding the right bull to improve my herd. My brother runs the estate his own way."

Rutledge studied him for a moment. "That's how he was lured out of his house. A request to inspect a prize bull."

"Don't look at me. I had no reason to kill him. And I don't know what I would do with said bull if I found *him*. My brother wouldn't listen if I brought in a dozen for him to choose from."

"What went wrong with Templeton's war? You were in France. You must have heard rumors."

There had been a subtle change in Robin Hardy's expression at the mention of Templeton's war.

"You were in France too," Hardy countered. "What did you hear?"

"I didn't know Templeton before the war. I never met him during it. I commanded in a Scots regiment."

"Did you now. I don't know how you managed the pipers. It was more than I could take, hearing them. Sent shivers up my backbone."

Rutledge wasn't about to be sidetracked. "I need to know. Two men are dead. I'd not care to see the number rise to three."

"Wentworth wasn't in France. He was on the high seas."

"Did Stephen Wentworth ever ask you about a gate keeper?"

Hardy stared blankly at him. "And what, pray, is a gate keeper?"

"I wish I knew." Rutledge went back to his previous question. "What happened to Templeton in France? He wrote something to his wife, something about being ashamed. What was that about?"

Hardy rose. "The poor man is dead. Let that die with him," he said roughly. "Besides, it couldn't matter here. Wentworth was in the North Atlantic. If you want to find their murderer, it has to be something that linked the two in Suffolk. Otherwise, it doesn't make any sense."

Rutledge stayed where he was. "If I find out why Templeton had to die, it could well explain Wentworth's murder too."

"Then it wasn't the damned war, I tell you."

Hamish said so clearly that the words seemed to echo around the sitting room, "It's no use. He willna' talk."

Rutledge got to his feet, nearly stumbling over one of the legs of his chair.

"Are you all right?" Hardy demanded. "You look like you've seen a ghost."

Rutledge almost laughed. Recovering as best he could, he said, "Sorry. A war wound."

Hardy said sympathetically, "I carry a piece of shrapnel near my spine. Sometimes it catches when I least expect it. The pain is little short of agony. But thank God it never lasts long."

Rutledge said, "No. Not long at all."

He left then, taking a deep breath of cold December air as the house door swung shut behind him.

Hamish had nearly betrayed him again. Rutledge was angry all the way back to Wolfpit.

A s he was slowing to make the turn into The Swan's rear yard, he saw a woman just walking through the inn door. He didn't recognize her and found himself thinking she might be Rose Templeton's sister and her husband's heir.

He left the motorcar and hurried in after her. She was standing at the desk, speaking to the clerk, and the man nodded in Rutledge's direction as he came through the door.

She turned to him. She was quite pretty, he thought, with fair hair and dark blue eyes. She was wearing a handsome blue walking dress under a coat cut in the latest style, and her fingers were smoothing the small handbag she carried with her.

He realized she was anxious.

"My name is Rutledge," he said, smiling. "How can I help you?"

"Inspector Rutledge?" she asked, as if men by that name were thick on the ground in Wolfpit.

"That's right," he replied. And to the clerk, he said, "Is there a quiet room where we could talk, and perhaps have tea brought in?"

The clerk led them down the passage that ran past the stairs, opening a door on his right. "There's no fire," he said.

"There's no need," she replied quickly, losing her nerve and turning to go.

But Rutledge was blocking her way. "Tea," he reminded the clerk, and ushered the young woman past him and into the room, shutting the door behind him but not quite latching it. That, he thought to himself, should satisfy decorum, if that was what was worrying her.

She stopped in the middle of the room and turned to him, her anxiety pronounced. "I shouldn't have come," she began, but she didn't quite have the courage to brush past him and leave.

"Perhaps not," he said pleasantly, "but now you're here, it's best to finish what you've begun."

"Alice was coming to speak to the milliner—she prefers her to our own—and I said I'd come. Just for the outing."

"Just so," he agreed. Then he added, "I've given you my name. Can you tell me yours?"

"No. Yes. I'm Carrie Reed." She said it in such a way that he knew she expected him to recognize it.

Not the sister then. Inspector Reed's bride.

"Yes, of course. And you've come to help us find out who killed Stephen Wentworth." He expected that to put her at her ease. Instead, she looked stricken.

"No. That is, I don't know anything about his death. I—I wanted—"

She froze as the door opened and one of the women from the kitchen brought in a tray with two cups and saucers, a pot of tea, a bowl of honey, and a jug of milk. "The kettle had just gone on the boil," she said cheerfully, and with a nod to Rutledge she disappeared, closing the door behind her.

He walked to the tray. "I've missed my lunch," he said quietly, and poured two cups, giving her time to collect herself.

When he held out a cup to her, he thought she was going to drop it, her hands were shaking so. But she got herself together, accepted it, and sat down in the nearest chair.

The room was cold, but they were both still wearing their coats. He took a chair on the far side of the table, and said, "You wanted . . . ?"

The tea nearly scalded her as she tried a sip, and she looked at him in desperation. He put a teaspoon of honey in it, and added milk without asking her.

"You wanted to know how Stephen Wentworth died." It wasn't a question.

She tried the tea again, and drank a little. It seemed to bolster her courage. "He won't tell me. I don't know why he should be so jealous. Or, yes, I expect I do. Once when we were courting, I told him that if he couldn't take me to a party, I'd ask Stephen to take me. I'd known Stephen forever. He was always in the bookshop when he wasn't away at school, but I'd never have done it. I'd have been so embarrassed if he said no. But I thought—I wanted to go very badly, you see. All my friends would be there. And my husband—well, he wasn't my husband then—was reluctant to take me. I knew what would happen, he'd go by himself and spend time with *his* friends, while I stayed at home. So I taunted him. I shouldn't have done it, it was wrong of me. I thought he'd laugh it off or dare me. I just wanted to have a bit of fun. And I couldn't very well go alone."

"And he's still jealous?"

"I had no idea how possessive he would be when I married him. I love him, I truly do, but he's wild sometimes."

"Has he ever struck you?"

She quickly rose to Reed's defense. "Oh—no, it's not that. It's just the way he questions me, wants to know everything. As if I'm a suspect and he's the policeman. But I'm not, I'm his wife. Still, he makes me feel guilty when I have done nothing *wrong*."

"That's not why you came to see me today."

"I can't ask him, you see. He'll start hounding me, wanting to know why it matters to me, if I'm still in love with him. But I need to know."

"He was returning from a party. Someone stopped his motorcar just outside Wolfpit, and when Wentworth got out, the man simply shot him and walked away."

The stricken look returned. "How do you know what happened? Was—was there a witness?"

"Do you think your husband killed him?" he asked gently.

"No. Of course not. No—" And yet she had come here, taking quite a risk. Mrs. Reed made an effort to change the subject. "I've always liked Stephen. He was nice to me. Not in any special way. I didn't see more there than courtesy. I was just the greengrocer's daughter, hardly someone he might care about. But it was lovely, when he was kind, and I enjoyed it. It made me want to be more than the greengrocer's daughter, and I worked in the milliner's shop, and learned something about clothes and how to do my hair. That's how I met Larry. He brought his sister to the shop to choose something for their mother's birthday."

When she paused to draw a breath, he brought the subject around to Stephen Wentworth. "Do you know any reason why someone would want to kill him?"

"He must have been mistaken for someone else. That's the only reason I can think of."

But Wentworth didn't look at all like Templeton. Even in the dark, someone coming face-to-face with him wouldn't have made that mistake.

"The problem is, you see, there's been a second murder. This time it was Frederick Templeton who was killed. In much the same circumstances."

Her mouth fell open. And then she seemed to rally, as if he had just proven to her that her husband wasn't guilty.

"He was? I didn't know—no one said anything—but why?" she asked disjointedly.

"That's what I'm here to discover. Did you know Templeton?"

"Well, I knew who he was. His wife often came into Georgine's shop. She was such a pretty lady and she looked quite elegant in hats. Sometimes he came in with her and helped her choose. They laughed together, you could tell they loved each other very much."

This is what a marriage ought to be . . .

He could hear the words as clearly as if she'd spoken them aloud, for it was there in her eyes, a sadness that recognized the state of her own marriage. She was too loyal to admit to it.

"Did you ever see anyone quarrel with Frederick Templeton? Did he have any enemies, anyone who might have worried his wife, because he was worried? Women sometimes—talk—while they're trying on a pretty hat." He'd nearly said "gossip."

Frowning, she shook her head. "The only time I ever saw him lose his temper was one evening in the autumn. Early October, that was. I was leaving the shop later than usual, because Georgine told me I might work on the design for my wedding veil after hours, and as I came down the street, Mr. Templeton was standing just outside the solicitor's, talking to Mr. Blake. I hadn't realized—they were keeping their voices down, you see, trying not to let the world and its brother know how angry they were. And by the time I saw it myself, it was too late to cross the road. Mr. Blake stopped in midsentence, tipped his hat to me, and Mr. Templeton turned quite abruptly, saw me, and raised his hat as well. I walked on past them, and I didn't hear anything else."

He kept his voice light, as if only mildly curious. "But you did hear something?"

She nodded. "Just a few words. Mr. Templeton had said something like 'I tell you, it's best to ignore it. What else can I do?' And Mr. Blake was starting to say something like, 'But it's wrong, don't you see?' just as he noticed me." She smiled deprecatingly. "I have a good memory. I can recall things people said and did when I was only a child."

"A gift," Rutledge agreed, then asked, "You never saw them quarrelling again?"

"I never even saw them together again."

"Thank you for coming and speaking to me," he said as she set her cup, still half-full, back on the tray. "It helps, when people are willing to cooperate with the police."

But that caused a new anxiety. "Must you—will you tell my husband I was here?"

He might have to, if there was anything to her description of the argument between Blake and Templeton. Blake had said nothing about it, which was also interesting. Still, he said, "You've come to me in confidence. I respect that."

Rutledge thought she was about to burst into tears of sheer gratitude. He saw her out and watched from behind the door, well out of sight, as she hurried across the street and turned toward the milliner's shop.

When he was certain that she had gone inside and no one would connect his departure with hers, he also crossed the street and went to Blake and Sons, hoping to verify what he'd just learned.

Mr. Blake, he was told by the clerk, was still in St. Albans, where he had gone to inform the heir to Templeton's estate of her brother-in-law's death.

"I was told not to expect him until tomorrow morning," he said, and Rutledge thanked him.

He stepped out and stood there by the road, debating with himself as he watched what traffic there was weaving its way through toward either Stowmarket or Ipswich.

Hamish said sternly, "You canna' go to Surrey. Ye canna' step into yon Inspector's inquiry."

Rutledge answered impatiently. "I'm well aware that it would be unprofessional. But damn it, it would help if I could know whether or not Surrey is related to these murders. If it is, then I'm wasting my time searching here in Suffolk. He's moved on, and that means that Stevenson won't find him either. He'll kill in Gloucester or Lancaster or even Yorkshire, and no one will think to look in Suffolk or Surrey for his earlier victims. By the time we've managed to put all the facts together, he'll be in Durham or Whitby. Or even in Scotland, where no one will expect him to be."

"Aye," Hamish answered him. "But if you discover what's behind these murders, ye'll ken to *look* in Surrey or Northumberland. Ye'll be ahead of him."

"I know that, of course I do. The problem is waiting to see if anything turns up in Surrey." He turned toward Templeton's house. He would speak to Templeton's housekeeper again in light of what he'd learned from Mrs. Reed. That would have to do until Blake returned from St. Albans.

But Mrs. Cox shook her head. She knew nothing about a quarrel between the solicitor and Mr. Templeton.

Although Constable Penny had taken statements from them, and he had read them, Rutledge took the opportunity to interview the staff, but as he expected, they had neither seen nor heard anything the night that Templeton walked down the drive to meet Mr. Young.

They had gathered in the kitchen, washing up after the meal and enjoying a quiet evening of their own, with Templeton expected to be away overnight. He could sense a feeling of guilt, that no one had ventured down the drive and found Templeton sooner.

The head housemaid, Sally Beddoes, said, "He sometimes went out to smoke, and then did the locking up. But it was Mrs. Cox who saw to it that evening, didn't she? The horror of him lying out there, all alone—it's enough to make you cry, thinking about it. I've had nightmares, truly. Are you sure he didn't suffer? Mrs. Cox told us it wasn't a lingering end, but then you'd know what Doctor had to say, wouldn't you?"

"No. He didn't linger. Even if you'd found him straightaway, it would have been too late. Tell me what you know about his service in France."

All they could tell him was the little his wife had felt she could share with them when his letters came. Small matters, a thank-you for a packet sent on his birthday, a reminder to look after their mistress in his absence, a word or two for each of them at Christmas. When he'd been wounded and in hospital, Mrs. Templeton had kept them apprised of his progress. But what else she had gleaned from his letters, what the censors had seen fit not to cut out, she kept to herself.

He thanked them and left soon after. He could see that while Mrs. Cox in her position as housekeeper had been of necessity aware of Templeton's comings and goings, and had often been told more than was usual after his wife's death, he hadn't confided in her, nor in any of the other staff.

It wouldn't have occurred to him to confide in them.

Returning to Wolfpit in a wind-driven rain that had come up while he was at the Templeton house, he could feel the winter cold seeping into the motorcar. He found himself thinking about Frances on her wedding journey and hoping that she had sunnier days. He'd tried to push any thought of the wedding out of his mind, and for the most part he'd succeeded. Not that he grudged her happiness. Not that he was jealous of it. But she shared her life with someone else now, and he would perforce take a different role. They had been close since the deaths of their parents, and this change left him feeling isolated, cut off. He couldn't be sure how much of what he told her now she would confide in her husband. Not that she knew about his shell shock—or Hamish. But she had always been there if ever he'd found the courage to speak of the war. Now she was not.

There was always Melinda Crawford, he told himself. But he knew he would never tell her, any more than he'd be able to tell Frances. Shell shock carried a stigma. And it didn't matter how many mentions in dispatches or medals he'd received, how well he'd served King and Country, it still branded him a coward. A man who lacked moral fiber, who couldn't be counted on by his fellow soldiers. It wasn't true, he'd let no one down but Hamish. But who would listen to any of that, once they knew?

He made a dash for The Swan's door, and arrived wet and cold. Rutledge went up to his room, opened the door—and came face-to-face with an angry Inspector Reed.

"Damn it, this is my room, and the door was locked," he said, incensed.

"What business did you have, questioning my wife when my back was turned?"

"Hardly questioning her," Rutledge retorted. "She came to call in at the milliner's with a friend." He had no idea how much Mrs. Reed had told her husband. "I've asked people who knew Wentworth the same question, whether he had enemies. I'm beginning to think you may be one of them."

For an instant he expected Reed to lunge at him. But the policeman got himself under control with an effort that was visible.

"Did she tell you that?" he shouted, fists clenched.

"Why should she? She's so much in love with you she's blind to what a bastard you are."

Whatever Reed was about to say, that stopped him. "*Damn you.*"

"It's time you put your personal life behind you and concentrated on dealing with two murders. Or I'll have you reduced to Constable."

"You can't do that."

"A word with the Chief Constable will be sufficient. Now get out of here, and find me a murderer." If nothing else it would keep Reed busy and out of his way.

Reed stared at him. "What did you say to my wife?"

"What did you expect me to say?" Rutledge countered. "That you're a fool? She probably wouldn't have believed me." He swung the door wide. "Out. Now."

Taking his time, Reed stalked past Rutledge with a look that could kill.

As soon as he was across the threshold, Rutledge shut his door with some force. And later, when he was in control of himself once more, he went down and had a word with the clerk in charge.

"Give Inspector Reed the key to my room again, and I'll have you locked up for aiding and abetting a trespass. Do you understand?"

"Yes, sir. He told me it was police business. Sir."

"Police business is conducted in the police station, not my room. Have I made that clear?"

"Yes, sir." The clerk looked frightened, and Rutledge regretted that he'd put the man in a difficult position, but he'd had enough of the Inspector.

But as Rutledge climbed the stairs back to his room, Hamish said, "He's no' Inspector Stevenson."

"I'm well aware of the difference," he retorted, and closed his mind to Hamish as best he could.

14

Rutledge spent an hour bringing his notes up-to-date, and when he'd finished, he sat there looking at them. A great deal of information, but it appeared to lead nowhere except to the fact that something was still missing.

He leaned back in his chair, trying to organize what he'd learned in a different way. What was unique about Stephen? Traveling to Peru?

That appeared to be a reaction to his broken engagement to Dorothea Mowbray. And the war had brought him back. But what had Wentworth done there? Where had he gone? Who had he seen there?

Had anything—anyone—from Peru followed him back to Suffolk?

It would have been easier to believe that if Frederick Templeton hadn't been killed soon after Wentworth's death.

The war?

But the two men had served in different branches of the military.

That left the bookshop.

To put it simply, a bookseller sold books. He ordered them from publishers and displayed them in a shop in order to attract buyers. Hardly a hotbed of criminal activity.

He was about to relegate that to the UNLIKELY list in his head when he suddenly recalled something he'd seen in one of his books as a boy. A pen-and-ink sketch of a monastery library where large hand-bound books were chained to tables. Accessible but not to be removed without permission.

Books could be valuable for more reasons than just their contents. Shakespeare's Folios, the Book of Kells in Ireland, the original Gutenberg Bible . . .

He reached for his hat and coat, made certain the bookshop key was in his pocket, and was halfway down the stairs when he realized that he hadn't locked his room door. It didn't matter.

The rain had let up, but only a little. Keeping his head down, Rutledge crossed the oddly shaped square and made his way to the bookshop. Letting himself in, he locked the door behind him, and without a light, found his way to the little room where Wentworth had done his orders and accounts.

He closed the door, found the lamp, and lit it. In the drawer of the desk were the orders that Wentworth had kept in a folder. He had already gone through them twice, first to see what they were and again to look for the title *Gate Keeper*. He had seen the names of the publishing houses, all well known and reputable. Most of these orders were to stock or restock the shelves. But what about people who had requested special titles? He'd come across a listing of those, he'd scanned them twice, and nothing had leapt out at him then. Besides, they were fairly recent. Where would Wentworth have kept records of past orders? These must exist, if only to keep the shop's accounts in good order.

Accounts.

On the shelf was what he was looking for. He groaned inwardly as he realized the accounts ledgers must go back through the years that Delaney had owned the shop. When he had scanned them sufficiently to establish the system, he was still no closer to finding the current year. It should have stood at the end—or the beginning. Instead, he discovered that Wentworth had set the current ledger in the middle of the long line, apparently because it was closer to hand at the desk.

Rutledge sat down in the desk chair and began to go through it, starting with January 1920. He could see that it was going to be a long night, because the names of buyers were interspersed with regular orders and the cost of keeping the shop open. Coal, oil for lamps, stationery, pens, ink, a new blotter, small diary, even the wages of the man who emptied the dustbins, all written in a stylish hand, neat and—thank God—in a dark ink that made them easier to work through.

The church clock was striking midnight when he reached mid-April, making notes of purchases as he went. Templeton, for instance, was a regular client, ordering books from Holland on irrigation and water management, from Italy on the care and maintenance of public fountains, from Austria on horse breeding. The solicitor Blake had ordered several volumes on jurisprudence, and the owner of the tea shop had asked for a French cookbook.

By now his shoulders were aching, but he soldiered on, finishing April and just beginning May when the telephone rang.

He raised his head, hearing the faint sound through the closed door. And then he was out of his seat and hurrying into the shop, praying that this was Sergeant Gibson with news from Inspector Stevenson.

The voice at the other end of the line was sharp with irritation.

"You're a damned hard man to find, Rutledge."

It was Haldane.

Rutledge swiftly reorganized what he'd been about to say, and replied, "This is the only telephone in Wolfpit. Sorry. I'm at the inn across the way."

"Yes, well, I have the information you were after. There's nothing in the career of Captain Wentworth that might lead to murder. His service record is excellent, and his superior officers thought highly of him."

Rutledge hadn't mentioned murder in his call to Haldane, but it must have been clear that murder was at the bottom of this request.

"Thank you. It doesn't make my task any easier, but I find I'm glad there is nothing untoward." There were already enough secrets in Wentworth's life.

"Templeton also has an exemplary service record. He rose quickly to Major because he was an excellent officer and a skilled tactician."

The man who had dealt only with vegetables and breeds of farm animals had hidden talents.

Rutledge was about to thank Haldane again when he went on, "There is no blemish on his record, of course. But I discovered there was an incident late in 1917 where he was a witness in a court-martial."

"Was he indeed?" Rutledge felt cold. "What was the charge?"

"Cowardice and desertion."

Dear God.

Rutledge said, keeping his voice steady with an effort of will that left him shaking, "Who was charged?"

"A young private soldier. When his batman was killed, Major Templeton chose Andrew Watts in his place. Hoping to protect him, I should think. Watts was a new recruit, and rather shy. Often the butt of jokes and taunting. Templeton thought he could make a difference, and took him on. But at the start of a dawn attack, Watts froze, wouldn't let go of the ladder, holding up others. The Lieutenant in his sector had to knock him down to make him release his grip. And he cowered in the trench while his company went out to fight."

Rutledge took a deep breath. That wasn't like Hamish. Hamish had fought with courage and intelligence.

He said, "And the upshot of the court-martial?"

"Sentenced to hang."

It fell into place. The words Templeton had written to his wife, surely just after the verdict had been sent down, the coiled rope on the chair in the attic. Even the photograph of the young soldier in a drawer in the master bedroom.

"Templeton tried to talk the Lieutenant out of bringing charges, but he was incensed and wouldn't hear of it. Templeton spoke in Watts's defense. But it did no good."

"What was Watts like? Where did he come from?"

"He was a farmer's son in Hampshire. Bright lad, according to his training reports. He told one of his Sergeants that he was interested in grafting, that's to say growing a better but weaker plant on sturdier root stock."

Rutledge knew what grafting was. Had Templeton seen Watts as the son he might have had, and tried to protect him? He'd failed, and Watts had been executed.

"Templeton, to his credit, insisted on being there when the sentence was carried out."

He had watched the young private die. And possibly had given him the courage to face hanging with some semblance of grace.

The man on the other end of the line added in a slightly different tone of voice, "The Lieutenant was a fool. Men broke. And healed. And did England proud."

Rutledge drew in a breath before he could stop himself. Had Haldane looked at *his* records? Was this his way of letting Rutledge know? But there weren't any records. Only what he'd told Dr. Fleming at the clinic. And Fleming would never allow even someone like Haldane to read them.

He realized, before it was too late, before he gave himself away, that there had been an Andrew Watts in Haldane's life. And Haldane was remembering. It was the first sign Rutledge had ever seen that the man was human.

"Yes" was all he could manage to say. And then he thanked Haldane.

There was silence for a moment on the other end of the line, and then Haldane asked, "I'd like to know. Is Templeton the victim? Or a suspect?"

"Victim. Someone shot both men. Wentworth and Templeton."

"Well, it can't be this lad's death that led to murder. Wentworth was at sea at the time."

"No. I am grateful for your help."

"Any time, Rutledge."

The connection was cut.

Rutledge stood there, still holding the receiver in his hand. And then he gently put it back.

He was no longer in the mood to sift through lines of ledger entries.

Walking back into the little office, he turned down the lamp, shut the door behind him, and went back to The Swan.

He was halfway across the street when he realized that he should have asked Haldane if Harvey Mitchell, the Surrey solicitor, had been involved in that court-martial.

It would have to wait.

H e didn't sleep well, and Hamish kept up a running battle in his mind, making it nearly impossible to close his eyes.

He could understand Templeton. He himself had fought one long, terrible night to persuade Hamish to change his mind before the next attack. Alternately talking to him across the flickering glow of a candle stub and trying to persuade him that his refusal to lead his men back across No Man's Land would not save them or Hamish himself. But the young Scot had had enough of death, of watching men die. He should have been sent back, but Rutledge had tried until the last possible moment to save him.

He knew how Templeton must have felt.

Only he, Rutledge, hadn't just watched Hamish die. He had delivered the coup de grâce with his own revolver.

T here was a fog hovering over Wolfpit in the morning. The bare tops of trees were ghostly in the soft light, and the tall spire of St. Mary's had disappeared completely. Condensate ran down the dining room windows like tears.

Rutledge asked for a pot of tea and drank it without milk or sugar, to clear his head.

He could think about Templeton and Andrew Watts more dispassionately this morning, and Hamish had already been at him over the possibility that Watts's family had been exacting a little private revenge. But unless they had mistaken Wentworth for Templeton, it was a rather far-fetched possibility.

Surely whoever this killer was, if he had gone to such lengths to draw out his victims, he would also have made it a point to see them on the street somewhere, so that he could recognize them when he was ready to question them.

Still, he understood now how Templeton's war had changed him.

Finishing his tea, he pulled on his coat and went out into the street. The fog was cool and damp against his face, and sounds were disembodied, confusing. He heard the clock in St. Mary's sound the hour, but it seemed to float over his head, surrounding him with no clear definition of the church's location.

Knocking at the door of the solicitor's firm, he expected the clerk to tell him that Blake was still away. Instead Danby nodded to him and informed him that Blake was in and just finishing some business with another client.

Hiding his impatience, Rutledge sat in Reception until an older woman, smiling and obviously relieved, came through the inner door, chatting with the clerk about trusts. When he had shown her out and closed the door behind her, he turned to Rutledge and offered to show him back to Blake's inner sanctum. But Rutledge said, "Thank you. I believe I know the way."

Blake was finishing signing some papers, and he looked up as Rutledge came through his door.

"Two minutes," he said with a wave of his pen, and Rutledge sat down, staring the rhino in its glass eyes. It was an enormous head. The desk had had to be moved forward several inches so that Blake could pass under the heavy jaw to reach his chair. Rutledge had never cared for such trophies, preferring the living animal in the wild to stuffed proof of nothing more than good aim.

Blake signed the last sheet, slid the papers into a folder, and set it aside for his clerk to file later.

"It was hell," he said without preamble. "I'd told Mrs. Gentry that I would be coming, because I didn't want to break such news over the telephone. And she thought it was something to do with the will, that Templeton had found someone he wanted to marry. We talked at cross-purposes for all of a minute before I could make it clear that Frederick Templeton was dead, and she was his heir. As it happens, her husband isn't well—lumbago—and she was afraid that she would be expected to move into the house here in Wolfpit. *That* was sorted out, and then she began to cry. I can most certainly understand why Frederick Templeton married the elder sister."

Rutledge said mildly, "The lot of the solicitor and the policeman."

"Yes, well, you didn't have to spend the night, so that you could explain the will all over again." He capped the fountain pen and set it in the dish at the edge of the blotter. "I hope you've come to tell me some good news. Although Danby didn't mention any arrests when I came in this morning."

"Why didn't you tell me about the court-martial of Andrew Watts?"

Blake's eyebrows flew up. "Who told you about that?"

"What matters is, it wasn't you."

"All right, I didn't think it was pertinent to your inquiry. It upset Frederick and we quarreled about it several times. He wanted to try to clear Watts's name, or else do something for the family. I told him it was unwise."

"He cared about Watts."

"I think he saw himself in the man. That same love of the land. But Watts wasn't his son, and someone should have seen to it that he was treated as a conscientious objector long before he ever reached the trenches. He wasn't fit to be a soldier. You know that was true in some cases. Before he enlisted, I don't think he'd ever traveled more than five miles from where he was born, and when he did, they gave him a rifle, taught him how to shoot it and drive a bayonet into a straw man. Then they shipped him to France. Once he got there, he didn't want to let the side down. But in the end, he broke. Good men did."

"His father could have found out who served on the court and tracked them down."

"That doesn't explain why Wentworth was killed. What's more, Frederick did his damnedest to stop the court-martial, and when that didn't work, he tried to have the sentence commuted on humanitarian grounds."

"All the same, I should have been the one to decide whether Watts was important or not."

"Well," Blake said, his voice bleak, "you know now. Does it change anything?"

"I don't know. I won't know until I'm closer to finding the killer. The question is, what else have you decided it wasn't necessary for me to learn?"

"That's it. That's all. I give you my word."

"Do you know if a man called Harvey Mitchell was sitting on that court-martial?"

"I was never given the other names. I think Frederick was too ashamed of them to want to name them."

Rutledge reached into his pocket and brought out the two small carvings of the wolves.

"Hello," Blake said, holding out his hand for them. "These are quite nice. How did you come by them?"

"That one," Rutledge said, pointing, "the one that isn't as well polished, was in a muddy rut just where Wentworth was stopped. The other one I found on Templeton's drive, not far from his body."

"The devil you say! But what on earth were they doing there?"

"That's what I'd like to know. The killer's calling card? An effort to throw us off the track? I can't believe it's coincidence."

"No," Blake said slowly, turning them on his palm. "Do you think it means the killer is here, in Wolfpit?"

"That's possible. Do you know anyone who carves as a pastime? No? Or they might have some significance to Wentworth and Templeton. Something they would recognize or might have seen before."

Blake gave them back to him, and he dropped them into his pocket again.

"This business is getting on my nerves," Blake said irritably. "I wish you could end it. When are you holding the inquests?"

"There's little enough information to do more than conclude person or persons unknown."

"That's true." Blake sighed. "Danby was saying that people are worried. They're keeping their children close and staying in of an evening themselves. Well, I can see why. They know damned little, just that there have been two murders, with the police at a standstill. You can't blame them."

It sounded like Inspector Reed stirring up trouble, Rutledge thought. Ignoring the comment, instead he said, "I can see from the ledgers that Wentworth often filled special orders for people, books they particularly wanted and couldn't find locally."

"Yes, I've gone to him several times myself. I don't get to London very often, and there are books on law that I'd like to have, references mostly. The world my father and grandfather knew is changing, and I need to change with it. I don't want to be labeled a country solicitor while my clients turn to larger firms elsewhere."

"What did he order for Templeton?"

"Books on irrigation and farming. As you'd expect. Although—" He hesitated. "It's probably not important. But there was a book that Frederick ordered late last summer. It was an older work, I have no idea where Stephen found it. A book on apple varieties, all the old ones from France and from abbey orchards here. It was quite lovely, actually. Stephen showed it to me. Folio, beautifully re-bound in cordovan leather at some point, and with the most marvelous drawings, all in quite amazing color. The trunk, the stems, the leaves, the blossoms, and then the fruit, carefully done. And wonderful old names, in medieval English or French. Pearmain was one, and Calville something or other. I really don't remember now. The point is, it came in with the post, and Stephen opened the wrappings to be sure it was what Templeton wanted. I'd dropped by, and he showed it to me. We locked up and we went to Stowmarket to dinner with friends. The next morning, the latch on the rear door of the bookshop had been broken, and the odd thing was, nothing was stolen except for that book on apples."

"Did he call in the police?"

"Yes, of course. But the book was never found, nor was the person who had broken in. Stephen finally managed to find another copy of the book. They aren't easy to come by—only a handful or so still exist, and those are in private collections. He was quite lucky, actually, but this one wasn't as beautifully bound. A pity. And there was some damage around the edges. Templeton was pleased, needless to say. Of course he hadn't seen the first one. Stephen suggested he could have his re-bound, to preserve it better. I don't know whether Templeton looked into that or not."

How could a book on apples lead to murder? But here at least was a connection where earlier he'd had none.

"You're certain you don't recall where Wentworth found the book?"

"Sorry. Probably from some library up for sale. Happened often enough after the war. Heirs dead, death taxes, estates broken up."

"You say it had been re-bound?

"Yes. Tooled leather."

Still, it made no sense.

He thanked Blake, and went from the solicitor's office to the bookshop.

He had a date now, and he began searching in the pages of the ledger that covered the month of August. But it was in early November that he found the first entry. It was not particularly helpful.

Stephen Wentworth had sent letters to several purveyors of rare books, asking if they could tell him who might own a copy for sale. One of them had written to say that he thought he could put his hands on a copy, and the upshot of that was a private sale, with the rare-book dealer acting as intermediary. Because Templeton had deep pockets, he hadn't quibbled over the price, and the book on medieval varieties of apple was bought for him.

When it was stolen, Wentworth had absorbed the loss himself, and after some trouble managed to find another edition in poorer condition but with all the pages intact. He made note of that in the margin of the accounts ledger, and offered the book to Templeton.

The matter was closed. The person who had stolen the original book was never caught. In early December, Wentworth had noted that the police in London had come to the conclusion that another collector had got wind of the purchase and had stolen the book. Rutledge was fairly certain Wentworth had chosen not to work with the local constabulary, for fear news of the theft would reach Templeton's ears.

He'd added that the police suspected that an employee of the book dealer had tipped off the collector, but there was no way of proving it. That had occurred in two of the smaller auction houses, and both prosecutions had ended in no conviction.

Rutledge went to the file in which Wentworth had kept his book orders and eventually found the name of the rare-book dealer in London who often handled Wentworth's special requests.

Using the bookshop telephone, he put through a call to the dealer, and after some persuasion, arranged a meeting with the man.

This meant driving back to London. Reluctant, Rutledge considered asking the Yard to send someone round to the dealer's shop, then realized that he must see to this himself.

But first there was Wolfpit to protect.

He drove to Stowmarket and found Inspector Reed in the police station.

"What brings you to call on us?" he asked sarcastically as Rutledge was ushered in by the Sergeant on duty. "Don't tell me you've realized you aren't the man for this inquiry?"

Rutledge sat down without being asked.

"Did Constable Penny request extra Constables for a few days?"

"Yes. I haven't decided whether I can spare them or not."

He stood up again. "Then I'll put my request through to the Chief Constable." He turned to go.

"All right, then. You can have Constable Talley and Constable Neal. But only for a few days. You'll be leaving me shorthanded as it is."

"Not for long. I've got my motorcar outside. Give them instructions to report to Constable Penny. I'll take them back with me."

"Here—" Reed began, rising as well.

"If you delay, and there's another death, I'll see that you take the blame for it," Rutledge said shortly, and left.

Fifteen minutes later, the two Constables came out to meet him, and he took them to their respective houses to pack what they needed.

He was returning to Wolfpit later than he'd wanted, and it took him another hour to settle in the two Stowmarket Constables.

With a thermos of tea beside him, Rutledge finally turned the bonnet on the road out of Wolfpit and set out for London.

He arrived late, but slept in his own bed. Sorting through the post the next morning, he found a note from Frances, mailed from Calais.

Opening it, he pulled out the single sheet and read it.

Darling Ian,

Thank you for everything. It was such a perfect day, and I'm happier than I ever thought I could be.
   My dearest love,

Frances

The words had been dashed off in haste, but he found himself smiling as he put the note back into the envelope and took it to his sitting room. Opening a drawer in his desk, he set it inside, then went back to shave and dress for his meeting.

The book dealer's shop was in the City, a narrow building not far from St. Clement's, but he owned all four floors. It was closed because this was Sunday, but Matthew Williamson had not had a problem with meeting him this morning. Every available surface seemed to be crammed with books. Rutledge found himself thinking that it was a far cry from Wentworth's shop, where the shelves were arranged to give a sense of light and space.

He was taken up two flights of stairs to a room in the back where there was the windowless office of Mr. Williamson.

The man behind the cluttered desk was in his early fifties, thin and balding. But his dark eyes were sharp with intelligence—and curiosity—as he stood up to greet his visitor.

"Mr. Rutledge. You told me that this was urgent business to do with Stephen Wentworth's loss of the book we sold to him." It wasn't a question.

"Yes, I represent Mr. Wentworth. It's imperative that I speak to the person who owned the book that was purchased by Mr. Wentworth for one of his customers. There's new information that may show that the previous owner is in imminent danger. I'm here to ask you for his name. You were the intermediary in the sale."

"I was. The owner wished to remain anonymous."

"I am sure this is true, and I'd be willing to accept it if there wasn't an urgent need."

"You haven't told me what that need is."

Rutledge smiled. "No, I haven't. The problem is, I can't prove what I'm about to tell you. But I feel strongly enough about this that I've driven all the way from Suffolk to ask for your help."

"I am in the business of selling books for people who have personal reasons for parting with rare treasures. A death in the family, a financial loss—it varies. Most of them wouldn't care to have such information made public knowledge. And I will lose my best source of income."

"I understand. But two people who have been associated with this book have been murdered."

It was Williamson's turn to smile. "Are you suggesting that a book on medieval apples is cursed? That's rather far-fetched."

"It's not so far-fetched, if you stop to consider that someone stole the book from Wentworth's shop. Perhaps it's not so much a curse as someone else's greed. Whatever it is, I need to find the original owner and learn why that book is far more valuable to someone than the price Wentworth paid you for it."

"You said that two people were murdered. In Suffolk?"

"Yes."

"What were their names?"

"Wentworth himself was the first victim. The second was the man for whom the book was purchased. Frederick Templeton."

"How did they die?"

Rutledge told him.

Williamson was silent for a long moment, and Rutledge thought he was debating with himself whether or not to tell him what he wanted to know.

Instead he asked, "Exactly who are you, Mr. Rutledge? You tell me that you are here representing Stephen Wentworth, and then you tell me that Stephen Wentworth has been murdered."

"An inspector at Scotland Yard."

"May I see some identification?"

Rutledge passed it across the desk, and Williamson studied it carefully before handing it back.

What he said next left Rutledge speechless.

"I'm afraid you're too late, Inspector. I don't know who owned this book before it was sold to Wentworth. And that is the truth. The sale was handled by this person's solicitor. His name was Harvey Mitchell, and I have been told that he was killed earlier this week."

15

Rutledge's first reaction was to swear.

Inspector Stevenson's inquiry.

And he'd told Sergeant Gibson that it should have been his.

But more important than whose inquiry it should be was the fact that Harvey Mitchell was dead and couldn't tell him who had owned this godforsaken book and why three people had had to die because of it.

Williamson was saying, "I can see that you didn't expect this news. But I'd have thought that if you are indeed with the Yard, you'd have been aware of Mitchell's death."

"I am aware of it," Rutledge said. "It wasn't thought to be connected with my inquiry, and so it was given to another Inspector at the Yard. It will save time if you will tell me where in Surrey I can find Mitchell's firm."

"It's a small village by the name of Singleton. It's not very far from Guildford. Are you certain that this book is the reason for three deaths?"

"Not at all certain. But now I have a feeling that it isn't the book itself so much as what it must represent to someone. How old is it? Do you know?"

"Sixteenth century. As people were building grand manor houses instead of castles, there was an upsurge in interest about gardens, parks, orchards, and the like. Beautifying the surroundings rather than fortifying them, if you will. This book isn't all that rare, there must be close to twenty copies still extant. But it *is* quite a treasure. Unfortunately, several copies were unbound and the illustrations framed for individual sale in the early 1800s, reducing numbers even further. The survivors as it were are in private hands and seldom come on the market. That brings us to a different kind of rarity, the rarity of opportunity. I was fortunate to find two books for Mr. Wentworth, but only because the sellers were in need of funds. Indeed, the seller of the original copy Mr. Wentworth purchased asked for assurances that this copy wouldn't be destroyed."

"What do you think became of the book? Why was it stolen from Wentworth?"

He smiled again. "That's your task, isn't it? You're the policeman. But if you find the book again, I'm still interested in buying it, if the original owner is agreeable. This time not for any of my clients but for my own collection. I really was of two minds about letting Wentworth have it. It is a handsome book in a quite lovely binding, and I must tell you I was not happy when he told me it had been stolen."

Testing the waters, Rutledge said, "Mr. Templeton's copy may soon be on the market as the estate is settled."

Williamson thanked him, saying, "I will keep that in mind, but only as a last resort. I fancied the other copy."

For an instant Rutledge wondered if he had had a change of heart and had stolen the book himself. And then decided it was unlikely. Williamson's reputation depended on his honesty.

He said, "If you had kept it, perhaps three men would still be alive."

"And I might not be," Williamson replied dryly.

Rutledge left then. By the time he'd reached his motorcar, he had already debated with himself about going to the Yard and explaining to Sergeant Gibson the connection between Suffolk and Surrey. But he had a feeling that he would only waste time, and Chief Superintendent Markham might still refuse to allow him to interfere in Inspector Stevenson's inquiry. He knew, if the Yard didn't, that he wouldn't learn what he needed to know through secondhand accounts.

And so he set out for Surrey. If he was careful, he might get in and get out without Stevenson being aware of it.

"That's all well and good," Hamish said, "but if yon solicitor is deid, how do you propose to find out where the book came from?"

Rutledge took a deep breath. "His clerk. The one who celebrated his birthday the night Mitchell was killed. He might be able to help me. Surely if Mitchell acted for a client, there will be a record of it. Failing that, there's his wife."

"Ye ken, yon book was re-bound."

"Yes, I thought of that as well. Perhaps it was what was taken off—or what was put on—at the time that makes the book so valuable."

"I do na' ken why."

"Neither do I," Rutledge answered, and settled himself for the drive out of London and into Surrey.

The solicitor's office in Singleton was smaller than Blake's in Wolfpit. But then the village was smaller as well. Relatively prosperous, it clustered around the main road from London and boasted three inns, one small church, and a pretty square. Just outside the churchyard wall were the stocks, and the police station appeared to be nearly as old. Rutledge left his motorcar by the church before walking on toward his destination. He was fairly certain Stevenson could recognize it.

Rutledge had just found the solicitor's door when he saw Inspector Stevenson stepping out of the police station. There was a lamp burning in the window, and he had been about to knock. He reached for the handle and his luck held. The door opened and he got himself inside before Stevenson turned his way.

The Reception rooms were done up in a staid green wallpaper, with prints of private gardens in Cambridge colleges. Looking at them, Rutledge realized that they must have been plates from an illustrated book, taken out and framed. He saw then what Williamson had meant, that they belonged between the covers of a book rather than in frames on a wall.

Still, they were better than the stuffed heads surrounding Blake's desk.

Mitchell's clerk came through an inner door, nodding to Rutledge and asking if he could be of assistance. He was in his fifties, with broad shoulders and a quiet manner. But the tiny, spidery veins spreading across his nose suggested to Rutledge that he enjoyed his drink.

"We are closed, I'm afraid. A death in the family," he added apologetically. "But I will do what I can, in the circumstances."

"I've been notified that Mr. Mitchell is dead," Rutledge said with a sympathetic smile, "but I'm also dealing with a death in the family, and I'd like to find out about a book that Mr. Mitchell sold for a client. I'd like to ask the client if he or she would care to have the book returned. I understand Mr. Mitchell worked through a dealer in rare books in London. Williamson is his name."

He could see a fleeting look of recognition in the clerk's eyes, and knew at once that he'd come to the right source.

But the man said firmly, "Mr. Mitchell's death is being investigated by the police. I've been asked not to discuss our firm's affairs with anyone."

Rutledge groaned inwardly. He'd have done precisely the same thing in Inspector Stevenson's shoes, and that was the frustration. He couldn't fault the clerk for following orders.

"What's your name?"

"Broughton, sir."

"Thank you, Broughton. I'll speak to Inspector Stevenson myself."

He left, and began to search for Stevenson. He wanted to avoid the police station if he could, and so he walked up one side of the High, and down the other, glancing in shop windows. He was just coming to the slight broadening in the road that was euphemistically called Market Square when he spotted his quarry stepping out of the bakery with a pork pie in his hand. He'd bitten into it before Rutledge could catch him up, and when he heard his name called, he turned with a frown, as if resenting being disturbed at his lunch.

"What is—oh, hallo, Rutledge. I wasn't expecting you. Sent by the Yard, were you, to tell me to get on with it? Well, so far I've hit a stone wall." There was still a faint hint of his Scottish birth in his *r*'s, reinforced by his red hair and freckles he'd never outgrown. His green eyes were wary.

Rutledge said, "Is there somewhere we might talk quietly? Preferably not at the police station."

The frown returned. "I don't like the sound of this."

"Nothing to do with your inquiry, I assure you. What brings me here is one of my own."

"Does it indeed?" He finished the last of the pork pie and wiped his fingers on a handkerchief. "There's a bench in the churchyard. A memorial to someone who died in the Boer War. We can talk undisturbed there."

He led the way to the churchyard surrounding the rather simple stone church with its squat tower. The bench was beside a flourishing yew tree, the only thing still green to be seen. They were out of the wind as they sat down in its shelter. Services had ended. They had the bench to themselves.

"All right, tell me," he said briefly.

Rutledge had had time to consider how to approach his request, and he'd come to the conclusion that until he knew more about his own search, it was best not to connect it in any way with Mitchell's murder.

"I've got two murders in Suffolk. And the only link I can find between them is a book. Yes, I know," he added, seeing Stevenson's expression of disbelief. "But it isn't an ordinary book. It's sixteenth century, and while it's valuable, it isn't worth a young fortune. It disappeared in November, which is why I'm interested in finding out more about it. I just came from London where I spoke with the rare-book dealer who acted as intermediary. And he told me that the anonymous seller's representative was his solicitor. Who happens to be your victim, Harvey Mitchell."

Stevenson had listened carefully. Now he said, "Do you think his death might be related to this book? I find that hard to believe. I haven't come across any connection with Suffolk, not so far."

"The book wasn't his," Rutledge pointed out. "It belonged to a client. I'd like to find that client and ask him if there was something about the book that I haven't been told." Even to his own ears the excuse sounded lame. He wondered how Stevenson would take it.

He'd stirred, crossing one leg over the other, as Rutledge explained. Now he said, "What's the book about?"

"Apples," Rutledge said firmly. "It's a guide to medieval varieties. One of the dead men was a farmer interested in such matters."

Stevenson grinned. "My God, Rutledge, you do have a strange inquiry on your hands. All right, I'll have a word with Broughton. But limit yourself to apples, mind you."

It was a polite warning not to meddle in other matters.

Rutledge said, "I wouldn't think of it."

Fifteen minutes later he was seated in the clerk's small office, repeating his reasons for coming. Stevenson had left after giving Broughton his permission, but Rutledge was still circumspect.

He explained again about the book, although he was certain the clerk hadn't forgot what he'd said earlier.

"I remember the transaction, sir," Broughton said.

And Rutledge had been certain he would.

"It's a very personal matter, and I ask you to be careful in approaching the seller. She was reluctant to part with the book, but it was all she had to sell. She lives on a pittance of a pension that has shrunk to almost nothing over the past twenty years."

Surprised, Rutledge repeated, "She? Mitchell's client was a woman?"

"She was governess to a family somewhere north of London. She's never said where. She left their employ in October 1899, and was given a pension, even though she was still quite young. Twenty-six. She had been ill, and the family was concerned that she wasn't strong enough to resume her profession." He cleared his throat. "What they didn't know was that she was pregnant when she left. The father unknown, but there were two young men in the house at the time, and several footmen." There was a defensiveness in his tone now, as if he was prepared for Rutledge's disapproval.

"Go on."

"Her parents were still living here in Singleton, and she came home to them. There was gossip at the time. One of the sons of the family—the younger one—visited once or twice, to be sure she was all right, but she asked him not to come again. On his last visit, he brought her a gift. The book on apples. She had been fond of it, and had used it to teach his young sister her lessons in art."

"You seem to know a great deal about her past," Rutledge observed.

"I lived nearby. I would have married her if she'd have me. In spite of the boy."

"Go on."

"She needed money to pay her son's university fees. The bank that had made her a loan was calling it in. And she came to Mr. Mitchell one day and asked him to sell the book for her. She was afraid that if she tried on her own, she might be cheated. That was in the summer, and Mr. Mitchell had some difficulty finding the proper dealer. And then one of them wrote him to say there had been an inquiry about just such a book, and should the dealer pursue it. He was willing to pay any sum.

Mr. Mitchell said yes, funds were sent to us through his bank, and he posted the book to the dealer. We discovered through the bank that the buyer was a Mr. Wentworth in Suffolk."

"Mr. Wentworth was murdered last weekend."

"Good God," Broughton said blankly. And then, "Have you caught *his* killer?"

"We haven't. I'd like to speak to the owner of the book."

"I've told you all the details. I don't see any reason to disturb her."

"Nevertheless."

Rutledge was adamant, and the clerk did his best to dissuade him, but when they reached an impasse, Broughton said, "I shall have to ask if *she* is willing to speak to you."

They left it there, and Rutledge went to find a late lunch. He had been sorely tempted to follow Broughton, but he kept his promise to come back to the solicitor's at four o'clock. It would delay his return to Suffolk, but there wasn't much he could do about it.

He was just finishing his meal when Inspector Stevenson, walking past, glimpsed him in the window, and turned around to the door.

Coming across to Rutledge's table, he said, "Any luck with Broughton?"

"He's gone to speak to the seller now. Apparently there's a desire for anonymity on the seller's part."

"Well, if it was a matter of shoring up the family's finances, that's understandable. One doesn't want his neighbors knowing about problems of that nature. How was the ham? I'm starved."

He'd eaten a pork pie an hour ago. Rutledge thought he was intent on keeping an eye on him.

They talked about the Yard, about motorcars, and about the war, always careful not to find themselves discussing inquiries.

Rutledge was relieved when he could excuse himself and return to the solicitor's.

He half expected Stevenson, who had all but wolfed down his own meal, to insist on coming as well.

"She doesn't want to see you, sir," Broughton told him as he stepped through the door. "I'm sorry, sir."

He had found the seller. Hamish was telling him that it was enough. But Rutledge had learned long ago that tenacity sometimes paid dividends.

"I intend no harm, Broughton. But if Wentworth was killed because of that book, then I must find out why."

"I've never heard of someone being murdered over a book, sir."

Exasperated, Rutledge said, "If I must, I'll have the police here in Singleton knock at every door in the village until we find this woman. You've told me enough about her that I could give them sufficient information to recognize her when they find her."

Cornered, Broughton said, "No, sir, that's not necessary. Let me try again, and see if I can persuade her."

"That's no idle threat, Broughton," Rutledge warned him.

This time he waited in the solicitor's office, tempted to pore through the boxes arranged so neatly on the shelves until he found the right client.

Finally Broughton returned, and this time he wasn't alone. A very attractive woman in her forties came with him. She was dressed nicely but not fashionably, her dark hair, still untouched by gray, swept up from her face in a prewar style. There were signs of tiredness around her blue eyes, and she appeared to be upset.

Broughton didn't introduce her, except to say, "This is the owner of the book in question." It was clear he wanted to stay, but Rutledge ushered him out of the room and firmly closed the door in his face.

He came back not to the solicitor's desk but to the chair beside hers.

"I'm so sorry to put you through this, but there are very good reasons. Otherwise I wouldn't have insisted on seeing you." He kept his voice level and unthreatening. "I'm in a quandary, you see. There have been two murders with only one connection between the two men. Your book on medieval apples. I can't think why it should matter enough to kill for it. Perhaps you can tell me."

"There's no reason, absolutely none, for that book to lead to murder," she said, facing him squarely, her gaze meeting his. "I sold it in good faith. I needed the money." It was a hard admission to make, but she admitted it, and dared him to doubt her.

"I understand you have a son."

She was suddenly tense. "He has nothing whatsoever to do with this matter." But the anxiety in her voice was noticeable.

Rutledge found himself wondering if her son could have been the killer. Searching for his mother's book? It had gone missing nearly a month before . . .

He said, "Tell me about how you came to be in possession of this book. Was it always yours, something you'd inherited from your parents?"

"No. It was a gift. From someone I didn't particularly like. But I loved the book, and it brought back—memories. I couldn't refuse it."

"It was a rather expensive gift," he reminded her.

"Yes. I'm well aware of it. And it was foolish of me to accept. But I was young, vulnerable, and I loved it," she said again.

"Was the giver of this gift the father of your child?"

Her face flamed. "Great God, *no*."

Rutledge believed her, although he could hear Hamish warning him about her.

Silently, he told Hamish, *If she lied about everything else, she didn't lie about this.*

He said, "I'm sorry. It was a natural assumption, given the value of the gift."

"I've told you. It meant more to me than its value. I was grateful for the kindness."

Rutledge wasn't quite sure what to make of her. There was something about her that was intriguing. She might be the mother of an illegitimate child, but she felt no shame, she faced him as an equal and made it plain that she was not the sort of woman he seemed—in her mind—to be suggesting.

"Do you know the name of the father of your child?" he asked gently.

Anger filled her eyes. "I'm not a slut, Mr. Rutledge. I've known only one man, and I was married to him. I've not told anyone else that, not even my parents. I couldn't prove it—he was dead, he never saw his son. But I want you to understand that I have done nothing wrong. The book was mine to sell—or not, as I pleased. I have broken no laws, either of God or man, and I will not be treated like this."

She rose to go, but he rose as well, stopping her. "Please. I meant no insult. It was pity, I think—"

But that was wrong too. He knew the instant he said the words that it was wrong.

"What do you want, Mr. Rutledge?" she asked, her voice husky with her anger, her eyes blazing.

And he thought, *Whoever her husband was, he was a lucky man . . .*

When he didn't answer her, she demanded, "Is it the money? Or the book you've come for? Have the decency to tell me, and I will settle this matter right now."

Rutledge stared at her.

She carried on, buoyed by her anger. "I've no proof, of course. But I am not lying about this. The buyer didn't wish to keep the book after all, but he was generous enough to send it back to me, and allow me to keep the money. I was in need of money just then, and I was so very grateful. I didn't question his kindness. I accepted it. I don't quite know how he learned of my situation, or what the book meant to me, why I had to sell it. Perhaps it was wrong of me, perhaps I should have written to him and told him I would return the money. But I didn't have it. It had gone to pay the bank over my son's school fees at Oxford. And I was already worrying about where I could find more. But I couldn't—I wouldn't—sell the book again."

She was about to walk away, but he touched her arm and said, "Forgive me. I knew none of this, I haven't come for the money or the book. I am trying to find a murderer. And your book appears to be the only connection I've found between the two victims."

"Who were they?" she said, stopping in the middle of the room.

"The bookseller who had been seeking the book on medieval apples, and the client who'd asked him to search out one."

"Small wonder you think so ill of me," she said, the anger draining away. "Do you think I killed these men? But why should I? I had the note telling me that I was free to keep both."

"Do you still have that note?" he asked.

She reached into the pocket of her coat and drew out an envelope. "This was in the package with the book. It was posted from London."

He took it from her and pulled out the single sheet of paper inside.

Hamish was already certain. "That's no' the handwriting of the Suffolk bookseller."

God knew, Rutledge thought to himself, he had spent enough hours on the ledger. Wentworth hadn't written the note.

And he thought, studying it carefully, that someone had attempted to disguise his handwriting.

His mind was working furiously now. The book had been stolen from Wentworth's bookshop. And he had informed the London police. If for some reason he'd wanted to return the book, he had only to do it, and tell Templeton anything he chose to say—the book was damaged in the post, it was not a fine copy, as it had been advertised to be. Besides, the ledgers listed a sale. And a loss. Not a return.

"Please sit down," he asked her gently. "I have this backward, I think, and I've only just realized it."

She glared at him, unconvinced.

"I don't want the book. The man who did is dead, and it would do no good now to take it back from you. As for the money, the man who paid for it is also dead, and he was wealthy enough that no one will care about the cost of a book. Even that book. He had already posted it as a business loss."

Slowly, warily, she came back to sit down.

"Go on."

"I want to know *why* that book has cost the lives of three men. Help me answer that, and I'll go away."

"You said three men."

"I've reason to believe that Harvey Mitchell was one of them."

"He was my solicitor. And a friend. You can't be serious, that he was killed because of this book? No. Scotland Yard has sent someone to Singleton to look into his death. They've been searching through his files to see if there's something in there. That's what Mr. Broughton told me."

"And there may be." He reached into his pocket and pulled out one of the little wolves. "Ever seen anything like this before?"

She sank back into her chair, her face pale. "Where did you get that?"

"I found it near where Wentworth—the bookseller—was killed. You recognize it, don't you?"

"I—this makes no sense." She reached for the little carving, turned it over in her fingers, smoothed the beautifully carved fur.

"The village where the bookseller and the book buyer were killed is called Wolfpit."

She didn't answer, still looking down at the little figure. Rutledge would have sworn it was important to her. But then she handed it back to him, and said, "No, I'm—I'm wrong, it's just that it reminded me of something from a very long time ago."

After a moment, Rutledge asked, "I've driven a long way to find out about this book. May I at least see it?"

He expected her to refuse, it was there in her face. And then she shrugged. "I expect there's no harm in it. But I'd rather you didn't come to my house. It will cause talk." She added wryly, "I've fought very hard for my reputation. I've told lies and pretended not to care and cried myself to sleep when it hurt too much. The only male who comes to see me is five years old, and his mother is a friend."

He laughed, as he knew she expected him to, and waited patiently for her to go home, fetch the book, and come back. He wondered if she would . . .

Ten minutes later she opened the door and walked in, a large object swathed in a scarf carried in her arms. He sprang to his feet and went behind her to close the door while she carried her burden to the desk. There she began to unwrap the scarf.

Rutledge watched as a beautifully bound folio-size book appeared.

It was bound in exquisitely tooled cordovan leather, the title in gold lettering. She stood back, an expression of love transforming her face.

Reaching out, he turned several pages, until the plates appeared.

He drew in a breath. He'd been told what was in the book, but the drawings were stunningly beautiful. The text was in Latin, but the color was as fresh as if it had been painted yesterday. Protected from the light, the illustrations seemed to glow. The bark, the parts of the flower, the shape of the leaves were masterly. But the skins of the fruit, from dark crimson, nearly the color of blood, to the palest green with red striations, were perfectly shaded to give the contours an almost three-dimensional quality, as if the reader could reach into the page and touch them. Each fruit had been shown cut open, to view the flesh and the seed. And the origin of each variety was displayed in the accompanying text.

Rutledge could understand why Templeton, with his interest in orchards, would have wanted to own a copy of this book. The drawings were hand painted, there couldn't be all that many done. It was worth every penny Templeton had paid for his copy.

"I can see why you love it so much," he said finally.

"My husband's brother—Eric's uncle—gave it to me. He said Lawrence would have wanted me to have it. I'd found it in the library while I was looking for something to show my young charge different techniques in painting. She had a small talent, and I wanted to encourage it." She broke off then, turning away, as if she'd said too much.

"Where was this?" he asked lightly, running his forefinger over the binding. He remembered that the book had been re-bound. Not many firms could do anything half so beautifully. Turning it over, he saw in the corner of the back cover, closest to the spine, that there was a small ornate *G*. She hadn't answered his question. He looked up. "You haven't told me your name. I can ask the local police. I'd rather you tell me."

"Vivian Moss. It won't help you, you know. It's the only name anyone knows here."

"You called him your husband."

"He was. We married quietly, by special license, one month before he came into his inheritance. He was a year younger than I was, and we thought it would be best not to tell anyone until then. But there was a war in South Africa, and his regiment sailed for Cape Town. It was going to be a short war. It was, for him. He died of a fever three months later. And I had discovered I was pregnant." She shrugged. "They were locked in grief, his family. I had to hide mine. I couldn't prove we were married. And I had too much pride to face them down. So I left."

She reached for the shawl and then took the book from him. "I hope this has helped you find a killer."

"Who carved those wolves? You know, don't you?"

Vivian Moss turned away. "I thought I did. I was wrong. He's dead. I'm sorry."

She walked out of the room.

He couldn't force her to tell him. But he had other means now of finding out what it was he needed to know.

16

Rutledge waited until he heard the outer door open and shut behind Miss Moss. And then he went looking for the solicitor's clerk.

His office was at the other end of the passage from Mitchell's. It was surprisingly tidy, although with the shelves of files ranging around all four walls, there wasn't much room for the desk and two chairs.

Broughton was going through a file, making notes. He looked up as Rutledge came in, and said, "There were some matters that Mr. Mitchell hadn't finished. I'm trying to prepare a list of them for whoever takes over his clients. It will be someone outside Singleton. Unless someone wishes to buy the firm. But that will be up to his family, I expect."

Rutledge said, taking the chair on the far side of the desk, "You stole the book belonging to Miss Moss from Wentworth's bookshop. The one he was forced to replace for his client."

Broughton flushed. "I don't understand you, sir."

"Yes, you do. You knew she didn't want to part with it. You saw to it that she got it back. I expect I could ask Mrs. Mitchell if on the dates in question, you had taken several days of leave from the firm to attend to personal business. I'd rather not intrude on her grief."

"I don't know that Mrs. Mitchell took an interest in the day-to-day running of the firm."

"She may not have. But she will remember her husband complaining about the extra work he had had to take on—or work that was left undone while you were away. It was probably only a matter of four days. From here to London, from London to Suffolk, changing trains, and the return. Nothing else in the shop was taken or disturbed. And you would have known when the book was put into the post, and when it would have been delivered. It was a tight schedule, you had no idea when Wentworth would turn the book over to his own client. Or were you there when he collected it from the post office?"

Rutledge was watching Broughton's face, and he saw that he'd hit his mark.

"Don't lie to me," he said harshly. "Miss Moss is once more in possession of the book. She doesn't know it was stolen from the new owner. And so she has kept the sum Wentworth paid for it. Still, I could arrest her for having it. And let the courts decide if she should be punished as an accessory."

Broughton looked at him. "You wouldn't do that to her."

"Only you, Mr. Mitchell, the dealer in London, and Wentworth knew that her book had been sold. That's a very small group of suspects. Wentworth is dead, and so is Mitchell. That leaves me with two. I have spoken to the dealer in rare books, and I believe him when he says that his reputation has to be safeguarded, or he's out of business. That leaves you. Someone else appears to be looking for that book now, and he doesn't know where to find it. He killed Mr. Mitchell, searching for it."

"You don't know if that's true," Broughton protested. "Inspector Stevenson hasn't taken anyone into custody yet."

"Perhaps I'm wrong. Perhaps *you* killed Mitchell because he discovered the truth about what you'd done—and was about to tell Miss Moss everything."

Broughton flushed and then went pale as he slowly got to his feet. "My God, you can't seriously think—I served Mr. Mitchell and his father before him—I was here the day he joined this firm—he came to my birthday party that night—"

Rutledge watched him sink back into his chair, then said, "I'm satisfied that I've uncovered a thief. Now the question is, what am I to do about it?" When Broughton didn't answer, Rutledge changed his tactics. "If the man who shot Harvey Mitchell discovers who has that book now, he'll find Miss Moss, just as he found Mitchell. He's killed three people so far. Do you think he'll have any qualms about killing *her*? I won't be here to prevent it. I'm leaving in an hour. She'll be at his mercy. And there's nothing on earth you can do to protect her."

Broughton shook his head in defeat. "No, you can't do that to Miss Moss. She didn't know anything about what I did. I told her the buyer wished to remain anonymous, and she mustn't tell anyone about his generosity. She was so grateful, you should have seen her, it nearly brought me to tears as well. I had no idea that the book was connected to Mr. Mitchell's death. You can't just walk away and leave her in danger. At least speak to Inspector Stevenson. *Do something.*"

"You should have thought of the consequences before you broke into Wentworth's bookshop."

"I only meant to help. She's had a struggle. It hasn't been easy. If she's caught up in what I did—if she's somehow drawn into what happened to Mr. Mitchell—it will undo all she's worked so hard to make up for. The talk will all be dredged up again, and this time her son isn't just a child, he'll suffer with her."

"Where did she work before she returned to Singleton?"

"I don't know. I expect no one did, except perhaps her parents. They're gone now. It was wrong of me, but I've looked in Mr. Mitchell's file on her, and there's nothing in it about the years she was away. There's just her pension, paid into her bank every quarter. It comes from the account of a firm in London. There's no way of knowing who their client is. I can show you the box, if you like. It also contains her will and the deed to her parents' property. It's as if her past didn't exist, except for the fact that she has a son. That's usually the way such matters are handled. A discreet income in return for silence."

That was all too often the case, although many women used Mrs. instead of Miss, to allay gossip. Something Miss Moss couldn't do, coming home to her parents and a village that knew who she was.

Rutledge took out one of the wolves and set it on the desk between them. "Have you ever seen a carving like this?"

Confused by the shift in subject, Broughton looked at it, then shook his head. "Should I have? Is it important?"

Rutledge picked up the little carving. "No. It's a Suffolk matter. Does the phrase *gate keeper* mean anything to you?"

"No, sir. But what are we to do about Miss Moss?"

"I'm going to find this man as quickly as possible and put a stop to his killings. Meanwhile, if you've lied to me, Broughton, I'll see you taken into custody. Whatever the repercussions are for Miss Moss."

As Rutledge got up to leave, Broughton reached out a hand, pleading. "You'll make certain she's all right. Please?"

"The best way to do that is for both of you to keep absolutely quiet about who has this book. If this stays a secret that only three people know, she'll be reasonably safe."

"If he killed Mr. Mitchell, whoever he is, do you think he'll come back to look for me?"

"Let's hope not. But I'd advise you to stay in after dark, and think twice about answering a sudden summons. Even if you think it comes from a client."

He walked out the door, leaving the clerk sitting there staring after him, fright in his eyes.

As he stepped out of the solicitor's office, he saw Inspector Stevenson standing in a doorway across the street, out of the wind, waiting for him.

"You've been busy," he said cheerfully, catching Rutledge up. "What's taken you so long?"

"Disappointment," Rutledge said shortly. "I've reached a dead end. By the way, did you find any small carvings where Mitchell was murdered?"

"Sergeant Gibson was going on about that. The answer is no. Nothing of the sort. Where did that thought come from?"

"From Suffolk. It wasn't likely that our inquiries overlapped. But no harm done making certain."

They were walking along the High together, holding on to their hats as they did. Stevenson looked up at Rutledge out of the corner of his eye. "You have a reputation for going your own way in handling an inquiry. Do you know anything you haven't told me about Mitchell's death?"

"I wasn't here, I didn't see the body. You'll probably find an answer among Mitchell's files."

"Broughton and I have gone through them. Spent one whole day, as a matter of fact, looking at each of Mitchell's clients. We didn't find anything I could use."

"A pity," Rutledge said sympathetically.

"Who was the young woman who came and went twice while you were there?"

He shook his head. "Another dead end. She didn't know anyone in Suffolk."

"A pity," Stevenson said, and Rutledge couldn't tell whether he was being sarcastic or simply echoing his own comment. With his hand holding the brim of his hat, Stevenson's face was half-hidden.

They shook hands—perfunctorily—when Rutledge reached his motorcar, and Stevenson volunteered to turn the crank. "How does she drive?" he asked as he stepped away from the bonnet.

"Wonderfully well," Rutledge answered.

"Been thinking about finding one for myself," Stevenson said. And then he stood aside, watching Rutledge out of sight.

"Ye didn't play fair wi' him," Hamish was saying.

"He's not going to solve his murder."

"Ye canna' be certain of that. There wasna' a carving found by the body. The killer could be someone else. Yon clerk, as ye said."

"I doubt it. On both counts. But if our man is in fact looking for that book, the last thing I want is to drag Miss Moss into it."

"You threatened to do just that with yon clerk."

"I had to know if he'd stolen that book. And she seemed to be the one weakness in his armor. It worked."

R utledge stopped briefly in London, paying a visit to Somerset House and the records there. He located Miss Moss and then her son. The father's name wasn't given.

He found a telephone in a hotel and put through a call to the Yard.

"I've been to Surrey," he said, knowing full well that Stevenson would report his visit to the Yard. "It was possible that the murders were connected. I spoke to Stevenson while I was there."

Sergeant Gibson was not best pleased. "You shouldn't have done that, sir. Not without clearing it with the Chief Superintendent."

"No harm done," Rutledge said easily. "There was a person of interest living in the village. I wanted to interview her myself." He considered asking Gibson to find out what he could about Vivian Moss. But the Sergeant might see fit to mention her to Inspector Stevenson, and that was the last thing Rutledge wanted to happen.

Rutledge could hear the rustle of papers. He'd caught Gibson at a busy time.

Then Gibson said, "Where are you presently, sir?"

"On my way back to Suffolk. That reminds me. What did you discover about Oliver Pace?"

"As to that, sir, we've come up with nothing. The Yorkshire police I've contacted have no record of taking anyone into custody by the name of Oliver Pace. I've even asked the Chief Super. The consensus is, if he has had a run-in with the police there, he's changed his name."

Which made sense. If Pace had intended to start over in Suffolk, the first step would have logically been to change his identity.

"Thank you, Sergeant."

He put up the receiver, stepped out of the stuffy telephone room, which smelled strongly of perfume, and walked out of the hotel.

R utledge didn't go directly to Suffolk. Instead he turned toward Kent and Melinda Crawford's house. She was at home and, late though it was, very pleased to see him, telling him that she had also had a brief note from Frances.

"It makes my heart sing," she said, smiling. "I can still remember how it was when I was married. We went to Agra on our wedding journey, and sat in front of the Taj Mahal in the moonlight. Did you know it isn't white by moonlight—it's the loveliest soft blue. Quite magical. And in the first light of dawn, it's the color of pearl and apricot. We spread a blanket in the garden there and watched the sun rise."

She had not married again, although Rutledge was sure she had had many offers over the long years of her widowhood. And unlike Queen Victoria, who had become the reclusive Widow of Windsor after Albert's death, Melinda Crawford lived a full and exciting life on her own.

Putting aside her memories, she grinned up at him. "My dear, I was about to have my tea. Come and join me. I expect you to spend the night, you know."

"I can't," he said. "I'm overdue in Suffolk even now."

When they were finishing their tea in her drawing room by a roaring fire that would have roasted an ox, she asked him if there was any way she could help. "Because you know, Ian, that I can tell when it's my own charming self you've come to see, and when it's something to do with one of your inquiries."

He laughed. "Am I so transparent? I'm afraid you're right. There was something you mentioned—it must be years ago. You said that your books had arrived from India in poor condition and you had had to have them restored and re-bound."

"You wouldn't have believed your eyes. Some of them were thick with green mold, long and hairy, as if they'd grown beards. It was the leather, you see. Thank God the pages inside were still in good condition. I sent the lot by train to London, where the binders met the boxes, and seven months later they presented me with beauty instead of a beast. Why do you ask? Is there something you need to rebind?"

"Luckily, no. But there's a particular book where the original binding was replaced, and I'd like to find out more about it. And possibly about who had ordered the work."

"Ah. The inquiry in Suffolk. As a matter of fact, I do recall the firm. It was Garamond, spelled like the typeface. I have no idea if the family is connected. The firm uses a particularly pretty *G* as its trademark. Garamond—the firm—served an elite clientele because it did such exceptionally fine work. And charged accordingly, of course. I'll show you." She led him into her library and at random pulled several books from the shelves. The Jane Austen books were bound in a soft rose leather, a history of India was in a rich cordovan, and the Greek tragedies were black with silver lettering.

He found the stylish *G* on all of them.

"You must know the present owners of the firm quite well."

"Yes, I send them work from time to time. I found a clean but undistinguished collection of Cicero that I had re-bound as a presentation for Winston. He'd worn his pages out, he said."

"Could you telephone them for me and ask about a certain volume they re-bound perhaps twenty years ago? I don't know who ordered the work done, and that's rather important."

She restored the books to their proper places on the shelves and handed him a sheet of paper. "Describe what it is you do know, and what it is you would have me ask about."

He sat at her mahogany desk and described the book and the binding.

While she put through the call to London, he paced the passage outside of the telephone room until she ordered him to stop. "Darling Ian, there's a decanter of whisky in the drawing room. You know which one. Pour a drink for both of us."

Rutledge did as he was told. When he returned, she was speaking to a clerk in the firm, asking after his children and congratulating him on a prize one of them had won at school. He forced himself to stand there, glasses in hand, and listen to her side of the exchange.

Eventually she got around to the favor she had telephoned to ask, and she gave the information clearly and efficiently, as he had spelled it out for her on the sheet of paper. She looked up and smiled at him, then attended to the conversation on the other end of the line.

Finally she thanked the clerk and hung up the receiver.

"He's going to have a look at their ledgers to see if he can find what you want. But it will take time, I'm afraid. More time than you're likely to have."

"I wish I had a date for the rebinding. But Miss Moss was reluctant to tell me anything about her past. I could only estimate the year."

"Will you at least dine with me? In the event the clerk is able to find the information more quickly than he expects."

He shook his head. "I can't. I've been away longer than I should be, as it is. You can telephone me at the bookshop. I'll make certain I'm there more frequently."

She knew when she'd lost. "Then I'll ask Shanta to fill a thermos for you and put up some sandwiches."

Melinda saw him off some twenty minutes later, promising to let him know as soon as she had any news.

I t was quite late when he reached Wolfpit. The main door of The Swan was unlocked, and he went directly to his room. It was another hour before he could fall asleep.

Monday morning was market day in Wolfpit. As he finished his breakfast, he could see early shoppers already walking among the stalls, chatting with the owners, and he realized it was a Christmas market, the first since the war. Among them, strolling about, was one of the Constables he'd brought from Stowmarket.

He went directly to speak to Constable Penny.

But Wolfpit had been quiet while he was away.

"We kept an eye on Miss Frost and Miss Dennis, and the solicitor, Mr. Blake. And Mrs. Delaney, of course. And there wasn't any trouble at all. Mrs. Wentworth came, looking for word about the inquiry. She blows hot and cold, sir, one minute seeming not to care, and in the next worrying about progress. I put her off, but she was not very happy about that. If you ask me, she's got something on her mind, and it's eating at her."

But Rutledge couldn't risk the long drive to Norwich and back. It was important to be close by the bookstore for Melinda Crawford's call.

He spent an hour at the market, looking at housewares and farm sausages and round loaves of bread. One man was roasting chestnuts over a brazier, and another was selling little cups of mulled wine to the marketgoers. There was a decidedly jolly atmosphere around his stall. Others had Christmas decorations and fruit cakes and gingerbread, and baskets of holly and other greens.

Rutledge even scanned the handmade toys for sale, but there were no small wood carvings that matched the skill needed to create the little wolves.

He spent much of his time on the side of the market nearest the bookshop, in the hope that he would hear the telephone if it rang. As more and more people gathered in the square, that became increasingly unlikely.

Blake found him standing near a stall filled with jams and jellies, and asked if there was any news, but Rutledge shook his head.

"I've made inquiries in London," he said. "We'll see what that turns up." And then he asked, "Did Wentworth know the name of the owner of that book on apple varieties?"

"No, it was handled through a London dealer."

And the dealer, Williamson, would have known the name of Miss Moss's solicitor as well as Wentworth's name. But that wouldn't bring them any closer to the previous owner, some twenty years ago. He was counting on Melinda.

There was the rub, he thought, as Blake walked on. What if even the most diligent clerk failed to find a name? It was such a slender thread on which to pin his hopes.

Hamish said, "Why are ye sae certain that the murders have to do with Miss Moss's past?"

Why is the book so important? he countered silently. *There must be something about it that matters to someone. And damned if I know what that is. Yet.*

H e let himself into the bookshop and sat by the telephone for an hour or more, willing it to ring.

And it crouched there on the wall without making a sound.

Finally, around eleven o'clock, he called Melinda Crawford himself.

"Patience, Ian. A search of this nature takes time."

He understood, having searched through Wentworth's ledgers, but it did nothing to help him endure the wait.

He walked from one end of Wolfpit to the other and back again, and was not twenty yards from the Wentworths' house when he saw their motorcar draw up in front.

As Mr. Wentworth stepped out and turned to help his wife get down, he saw Rutledge coming toward them, and said something to Stephen's mother.

She stood there by the gate, staring at him as he approached, a cold dislike in her face.

"Good morning," Rutledge said, removing his hat.

"Why are you strolling about the streets of Wolfpit, when there has been no inquest into the murder of my son and Frederick Templeton?"

He said nothing.

"I have written to Frederick's sister-in-law, offering my condolences. She's understandably upset. And so are his many friends. I can't leave my daughter's house without being asked about the progress being made finding the murderer. And I am left to tell them that Scotland Yard has sent its most incompetent Inspector to handle this inquiry."

"I'm sorry you're not pleased with the course of events," he said.

"It seems impossible that Frederick is gone," Wentworth said in the brief silence that followed, trying to ease the tension between his wife and the man from London. "I'd seen him barely a fortnight ago at a dinner party. I remember how enthusiastic he was about a recent purchase, a book dealing with varieties of apples—"

Rutledge broke in, his voice urgent. "When was this dinner party? Why hadn't you mentioned it before this?"

"I saw no reason to mention it. It had nothing to do with my son's death."

"Where was this dinner party? And who attended it?"

"I'm not sure I recall everyone who was there. Why should it matter?"

Rutledge wanted to curse him for a fool but held his temper in check. "I need as much information as you can give me. Shall we go inside?"

"You are impertinent," Mrs. Wentworth said, "inviting yourself into my home without a by-your-leave."

"This is police business," he told her bluntly, and took her arm. She shook him off and marched ahead of them while Wentworth, protesting, followed.

Opening the door, Mrs. Wentworth started for the stairs, but Rutledge stopped her.

"I'm rather tired from the drive down from Norwich," she told him, but he shook his head.

"You can speak to me here," he said coldly, "or at the police station. It's your choice."

She stared defiantly at him, daring him to carry out his threat.

Wentworth stepped forward. "My dear. The sooner we finish this business, the sooner he will leave. Please. The drawing room?"

She glared at him as if he had betrayed her, then marched into the drawing room and sat down.

The drapes were still closed and the room was chill. Clearly no one had warned Lydie they were coming. Wentworth went forward and took a match from the mantelpiece, kneeling to light the fire ready laid on the hearth. For a moment only the crackling of the flames as they found the tinder and began to lick at the coal filled the room. Dusting his hands, Wentworth sat down halfway between Rutledge and his wife, as if expecting to referee the match to come.

Rutledge waited until he had their full attention. "When I asked you about Templeton, you told me about a visit when he was ten years old. When was this dinner party you neglected to mention?"

"It was a weekend before Stephen—before all of this began," Wentworth answered. "It was in Kent, actually. Old friends, an early Christmas gathering. They're spending the holiday in Ireland with their son and his family. I was surprised to see Templeton there, but FitzSimmons owns cherry and apple orchards, and I expect that's the connection. I didn't ask, of course, it would have been rude."

"How was he? In good spirits? Behaving normally, as if nothing was worrying him?"

"Oh yes. Quite himself." He glanced toward his wife, but she was maintaining a stony silence.

"Go on," Rutledge ordered curtly. "You mentioned a book?"

"Oh. Yes. The subject of the book came up rather by chance. Mrs. FitzSimmons was telling us about the gifts she'd collected for her grandchildren. And Frederick said something about a book he considered an early gift to himself, and he added that he ought to have brought it with him, because FitzSimmons would find it interesting, but he was about to send it out to be restored. The cover wasn't quite what he'd like. Then he looked our way and added that Stephen had found it for him, and that Stephen was going to contact a book binder before Christmas. Naturally FitzSimmons wanted to hear more, and so Frederick went on to describe the plates. I wasn't particularly interested in medieval apple varieties, I wasn't paying strict attention. Someone, I forget who, asked where the book had come from, and he replied that he didn't know, but he could ask Stephen." He glanced again at his wife. "My wife told everyone then that she was surprised that Stephen hadn't kept the book himself, if it was so beautiful, or at least have found one for himself. That he was attracted to books the way a magpie was attracted to bright objects. She suggested that he could find a copy for FitzSimmons as well. For there must surely be other copies available."

Listening to him, Rutledge realized that Mrs. Wentworth might well have, wittingly or not, sent a killer after her son.

And she said, as if defending herself against his condemnation, "Well, it's quite true. He cares for that bookshop more than he has ever cared for us." Forgetting to use the past tense, as if she hadn't yet come to terms with his death. Or wasn't willing to give up a lifetime's anger simply because death had intervened.

"What happened then?" Rutledge asked.

"The conversation moved on, the way it generally does at dinner parties. I think one of the guests asked if FitzSimmons would be looking at brood mares while he was in Ireland."

"Will you give me a list of the guests at the party?" It was framed as a question, but there was an edge to Rutledge's voice.

"They were the guests of FitzSimmons and his wife, I don't think that it would be appropriate for me to give their names to you," Wentworth objected.

Rutledge wanted to shake the pair of them. "It will be far more embarrassing to everyone if I am forced to call on Mr. FitzSimmons and ask him for their names. He won't thank you for drawing him into a murder inquiry just before he's set to leave for Ireland."

Wentworth flushed. "Very well." He excused himself, and came back presently with paper and pen. He and his wife conferred and finally agreed on the list.

"If you know where each of the guests lives, add that as well, please."

With poor grace they did as he asked.

Handing the completed list to Rutledge, Wentworth said, "Now I must ask you to leave us in peace."

"There is one other matter," he said, and took out the little wolves to show the two of them. Mrs. Wentworth barely glanced at them, but Wentworth seemed to find them interesting.

"Where did these come from? And what do they have to do with my son's death?"

"I don't know. This one was found near his body. The other one close by Templeton's. Rather too much of a coincidence to ignore."

Mrs. Wentworth rose as he returned the carvings to his pocket. "Good day, Inspector." It was dismissal.

He rose politely but wasn't finished with them. "Do you know why the words 'gate keeper' meant something to Stephen?"

Mrs. Wentworth's face flamed. "How dare you?" she demanded, her voice low and vicious. "How dare you throw that up at me in my own home!"

Wentworth stepped forward, his hand raised, as if to stop her from attacking Rutledge physically.

"You'd better go," he said to Rutledge. "Please. We've done as you asked."

Rutledge turned to leave. He hadn't taken off his coat, for the room had been too cold. Picking up his hat, he said, "Thank you," and walked to the door.

He was in the foyer when he heard Mrs. Wentworth cry out in fury, "If you let that man into my house once more, I shall never speak to you again. Do you hear me?"

Her husband's response was lost as Rutledge walked out the door.

He didn't look at the list of names until he had reached the book-shop. Shutting himself in, locking the door, he went to the room where Wentworth sat to read, and lit the lamp before settling himself into the chair.

Hamish was saying, "You've made too much of that party. You canna' be sure the killer's name is on yon list. Or that Templeton hadna' spoken of yon book before. One of the ither guests could ha' mentioned the party to someone else."

"It's a start. It's all I have." How many leads had already vanished like smoke?

He unfolded the sheet of paper and read through the names. He didn't recognize any of them, but that could be remedied. If Melinda Crawford didn't know them, he could ask the Chief Constable in Kent to tell him who they were.

Going through it a second time, he sorted them by county. Two couples from Suffolk, including the Wentworths, Templeton, two couples from Essex, one of them with their daughter, and four couples from Kent, in addition to the host and his wife. Twenty guests in all.

He put through a call to Melinda Crawford and was told by Shanta, her Indian housekeeper, that she was spending the day with friends in Sevenoaks. She would also be dining with them that evening.

"Has she had a telephone call from London? She's been waiting for one."

"Someone telephoned earlier. I don't know if it was from London."

"Tell her I've called, will you please, Shanta? I have a list of names to read to her."

On the off chance that Sergeant Gibson had found something that would help sift through the names on the list, as soon as he'd finished the call to Melinda, he put in one to the Yard.

Gibson wasn't on duty, and the Sergeant who was could find no notes set aside for Inspector Rutledge.

"Sorry, sir. There's nothing here."

Rutledge said, "Has Inspector Stevenson closed his inquiry in Surrey?"

"Ah. That must have been what Gibson was talking about before he left, sir. He said there's a complaint from the Inspector, something about poaching, sir. The Sergeant said he was going home to a Guinness and his newspaper. That was at midnight last night." Rutledge heard him clear his throat, as if he'd remembered who he was speaking to. "Sorry, sir."

Rutledge thought wryly that if Stevenson had any idea of just how far his patch had been poached, he'd be lodging a complaint with Markham, not Gibson.

He put the receiver up, listening to the voices outside. A sudden burst of laughter echoed in the bookshop, out of place in the silence around him.

Rutledge looked at the shelves ranging around the room. It was likely that he could put his hand on any title there after searching them and the orders and the ledgers so many times. It was another man's life, and he had come to know it well.

He had also come to know Stephen Wentworth rather well over the past week, and he had liked the man. He'd liked Templeton too. They hadn't deserved to die at the hands of a murderer, and nothing would bring them back, not even taking their killer into custody.

"What the hell," he wondered aloud, "was so important about that lovely book that it cost three lives?"

Hamish said, "It isna' the book."

Rutledge had been about to put out the lamp by the chair, and he stopped, his hand reaching for the shade.

It had been re-bound . . .

But that was years ago. Why was it suddenly so important *now*, in December 1920, that murder was done?

17

Rutledge went out into the crowded square, hoping to find Mrs. Delaney among those enjoying market day. When he didn't see her, he looked into the dining room at The Swan in the event she might be having lunch with friends.

Making his way through the throng of people, he walked on to her house and knocked.

It was several minutes before she came to the door, and he was beginning to feel more than a little concern.

She said, "I've taken a chill, Inspector. You may be afraid to come in."

"I just came to look in on you. And to ask if you know any of the names on this list."

She took it from him, turning away to cough.

"Shall I send Dr. Brent to see you?"

Shaking her head, she said, "It will be over in a day or two." She scanned the list.

"The Wentworths, of course. And here's Frederick Templeton. The other Suffolk couple, the Drysdales, live in Colchester. Lovely people. We've ordered books for them before. They were friends when my husband was married to Josephine, and became our friends after he married me. I don't know the families in Essex or Kent. Sorry." She looked up. "Where did you get this?"

"From Wentworth and his wife. When I spoke to them earlier about Templeton, they neglected to mention attending a dinner party where he happened to be among the guests. It's too close to his murder to ignore."

"Well, I should think that's typical of them. Too haughty by half. But you can ignore the Drysdales. I can vouch for the sort of people they are."

"You shouldn't be standing in this wind. Are you sure I can't help in some way?"

"You're kind to ask. But no, I'll be just fine."

He let her go, then, glad to cross the Drysdales off his list.

That left Kent and Essex.

He ran Blake to earth in his house, two doors down from the solicitor's office.

But Blake shook his head when he'd scanned the list. "I've met the FitzSimmonses a time or two. I don't know the others. When was this party, did you say?"

"Before the murders."

"I don't quite see how this might have had anything to do with Stephen's death. Templeton's, perhaps, since he was present at the dinner. You're on thin ice, Rutledge, trying to prove this damned book had anything to do with murder. Surely there's some other reason?"

He couldn't explain about Vivian Moss. Or Harvey Mitchell. Instead, he smiled and replied, "Do you have a suspect in mind?"

"I'm a country solicitor, for God's sake. Not a policeman. Which reminds me, why are there two constables from Stowmarket roaming about Wolfpit?"

"A precaution. Penny was hard pressed to keep an eye on the village night and day."

Blake said, "You think I'm still at risk?"

"Truthfully? I don't know. If I'm right, you're in the clear. If I'm wrong, then we'll have to start over again."

He was at sixes and sevens, waiting for Melinda Crawford to come home from her dinner party, and the rest of the day dragged. He stood in the window of his room, watching the market stalls being taken down as dusk approached, and a handful of men sweeping up the debris that had been left behind. It was still at least two hours before dinner, even an early one.

At nine o'clock he went back to the bookshop and sat in Stephen Wentworth's chair, hoping that Melinda would telephone him as soon as she got in and put him out of his misery. He hated idleness, but there was nothing he could do until he heard from her.

He had uncovered the secrets in Wentworth's life and in Templeton's. Vivian Moss was turning out to be even more difficult. He wished himself back in Surrey, where he might have an outside chance of convincing her to trust him and confide in him. But she had kept her own counsel for twenty-some years, and it wasn't likely that she would break her silence now, however much he might wish it.

When the bookshop telephone rang shortly after eleven o'clock that evening, he all but leapt for it.

Melinda's voice came through clearly. "Ian, I'm so sorry. It was an obligation I couldn't get out of. I did speak to the clerk at Garamond's just before I left for Sevenoaks. And he has found a reference in the firm's ledgers that could be just what you are looking for. A book on medieval apple varieties was re-bound in 1900, at the request of one Desmond Montgomery of Essex. He came to London with it, paid for the book in person when he collected it, and took it away himself."

He needn't look at the list of names from the dinner party. Desmond Montgomery was there, along with his wife, Prue. He felt a surge of satisfaction. And be damned to Blake and his thin ice.

"Melinda, you're a worker of miracles. Where in Essex? Do you have any idea?"

"I looked it up for you, before I telephoned. It's a village called Little Tilton."

"You have my gratitude and love," he said, preparing to hang up. "I'll let you know if this is the man I'm after. Good night."

"Wait, Ian, there's more," she said quickly, stopping him. "I don't know if this matters, but this man Montgomery asked that something be placed between the old cover and the new leather binding. The clerk says the note in the ledger referred to something to do with a marriage."

He was silent for so long, she said in alarm, "Are you still there, Ian? Have we been disconnected?"

"No, I'm here. I'm just taking in what you've found out. And I expect that was worth killing for. Not a book about apples."

"Are you thinking what I am? That this is the proof that that young woman was married to her young man?"

"Yes. I'm sure of it." And then he remembered the thin ice, and added, "What else could it be?"

"But why put it in the binding, then give her the book?"

"Cruelty," he said, his voice grim. "He could have destroyed it. Instead he has had the satisfaction of knowing she will never find it. She loved that book, she thought it was a kindness, to be given it. And she would never countenance having it taken apart. She even put a stipulation on the sale, that the plates were not to be taken out and framed. She cared that much, even though she was in such dire need of money."

"Then I'd be very careful, Ian, going after this man. He will be very dangerous."

He promised, his mind already on the morning.

After he'd hung up the receiver, he changed his mind and went directly to his room in The Swan. He took the smaller of the two valises, put what he needed in it, and went down to his motorcar.

The night was cloudy, no stars and no moon to light his way as he drove out of Wolfpit, gathering speed as he left the village behind.

He drove with care, for there were stoats and hares and even a fox or two trotting along the road in the dark, then hypnotized by the brightness of the two large headlamps that pierced the night and showed him his way.

Following finger boards into Essex, he passed through silent villages, saw the silhouettes of farms just off the road, and once glimpsed the gates of a large manor house, shut at this hour of the night.

It was well after three when he reached the outskirts of his destination. A cold wind had come up, sending the clouds scudding. The church tower was stark against the sky, and he saw two small pubs, the police station, and a number of shops along the High. When he had come to the far side of the village, he turned and drove back to the church. He'd noticed a stand of yews just where the churchyard wall ran back toward the rectory. The deeper shadows there were exactly what he had hoped to find, and he left the motorcar there, where it would be almost invisible until someone was nearly on it.

Carrying his torch with him but using it sparingly, he began to hunt for the Montgomery house. He found it down one of the two lanes that crossed the High, at the end of a street of more prosperous houses. There were high stone posts topped with what appeared to be a bird of some sort—a falcon, he thought—and the gates between them were shut. Taking his torch with him, he followed the high wall for some distance and found another gate, this time into a muddy lane. It stood open. He went down that lane, coming at length to a yard formed by the stables and a barn. He could hear horses moving about their stalls.

A dog began to bark in the distance, in the direction of tenant cottages whose rooflines he could just pick out, dark against the darker sky. He stayed by the yard until the barking had stopped, then found his way to the house.

It was larger than Templeton's town house, with extensive gardens laid out around it, tenant farms, and barns. There was a sheltered walk formed by yews, a more formal garden leading up to the terrace, and a large pond currently occupied by geese.

Rutledge recognized the large white shapes in time to stop short. The Romans had used geese as watchmen, alerting the city to invaders. He gave them a wide berth and came to the front of the house. Looking up, he could see that it was handsome enough but architecturally rather plain.

An hour later he knew his way around the estate even in the dark. He had found all the doors from the house to the gardens, the kitchen yard, and the terrace. He knew where the family's motorcar was kept and how the drive and the farm lane twisted and turned.

He wasn't certain what he was going to learn, come the morning, but he was prepared. He made his way back to his motorcar and found a village some ten miles away. Far enough that news of his presence wouldn't reach the Montgomery household before he arrived there himself. The village had only one inn, but after some effort he roused the clerk and was given a room for the night. It was cramped and the fire was pitifully small, but that didn't matter for the few hours left before dawn.

The next morning, shaved and carefully dressed, he drove back to Little Tilton. When he reached the house, he remembered something that Robin Hardy had said, that he would have loved the family estate, while his brother saw himself only as a caretaker for it. Had there been the same feeling here, the elder son inheriting by right and not by choice? He had joined the Army . . .

He would soon know. He was about to tell the present owner that he was not the true heir. And there was proof.

He lifted the brass knocker and let it fall. Almost in the same instant a woman in riding clothes opened the door to him.

"You're early, Sally—but you aren't Sally, are you, worst luck. Are you here to see Desmond? He's in the estate room."

She was tall, lithe, and accustomed to taking charge. Not attractive, but striking in her own way, with fair hair and green eyes. She led him toward the back of the house to a room at the end of the passage. Throwing open the door, she said, "Darling, your friend is here."

Montgomery looked up from the letter he was reading. He was dark with brown eyes and a strong chin. He looked at Rutledge, then frowned.

"Who are you?" he demanded. "Prue, what is this stranger doing here?"

She turned to stare at him as well. "Oh dear. I thought it was the man you'd contacted about the new motorcar."

Rutledge said easily, "My name is Rutledge. I've come to ask you about Vivian Moss."

The consternation in their faces told him all he needed to know. They recognized the name, and they knew who she was.

"Yes, I thought you might remember her," he said affably, moving into the room and stopping where he could face both of them.

Prue Montgomery glanced behind her to see if anyone was in the passage, then shut the door and stood with her back against it.

Montgomery turned to her. "They'll have brought your horse around. I'll deal with this man."

"We'll deal with him together."

Still watching her face, Montgomery asked warily, "What does she want? Vivian Moss?"

"Nothing—yet. She sold that book about apples. The one you gave her. Did you know? She needed the money. Too bad she never realized what was behind the handsome leather binding. But I did. And I happen to know where it is at the moment."

"Are you from the binders?" Rutledge had all his attention now. "No, you can't be, you're not old enough to have been working there at the time. Your father, then. Did he work for them?"

Prue took a step forward. "Don't—"

Ignoring the interruption, Rutledge said, "It occurred to me that you might be interested in seeing it safely back in your hands."

"That's blackmail," Montgomery blustered, flushing.

"What an ugly word. I'm simply asking how much proof of her marriage to your brother is worth to you. A simple business transaction." He gestured toward the ledgers on the shelf behind the desk. "This house and the grounds appear to be rather prosperous. You've had the use of them for twenty-some years. Perhaps you've developed a taste for living here, and you might be willing to pay well to go on feeling secure. Or if you tell me you'd rather not do business with a stranger, I can offer my services to Miss Moss. She can't pay me a farthing now, of course, but when her son comes into his proper inheritance, I am sure she'll be very grateful. I warn you, she may not feel kindly enough toward you to offer you even the same pittance of a pension you gave her."

Prue started to speak, but he raised his hand to stop her. "I won't have it, do you hear?" he told Rutledge. "This is not my fault. Lawrence wanted to be a soldier. He didn't care tuppence for his inheritance. I haven't taken anything from him that he valued. He paid with his life for choosing the Army instead of this house. He should have realized that such a hasty marriage left Vivian vulnerable."

"But you took advantage of her. And when you discovered she'd had your brother's child, you did nothing about it. The courts might see this matter differently. Her son's old enough now to understand what you did. Have you asked *him* whether he might wish to bear his father's name? He uses Eric Moss at present. He's just come down from Oxford, and there's a mountain of debt. Do you have a son?"

He directed that last question to the woman.

"Yes," she snapped. "He chose Cambridge. All the Montgomery heirs have gone there."

"Sadly Eric didn't know that." So Prue was Desmond's wife . . .

She flushed, but he thought it was with anger and not shame. Turning to her husband, she said, "You can't trust this man. You know that, don't you? He'll be back for more, and then even more, till there's nothing left for Julian."

He turned on her. "I should never have told you about this, Prue."

"Then you shouldn't have come home and got drunk after that dinner party. You sat there in the drawing room, drinking whisky after whisky, until the whole sordid affair came spilling out. I can't believe you've kept it from me all these *years*. If they hadn't been talking about that godforsaken book at the dinner table, would you never have told me? If you'd wanted to keep the marriage lines away from her, why not simply burn them?"

"I couldn't. What if at some time in the future, I'd needed to produce them? He was my elder brother, in spite of everything. My sister loved him. I'd done my duty, I'd given the lines back to his widow. Even if she wasn't aware of it." He glared at her. "And *you* told me that there must be a dozen such books on apples. Well, you were wrong, weren't you. This *was* the book I'd given Vivian. Or this man wouldn't be here."

Ignoring that last, she went back to her first concern. "And when, pray, would you ever need to produce her marriage lines? I remind you that you have a son of your own."

This was clearly a sore subject between man and wife. His conscience and her fear for her own child. Rutledge made an attempt to redirect the conversation.

"You can quarrel over what happened later. We were discussing the future, not the past."

"Why should you care what happens to Vivian Moss and her son? Are you related to them? Is that why you're here?" Montgomery demanded.

"No, I'm just aware of a piece of information that might in some quarters be valuable. I'm asking what I ought to do about it."

He could feel the rising tension in the room. And Hamish was already warning him that he had gone too far. He could see that Montgomery had one of the desk drawers open, but he was too far away to look inside. Was that where the man kept his revolver?

He answered Hamish silently. *He can't kill me here. Not in the house. Not in front of his wife. Not where the servants might hear.*

Montgomery said, "You've come here without any warning. I need time to think. I can't make a rash decision. And I don't care for threats."

"Go to the police, if you like," Rutledge said, smiling. "I don't mind. I'll lose what I came for, and you'll still lose this house. But Miss Moss might still be grateful enough to reward me." He looked from one to the other. "I think you'll have made the worst of the bargain."

"Desmond?" his wife said sharply. "This is getting out of hand, don't you see?"

"Leave this to me, Prue. Stay out of it," he warned her again. He turned back to Rutledge. "Give me twenty-four hours. I can't think like this, I tell you, it's not fair to me."

"Why should I wait? I have the upper hand now."

"Look, whoever you are, for one thing I don't keep large sums here in the house. For another, I prefer to consider my choices. For all I know, you're bluffing. And I'm no fool, understand me there. I'll see proof before you see a ha'penny." Montgomery was recovering from his initial shock and starting to think more clearly. "My wife is my witness, she will swear that I've admitted to no wrongdoing this morning. And we will be believed, because Constable Wiggins looks up to this family. Take it or leave it. Twenty-four hours. Where are you staying? I may need to reach you sooner."

"Ah, but that's my little secret," Rutledge said brightly. "Twenty-four hours. Not a second longer. Meanwhile, if you try to cause me any trouble at all, you'll pay dearly. I'll see that the evidence in my possession goes directly to the police. And I'd rather you didn't contact Vivian Moss. I haven't decided just how much I intend to share with her. I see no need to make her aware of her situation at this stage."

"Yes, I thought you were out for yourself, damn you," Montgomery said trenchantly.

"Well," Rutledge said reasonably, "if I don't look out for myself, who will?"

Prue Montgomery stayed where she was by the door. "I believe you're wrong, Desmond, to deal with him. There must be some other way around this."

"The choice isn't yours, Prue. It's mine. I was convinced that without the marriage lines, she would never dare to confront me. And I was right about that. I just never counted on someone like this man coming along. How *did* you find out what was behind the binding?"

Rutledge laughed. "I've Stephen Wentworth to thank for that. He had no idea what he possessed. I was far more curious than he was. And my curiosity was rewarded tenfold. The rear door of his shop has a latch a child could open. When you came to search the shop, you didn't get in, did you? No, I thought not." It was a wild guess—that the night he'd chased a figure through the schoolmistresses' back garden, the killer was looking for the book. It hadn't satisfied him that Wentworth and Templeton were dead.

He started toward the door, and after a moment Mrs. Montgomery reluctantly moved out of his way. He paused on the threshold, on the point of taking one of the little carvings out of his pocket, then thought better of it. They were connected to two murders, and he was wary of pushing Montgomery too far. It was one thing to appear to be blackmailing him about his inheritance, and quite another to indicate that he could send this man to the gallows. He said, "I never thought I'd make my fortune in such a fashion. Your wife is right, you'd have been wiser to destroy the marriage lines. As it happens, I'm very glad you didn't. But I'd be curious to know what it was—other than the inheritance—that made you so willing to cut your brother's son out."

He saw the look in Montgomery's eyes. A burning jealousy that the years hadn't dimmed.

"My brother had a number of talents. He could have made his living with any of them. I had none, and there was only the inheritance from an uncle for this younger son. Hardly more than a pittance. It was so unfair."

"What sort of talents?"

"He was a damned fine soldier. He had a good head for business, he could have made his way in any firm in the City. He was always carving something or other. He might even have made a living selling them. Especially the birds. They were perfect down to the last feather. My parents wanted me to study for the church. I'd have hated visiting the sick and holding the hands of the dying or baptizing screaming babies. The Army would have been even worse. I was damned lucky to survive the last war."

Prue Montgomery interrupted him. "You're telling him too much."

But Rutledge said, "If you envied your brother as much as you say you do, I'm surprised you didn't rid yourself of him."

"South Africa did that for me. And I did give his widow her marriage lines. I can't help it if she didn't know where they were. And a pension."

"How fine of you," Rutledge commented sardonically, in spite of himself. He turned and started down the passage to the main door.

The space between his shoulder blades felt all too vulnerable, but he didn't look behind him until he had reached the outer door and stepped through it. Glancing back as he closed it, he saw Montgomery standing in the passage outside the estate room. And his fists were clenched as he watched Rutledge go, his face taut with fury.

It wasn't very sensible to spend the night in Little Tilton. He was tired from lack of sleep the night before. On the other hand, a room in the larger of the two pubs in the village might tempt Montgomery to do something rash. The book on medieval apples and a pair of wood carvings were hardly sufficient proof of murder, not in a courtroom. Montgomery might lose his inheritance when the book came to light, but he'd deny that the carvings had been done by his late brother, more famous for his birds. Even Vivian Moss's testimony wouldn't be enough—she hadn't seen those carvings for twenty years, and Montgomery and his wife could swear they'd been sold as well, long ago.

Would Prue Montgomery stand by her husband, if he was accused of murder? In the hope that she and her son would be better off if he could be cleared? Could she go on living with a man who was accused of murder, whether it was proven or not? Or divorce him after he was cleared, and ask for a sizable settlement?

It was likely a matter Desmond Montgomery was considering even now. And it would be imperative to rid himself of Rutledge. A fourth murder to end the threat against his inheritance? A small price to pay, surely.

Hamish said, "No one saw you at the house. It was Mrs. Montgomery who opened yon door. No' the maid. And likely she'd say naught, for her son's sake."

"He thinks I have that book in my possession. He'll need to bargain with me to get his hands on it, before he tries anything. Once he's destroyed it, he's safe from Vivian Moss as well."

"I wouldna' count on it," Hamish said darkly. "Ye ken, the book isna' important if ye do na' know its secret."

But Rutledge had come to the end of the drive, and had to make a decision now.

"In for a penny, in for a pound," he said, and turned back into Little Tilton. "You may be right. He may decide to find a solution quickly. It would be a chance worth taking, if he thinks he can get away with it. If I haven't connected him with the murders yet, he knows I soon will, and that will spur him on. Before his wife hears about them."

"He'll keep killing you fra' his wife. Until he's drunk too much again."

"Which means he won't leave the house until he's certain she and the staff are asleep. I ought to get some rest while I can."

People were hurrying toward their work, and he realized it was Tuesday. They glanced curiously at him as he passed, and he thought this would only complicate matters for Montgomery. Would he wait and pay off the stranger—then ambush him on an empty road well away from the village? It was how Wentworth had been murdered.

Worth remembering that, he thought.

There was no one in the pub at this hour, but he found a woman in the kitchen preparing a chicken for roasting. She wiped her hands on her apron and went with Rutledge to the bar.

"There's but the two rooms," she told him. "They're not very fine."

"It's no matter," Rutledge said. "I'll only be here one night."

"Will you be wanting breakfast in the morning, before you leave?"

He hadn't thought that far ahead. "Yes. Yes, I think so."

"I'll leave a note for Teddy, then." Opening a drawer, she handed him a key. "I doubt it works," she said. "We don't generally lock our doors. Through that door you'll find the stairs. First room on the right."

"Does it look out on the street?"

"That's on your left, that room. It's not as large. And there's no difference in price."

"All the same, I think the front room will suit me better."

"Your choice," she said. Excusing herself, she hurried back to her hen.

He took the narrow stairs two at a time and opened the door into the front room.

It *was* small, he saw, with a narrow bed, one chair, a washstand, and a wardrobe that took up most of one wall. What's more, the front walls slanted inward at shoulder level. He could feel his claustrophobia clutching at his throat as he shut the door. A child, he thought, would be hard-pressed to find this room comfortable. Walking to the window, he parted the curtain and realized that this was one of the dormers above the pub door.

He was about to turn away when he heard the sound of hoofbeats. He waited, and Mrs. Montgomery came into view, trotting down the center of the High. She was a superb horsewoman, he saw, moving with the horse so perfectly that they were the epitome of grace. Except for her face, which was set and angry.

Apparently she and her husband had had words after Rutledge left. And her husband looked to have won.

When she was out of sight, he went down to the motorcar, took out his valise and a torch, then moved the vehicle to the far side of the street, where he could see it clearly from his window. And anyone showing an interest in it.

A wrecked motorcar could kill as easily as a revolver, if not as surely.

He went upstairs and settled himself for the long wait to come.

Hamish was restless, leaving Rutledge with a thundering headache.

"If he comes," he reminded Rutledge, "and you've found your murderer, ye'll have no excuse. Ye'll have to return to London."

"I'm aware of that."

"Yon bride and groom will be returning soon enough fra' the wedding journey."

"They can't stay in Paris forever," he retorted irritably.

"Aye. It will be verra' different now."

"I've managed before. I can manage again."

"Oh, aye? Weil, we'll see. Ye ken, if Montgomery doesna' miss when he shoots, you willna' ha' to find oot."

Rutledge got up and walked to the window, trying to shut out the voice.

He stood there and watched children hurrying toward school, women setting out to do their early marketing. A few men stopped to have a look at his motorcar, but they walked on soon enough. The High was empty after that, for a cold wind had come up.

The chimney in his room wasn't drawing well, the smoke irritating his throat. He finally went down to the kitchen to ask for a plate of chicken and an ale.

A few minutes later, someone from the pub brought up a tray with his meal, and an hour later, he carried it back down again, ordering the other half.

He brought it back and set the glass on the tiny table by the bed. He slept for several hours, but not deeply enough to dream.

The day seemed to drag by. And then the light began to fade, helped along by a bank of clouds hovering in the west.

Watching the street, he saw someone walk as far as his motorcar, then turn and go back the way he'd come, his hat pulled low over his face. Montgomery now knew where he was staying—and how many rooms the pub boasted.

He tried to sleep for another hour or two, but the silence left him restless. The pub must have closed early. Or wasn't all that popular.

He had the place to himself now. The old building seemed to creak and groan around him, pressed by the wind, which hadn't dropped at sunset.

The rain came close on to ten o'clock, but lasted for only an hour before moving on. The street outside glistened wetly, and not even a cat was out there.

Another hour came and went. He crossed to the other room and gathered up pillows and blankets, arranging them on his bed to give the appearance of someone sleeping. He took a pair of trousers and a shirt out of his valise and draped them over the only chair, as if he'd undressed for bed. Then he put on his heavy coat, banked the fire— and waited.

18

He eased his shoulders as the church clock struck midnight. Standing in the deep shadow on the far side of the wardrobe was tiring, but the room was too small for him to conceal himself anywhere else. What's more, he could just see the motorcar from there.

One o'clock. Montgomery would have to wait until he was sure his household was asleep. Stifling a yawn, Rutledge leaned his head back against the wall. In the trenches he'd learned to sleep anywhere, even standing up, but now he fought sleep, alert to every sound in the pub, from the creaking of the stairs to the groaning of the structure as the night temperatures dropped.

It was almost two by his calculations when he heard a different creaking from the stairs. A rhythm to it, not random this time.

Someone was coming.

He stayed very still. It would do no good to give himself away before the shot was fired.

Someone was standing outside his door now. Listening for his breathing? He swore silently, then put his hand over his mouth and smothered a cough as if rousing a little from his sleep.

Minutes passed.

Over the top of the wardrobe, he saw the door open quietly, first a crack, and then wide enough for the figure on the bed to be visible. There was just enough light from the hearth to make it look quite real.

He waited. He couldn't see whoever it was, but he could hear the hammer pulled back on the revolver. And the pillow and blankets jumped as the room filled with the sound of the shot. A second shot followed, then someone was feeling for the key. The door closed and then the key was turning in the lock.

Rutledge sprang forward, racing to reach the door before the key sent the bolt home.

But he was too late. Footsteps clattered down the stairs as he grasped the knob and tried to open the door.

He was locked in.

Swearing again, he kicked at the door, but it opened inward and he had no leverage. Giving that up, he tried to pull the hinge pin out at the top of the door, but it appeared to have rusted in place. He took out his pocketknife and worked at it, and suddenly it popped out. The bottom hinge pin was easier, coming out straightaway. He caught the door as it came toward him, shoved it against the wardrobe, and was down the stairs and out the main door of the pub, racing for his motorcar.

Montgomery had a head start, and Rutledge was counting on overtaking him before he reached the drive up to his house.

But Rutledge drove as far as the house door at the head of the drive without encountering anyone. Had he cut across the small park to another door?

Leaving the motor running, he started around the house. He glimpsed a figure ahead of him now, hat pulled low, greatcoat flapping, and he followed. Montgomery reached the terrace, dashed across it, and the door into the garden room opened and closed.

Rutledge leaped up on the terrace and raced for the door, hesitating only an instant. It opened easily, and that should have warned him.

Hamish was shouting "*'Ware!*" as he stepped into the room.

Rutledge threw himself to one side, felt the shot pass close enough that he heard the familiar, deadly sound of a bee at his ear. Glass in the terrace doors shattered.

The killer fired again, this time hitting the wall just to one side of Rutledge's shoulder.

Four shots. Only two left.

He dropped like a stone behind a table, reached up for anything his fingers could find, and touched a glass paperweight. He hurled it toward the hearth just as the door to the passage opened and then closed again.

He got through it fast, ducking into the shadows of the staircase.

He could hear voices now, servants calling to one another. And a lamp glowed at the top of the stairs.

The revolver clattered to the floor and was kicked in his direction.

And then a woman's voice cried, "Help, help me! He's armed!"

Rutledge realized that he'd walked straight into a trap.

Footsteps hurrying down the stairs, another lamp shining now, and he could just see Prue Montgomery standing in the middle of the hall. She was wearing a nightdress, her hair down her back.

He wheeled, heading for the garden room. But it was too late. Montgomery, roaring with anger, was at his heels.

Someone was coming the other way, through the shattered doors, and Rutledge knew that he was well and truly caught.

Montgomery seized him and was dragging him toward the foyer, where lamps were blindingly bright after the darkness. A gardener or chauffeur, still in his nightdress, blocked the passage door, and Montgomery himself, in nightdress, with his hair tousled, was shouting something.

And Mrs. Montgomery, crying now, one shoulder of her nightgown torn, was clinging to an older woman, who appeared to be a housekeeper.

"I heard a noise," she whimpered, "and I came down to investigate. He was in the garden room, and he fired at me twice. He meant to kill me."

"But who is he?" the housekeeper was asking, staring at Rutledge.

Montgomery was standing just to his left. Without warning, he whirled, raised his fist, caught Rutledge on the side of his jaw, and sent him staggering back against the wall. "Break into my house, will you, attack my wife? I ought to kill you!"

The other man walked into the foyer and picked up the revolver, looking at it. "It's been fired recently," he said, handing it to Montgomery.

His hand unsteady, Montgomery pointed the revolver at Rutledge's chest.

"I'd rather you didn't," Rutledge said, shaking his head to clear it. "My name is Rutledge. Inspector, Scotland Yard. I'm here to take you and your wife into custody for the murder of three men."

He thought Montgomery was going to pull the trigger out of sheer surprise.

"Liar!" he shouted. "You were here blackmailing me earlier this morning. Yesterday morning."

Mrs. Montgomery said sharply, "Desmond, no! Just shoot him."

Rutledge slowly reached into his pocket and pulled out his identification. As he did, one of the little carvings fell out and bounced on the floor.

All eyes were drawn to it.

Except for his. He was staring at Prue Montgomery.

Rutledge said quickly, "Look at Mrs. Montgomery's feet. She's not barefoot like the rest of you. She's wearing boots, and they're muddy. And," he added, "if you go to my room upstairs at the pub, there are two shots in the pillow where my head should have been."

The other man held out his hand for the revolver. "I think it's best if I send for Constable."

"Damn it, no, I'll deal with him myself," Montgomery objected, but his gaze was still on his wife's feet. "I'm the magistrate."

"You'll find a man's hat and coat and trousers in the garden room. The hearth? Behind one of the chairs? Where they could be put away later. As you can see, they aren't mine. I'm wearing my own," Rutledge told anyone who would listen.

The housekeeper was listening. Moving away from her mistress, she went into the garden room, and he thought she was intent on proving him a liar. But after a moment, she came out again with a bundle of clothing in her arms. "These are Mr. Julian's things," she said, looking at Montgomery. "But he's at Cambridge now."

Montgomery stood there, frozen. After a moment he said quietly, "What have you done, Prue? Whose revolver is this?"

"He's lying," she began. "Don't you see?"

"You said three men," Montgomery asked over his shoulder to Rutledge. "Who were they?"

"Stephen Wentworth, the bookseller in Wolfpit. Frederick Templeton, who ordered a book through Wentworth's shop. And Harvey Mitchell, Miss Moss's solicitor."

"But why?" Montgomery demanded.

"To find that book and destroy it. It had been safe enough in Miss Moss's possession. She wasn't likely to remove the bindings. But Wentworth had bought her book for Templeton, then had to substitute another one. Templeton didn't even know he hadn't been given her copy. Nor did you. When he talked about the book about apples at dinner, you recognized it at once, and then heard him say something about having it re-bound. That could prove disastrous. He probably mentioned that it was a rare find, and you had no reason to think otherwise. You were in a panic. Wentworth had to be stopped before he could send that book to the binders. Templeton had to be killed because he knew Wentworth would be seeing to the binding for him. The third victim, Mitchell, didn't have to die. You didn't know it was a blind sale, didn't know he wasn't even acquainted with Wentworth and Templeton. I don't know how you found him—possibly through the bank that handles the pension you set up for Miss Moss.

He represented her. Something else you didn't know. That book was already back in Miss Moss's hands, none the worse for wear. Three men died for no reason at all."

"Who is this Miss Moss?" the housekeeper asked.

Montgomery ignored her. "Prue?" he asked his wife, his face ravaged by fear and anger. "Please tell me he's lying."

"That night after the dinner party," she said furiously, "you told me all this. You were drunk and maudlin. All but helpless with fear of what was about to happen. *And you were going to let it happen!* I couldn't believe my ears." When her husband went on staring at her as if she were someone he didn't know, she exclaimed, "This is Julian's birthright. Did you think I would sit idly by and let it be taken from him by someone like that? For all you know, your brother was tricked into marrying that woman. And her bastard had no right to this house. But once that piece of paper got out, who knows what the courts would decide? If she was pathetic enough, they might find for her."

The other man there in the entry had been listening silently. Now he spoke up. "I'll send someone for Constable. Let him sort this out."

"Who are you?" Rutledge asked.

"I live on one of the tenant farms. The nearest one. I heard the shots." And he walked away, had second thoughts, and came back for the revolver he'd set on the table by the door.

"My motorcar is out front," Rutledge said. "Take it. It's faster."

And they stood where they were like a tableau vivant until the front door opened again, and a man in the uniform of a Constable stepped in and said, "Now then, what's this all about?"

I t took an hour before Constable Wiggins had sorted it all out. His sleep had been interrupted, and he hadn't even taken time to shave. He was in no mood to trust anyone's word.

But he had gone back to the pub to look at the pillows in Rutledge's bed, and found the door to his room battered and off its hinges.

What's more, the key was in the trouser pocket of the clothes that Mrs. Montgomery had worn. Sniffing at them as he examined them, Wiggins said, "That's her perfume, all right." He had them put aside as evidence.

Rutledge, waiting for Wiggins to question the staff, said to Montgomery, "Do you smoke at all? Cigarettes? A pipe?"

He thought the man, sitting across the room with his head in his hands, wasn't going to answer him. But he looked up after a moment and said, "I smoked a pipe some years ago but gave it up. Why does it matter, in the midst of all this trouble?"

"And the little wolves?"

"We moved all of my brother's belongings to the attics. They're probably still there, along with the rest of his carvings. I didn't care to look at them. His birds were larger. We sold them to a collector. The irony was, he'd have taken more if we'd had them. I was glad to be rid of them. He hadn't wanted the smaller pieces, the wolves and horses and other creatures. Only the birds. In God's name, why did she take them? Did she believe she was being clever?" He dropped his head into his hands again, then said, his voice muffled, "What's to become of Prue?"

"When Constable Wiggins is satisfied, I'll take her back to Wolfpit for the inquest. And she'll be charged with the murder of Wentworth and Templeton. I'll have to inform Inspector Stevenson that Mitchell's murder is also solved. But I expect Wolfpit will take priority in the matter."

"What possessed her to do such things?"

"You should never have told her about your brother's marriage or where the lines were hidden. She couldn't take the risk that someone else would find them."

"It was on my conscience. I had to tell someone."

"It must not have bothered your conscience too much to give that book to Vivian Moss, knowing that it held the proof of her marriage to your brother."

"I discovered the marriage lines in his room. I told her he must have taken them to South Africa with him, and that they weren't in his belongings when the Army sent them back. I told her they were probably on his body when he died, and they'd had to burn his clothing because of the virulent fever."

"It doesn't matter. As soon as Wiggins is satisfied that I'm right about your wife, he'll have to know about the inheritance."

"You can't do this to Julian."

"You did it to Eric Moss."

Disgusted, Rutledge got up and went to pace the terrace until Constable Wiggins sent for him.

"They claim you tried to blackmail them," Wiggins said as he read over Rutledge's statement.

"I let them think that's what I was offering. If I hadn't, we'd never have found out what Mrs. Montgomery had done."

"Such a fine lady, a pillar of the church—I can't quite wrap my mind around it. I'd find it easier to accuse her husband, strange as that may sound."

"I had expected it to be him. She's nearly as tall as he is."

"Well, that about finishes it, sir. Do you need me to accompany you to Wolfpit? I wouldn't trust her, if I were you."

"I'll manage. But there's another matter, one you'll need to take up with the Montgomery family solicitor," he said and watched the Constable's face change as he explained about Vivian Moss.

"But I remember her, sir. Such a sweet little thing. She left abruptly, and there was gossip about her carrying on with young Lawrence. I found it hard to believe. And then he was killed. Nearly killed his mother too. But you say they were *married*, sir?"

Rutledge explained once more, and Wiggins nodded. "Mr. Warren, the solicitor, is a solid man, sir. He'll want to look into this. If you'll write out Miss—Mrs. Montgomery's direction, sir, I'll give it to him."

It was after three o'clock when Mrs. Montgomery was settled in the motorcar, a small valise in the boot. Her husband stood there, trying to find words as Rutledge shut the motorcar's door and went to turn the crank. Finally he said, "What shall I tell Julian? I'll have to tell him something."

But she didn't answer him.

I t was a long drive back to Wolfpit, and Rutledge was already tired. Mrs. Montgomery seemed to understand that, and watched him with hawk-like intensity.

Halfway there, she said, "I have money. I can make your life very comfortable. You have only to stop along the road, and let me disappear. It's for the best."

"What did you ask Wentworth, that night on the road? About the book? Or Templeton?"

She laughed. "I simply asked if he was Stephen Wentworth. And he said yes. It was all I needed to know. I didn't want to shoot a complete stranger. Frederick I knew. He didn't recognize me at first. It was quite dark there at the foot of the drive."

"You left the pipe tobacco and the carvings to confuse the police?"

"Yes, of course. Do you think I wanted to get caught?"

"How did you know how to find Wentworth? Along that road at that hour of the night?"

"I didn't. I came to Wolfpit to look for him. And I saw him leave the bookstore, go home to change, then drive out of the village with a woman beside him in the motorcar. I went out the road he'd taken and decided to wait for him to drive back. I'd brought the revolver, the pipe, the tobacco. I didn't count on having to stand about until three in the morning." She shrugged. "I'd already told Desmond that I was going up to London for a little shopping. I couldn't very well reappear too soon. I had to make the best of it. I hid the motorcar two miles away and waited in that wretched hayfield for hours and hours."

He'd been listening to her, his eyes on the road, and he hadn't seen the look on her face as she finished speaking.

She lurched for the wheel, fighting him for control. A strong woman, bent on having her own way, she gave no quarter, nearly sending them both headlong into a ditch. He managed to shove her away, wrenching the wheel with one hand, fending her off with the other. Her nails raked his face as one tire slipped on the crumbling edge of the ditch, and then he had the motorcar back on the road. It had been a near run thing. And still she fought him.

He pulled to the verge, his face a thundercloud. "Try that again," he warned her through clenched teeth, his grip on her arm like a vise, "and I'll drag you the rest of the way on a rope behind the motorcar."

He was angry enough, his voice thick with it, that she believed him.

The rest of the journey to Wolfpit she hunched against her door and had nothing more to say.

I t was nearly dawn when he pulled up in front of Constable Penny's cottage and woke him from a sound sleep.

"Inspector Rutledge?" he said, peering out into the darkness at the figure he could just see sitting in the passenger's side of the motorcar.

"I've brought in the killer of Stephen Wentworth and Frederick Templeton," he said formally. "Prudence Margaret Alice Howard Montgomery, late of Little Tilton village in Essex. We can hold the inquest tomorrow if you like. Today," he amended.

"I don't understand," Penny said. "What's happened to your face?"

"It's late, man, just bring your keys and let's be done with it."

It took several minutes before Penny reappeared in his uniform and accompanied them to the police station in the rear seat of the motorcar, crowding Hamish.

Mrs. Montgomery was taken back to the single cell, and she asked if she could have her valise with her. But Rutledge refused. The last thing he wanted was to find her hanging in her cell by morning.

When she had been locked in, and the outer door had been closed as well, Penny said, "Are there witnesses, sir?"

"I'll give you a list tomorrow. Today. Go back to bed. I have several telephone calls to put through before I sleep."

He let himself into the bookstore, put through a call to the Yard, and when he reached the Sergeant on duty, he informed him of the arrest of Mrs. Montgomery and added that he had evidence that she had been the killer in Inspector Stevenson's inquiry as well. Gibson was sent for, and he asked a number of questions. Rutledge dutifully answered them.

When at last he could hang up, he put the next call through to Melinda Crawford, early as it was, and told her his news.

She listened without interruption, then said, "I'm glad it's done, Ian. I'm glad it's finished. You sound very tired. Go to bed, and rest. You'll need to be fresh tomorrow. Today."

He took her advice. He lit the fire laid ready for him on the hearth of his room, looked around at its spaciousness compared to the little dormer room, and then undressed for bed.

Even Hamish couldn't intrude that night.

For once Rutledge slept without dreaming.

Later that morning he went to speak to Blake, giving him the news. His next stop was at Mrs. Delaney's. He was afraid she was going to cry.

But she squared her shoulders, looked toward the street, and said bitterly, "I hope she hangs for what she did. It won't bring Stephen back, will it? At least there will be justice done."

Rutledge didn't think she found much comfort in that.

He called on Miss MacRae and her aunt, telling them that Wentworth's killer had been found, and watched their relief.

Elizabeth MacRae shook her head. "A woman? But I find that hard to believe. I'm certain it was a man."

"You saw what you were expected to see. Someone in a man's clothing, striding up to the motorcar with such confidence? It all happened too fast for you to have time to notice anything else."

"Still," Audrey Blackburn argued, "you'd think she'd have been nervous, uncertain."

"You haven't met Prue Montgomery," he said dryly, remembering how she had fired into what appeared to be a sleeping man in a bed. Without thinking, without remorse.

It was Dr. Brent who had protested the strongest. "The shots were too well placed. It had to be someone from the war, who knew what he was doing."

It had been Constable Wiggins who had given Rutledge the answer to that. He had shaken his head in disbelief as he handed over the statements he'd taken from the household staff and Montgomery himself. "You don't expect it from the likes of Mrs. Montgomery. She's a *Howard,* for God's sake, connected to the Northumberland Howards. Her mother's father was a respected Harley Street surgeon, top of the line. She's a *lady.*"

She was also a mother, Rutledge had had to remind the doctor. And she was willing to kill for her son's birthright.

Dr. Brent, only partially mollified, retorted, "A woman handling a revolver that well? Not trembling at the thought of doing murder?"

"I'll be happy to introduce you to one who will prove you wrong," Rutledge answered, thinking about Melinda Crawford. She was a crack shot.

He had left the Wentworths until last, after speaking with Mrs. Cox. It wasn't a visit he relished. But it was his duty to inform them that the murderer of their son was in custody, and that the inquest into his death would be held the next morning.

Mrs. Wentworth listened without comment. He might as well have told her the weather over the past few days had been drearier than usual for December.

Wentworth was visibly relieved. What else he felt was hard to tell. He'd been used to hiding his feelings for most of his married life, choosing his wife over his son again and again.

Rutledge found himself thinking that the elder Wentworth and

Montgomery had much in common, weak men who valued their peace more than their duty.

Hamish said, "Montgomery couldna' ha' known his wife would kill."

And Rutledge had answered him silently. *He told her about the re-binding of the book. If he hadn't, three men would still be alive.*

Hamish persisted. "But he didna' *know*."

As Wentworth saw him to the door, Rutledge said, "There's one last matter I need to clear up. What does *gate keeper* mean to Mrs. Wentworth?"

Stephen's father looked away. "I'd rather not answer that."

"I can ask it at the inquest, when you're under oath to answer."

Wentworth looked over his shoulder to be sure his wife wasn't within hearing.

"Please, you mustn't do that. She told Stephen once—years ago, when he was perhaps six or seven—that she was the gate keeper of his life, and she would see to it that happiness never reached him as long as she lived and could stand in its way. That it would be her revenge for taking away her beloved boy."

"And you let her tell your son that?" Rutledge demanded, appalled.

"I tried to explain it to him afterward. I'm not sure it did much good. But I did try."

Rutledge turned on his heel and left him standing in the doorway.

A fter the inquest into the deaths of Stephen Wentworth and Frederick Templeton was finished, and Mrs. Montgomery was bound over for trial, Rutledge left the stuffy room in The Swan where it seemed everyone from the village had crowded in to hear the proceedings. Even Robin Hardy was there, and he'd brought Evelyn Hardy with him. Rutledge noticed that her left hand was bare of rings. Her engagement had ended. He could only think it was a good thing.

Hardy nodded, not speaking, when Rutledge greeted the two of them. And then before Rutledge turned away, he said, "You give sound advice. For a policeman."

"You listen well," he replied, "for a rebellious man."

Hardy grinned, but didn't answer.

Templeton's sister-in-law, a quiet woman in the heavy black of mourning, sat stoically in a back row, her head down, through the giving of evidence. Miss Blackburn and her niece kept her company. Miss Mowbray had not come from Cambridge, and he hadn't expected to see her. Mr. Wentworth was there, and so was Inspector Reed's wife, defiantly facing her disapproving husband as he was questioned.

One other person besides Mrs. Wentworth hadn't been there, and Rutledge searched the churchyard for the sexton.

He ran him to earth in the vestry.

Taking out the note he'd found in his room shortly after arriving in Wolfpit, he held it out.

"You wrote this, I think."

Pace shook his head. "No, you're wrong there." He relished saying it, grinning at Rutledge.

"Then Mrs. Wentworth wrote it, and you delivered it."

"I'm not admitting anything. Think what you please."

"Why are you so loyal to her? She was vicious to her son."

"I grew up on her father's estate. And I followed her here when she wed. I've kept an eye on her all these years."

"And you buried her dead son."

"Well, I buried the little casket. But he's not under the lamb. She wanted to keep him with her. And so I buried him under the sundial in the walled garden of that house, while everyone was at the funeral. It was what she wanted."

Rutledge shook his head. "I don't believe you."

The grin was gone. "It doesn't matter what you believe. It only matters what she believes."

And he walked away.

I t was late Friday evening when Rutledge unlocked the door of his flat in London, and stepped inside.

It had seemed foreign, a place he hardly knew, on the Saturday evening after his sister's wedding.

Now it seemed to welcome him. It wasn't home. Home was still the large white house on the square where his sister and her husband would live. But this was the place he'd chosen for himself, and it would do.

It would have to do.

He went through his post and found a letter from Frances. As he read it, he could hear her voice, brimming with happiness. He was glad for her. He would always be.

The other letter was in a handwriting he recognized at once.

It was from Kate Gordon, inviting him to a Christmas Eve party at her father's house.

He held it for some time, looking at it, tempted.

Then he put it back in the envelope and set it in the drawer of his desk.

There were still several days until Christmas Eve.

There was still time to think about it.

About the author

2 Meet Charles Todd

About the book

3 The Story Behind the Story

5 Discussion Questions

Read on . . .

7 Inspector Ian Rutledge: A Complete
   Timeline of Major Events

Insights,
Interviews
& More . . .

Meet Charles Todd

Michael Frost Photography

CHARLES TODD is the author of the Bess Crawford mysteries, the Inspector Ian Rutledge mysteries, and two stand-alone novels. A mother-and-son writing team, they live on the East Coast. ∾

The Story
Behind the Story

Driving through Suffolk one day, we came across a very pretty village by the name of Woolpit. While walking around, we noticed several depictions of a howling wolf, and the story behind them was interesting: here the last wolf in England was caught and killed.

Other places have made the same claim—not surprising because in medieval England, there was no CNN to tell Cornwall that Suffolk had got there first.

Woolpit—Wolfpit. Hmmm.

Of course there were no real wolves in Rutledge's day, unless you counted human predators. But we liked the silhouette of the howling wolf, and there was a possible way to work that into the story as a carving. We also liked the dark and lonely stretch of road that comes into the town—dark and lonely in Rutledge's day, that is.

What we actually wanted to do in this book was put Rutledge on the scene right away, almost as soon as the murder occurred. Usually, because of the state of the roads at the time, he arrived a day or even two after the fact and saw the murder scene through the eyes of the local constable. How would being there at the very start change the course of his investigation? If he could walk the ground before it had been ▶

3

contaminated by others? If he could see the shock in the eyes of the woman who might—or might not—be the killer? This was intriguing, and Frances's wedding gave us the perfect opportunity to put him on that lonely stretch of road in the middle of the night, uncertain whether he had heard the shot that killed Stephen Wentworth—or whether what he heard was part of his waking nightmare. The rest fell into place as we looked at Stephen's life. Why was he so respected by everyone who knew him, while his own family reviled him? What was the key to his death? Lots of questions to find answers for, but that's what a mystery is: a puzzle with all the pieces at your fingertips, and the challenge of putting them together in the most exciting order. ❧

Discussion Questions

1. Hamish's voice often acts as a devil's advocate, pushing Rutledge to reinterpret information or his own feelings. Why do you think Hamish has taken on this role in Rutledge's mind?

2. What do you make of Rutledge's feelings toward Kate Gordon? How would you like to see their relationship play out?

3. What was your first impression of Elizabeth McRae when Rutledge finds her on the road? She is an outsider in Wolfpit. Does that make it easier for you—and the local people—to suspect her?

4. The local authorities and even his colleagues at Scotland Yard often present roadblocks for Rutledge when pursuing a case. The Yard mistrusts his way of seeing a case through, while the local people often resent his taking charge. Do you feel that this is true in police work today?

5. There are many conflicting reports from witnesses about Stephen Wentworth's character. Who did you believe or disbelieve? ▶

Discussion Questions *(continued)*

6. How do you interpret Rutledge's relationship with Melinda? Why do you think he allows himself to trust her more than others in his life? And yet he continues to hide his shell shock from her. Why?

7. As other victims turned up dead, did you foresee the connection between the murders? Did the initial comparison of the lone wolf with a human predator distract you? Did it help you?

8. Did the identity of the killer surprise you? Did the killer's motive surprise you?

9. There are several mothers in this story. Each one has a different way of relating to her son, and one pushes her daughter toward a loveless marriage. How did you feel about them?

10. What is your impression of society's view on the roles of women on the heels of World War I? What role does gender take in this case?

11. Do you think Rutledge is compelled to pursue this case out of professional obligation, a hunger for the truth, or to avoid facing his own demons? Or is it something else? ∼

Inspector Ian Rutledge:
A Complete Timeline of Major Events

JUNE 1914—*A FINE SUMMER'S DAY*

On a fine summer's day, the Great War is still only the distant crack of revolver shots at a motorcar in faraway Sarajevo. And Ian Rutledge, already an inspector at Scotland Yard, has decided to propose to the woman he's so deeply in love with—despite hints from friends and family that she may not be the wisest choice. But in another part of England, a man stands in the kitchen of his widowed mother's house, waiting for the undertaker to come for her body, and stares at the clock on the mantel. He doesn't know yet that he will become Rutledge's last case before Britain is drawn into war. In the weeks to come, as summer moves on toward the shadows of August, he will set out to right a wrong, and Rutledge will find himself having to choose between the Yard and his country, between the woman he loves and duty, and between truth and honor.

JUNE 1919—*A TEST OF WILLS*

Ian Rutledge, returning home from the trenches of the Great War, breaks off his engagement to Jean during his long months in hospital suffering what is ▶

now called post-traumatic stress disorder. Facing a bleak future, and fighting back from the edge of madness, he returns to his career at Scotland Yard. But Chief Superintendent Bowles is determined to break him. And so Rutledge finds himself in Warwickshire, where the only witness to the murder of Colonel Harris is a drunken ex-soldier suffering from shell shock. Rutledge is fighting his own battles with the voice of Corporal Hamish MacLeod in his head, survivor's guilt after the bloody 1916 Battle of the Somme. The question is, will he win this test of wills with Hamish—or is the shell-shocked witness a mirror of what he'll become if he fails to keep his madness at bay?

JULY 1919—*WINGS OF FIRE*

Rutledge is sent to Cornwall because the Home Office wants to be reassured that Nicholas Cheney wasn't murdered. But Nicholas committed suicide with his half sister, Olivia. And she's written a body of war poetry under the name of O. A. Manning. Rutledge, who had used her poetry in the trenches to keep his mind functioning, is shocked to discover she never saw France and may well be a cold-blooded killer. And yet even dead, she makes a lasting impression that he can't shake.

AUGUST 1919—*SEARCH THE DARK*

An out-of-work ex-soldier, sitting on a train in a Dorset station, suddenly sees his dead wife and two small children standing on the platform. He fights to get off the train, and soon thereafter the woman is found murdered and the children are missing. Rutledge is sent to coordinate a search and finds himself attracted to Aurore, a French war bride who will lie to protect her husband and may have killed because she was jealous of the murder victim's place in her husband's life.

SEPTEMBER 1919—*LEGACY OF THE DEAD*

Just as Rutledge thinks he has come to terms—of a sort—with the voice that haunts him, he's sent to northern England to find the missing daughter of a woman who once slept with a king. Little does he know that his search will take him to Scotland, and to the woman Hamish would have married if he'd lived. But Fiona is certain to hang for murdering a mother to steal her child, and she doesn't know that Rutledge killed Hamish on the battlefield when she turns to him for help. He couldn't save Hamish—but Rutledge is honor bound to protect Fiona and the small child named for him. ▶

Inspector Ian Rutledge *(continued)*

OCTOBER 1919—*WATCHERS OF TIME*

Still recovering from the nearly fatal wound he received in Scotland, Rutledge is sent to East Anglia to discover who murdered a priest and what the priest's death had to do with a dying man who knew secrets about the family that owns the village. But there's more to the murder than hearing a deathbed confession. And the key might well be a young woman as haunted as Rutledge is, because she survived the sinking of the *Titanic* and carries her own guilt for failure to save a companion.

NOVEMBER 1919—*A FEARSOME DOUBT*

A case from 1912 comes back to haunt Rutledge. Did he send an innocent man to the gallows? Meanwhile, he's trying to discover who has poisoned three ex-soldiers, all of them amputees in a small village in Kent. Mercy killings or murder? And he sees a face across the Guy Fawkes Day bonfire that is a terrifying reminder of what happened to him at the end of the war . . . something he is ashamed of, even though he can't remember why. *What happened in the missing six months of his life?*

DECEMBER 1919—*A COLD TREACHERY*

Rutledge is already in the north and the closest man to Westmorland where, at the height of a blizzard, there has been a cold-blooded killing of an entire family—save one child, who is missing in the snow. But as the facts unfold, it's possible that the boy killed his own family. Where is he? Dead in the snow or hiding? And there are secrets in this isolated village of Urskdale that can lead to more deaths.

JANUARY 1920—*A LONG SHADOW*

A party that begins innocently enough ends with Rutledge finding machine gun casings engraved with death's heads—a warning. But he's sent to Northamptonshire to learn why someone shot Constable Ward with an arrow in what the locals call a haunted wood. He discovers there are other deaths unaccounted for, and there's also a woman who knows too much about Rutledge for his own comfort. Then whoever has been stalking him comes north after him, and Rutledge knows if he doesn't find the man, he will die. Hamish, pushing him hard, is all too aware that Rutledge's death will mean his own.

MARCH 1920—*A FALSE MIRROR*

A man is nearly beaten to death, his wife is taken hostage by his assailant, and Rutledge is sent posthaste to Hampton Regis to find out who wanted Matthew Hamilton dead. The man who may be guilty is someone Rutledge knew in the war, a reminder that some were lucky ▶

enough to be saved while Hamish was left to die. But this is a story of love gone wrong, and the next two deaths reek of madness. Are these murders random, or were the women mistaken for the intended victim?

APRIL 1920—*A PALE HORSE*

In the ruins of Yorkshire's Fountains Abbey lies the body of a man wrapped in a cloak, the face covered by a gas mask. Next to him is a book on alchemy, which belongs to the schoolmaster, a conscientious objector in the Great War. Who is this man, and is the investigation into his death being manipulated by a thirst for revenge? Meanwhile, the British War Office is searching for a missing man of their own, someone whose war work was so secret that even Rutledge isn't told his real name or what he did. Here is a puzzle requiring all of Rutledge's daring and skill, for there are layers of lies and deception, while a ruthless killer is determined to hold on to freedom at any cost.

MAY 1920—*A MATTER OF JUSTICE*

At the turn of the century, in a war taking place far from England, two soldiers chance upon an opportunity that will change their lives forever. To take advantage of it, they will do the unthinkable and then put the past behind them. Twenty years later, a successful London businessman is found savagely and bizarrely murdered in a medieval tithe barn on his estate in Somerset. Called upon to investigate, Rutledge soon discovers that the victim was universally despised. Even the man's wife—who appears to be his wife in name only—and the town's police inspector are suspect. But who among the many hated enough to kill?

JUNE 1920—*THE RED DOOR*

In a house with a red door lies the body of a woman who has been bludgeoned to death. Rumor has it that two years earlier, she'd painted that door to welcome her husband back from the Front. Only he never came home. Meanwhile, in London, a man suffering from a mysterious illness goes missing and then just as suddenly reappears. Rutledge must solve two mysteries before he can bring a ruthless killer to justice: Who was the woman who lived and died behind the red door? Who was the man who never came home from the Great War, for the simple reason that he might never have gone? And what have they to do with a man who cannot break the seal of his own guilt without damning those he loves most?

JULY 1920—*A LONELY DEATH*

Three men have been murdered in a Sussex village, and Scotland Yard has been called in. The victims are soldiers, each surviving the nightmare of the ▶

Great War only to meet a ghastly end in the quiet English countryside. Each man has been garroted, with a small ID disk left in his mouth, yet no other clue suggests a motive or a killer. Rutledge understands all too well the darkness that resides within men's souls. His presence on the scene cannot deter a vicious and clever murderer, and a fourth dead soldier is discovered shortly after Rutledge's arrival. Now a horror that strikes painfully close to home threatens to engulf the investigator, and he will have to risk his career, his good name, even his shattered life itself, to bring an elusive killer to justice.

AUGUST 1920—*THE CONFESSION*

A man walks into Scotland Yard and confesses that he killed his cousin five years ago during the Great War. When Rutledge presses for details, the man evades his questions, revealing only that he hails from a village east of London. Less than two weeks later, the alleged killer's body is found floating in the Thames, a bullet in the back of his head. Rutledge discovers that the dead man was not who he claimed to be. The only clue is a gold locket, found around the victim's neck, that leads back to Essex and an insular village that will do anything to protect itself from notoriety.

SUMMER 1920—*PROOF OF GUILT*

An unidentified man appears to have been run down by a motorcar, and a clue leads Rutledge to a firm, built by two families, famous for producing and selling the world's best Madeira wine. There he discovers that the current head of the English enterprise is missing. Is he the dead man? And do either his fiancée or his jilted former lover have anything to do with his disappearance? With a growing list of suspects, Rutledge knows that suspicion and circumstantial evidence are nothing without proof of guilt. But his new acting chief superintendent doesn't agree and wants Rutledge to stop digging and settle on the easy answer. Rutledge must tread very carefully, for it seems that someone has decided that he, too, must die so that justice can take its course.

AUGUST 1920—*HUNTING SHADOWS*

A society wedding at Ely Cathedral becomes a crime scene when a guest is shot. After a fruitless search for clues, the local police call in Scotland Yard, but not before there is another shooting in a village close by. This second murder has a witness, but her description of the killer is so horrific it's unbelievable. Inspector Ian Rutledge can find no connection between the two deaths. ▶

Inspector Ian Rutledge *(continued)*

One victim was an army officer, the
other a solicitor standing for Parliament.
Is there a link between these murders,
or is it only in the mind of a clever killer?
As the investigation presses on, Rutledge
finds memories of the war beginning
to surface. Struggling to contain the
darkness that haunts him as he hunts
for the missing link, he discovers the
case turning in a most unexpected
direction. Now he must put his trust
in the devil in order to find the elusive
and shocking answer.

AUTUMN 1920—*NO SHRED OF EVIDENCE*

On the north coast of Cornwall,
an apparent act of mercy is repaid by
an arrest for murder. Four young
women have been accused of the crime.
A shocked father calls in a favor at the
Home Office. Scotland Yard is asked to
review the case. However, Inspector
Ian Rutledge is not the first inspector
to reach the village. Following in the
shoes of a dead man, he is told the case
is all but closed. Even as it takes an
unexpected personal turn, Rutledge
will require all his skill to deal with
the incensed families of the accused,
the grieving parents of the victim,
and local police eager to see these four
women sent to the infamous Bodmin
Gaol. Then why hasn't the killing
stopped? With no shred of evidence
to clear the accused, Rutledge must
plunge deep into the darkest secrets

of a wild, beautiful, and dangerous place if he is to find a killer who may—or may not—hold the key to the women's fate.

NOVEMBER 1920—*RACING THE DEVIL*

On the eve of the Battle of the Somme, a group of officers have a last drink and make a promise to one another: if they survive the battle ahead, they will meet a year after the fighting ends and race motorcars from Paris to Nice. In November 1919, the officers all meet as planned, but two vehicles are nearly run off the road, and one man is badly injured. No one knows which driver was at the wheel of the rogue motorcar. Back in England one year later, a driver loses control on a twisting road and is killed in the crash. Is the crash connected in some way to the unfortunate events in the mountains above Nice the year before? Investigating this perplexing case, Scotland Yard inspector Ian Rutledge discovers that the truth is elusive. Determined to remain in the shadows, this faceless killer is willing to strike again to stop Rutledge from finding him. This time, the victim he chooses is a child, and it will take all of Rutledge's skill to stop him before an innocent young life is sacrificed. ∾

Discover great authors, exclusive offers, and more at hc.com.